A MOMENT OF WEAKNESS

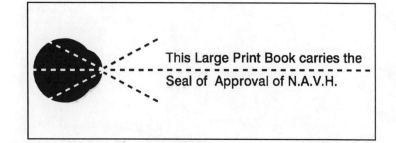

This Large Print Book carries the
Seal of Approval of N.A.V.H.

A MOMENT OF WEAKNESS

KAREN KINGSBURY

THORNDIKE PRESS

An imprint of Thomson Gale, a part of The Thomson Corporation

Detroit • New York • San Francisco • New Haven, Conn. • Waterville, Maine • London

THOMSON

✳ ™

GALE

Thomson Gale is part of The Thomson Corporation.

Thomson and Star Logo and Thorndike are trademarks and Gale is a registered trademark used herein under license.

Thorndike Press® Large Print Christian Romance.

The text of this Large Print edition is unabridged.

Other aspects of the book may vary from the original edition.

Set in 16 pt. Plantin.

LIBRARY OF CONGRESS CATALOGING-IN-PUBLICATION DATA

Kingsbury, Karen.
   A moment of weakness / by Karen Kingsbury.
     p. cm. — (Thorndike Press large print christian romance)
   ISBN-13: 978-0-7862-9382-7 (lg. print : alk. paper)
   ISBN-10: 0-7862-9382-9 (lg. print : alk. paper) 1. Custody of children —
Fiction. 2. Large type books. I. Title.
PS3561.I4873M66 2007
813'.54—dc22   2006101060

Published in 2007 by arrangement with Multnomah,
an imprint of WaterBrook Press, a division of Random House, Inc.

Printed in the United States of America on permanent paper
10 9 8 7 6 5 4 3 2 1

DEDICATED TO . . .

Donald,
My love song, my heart's mirror image, my
   best friend —
Who once upon a yesterday looked to God
   alone during our own
Moments of weakness . . .
And whose faith is today still my greatest
   strength . . .
Life with you is good; it's all good.
And since I can't slow the passing of time I
   am doing my very best
To savor it.

Kelsey . . .
My sweet girl, my most priceless treasure
   . . .
Your music is in my heart,
The voice of one whose love is the very
   definition
Of pure and whole and right.
Little Norm, can it truly be that you've

5

reached double-digits?
And that your little-girl time with us . . .
Is more than half over?

Tyler . . .
My handsome, lanky sunbeam . . .
You continue to give me bouquets of
Laughter and sunshine-filled memories . . .
I love everything about you, Ty.
No matter how tall you grow you'll always
   be
My little boy.

Austin . . .
Who races and rolls and rough-houses
   through our home . . .
Even the toughest athletes take timeouts
   . . .
And when you take yours and those sticky,
   baby arms make their way
Around my neck . . .
I think of the miracle you are . . . And I am
   gratetul.
Grateful beyond words.
Whenever I wonder how much God loves
   me, I never have to look further than you.

And to God Almighty, who has — for now
         — blessed me with these.

ACKNOWLEDGMENTS

My novels are not written without drawing on the research and true-life events that happen around me. For that reason, I'd like to thank several people for the help they have sometimes unwittingly provided me during the writing of *A Moment of Weakness.*

First, I'd like to thank the American Center for Law and Justice (ACLJ) for their tireless work in fighting for religious freedom in the United States. One day while listening to an ACLJ broadcast, I heard a woman call in because she was being sued by her husband for complete custody of her child. The reason? The woman was a Christian. And in that moment the story line for *A Moment of Weakness* was born.

Also, I'd like to thank my friend, Sherri Reed, aka Evil Buster. In the small town where she lives, Sherri started a campaign against Channel One — a real U.S. Department of Education program, which offered free televisions to public school classrooms as long as the students watch a fifteen-minute program each day. The program — which did not require parental approval — included government-chosen documentaries on topics that are at best questionable. Five minutes of the programming is commercial spots geared directly to school children. Over the course of a year, Sherri led a parent group that convinced the local school board to cancel the programming and give the television sets back to the government. I drew heavily from Sherri's experience in writing certain sections of *A Moment of Weakness.*

My medical scenes — no matter the book — are always written based on the expertise of my close friend and brother in Christ, Dr. Cleary. I am humbly indebted to him for allowing me, a would-be, self-appointed medical expert of the Verde Valley, to pick his brain at all hours of the day and night.

A very heartfelt thanks goes to my amazing editor, Karen Ball, whose God-given talent is responsible for making my fiction what it is today. And also to the entire staff at Multnomah, from Don Jacobson and Ken Ruettgers to the sales and marketing and publicity teams, to cover design, and editing. I am amazed at what God is doing at Multnomah and humbly blessed to be part of it. Thank you for believing in my work.

As with each of my books, I could not have written this one without the help of those who care for my precious children during crunch time. For that reason I'd like to thank Christy and Jeff Blake (and Butter for making Austin's naptime a bit cozier). And also my dear, sweet friend, Heidi, for making Tyler part of your family on so many occasions.

A special thanks to my parents who have believed in my writing since I was old enough to hold a pencil and to my extended family for their love and support.

Also thanks to my church family and friends, especially Christine Wessel, who knows my heart and has held me up in prayer on so many occasions; Michelle Stokes, who has a house with her name on it next door to mine; Lisa Alexander, who has been there from the beginning and always will be; and Heidi Cleary, who will take a piece of my heart with her when she moves away this summer. I love you all.

Oh, and thanks to the Skyview basketball team — you fiery, slam-dunking, hard-working, amazing guys who have given me so many reasons to cheer, even on deadline! Each of you and your families feel like a part of mine, and I cherish the fleeting moments we have together!

Finally, thanks to Grandma Polly Russell, who went to be with the Lord during the writing of this book. Thank you for teaching me what it truly is to love.

■ ■ ■ ■

PART I

■ ■ ■ ■

"For I know the plans I have for you,"
declares the LORD, "plans to prosper you
and not to harm you, plans to give you
hope and a future.
Then you will call upon me and come and
pray to me, and I will listen to you."
                              Jeremiah 29:11–12

ONE

The old biddies sat in a circle, their tightly knotted heads turning this way and that like vultures eyeing a kill. Only this time the carcass was the Conner family, and no one was quite dead yet.

Hap Eastman watched from a corner of the Williamsburg Community Church fellowship hall. He'd done his part. Started the coffee, laid out the pastries, set up the chairs. It was something he did every Saturday morning for the Women's Aid Society, and every time it was the same. The old girls started with a list of needs and prayer requests and ended with a full-blown gossip session.

Hap's wife, Doris, was president, and at forty-five the youngest of the group. So Hap hung around tinkering with fix-it jobs in the kitchen or perched on a cold metal folding chair in the corner, a cup of fresh brewed

French Roast in one hand and a Louis L'Amour novel in the other. Four days a week he was a jurist laden with a heavy workload and weighty decision making. Saturdays were his day to relax.

Hap had already heard the story from Doris and generally when the birds got going, he tried not to listen. But days like this it was nearly impossible.

"I don't care what anyone says. We need to talk about it." Geraldine Rivers had the floor, and Hap eyed her suspiciously from a distance. Geraldine was a talker from way back and in charge of the social committee. Generally when the gossip got going, Doris and Geraldine fanned the fires and battled for position. Especially in the heated sessions, and Hap figured this was about as hot as they'd ever get.

"We haven't read the minutes yet." Louella tilted her face in Geraldine's direction. The minutes were still tucked in her unopened Bible, so her comment was more for appearances than anything else.

"Minutes mean nothing at a time like this!" Geraldine nodded toward Doris. "Tell us what you know, will you, Dorie? Several of the ladies here haven't heard what happened."

The vultures nodded in unison, and Doris

took her cue.

"It's really very tragic, very sundry. I almost hate to talk about it at church." She paused for effect, smoothing the wrinkles in her polyester dress. "You all know the Conner family, Angela and her husband, Buddy —"

"Buddy's been drinking alcohol at the tavern lately. Louella's husband saw his truck there last week, isn't that true?" Geraldine knew this to be true but enjoyed her own voice too much to be silent for long.

Doris frowned. "Right. He's become a regular drunkard. Now, Angela . . . well, she's another story. A flirtatious type, not given to things of the Lord." She looked around the circle. "Nearly everyone in Williamsburg has suspected her of cheating on Buddy."

The old birds nodded again.

"Well, yesterday I got a call from Betty Jean Stevens . . . you've probably noticed she's not here today." Doris's face bunched up like it did when Hap forgot to take out the trash. "Seems all those rumors were true. Betty Jean found out last week that her husband's been seeing Angela Conner on the side. And I don't mean at the Piggly Wiggly."

A collective gasp rose from the circle, and

15

six of the girls started talking at once.

"Bill Stevens and that loose woman?"

"Why, that hypocrite!"

"A deacon at Williamsburg Community has committed adultery?"

"He'll need to make a public apology before I forgive him!"

"I knew something was happening between those two!"

The cacophony of accusations grew until Geraldine rapped her fist on the table. "Quiet, all of you! Quiet!"

They had obviously forgotten about Hap and his novel, and he gazed at them over the top of his book. The biddies fell silent again, and Geraldine lowered her gaze, trying to look appropriately indignant. "There's more. . . ."

Doris brought her hands together in a neat fold. "Yes." She drew a deep breath. "For the past few weeks Bill's been . . . taking a motel room with the Conner woman. Apparently she set about trying to seduce him for some time. And . . . well . . ."

"There's a temptress in every town!" Geraldine obviously intended to maintain her presence even if it was Doris's story.

"Betty Jean says Bill tried to ward off her advances. But last month . . . he gave in."

"I do declare, Angela Conner's a harlot.

16

She's always been a whore!" Geraldine snapped at a lemon pastry and dabbed fiercely at the filling it left on her lips.

"Yes, I believe she is." Doris looked glad that Geraldine had said it first. Hap sighed. "But the worst part happened last night."

The birds were nodding their interest, waiting breathlessly for the rest of the story.

Doris sipped her coffee, and Hap knew she was enjoying the way she held her audience captive. "Last night . . . Bill Stevens ran off with her. The two of them. Just like that, they up and left town."

Several of the women were on their feet firing questions.

"Where did they go?"

"Does anyone else know?"

Doris kept her back stiff, her nose in the air. Hap hated it when she got uppity, and this was one of those times. She answered their questions with all the condemnation she could muster.

"D.C."

"The capital?"

"Yes. Betty Jean says Bill sat her down last night and told her they were through. Told her he's in love with Angela, and they're starting a new life in Washington, D.C."

"Dear heaven, how's Betty Jean handling it?"

17

"She's ashamed, broken. But she saw it coming. About a year ago, Bill began meeting with Angela to talk about a business venture."

"Business venture?"

"I guess we all know what type *business*—" Geraldine spat the word the way boys spit watermelon seeds on a summer day — "that was, don't we?"

Doris hesitated. "Betty Jean's just thankful the children are grown and out of the house."

"Angela Conner was bad blood from the get-go. Last year, I think she was seeing that attorney in town. You know, the divorce lawyer."

"I'm sure you're right. Everyone this side of Richmond knows the Conner woman and how she was always sniffing around for a man to bed."

Hap raised an eyebrow. *A man to bed?*

"What about Buddy?" Again Geraldine was determined to keep the discussion alive.

"Buddy's disgraced, as well he should be. Any man who can't keep his wife at home *should* be ashamed of himself." Doris looked at Geraldine for approval. "And I have it on good word that he won't be back to Williamsburg Community Church."

"I certainly hope not." Geraldine finished

the pastry and wadded her napkin into a tight ball of crumbs and sticky paper. "The man's a drunkard."

There were several nods of approval, then one of the vultures gasped. "Oh, dear heaven. What's going to happen to little Jade?"

Jade. Hap felt his heart sink. He'd forgotten about the sweet ten-year-old, Buddy and Angela's only child.

Geraldine did nothing to hide her righteous indignation. "Isn't she the one who pals around with your Tanner?"

A deep crimson fanned across Doris's face. "The Conners live in our neighborhood, in Buddy's mother's house. Tanner is about the same age as the Conner girl, so it's only natural that the two play together. It doesn't happen often."

Doris wasn't telling the entire story, and Hap knew why. The reason was an ugly one. He and Dorie had two boys: Harry was twenty and worked for the city dump — a detail Dorie never told the girls at the Women's Aid Society. Then there was Tanner. Even at twelve years old, Tanner was everything Harry hadn't been. He was bright and handsome and the finest athlete in primary school. Doris thought he was going to be president of the United States

19

one day. How would it look if he had already made the social mistake of befriending the child of a woman like Angela Conner?

Of course, there were other reasons Doris detested the children's friendship. More complicated reasons. But Hap didn't want to think about those on a sunny Saturday in May when he was supposed to be relaxing. He shifted positions, but the biddies were too caught up to notice him.

"Didn't you say something about Buddy leaving town?" Geraldine was working on another Danish.

Doris lowered her voice. "Buddy's moving. Taking the child and getting as far away from Virginia as he can."

"He must've been planning it," one of the girls chimed in.

"Certainly he saw it coming."

Doris nodded. "I assume. Either way, Angela and Bill are gone, and by next week, Buddy and the girl will be gone, too."

"I feel sorry for the child." Louella fingered the pages of her Bible and the minutes, which remained unread.

Doris huffed. "Daughter of a woman like that! I say good riddance to bad rubbish. . . ."

Hap knew his wife was thinking about

their son. He and Jade were more than casual neighborhood pals. They were best friends, and for the past year, Tanner had insisted he was going to marry Jade when they grew up.

Doris was wagging her finger. "You know what the Bible says. Bad company corrupts good character."

Geraldine raised an eyebrow. "Tanner?"

Doris nodded, her cheeks flushed again. "My boy doesn't need a girl like Jade around to tempt him. He'll wind up a father before he's sixteen."

"Doris!" Louella seemed genuinely shocked.

"Well, it's true. I'm glad they're leaving. Especially after what they did to Betty Jean. She's my best friend, after all."

Geraldine clucked her tongue against the roof of her mouth. "Doris is right. Williamsburg is a place filled with old money, old family ties, and old-fashioned values. The Conners are trouble, pure and simple. The girl is sweet now, but with a mother like hers we all know how she'll wind up. Where are they moving?"

Doris cleared her throat. "Washington state somewhere. Buddy has a brother in a small town. . . . Kelso, I think it is."

"Pity the good folks of Kelso, Washington,

21

when a family like the Conners moves to town." Geraldine nodded her head decisively.

"Now, now . . ." Doris's tone was friendly again, and Hap saw she was making an effort to look the part of a righteous Christian leader. "Let's not be vicious. We need to concern ourselves with Betty Jean. After all, the Conners will be gone soon, out of our lives for good."

Hap knew Doris's last comment was more for his benefit than for anyone else's, and as she said it she looked right at him. None of the biddies knew the real reason Doris felt so strongly about Angela Conner, but Hap did. Her comment hit its mark, and Hap lowered his gaze back to his novel. What had happened between him and Angela Conner was decades old, but that didn't matter. No matter how many years passed, there was one thing Doris Eastman would never forget.

The sins of Angela Conner.

The children rode their bicycles into Tanner's driveway, laid them on the pavement and flopped down on a grassy spot in the center of his neatly manicured front lawn. The discussion had been going on for several minutes.

"I still don't get it. Where'd she go?" Tanner plucked a blade of grass and meticulously tore it into tiny sections.

Jade shrugged and gazed across the street toward the two-story house where she had lived for the past three years. "Daddy says she's gonna meet us in Washington. That's all I know."

Tanner chewed on that for a moment. The whole thing sounded fishy to him. Mamas didn't leave for no reason. And people didn't move without making plans first. "Do you think she's mad at you?"

"Of course she's not mad. She loves me. I know it." Jade tossed her dark head, and her eyes flashed light green. Tanner had never seen eyes like Jade's. Green like the water of Chesapeake Bay.

"Why doesn't she just come back? Then you wouldn't have to move."

"I told you, they already decided. We're moving to Washington. Mama went on ahead of us, and Daddy says she'll meet us there."

"In Washington?"

"Yes, Tanner. I told you she didn't *leave* me. She just needed some time alone."

Tanner plucked another piece of grass and twisted it between his thumb and forefinger. "But she didn't say good-bye, right?"

Jade sighed, and Tanner saw tears form in her eyes. "I *told* you, Tanner. She left early in the morning. Daddy said she probably knew I would be sad so she left before I woke up. 'Cause she loves me."

"Did she leave a note or anything?"

"Daddy said he didn't need a note." Jade swiped at a tear, and her voice was angrier than before. "He knows where she's going, and that's why we have to move. We need to get there so we can be with Mama again. She would never wanna be alone that long."

Tanner still didn't understand, but he saw that his questions were bothering Jade. He sat up and crossed his legs, studying her curiously. The only time he'd ever seen her cry was two years ago when she jumped a curb on her bike and flew over the handlebars. But that was different. Now Tanner wasn't sure what to do. He decided to change the subject. "How far away is Washington?"

"Daddy says" — she leaned back on her elbows and stared at the cloudless sky — "it's about as far away as heaven is from hell."

Tanner thought about that for a moment. "But you're coming back, right?"

Jade nodded. "Of course. We'll meet up with Mama, and then Daddy's gotta do a

24

job there. He said it could take all summer. After that we'll come home."

Tanner relaxed. That sounded all right. Even if the whole thing still seemed kind of weird.

"I gotta go." Jade rose and climbed back on her bike. "Daddy needs help packing."

Tanner stood and pushed his hands deep into the worn pockets of his jeans. "You leavin' tomorrow?"

She nodded and worked her toe in tiny circles on the pavement. For a moment Tanner thought she was going to hug him, then at the last second she pushed him in the arm like she always did when she didn't know what to say.

Tanner pushed her back, but not hard enough to move her. "Hey, I'm still going to marry you."

Jade huffed. "Shut up, Tanner. You're a smelly old boy and I'm not going to marry anyone."

"One day you'll think I'm Prince Charming," Tanner teased.

Jade couldn't keep a straight face, and she began giggling. "Oh, okay. Right. Sure . . . whatever you say." She shook her head dramatically. "I would never marry you, Tanner. Sometimes I think you're crazy."

"Got you smiling, though, didn't I?"

They grinned at each other for a beat and then Jade's smile faded. "I'll see ya later."

Tanner kicked at a patch of grass and sighed. "You better come back when summer's over."

Jade's eyes got watery again. "I *said* I'll be back." She began pedaling down his driveway. Halfway home she turned once and waved. Tanner raised one of his palms toward her. He'd heard his parents whispering about Jade and her daddy the other day. Tanner didn't catch all the details, but it was obvious his mother didn't think the Conner family was ever coming back.

It was good to know she was wrong.

As Jade disappeared into her house, Tanner felt a subtle reassurance that somehow, someday soon, the two of them would be together again.

Two

Doris Eastman watched the 727 angle across the Columbia River and make its final approach toward the runway. Seated somewhere inside the plane, Tanner would be waiting, excited to see her, anxious to be back in the Northwest.

The thought frustrated her. She would have done anything to keep him at Princeton where he belonged.

Hap must have been crazy to move here in the first place, and now that he was gone, Doris had every intention of getting back to Virginia. Poor old Hap. Retired from the bar two years earlier with dreams of being a lawyer again in Portland. For a tennis shoe company of all things. And despite his history of heart problems.

No matter how many times she thought about his decision, she'd never understand. They had had plenty of money in Virginia

27

and a reputation Hap had earned after twenty years of serving as a superior court judge. Countless social invitations, the best seats at their favorite restaurants, season tickets to the opera . . . they'd had everything they'd ever wanted. And of course, in Virginia they were closer to Tanner.

Hap hadn't been concerned with any of that. His buddy Mark Westfall, another attorney, had moved to Portland three years before. Mark had played professional basketball after college and eventually took a job in the legal department of the shoe company. It wasn't long until Mark had convinced Hap that Portland was the place to retire. No snow, no heat, no smog. Only beautiful greenery and endless opportunities.

Doris watched the plane taxi toward the gate and sighed. Good old Mark had forgotten that greenery comes at a price. The rain had been incessant and besides, what kind of retirement was it to take on a second career? And with Hap nearly sixty years old? She'd seen the heart attack coming, even if Hap hadn't. Too many fast-food lunches and too little exercise all heaped on a workload that seemed to grow every month.

They'd moved to Portland in November — to beat the cold Virginia winter, Hap had said. That year Williamsburg hadn't had an inch of snow all season. Oregon, meanwhile, had record-breaking rain.

Even now, with June already here, the cursed Northwest was shrouded in clouds and drizzle. Who could jog or even walk in such a dreadful place? Hap tried it for a while, jogging in the rain. But that lasted only a month. His heart attack came just after Easter.

Now she was still in the process of settling the estate, handling Hap's affairs and packing up the condominium. She planned to be back in Williamsburg by fall, and if she'd had anything to do with it, Tanner could have waited and seen her then. For the life of her, Doris couldn't imagine why her son would want to spend a summer in the Northwest.

He'd explained it a dozen times. Some sort of internship program with the Kelso board of supervisors. If it were anywhere else, Doris would have been pleased with the assignment. But Kelso? Of all the places in the world, her son had chosen to take an internship in Kelso, Washington?

Of course, Kelso was still big enough that the odds of them running into each other were slim. Even if they did, Doris doubted they'd recognize each other. Jade had moved away eleven years ago, after all.

Still . . . it worried her.

She remembered talking with Tanner about it last week. "Son, I don't understand. Why Kelso?" Doris was not about to mention the fact that Jade might still live there. Tanner hadn't brought up the girl's name in years; certainly he had no idea that she had moved to Kelso way back when.

"I told you, Mom. I want to spend weekends with you, going through Dad's stuff, helping you pack for the move. The board of supervisors had an internship available in Kelso. It's near Portland. I had all the qualifications. Seemed like a perfect match to me."

Doris tried to detect anything false in her son's voice, but there was nothing. He didn't remember Jade; wouldn't look her up. The whole thing was just a coincidence.

She moved closer to the window and wondered again why she was so worried. There were thousands of loose girls prowling about for a man like Tanner — and Jade Conner would certainly be a loose girl. Just like her dreadful mother. Poor Betty Jean had never been the same after Angela Conner ran off with Bill.

But Doris had her own reasons for hating the Conner woman. Reasons no one knew anything about. Doris felt the sting of angry tears, and she banished the memories from her mind.

She would hate Angela Conner until the day she died.

Five years ago Doris got word from one of the women at the Aid's Society that Buddy and Jade were still living in Kelso. Someone knew someone whose brother maintained contact with the family. Apparently Buddy was an unemployed drunkard, and Jade ran the streets. If that were true — and Doris was sure it was — then there was no need to worry about Tanner. He'd never be interested in a girl who ran the streets, a girl who probably slept around, a girl with a scandalous past.

A girl whose mother had very nearly ruined their lives.

The college girls Tanner dated were virginal types, clean-cut and wholesome. Even then there had never been anyone serious. His faith wouldn't allow it.

That was another irksome thing. Tanner's incessant faith.

She and Hap had brought him up in the church and left it at that. A modest faith could have been an asset to his political future. Instead he'd taken to reading the Bible and quoting Scripture. He attended

31

some crazy nondenominational church on campus and talked about God's will this and God's will that.

Doris hoped it was only a stage, something he'd outgrow. There was no room in public office for religious fanaticism. Especially in one who leaned as heavily to the right as Tanner did.

His obsession with religion would pass, Doris was certain about it. Just like his fascination with Jade. For three years after she moved he had asked about her and when she was coming back. Doris remembered the time when Tanner was nearly fifteen and he'd wandered into the backyard where she was weeding.

"Mama, tell me the truth. Jade isn't coming back, is she? Not ever." Tanner was gangly in those days, all knobby knees and giant blue eyes.

Doris had leaned back on her heels and shook the soil from her work gloves. "Why must you persist in asking such questions, Tanner? What is it about Jade? She's been gone nearly three years."

"I'm going to marry her one day, Mama. How can I marry her if she doesn't come back?"

Doris remembered feeling lightheaded at the suggestion of Tanner and Jade wedded in matrimony. She had forced herself to take deep breaths. The daughter of a harlot? Doris had to stifle the anger that rose within her. "Son, you're too young to know who you want to marry."

"I'm not too young, Mama. I know what I want, and I want to marry Jade Conner. I decided a long time ago."

Doris wanted to tell him the girl was worthless, trash. A weed in a garden chock full of roses. Instead she smiled warmly at the boy before her. "Well, dear, first she'll have to move back to Virginia. And honestly I don't see that happening."

"I can't remember where she moved. Where was it, Mama? Was it Washington, D.C.? Maybe I can get her address and write to her."

Doris stopped herself before spurting out the city and state. "I'm not really sure, actually. Out west somewhere, I think." She had resumed her gardening, loosening a weed and then pulling it out from the root.

Tanner had crossed his arms angrily. "I'm going to marry her one day, Mama. Even if I have to search the whole country and find her myself."

An attendant announced the arrival of Tanner's flight, and Doris blinked back her son's words, shuddering at the memory. If anything had been an act of God, it was the fact that Jade Conner never came back to Williamsburg, Virginia.

Doris folded her hands and noticed her palms were sweaty. Her fears about the girl were irrational, weren't they? Tanner couldn't possibly know Jade lived in Kelso. It was coincidence, pure and simple. What could go wrong when he would only be in town a single summer? The weeks would dissolve in an instant, and then he'd fly back to New Jersey, back to Princeton where he could prepare for his senior year.

Doris didn't know what his first assignment would be when he graduated, but she knew it would be political in nature. He had been groomed for public office since he was a small boy. Every friendship, every activity, every article of clothing, every class, each student government office, even his role as an award-winning athlete was a line on what had become a stellar resume. She'd designed a packet on Tanner's accomplishments midway through his junior year and touted it to all the Ivy League schools. Scholarship offers had been plentiful.

He and Hap had complained for a while, thinking Tanner would be better off at a West Coast school where he could play sports. But finally she'd convinced them. A

Princeton education would be priceless. Besides, the time had come to stop playing games. Tanner had a brilliant future at hand and not a moment to waste. Now he was nearly ready. He would graduate next summer, and the climb would begin, one rung at a time.

People were streaming through the gate with that bewildered look travelers wore. She moved closer, and there at the back of the pack she saw him. He was nearly a head taller than the masses, and he drew the stares of several women in the crowd. People had always noticed Tanner. He had a magnetic quality that couldn't be taught or trained. It was more of a birthright. As he drew closer, she saw his skin had lost the paleness of three months ago when he'd flown out for Hap's memorial service. He had some color now, and he was taking on a more pronounced jawline. *Perfect. The public loves a good-looking politician with a strong jawline.*

He was going to look wonderful in the White House.

"Mother, you look lovely as always." Tanner strode toward her, wrapped her in a hug, and grinned.

They made small talk, and he kept one arm around her shoulders as they headed toward the baggage department. After a few minutes, Tanner's tone grew serious. "How are you, Mom, really? Dad's been gone a while now. I've been praying for you."

Doris squeezed him tighter. "Thanks, honey. I miss him. But we had a wonderful life. I'm glad he didn't suffer."

"It's good you're moving back to Virginia. I think you've had about as much of the Northwest as you can stand." Tanner's eyes danced as he nodded toward a wall of windows and the thick, gray sky outside. "You'll feel better when you get back to sunny Virginia."

"Yes . . ." She paused. *The sooner the better.*

Tanner was telling her something about the internship and the projects at hand, but she wasn't really listening. She was wracked by thoughts of Jade and Tanner and Kelso, Washington . . . and the memory of a fifteen-year-old boy with earnest eyes insisting that one day he'd marry the girl.

Even if he had to search the whole country and find her himself.

THREE

Midday at Kelso General Hospital was typically a quiet time, especially in the children's unit. Most of the younger patients napped or watched afternoon cartoons; others were too sick to sit up, and they slept, usually until dinner.

But that Monday, the fourth of June, Jade Conner was at the nurse's station reading a book for her science class at Kelso Junior College when she heard whimpering. She worked three afternoons a week as a nurse's assistant in the children's unit, and she could hardly wait to finish her education and begin nursing. The children needed her. They were frightened, unsure of why they were sick and wondering whether everything was going to turn out all right.

The whimpering grew louder.

"Wanna check her, Jade?" The head nurse was buried in paperwork, and Jade nodded. She stood up, tucking a strand of short dark hair back behind her ear.

"Coming, little one. I'm coming." She worked her way across the hallway to Room 403. Shaunie Ellersby. Four years old. Recurrent kidney infections. Doctors were running tests, but there was a strong suspicion that the child's kidneys were failing. Shaunie had been in the hospital off and on for the past six months. This time she'd been in for more than a week, and her mother had finally taken to staying home between meals to tend to Shaunie's two younger sisters.

"Sweetie, I'm here. What's wrong, baby doll?" Jade cozied up next to the child and gently stroked her forehead. She knew she was Shaunie's favorite nurse, and the two had been fast friends since the girl first got sick.

"I miss my mommy." The little girl squeezed out the words between stifled sobs.

"Ah, it's okay, sweetie. She'll be here later, I promise." Jade kissed the child's forehead. "Want something to drink?"

Shaunie nodded, and Jade saw her sadness fade. "Apple juice."

"What's the magic word?"

"Please?"

Jade smiled. "Okay. Be back in a minute." When she returned with the drink, she took her spot once more on the hospital bed beside the little girl. Shaunie took several long sips from the straw. After the third mouthful she smiled up at her. "Thanks, Jade."

"Sure, sweetie. Hey, what say we talk for a little bit?"

Shaunie nodded. "Guess what? Mommy painted my bedroom."

"She did?"

"Yep. Pink and white with little flowers."

"Oh, I wish I had a room like that. Your Mommy sure is nice."

Shaunie nodded and finished her juice. "Jade, do you live here?"

She grinned and tousled the child's hair. "Here? At the hospital? Of course not, silly."

"Then where do you live?"

"At home, like everyone else?"

"With your mommy and daddy?"

A twinge of sorrow seized Jade. The answer never came easily. "No, sweetie. Just with my daddy."

Shaunie's face scrunched up. "What about your Mommy?"

Jade felt the sting of tears and blinked them back. "I don't have a mommy."

Shaunie's eyes grew wide. "Why not? Did she die?"

The child's innocent questions rattled

around in her heart like pebbles in an empty tin can. "She lives far, far away, baby doll. We never see each other anymore."

Sadness filled the child's face. "That's too bad. How 'bout your daddy. Does he paint your room sometimes?"

Jade thought of her father, passed out in his easy chair, beer bottles littering the living room floor. "No, sweetie, he doesn't. But think what a lucky little girl you are to have a brand new room waiting for you when you get home."

Shaunie considered that for a minute, and Jade ran her fingertips over the child's forehead. The little girl's skin had a yellow cast, and her eyes still looked tired from the infection that ravaged her body. The doctors had done more tests that week, and Jade hoped they wouldn't find anything seriously wrong with her.

"My mommy and daddy don't live too far away from me, do they, Jade?"

"Well, honey, no. But you don't live here, you live with your mommy and daddy."

"Sometimes I live here." Shaunie didn't seem distraught by the fact.

"That's true, I guess. But Mommy and Daddy are very, very close. They can visit all the time."

For now, anyway. Unless the county voted

to shut down the children's unit. A stab of fear set free a batch of butterflies in Jade's gut. There had been talk about closing the unit for months. Budget cuts were needed, and someone had designed a plan to eliminate the children's ward at Kelso General. If that happened, sick children like Shaunie would have to go an hour south to Portland for care. An hour that meant the difference between a child getting to see her parents several times a day or being left alone in a hospital with infrequent visits at best.

The city was going to discuss the idea at a meeting that afternoon. The plan made Jade furious.

"Yes, honey, you can see your mommy and daddy any time you want."

Shaunie nodded and wriggled about, an anxious look on her face. "I have to go potty."

Jade helped her out of bed, careful not to tangle her IV lines. When the ordeal was through, she eased the child back under the blankets.

"You're pretty." Shaunie yawned.

Jade smiled and kissed the little girl on the tip of her nose. "Thanks. You, too, princess."

"My mommy says you look like Meg Ryan with dark hair."

"Does she now?" Jade laughed.

"Who's Meg Ryan?"

"Oh, she's someone in the movies."

"I think you're prettier than her." Shaunie laid her head back on the pillow and rubbed her eyes. "I need to take a nap-time now."

"Okay, baby doll. You do that. I won't be here when you wake up, but I'll see you tomorrow."

"Where will you go, Jade? Home to see your daddy?"

She hugged the little girl close. *Only when I absolutely have to, honey.* "No, sweetie. I have to go to a meeting."

"Okay." Shaunie yawned again and her eyelids fluttered. "Night-night, Jade."

"G'night, honey."

Rarely had anything mattered this much to Jade. She slept in the house where her father lived, but the hospital was her home. She had volunteered in the children's unit since she was sixteen. Now that she worked there, she would fight the county with everything she had so Shaunie and Kelso's other sick kids would never have to be shuttled away to a hospital in Portland.

Jade returned to the nurse's station and glanced at the clock. It was nearly three. The meeting was at four and was expected to draw a hundred people.

Jade pushed aside her science book and began scribbling on the back of a blank admitting form. If she had a chance, she intended to talk about the kids at Kelso Hospital. Shaunie had given her an idea. She began putting her feelings on paper until she'd filled an entire page with notes.

The thought of Shaunie being separated from her parents made her throat constrict. *Help me, God. Let them see how badly we need this place.*

Jade was not religious — she didn't attend a church or read a Bible — but ever since she was a little girl she had talked to God, especially when she was alone. And she was alone often.

She thought about the townspeople who would attend the meeting and wondered whether they, too, wanted to keep the unit open. Jade would know many of them, she was sure, and she hoped her words would persuade them to join the fight. While the people of Kelso who knew her did not go out of their way to be friendly to Jade, most of them didn't seem to hold her father's alcoholism against her. Jade didn't care if they did. She didn't need anyone's approval. She didn't need anything at all.

Except the children's unit at Kelso General.

A unit whose fate was entirely in the
hands of the county's board of supervisors.

FOUR

The offices of the Cowlitz county board of supervisors for the city of Kelso, Washington, were located above city hall and adjacent to an auditorium where town meetings had been held for the past fifty years. Tanner had spent the morning in meetings and used his lunch hour to unpack his files, reference books, and rearrange his office.

Tanner surveyed the worn-out cubicle that would serve as his workspace for the summer. His mother would have been appalled. Nothing but cherrywood and inlaid carpets for Tanner Eastman. A politician on the rise needed the right type of office even if it meant having his mother come down and make over the place herself.

He ambled toward the last of his things, a stack of legal books that would barely fit on his desk. These were treasured books, and whether he'd need them or not during the internship, he intended to read them: *Reli-*

gious Freedom Fading Fast, Whatever Happened to God in America?, One Nation Under God?

He stood the books where he could see them, wondering what his mother would say if she knew what really interested him. Hogwash, no doubt. A waste of time. Silly notions. Extremism. Tanner smiled. The books were a secret, but they were nothing compared with the secret he harbored in his heart. The secret of what he really wanted to do with his life.

Fred Lang, one of the younger supervisors, peered around the pressed board that made up the cast wall of Tanner's new office. "You 'bout ready?"

"I think so." Tanner reached for a folder.

"You did read the file we sent, correct?"

"Four times." He handed Lang the folder. "I put together a few pages in summary, stating the board's reasoning, highlighting the profit and loss statement for Kelso General's children's wing. It's all in there."

Lang took the folder and glanced through it. "Impressive." He looked up at Tanner. "This is a hot one. Town's pretty riled up about it, what with a closure affecting sick kids and all." He hesitated. "What would you think about presenting your summary at the public meeting today? Since the townspeople don't know you yet."

Tanner shrugged. "Fine with me."

Lang's shoulders relaxed and the lines on his forehead were replaced with a broad smile. "Okay, great. We'll introduce you, tell them you're working with the board for the summer. Then hand you the floor. We'll handle the questions when you're done."

Tanner shot a glance at his watch. "The meeting's at four, right?"

"Right. We need to be there half an hour early to compare notes."

"One question."

Lang leaned against the particleboard but straightened again when it threatened to topple. "Shoot."

"The file wasn't real clear on the alternatives, other ways the county could cut the budget besides closing the children's unit."

Lang sighed. "To tell you the truth, there really hasn't been time. Elections are coming up this fall, we've got the police staff about to go on strike. Budget cuts are a reality, and this was an easy choice."

"Maybe not to the townsfolk." Tanner wasn't trying to be difficult, but if he was going to be on the front line, he needed to know how to respond to the fire.

"Don't worry, we'll take the heat. You just give 'em your presentation. Maybe then they'll stop thinking we have something against their kids."

"Small town syndrome?"

"Too small. Everyone on the board knows someone who's taking this thing personally. The town thinks we're a bunch of ogres who have it out for them."

Tanner wondered. "Nothing personal involved?"

"No. Just the simplest cut we could make. The one that took the least time to figure out and helped us make ends meet."

Tanner nodded. "Is there a Plan B?"

"Plan B?"

"The town's coming out for the meeting, right? What if there's more outrage than you're counting on? It's election year, after all. You said so yourself. Maybe we should have a Plan B."

"Such as?"

"Such as taking the summer and seeing if we can find somewhere else to cut the budget."

Lang gripped his chin with his thumb and forefinger and nodded slowly. "Not a bad idea." He let his hand drop. "But don't tell the people that."

Tanner folded his arms. "First rule of sticky politics: Work like you have a Plan B, talk like you wouldn't consider it."

Lang smiled. "I like that. But it wouldn't be us finding somewhere else to cut the budget. It would be you."

Tanner chuckled. "I figured as much."

Lang patted Tanner roughly on the shoulder. "Welcome to summer internships, my friend. We'll keep you so busy you'll look forward to final exams."

"I don't doubt it."

Lang had lightened up considerably in the past five minutes and seemed ready to make small talk. Tanner didn't mind that he'd been made chief scapegoat on the issue. He didn't know a soul in the state of Washington, and it wouldn't hurt to have a friend in Lang.

The man shot a look around Tanner's cubicle. "Public office, right? That's the goal?"

"How'd you guess?"

"Princeton degree in poli-sci, political internships, get elected to councilman or congressman. Maybe the big time, state senator, or even the White House." Lang huffed and a grin appeared on his face. "I've worked with you dreamers before."

"Yep." Tanner studied the stack of books he'd unpacked moments earlier. He suddenly felt like a load of bricks had been dumped on his shoulders. "That's always been the big dream. Public office. An elected servant of the people. It's something I've . . ." he searched for the right words, "known I'd do . . . as far back as I can remember."

The ten-member board of supervisors had finished its private meeting and now sat along a panel at the front of the auditorium. The room was filling fast, and Tanner could feel the tension. Scattered about were clusters of townspeople, whispering and gesturing and casting disdainful looks toward the board.

This wasn't going to be a discussion. It was going to be a lynching. They didn't want to lose the children's unit at Kelso General, and they appeared ready to demand the heads of the people who did.

Tanner scanned the room. Mostly older people, longtime residents, probably, and several serious-looking couples. Parents of sick kids, no doubt. He continued searching the room . . . and his breath caught in his throat.

She was in the back row, sitting by herself. She couldn't have been much more than twenty, slim and athletic looking with short, windblown hair the color of roasted walnuts. She was studying a pile of notes on her lap, and Tanner realized she was wearing a nurse's uniform. *Great. Another voice against us.* Despite the scowl on her face she was breathtaking. The girl glanced up and met his gaze, and for a moment a look of recognition flashed in her eyes. Then she looked quickly away.

For a moment, Tanner's political poise wavered, and he considered going to her. There was something familiar about her, though Tanner couldn't decide what it was. He watched her for another few seconds, then returned to his notes. The girl didn't matter.

If she worked with the children at Kelso General, then they were about to become enemies.

The meeting was underway, and several minor matters of business had been taken care of. Now Lang had the floor, and he was reading from Tanner's resume.

"We have a young intern with us for the summer. He's from Princeton University and —" he shot Tanner a look — "will probably become a household name one day in political circles. This afternoon he's going to brief all of you on the budget status and the intended closure of the children's unit at Kelso General Hospital." A chorus of grumblings began to build, and Lang was forced to raise his voice. "If you'll please give him your attention. Mr. Tanner Ghormsley."

Tanner hesitated for a moment. *Ghormsley?* Some great start he'd made in becoming a household name if his boss couldn't even remember what to call him. He didn't bother making a correction. He stood and felt a sense of serenity. Crowds did not make him nervous.

"Ladies and gentlemen, first let me thank you for coming. I understand that many of you have serious concerns about the closure of the children's unit at Kelso General." He paused, guessing that nearly two hundred people had packed the auditorium. Not one of them was smiling. His eyes found the girl in the back, but she was looking at her notes again.

He cleared his throat and began explaining in succinct detail the condition of the county's budget. When it was apparent how desperately cuts were in order, he began talking about the children's unit. The numbers told the story. Kelso General was owned by the county and simply was not making enough money to warrant a children's ward.

"Children's units are more costly because

equipment must be adjusted on nearly every level. Smaller beds, smaller machinery, smaller needles and tubing and testing devices." He looked for a softening among the crowd and saw none.

He went on to tell them how other units at the hospital were essential and that children could still be treated in the emergency room once the children's unit was closed.

"Children who need hospitalization will be transported to Portland's Doernbecher Children's Hospital. Of course that facility is one of the finest in the nation."

Finally, Tanner dealt with the most difficult truth of all. "The fact is, Kelso General is costing this county a lot of money. While none of you wants to see the children's unit closed, it would be far worse to see the entire hospital shut down."

He cited towns that had lost hospitals because of the drain on county funds. "The board of supervisors feels very strongly that this town does need a hospital. Kelso General has a tremendous reputation in the medical community, and the staff there has played a part in saving the lives of hundreds of Kelso residents. You may know someone who is alive today because of Kelso General. Perhaps you, yourself, are here because you had the privilege of living near a top-notch medical facility."

Tanner scanned the faces before him, relieved to feel the tension easing. "We all want to keep the children's unit. But if it means the difference between losing Kelso General or keeping it up and running in this great town, is there any question what the board should do? Thank you."

So much for Plan B.

Tanner sat down and watched as the clusters of people who had been frowning and grumbling quietly considered what he'd said. He could almost read their minds. Children were wonderful and all, but no hospital? Nowhere to go when chest pains struck in the middle of the night? Longview's St. John's Hospital was ten miles away and a far cry from Kelso General. Several elderly citizens in the back of the room stood and headed for the exit.

Tanner turned and looked at Lang. There was relief in the man's eyes, and Tanner silently thanked God. There was no doubt about one thing: The Lord had given him a gift of persuasion. The children's unit was as good as gone. Maybe his mother was right after all. Maybe he would love being a politician.

Lang stood up. "Are there any questions?"

54

Another batch of townsfolk stood and headed for the door. "All right then, at this point we'd like to —"

"Wait!" It was the girl from the back. She was on her feet staring at the people who were leaving. "Don't go! You can't give up that easily." She motioned toward Tanner. "He doesn't live here; it's not his hospital."

Lang coughed once. "Uhhh, Miss . . . Conner, is it? Do you have a comment you'd like to address to the board?"

The girl spun toward Lang. "Yes, sir, I do."

Tanner sensed that for some reason the crowd didn't like Miss Conner, whoever she was. Still, the citizens who had started for the door were turning around and making their way back to their seats.

"I believe we've already shared with you the fact that we don't want to cut the children's unit. We simply don't have a choice." Lang sighed impatiently. "But go ahead. Make your comments known."

The girl clenched her fists tightly and stood straighter, her eyes blazing. As she met the eyes of her fellow townsfolk, the look on her face softened. "Don't be fooled by some . . . some stranger who doesn't know us. The board of supervisors would never close down Kelso General. Not in a million years. That hospital is a source of pride and strength in this town . . . every one of you knows that."

She glared at Tanner, and he was struck by the color of her eyes. There was something hauntingly familiar about her, like the strains of a long-ago song that had once played over and over in his mind. *Have I seen her somewhere before? Do I know her?* He banished the thought. It was impossible; he'd never been to Kelso before in his life. He glanced down at his notes, preferring them to the penetrating anger in the girl's eyes.

Her voice was ringing with sincerity. "The county budget covers hundreds of items. Certainly the board can make their cuts somewhere else. And if the hospital isn't making money —" she waved her hand toward the board members — "well, then, maybe we need a new board of supervisors. A facility like Kelso General should be making money, or there must be something wrong with the people responsible for it."

A quick glance at the crowd told the story. Outrage was back in the people's eyes, and Tanner summoned his strength. Maybe Plan B wasn't dead after all.

The young woman reached down and picked up a snapshot of a blond child, four, maybe five, years old. "This is Shaunie. She has kidney disease." Her voice remained strong, but Tanner could see tears in the young woman's eyes . . . those green, gorgeous eyes. "She's spent most of the past six months at Kelso General's children's unit." The girl paused. "Today, Shaunie said something to me that I want you to hear. She told me she was glad her mommy and daddy lived so close."

Tanner shifted his gaze and saw a few women in the crowd with tears running down their faces. *Wonderful.* Apparently everyone in town knew little Shaunie.

"I held her in my arms and told her that her parents lived *with* her, not close by somewhere else. But Shaunie shook her head and told me as sweetly as she could that sometimes she lived at the hospital. And when she did, she was glad her mommy and daddy were close."

Handkerchiefs were yanked from purses and several women dabbed at their eyes. The sound of stifled sniffles filled the auditorium, and the citizens strained to hear the young nurse. "Medical research has proven that children heal more quickly, more thoroughly when they are happy. When they're not afraid."

She pointed to Tanner again, and he

wished he could disappear. The girl was stunning, and he could feel the fight leaving him. What was he doing arguing with her, anyway? *It's not my budget, lady. You can keep your children's unit . . . and anything else you want with eyes like —*

"That . . . that *man* wants to move Shaunie to Portland, more than an hour away. How well do you think she'll recover from kidney disease when her mommy and daddy don't live close by."

Her attention was back on the people. "Please. Don't let them close the children's unit without a fight. We need to stick together and tell this board that we won't reelect them this fall if they don't find some other way to cut the budget."

Tanner caught several of the board members exchanging glances. Obviously "reelect" was the buzzword. He could almost feel them implementing Plan B. The beautiful nurse was finishing her plea. "Let's take a vote. Please. Everyone who wants to keep our children's unit open, raise your hand."

Hands filled the auditorium, and Tanner watched as his persuasive presentation dissolved like sand in a stormy ocean wave. If he wanted, he could take her on, go head-to-head with her in debate, sway the people back to his way of thinking. But then, he wasn't up for reelection this fall. Besides, he'd angered the nurse enough already.

Lang looked to the other board members for approval, and Tanner saw several of them nodding. Leaning forward, Lang smiled politely at the townsfolk and spoke into the microphone. "If there are no other comments, the board wants all of you to know we appreciate your interest in coming to the meeting today. We also want to thank our new intern for his presentation. Although he has done his homework and made a strong case for closing the children's unit, the board wants to assure you that this matter is far from decided."

Tanner grimaced. Nice. Make it sound like the whole thing had been his idea. He'd be lucky if he got out of the building alive.

Lang was rhapsodizing about being a servant of the people and doing only that which was best for everyone, but the crowd was growing tired and more frustrated. Eventually Lang caught on. He smiled in Tanner's direction. "We have therefore decided to postpone any decision on this matter until the first week of September."

Tanner wasn't surprised. That was long enough for him to spend the summer researching a better way to balance the budget and save the children's unit, and late enough that the supervisors could take credit for it. *Ah, the life of a political intern.*

The meeting was over, and the atmosphere had done a one-eighty. The clusters of townspeople stood in bunches, congratulating each other. They had a lofty air about them now, as though they were far superior to the board of supervisors.

Tanner watched as several of them approached the girl who had championed the children's unit so well. Again he had the feeling he'd seen her somewhere before. What had Lang called her? The citizens talked to her in a manner that seemed far friendlier than their earlier reception. She remained aloof, an ice queen. But still there was something about her . . .

Lang approached him. "Tanner, great job up there. We almost had 'em."

"Eastman." Tanner's eyes were trained on the girl.

Lang's face went blank. "What?"

"My name. Tanner Eastman."

A beat. "What did I call you?"

"Tanner Ghormsley. As in Professor John Ghormsley. The man who arranged my internship."

Lang shrugged. "Oh well, they don't know who you are."

"Yeah, well, after what happened here

today maybe I should thank you." Tanner collected his file, but his eyes still followed the girl. Every move she made reminded him of something he'd seen before, someone he'd known before.

Lang followed Tanner's gaze and huffed. "She sure did us in. She's worked the children's unit for years. Obviously a bleeding heart —"

"Wait a minute!" Tanner's eyes widened and his heart pounded in his chest. It couldn't be, but then . . . Where had she moved? Wasn't it somewhere out west? Maybe even somewhere in Washington? Tanner's mouth went dry as he stared at her, still standing there across the room. "What did you say her name was?"

"Who?" Lang looked around, trying to make sense of Tanner's question.

The young nurse was gathering her things, making her move to leave, and Tanner was filled with a frantic sense of urgency. "The girl, the nurse. What's her name?"

Tanner knew he couldn't wait another moment. He had to know if he was right. He began pulling away, heading toward her, and for a single moment he focused his gaze on Lang, desperate for his answer. "Come *on,* what's her name? You said it earlier."

"Oh, her." Lang nodded toward the girl.

"Conner. What's this all about? The meeting's over, Tanner."

"I have to talk to her. What's her first name?"

"Ummm, I'm not sure. Wait a minute, I'll think of it." Lang concentrated and then pursed his lips, tapping a single finger on his chin. "Let's see. Jean, was it? No, not Jean. . . ."

Tanner thought his heart might burst. Lang was still concentrating. "Jane . . . no, that's not it."

"Think, Lang. I have to know." The girl was leaving, and he absolutely had to know her name, had to find out if it could possibly be her after all these —

Suddenly a knowing look crossed Lang's face. "I've got it. Unusual name. Jade, I think it is." Lang nodded. "Yes, that's it. Jade. Miss Jade Conner."

FIVE

Tanner stared at Lang and felt the blood drain from his face. For a moment he stood frozen in place. Jade Conner? The girl who'd fought so eloquently against him was Jade Conner?

Tanner shoved his papers at Lang. "I'll see you at the office." Lang took the documents, a bewildered look on his face, as Tanner ran toward the door where he had last seen Jade.

He scanned the area in both directions, and then he saw her, fitting a key into a newly washed Honda.

"Jade!" He wore Italian dress pants and a starched white button-down with the finest tie his mother's money could buy. But he dodged the mingling citizens like a wide receiver eluding tacklers. He was at her side in seconds.

She turned around and scowled at him. "What do you want?"

Tanner gulped. Where should he begin? His heart was pounding as he searched her face, her emerald eyes. It was Jade. Eyes as green as the water in Chesapeake Bay. No wonder she'd seemed familiar. "Yes, I . . . well, you're —"

"How did you know my name?"

Her question caught him off guard, and when he hesitated she pounced. "Listen, I don't care who you are or where you're from or what lofty Ivy League school you attend. You have no right coming to our town and trying to convince those people it's okay to close down the children's unit. That's our hospital, not yours, and personally I don't care if you have some kind of agenda to work out . . ."

She railed on him for nearly a minute, which gave Tanner enough time to catch his breath. He relaxed and studied her. She was beautiful. Much more so than his memory of her could have imagined. He watched her eyes flash the way they had back when they were children, and he felt himself smile.

Tanner soaked in the sight of her. Jade Conner. He'd actually found her after all these years.

She released a heavy sigh. "You know, you are an arrogant, wicked man." Her jaw was clenched, and Tanner felt a twinge of re-

64

morse for causing her such grief. "Kelso General is filled with sick children, children you care nothing about, and all you can do is walk in here, give your professional speech, and then stand there *smiling at* me. I wish you'd turn around and go back to wherever you came from." She spun around to her car and opened the door. "I have nothing more to say to you, Mr. Ghormsley."

Tanner paused. *Don't you recognize me, Jade?*

"Eastman . . ." He waited while the word hit its mark. "Tanner Eastman."

It took her a few seconds. Then slowly she turned around and faced him once more, only this time she leaned against her car for support. Some of the color had faded from her face, and her voice trembled when she spoke. "Your name is Tanner Ghormsley."

"No." Tanner took a step closer. "Mr. Lang got it wrong."

They stood there for what felt like an eternity, searching each other's eyes. Tanner saw her expression soften and then fill with disbelief. Finally her eyes grew wet and she shook her head. "No. It can't be . . ."

"Jade, it's me. Tanner."

Tears spilled onto her cheeks, and he circled his arms around her, drawing her

65

close as she did the same. All those years as childhood friends and they'd never hugged like this. But now, with the evening traffic whizzing by and the last of the stragglers from the meeting still filing past them, it felt like the most natural thing Tanner had ever done.

He pulled back, his arms still around her waist. She wiped her nose with the back of her hand and then pushed her fists into his chest like a petulant child. "So tell me, what do you have against our children's unit, huh?" Her tone was completely different now, almost teasing, but Tanner could tell she was bothered . . . and wanting to understand.

His voice was little more than a whisper. "I have nothing against your hospital, Jade. I'm an intern. They sent me a file and I wrote a brief. When I reported in this morning, they told me I was in charge of the presentation."

Jade released a shaky sigh and then, for the first time that afternoon, she gave a short laugh. "I should have known. Those snakes on the board used you as their scapegoat."

Tanner watched her, a dozen questions filling his mind. He ran a thumb along her cheek and allowed himself to get lost in the memories her face evoked. As he did, he felt his eyes brimming with unshed tears. "You never came back."

Jade could manage only a slight shake of her head as her eyes grew watery again.

He thought back to that afternoon on his front lawn, the day Jade said good-bye. It was all coming clearer now. "You were going to meet your mama in Kelso." He was transfixed, trapped in her gaze, carried back to the spring of his twelfth year. "You were supposed to come back when summer ended."

A wall went up in Jade's eyes and she stiffened. "We ended up staying."

"But why? What happened?"

She stared at her hands, and he had the strong sense that she was wrestling with something. Finally she sighed. "Mama never came back."

"She didn't?" Tanner frowned. "Where did she —"

"I don't know. Daddy still won't talk about it." Jade kept her eyes trained on her hands, and Tanner saw they were trembling. "I used to think she got killed in a car accident somewhere between Virginia and Washington."

"And now?"

"I found a letter from her a year after we

moved, postmarked D.C." Jade's expression was hard and Tanner realized the years must have been difficult for her. "She told Daddy to tell me she was sorry. That kind of thing."

The truth about what she was saying hit Tanner like a truck. Jade's mother had walked out on her with no intention whatsoever of coming back. No wonder Jade never moved back to Virginia. His heart broke for her, and he pulled her close again, stroking the back of her head as if she were still the ten-year-old girl he had grown up with. "I'm sorry, Jade."

She remained stiff and although she allowed him to comfort her, Tanner could tell she wasn't crying.

"Have you heard from her since then?"

"No. It doesn't matter. She's dead as far as I'm concerned."

Tanner got the point. The topic was closed. He pulled away again, this time completely. He had so much to tell her, so many years to make up for, but he didn't want her to feel like he was prying. He leaned back against her car so they were standing side by side.

"How old are you, anyway, Jade? Twenty, twenty-one?"

She smiled, and Tanner could see she was glad he'd changed the subject. "Twenty-one. And you're twenty-three." She studied him for a moment. "So . . . if you're an intern I guess you're staying in town?"

"Rented an apartment for the summer. Furnished. And one of the supervisors lent me a car. The internship lasts through August."

Jade cocked her head. "Where's Princeton, anyway?"

"New Jersey."

"Hmm." Jade hugged herself and looked away. "You like it?"

"It's all right." Tanner didn't want to talk about Princeton and politics and his well-planned future. "So what's it been? Twelve years?"

"Eleven, I think. A lot's happened since then."

Tanner gazed at the treetops behind city hall for a moment then back at Jade. "I thought about you all the time after you left, wondering what happened to you."

Jade hugged herself tighter. "The minute I saw you I thought . . . I thought you looked like my old friend, Tanner. The way I imagined you might look grown up."

Tanner watched her, how she brushed her hair back from her face and tilted her head just so. He was mesmerized by her, taken aback by the fact that his long lost friend wasn't a little girl anymore. She was the most beautiful woman he'd ever laid eyes on.

"Let's go somewhere. Talk, catch up." Tanner reached for her hand, but she pulled it back and again her eyes found something on the ground. He searched her face, but her troubled expression did nothing to explain her actions. Then it dawned on him . . . "I'm sorry . . . I didn't even ask. Are you married, Jade? Is there someone waiting for you?"

She viewed him through cautious eyes. "No. I just . . . people will talk. I like to keep my distance."

Tanner hesitated. "Okay. Sorry about the hand thing."

A slight grin appeared, and some of the caution in Jade's eyes faded. "Forgiven." She stared at him a moment. "I'm sorry for overreacting."

"No problem." Tanner was surprised at how he ached to take her in his arms and kiss her. From the time he was in high school he could have had his pick of beautiful women. They left notes on his car, messages at his dorm, and propositioned him to his face. He wasn't interested. He trusted God's plan for his life, and part of that plan was being sexually pure until he was married. Despite the women who sought after him, holding to that conviction had never been a struggle.

Yet none of them had ever made him feel the way he felt now, standing on a city sidewalk, Jade Conner filling his senses. Tanner had a feeling that whatever wounds Jade's mother had inflicted on her daughter's heart, they had left her scarred. He would have to move slowly if they were going to be friends again. "Wanna get something to eat?"

She nodded. "I know a great hamburger place."

He patted her car. "You driving?"

Her eyes twinkled. "If you trust a girl who can beat you in a bike race."

Tanner didn't smile. The emotions she stirred in him were too deep to make light of. "The question isn't whether I trust you . . ." His voice was softer, his face less than a foot from hers. "It's whether you trust me."

Jade said nothing, just considered his statement, meeting his gaze while a dozen emotions danced in her eyes. Finally she caught his neck with the crook of her arm and hugged him close. His arms circled her again, and he clung to her the way a brother might cling to a long lost sister.

He held her that way for nearly a minute all the while praying that she wouldn't see the truth. How the feelings that assaulted him now were far from brotherly.

Six

If train tracks had run through the town of Kelso, the house where Jade and her father lived would have been on the wrong side.

Their two-bedroom rental was sandwiched between a cluster of miscellaneous mobile homes and a weed-infested trailer park on Stark Street. The city dump was within eyesight, and a bitter stench drifted down the roadway whenever a breeze kicked up. What with the rusted washing machines and broken-down automobiles cluttering the yards up and down Stark, it was difficult to tell where the dump ended and the neighborhood began.

Crime had never been much of an issue in Kelso. A sleepy town that survived on industry along the Columbia and Cowlitz rivers, most of the people who lived there had done so all their lives. Still, when there was a domestic incident or a drug bust, inevitably it was on or near Stark Street.

Jade was used to her neighborhood. That night when she pulled into her driveway and stepped around broken engine parts and a Mustang that had died five years earlier, she didn't give a second thought to the condition of her home.

She had found Tanner Eastman. After ten years of sorrow and struggle she had come face to face with the one who had been a single ray of light in an otherwise cavernously dark past. Somehow, someway, despite the years gone by, he had found her, and she desperately needed to talk to someone about what she was feeling.

Jade opened the front door. "Dad?" It was Monday night, and if there'd been enough work at the garage to keep him past noon, he would have worked the whole day. In that case, he would probably still be sober enough to talk.

There was a crash in the kitchen, and Jade followed the sound. The cracked kitchen countertop was covered with a dozen empty beer bottles, the mangled remains of five fried chicken parts, and congealed pools of spilled gravy. Her father was leaning against the refrigerator, swaying slightly and standing in a pool of beer and broken glass.

He saw Jade and scowled. "Don't jus' stan' there!" He glared at her with bloodshot eyes. "Clean it up!"

Jade sighed. "Daddy, why do you have to do this?" She set down her purse and stooped to pick up the larger pieces of glass. "Did you cut your foot?"

"Footz fine. Hurry up. You think I like bein' stuck here?"

For as long as they'd lived in Kelso, Jade had had two fathers. One, a quiet, hardworking man who was humbly apologetic to her for his ineptitude at knowing what it took to raise a little girl. The other . . . the other stood before her now. A belligerent, drunken, miserable man who took out his frustration with life on Jade because she was the only one around.

Mornings were the best. He would wake up groggy and pained from the hangover, and his voice, his eyes, his entire countenance would be different.

"Jade, baby, could you be a doll and pick up some milk when you're out today?" he would say on his way out the door. Sometimes he'd search for her and hug her. Occasionally he would apologize for the night before. Always he wore regret in his eyes and the haunting shades of failure.

Jade took a rag and began cleaning the floor as her father stepped unsteadily around her and wiped his wet feet on the threadbare carpet. She was still picking up broken glass as he shuffled to his easy chair. She would never understand how he managed to hold a job at the garage, fixing cars and making enough money to get by, when he went to work each day ravaged by the effects of another hard-drinking night.

She could hear him pop the top on another bottle. "Where ya been?" He didn't talk when he was drunk, he barked. His voice was abrasive, short tempered, and full of accusation.

The glass was cleaned up, and Jade ran the cloth once more over the floor, hating the way it made her hands smell like beer. "I ran into an old friend, someone from Virginia."

Her father was used to holding conversations in a drunken state. He thought over Jade's comment and then bellowed. "What friend?"

Jade wiped her hands on a towel and took a spot on the sofa across from her father. "Tanner Eastman. Remember him?"

Her father belched loudly. "Eastman . . . Eastman. Oh, yeah. Snobby folks across the street."

Jade noticed the gravy stains on her father's undershirt and the chicken crumbs scattered on the floor around him. She wondered what he would think come morning if he could see how he looked now. "Tanner wasn't a snob. He and I used to play together."

"You did?"

"Yes." Where had her father thought she was all those hours she spent away from home? *He didn't care then, and he doesn't care now.*

"I don't remember it."

"It's true, Dad. Until we moved he was my best friend."

"Whas he doin' here?"

"An internship for the university he attends."

Her father scowled. "Told ya he was a snob." He raised his bottle and took a long swig. "Ahhhh. What about ol' Jim Rudolph? Whatever happened to him?"

"I'm not talking about Jim, Daddy."

Her father raised part way out of his chair in a threatening motion. "Don' get smart with me, y'ng lady. You might be grown up but you still haffa show a little respect."

Jade stared at her hands. Why did she bother?

Her father plopped back into his chair. "Don't get your hopes up, Jade."

"What?"

"That Eastman's a snob. 'S too good for

trash like you an' me."

Jade stood to leave. She'd had enough of her father's encouragement for one night. "Tanner's my friend. We had a nice dinner and caught up on our lives." She paused and felt the sting of tears. "And don't worry, I don't have any hopes about him."

"That's good. Jim Rudolph wouldn't like it if you took up with 'nother man."

A pit formed in Jade's stomach. Why must her father persist with talk about Jim? Hadn't she made herself clear?

"Daddy, I don't love Jim. I don't even like him. He asked me to marry him, and I turned him down, remember?"

Her father scratched his armpit and stared at a wrestling match on TV. "You're an idiot, Jade."

Her heart deflated like a two-week-old balloon. "I am not an idiot." There was no point carrying on a conversation with her father when he had been drinking, but sometimes Jade couldn't help herself. Most nights, these were the only conversations they had.

He faced her again and raised his voice another notch. "You're an idiot! Jim comes from good, hard-workin' family. He's gonna be a teacher, and you turned him down. I said it before and I'll say it again —" he

took another swig and finished the bottle —
"Jim Rudolph's the bes' thing ever happened to you, Jade." He tried to focus on
her, but his head bobbed unsteadily, and he
finally gave up and turned back to the
match. "You shoulda married him. No one
else'll ever want you."

Jade felt her shoulders slump. Every time
she let herself get sucked into a discussion
like this one she wondered the same thing:
Was it the beer, or did her father really hate
her?

He belched again. "Get me 'nother beer,
will ya?"

Jade stared at her father. Most of the time
she did as he asked, but this time he could
get it himself. Maybe break another bottle
in the process. She needed fresh air before
she let go and threw something at him.

She exhaled through tightly clenched teeth
and spun around. She was already outside
when she heard him stumbling toward the
kitchen. Apparently he'd forgotten about
her. Jade breathed a heavy sigh. The air was
warm and damp, hovering like a blanket
against Jade's skin.

The covered porch was the best part of
the house. It ran along the entire front and
was deep enough to find shelter even when
wind drove the Northwest rain sideways.

Jade had read hundreds of books on this porch, spent years here dreaming about a different life.

When she was a little girl, she had considered running away, moving in with somebody else's family where there would be a mom and a dad and dinner hours and laughter. But over time she had learned to fend for herself, avoiding her father when he was drinking and escaping to imaginary worlds on the front porch.

Jade wandered across the creaking boards. The porch was cluttered, of course, like everything else about their house. Jade would have loved to clean it up, to throw out the junk. But her father had collected most of it from his years as a mechanic. Parts that could be fixed and sold if he ever found the time, engines he could repair and use again if only he'd had a sober evening in which to work.

She spotted a cardboard box marked Starters and Ignition Switches. It had been there for at least five years, and Jade had used it as a chair so often it felt almost normal to do so. She pushed it out so she could see the dusky sky. Her heart felt bruised from her father's comments, and Jade thought about the irony. Men were easily struck by her looks, but the most important part, the place where her heart and soul lived, was battered beyond recognition. Her father was right. Why would anyone else want her?

Especially someone like Tanner Eastman.

Jade sighed and stared into the dimly lit sky. It was nine and night would settle within the hour. Maybe she should throw on a pair of sweats and jog. Her mind was racing far too quickly to think about sleep. Jade felt as if she'd drifted downstream in time and was being sucked into a whirlpool of memories. Memories she'd almost forgotten.

She smiled. Who would have thought after all this time . . . ? What if she hadn't gone to the meeting? What if he'd chosen an internship somewhere else?

Seeing him again made her ache for the little girl she'd been and the way she had missed him so desperately the summer after she and her father had moved to Kelso. For three years, they'd been best friends. His parents were busy and so were hers. Together they found time for each other, a world where they chased butterflies and jumped rope and played house. He was the father and she was the mother. Or she was the sister and he was the brother. Sometimes they would stay in character all day long.

Tanner's mother didn't like him going to other kids' houses, so most of the time they played at his. His backyard was the stage for a hundred games of make believe and mysterious monsters and unrivaled challenges and story lines.

Jade remembered one of Tanner's favorite games. She leaned her head back, and she could see them as they were more than a decade ago.

"Okay, Jade, close your eyes." Tanner would take her hand and lead her to the corner of the yard. "See how much you trust me."

"Not this again!"

"Come on, you love this one." Tanner had been persuasive back then, too.

"Okay." Once her eyes were closed he would lead her on an obstacle course through the yard. "Come on, Jade. Trust me; don't open your eyes."

"I won't! I promise."

And she hadn't. Her trust in Tanner had been absolute.

The sky was growing black, and a handful of stars poked their way through the darkness. Even now those days with Tanner stood out as the happiest time in her life. The years since then had been wracked with disappointment and insecurity. Everyone who mattered had let her down. Everyone but Tanner. He was the only person she'd ever truly trusted.

Back then she'd been certain she would marry him one day. Other kids teased them about it, but secretly in her little girl heart, she knew it wasn't a joke. How could she marry anyone else?

A lump formed in Jade's throat and she swallowed hard. Everything had changed since then. Jade knew more about marriage now, how it could make a person crazy.

She sighed. Every moment with Tanner tonight had been magical. They'd grown up in two completely different worlds, yet still they shared a bond that had not faded.

Tanner's words from earlier that night echoed in her mind now.

"I want to see you tomorrow and the next day, and the next . . ." He'd stared deep into her eyes. "I want to know what you're about now that you've grown up."

Jade wanted to see him, too. She wanted to bare her heart to him the way she had as a child. But while the bond between them hadn't seemed to change, their circumstances had. There was no way to bridge their worlds now. Tanner would never be interested in her. Besides his internship only lasted through the summer.

Still there was something about the way he had looked at her earlier that night that made her heart sing. If she hadn't known him better, she would have said he looked at her the same way Jim Rudolph did.

And Jim Rudolph's intentions were obvious.

Jade had met Jim when she was a freshman in high school. He was a senior that year, quarterback of the Kelso football team, a tall, stocky boy with a baby face. Most of the girls at Kelso dreamed of dating him, but Jade hadn't been interested. Throughout high school she enjoyed dozens of acquaintances, but no lasting friendships. Close friends would eventually want to come over and meet her parents. And Jade was not willing to share that part of her life with anyone.

So she remained aloof. Girls envied her; boys found her a challenge, but she was never concerned with any of them. She found comfort in running and biking and reading mysteries. In the controlled world she had created for herself there was no room for relationships of any kind.

But Jim Rudolph simply would not take no for an answer.

In Jade's freshman year he followed her around campus between classes and asked her to every one of the school dances. Jade always told him no, but eventually she allowed herself to make small talk with him. It was harmless. Jim wasn't a threat to her isolation.

After all, he could never love anyone the way he loved himself.

Still he persisted. Long after he moved to Corvallis and took a dormitory room on campus at Oregon State University, he continued his pursuit of her. He would stop by her house when he was home on break, chat with her father and wait for her to come home from school.

Jade made sure she never encouraged his attention, but he continued pursuing her all the same.

"I could have any girl I want, do you know that, Jade."

"I'm so impressed, Jim." She remembered busying herself in a magazine, staunchly ignoring his advances.

"Come on, Jade. You like me. Admit it."

She had been bored with the conversation. "No, Jim. I don't like you. I tolerate you."

Jim had laughed like that was the funniest thing he'd ever heard. "Do you know how many girls would die to be in your shoes right now?"

Jade had glanced down at her bare feet and sighed impatiently. "I'm not wearing shoes, Jim."

"You know what I mean."

"Not really."

He had studied her. "You play a better game of hard-to-get than any girl I know. You know what else?"

Jade was certain she hadn't looked up. She rarely gave Jim the privilege of eye contact. "What?"

"You're not so bad looking for a girl who plays it cool."

"Change the subject, Jim."

"Why?"

"Because I'm not interested. If you must come around and talk to me, then please stop pretending I'm your girlfriend. I'm not."

He'd seemed indifferent. "You seeing someone else?"

"No. I'm not seeing anyone. I don't *want* to see anyone. How much clearer can I be?"

"Fine. One day you'll wise up and come to your senses." Jim puffed out his chest. "But you better hurry. I won't be free forever."

Jade had a hundred memories of conversations like that one. Then, last summer, when Jim graduated from college, he did the craziest thing of all. She was working at a sporting goods store in town when he came in wearing a wide grin. He motioned for her and she followed him outside.

"Jade, I know this is a strange place to ask you . . ." He pulled a tiny velvety box from his pants pocket.

She remembered feeling deeply alarmed and then trapped, like she might suffocate. She knew what was coming, and she was helpless to stop it.

He opened the box and therein lay a smallish diamond ring. "I already asked your father. . . . What I'm trying to say is, I can't wait around forever, Jade. I want to offer you the chance of a lifetime. Your daddy said so himself." Jim had grinned and Jade thought she might hyperventilate. "What do you say? Marry me and let's stop playing games with each other."

She cringed now remembering her re-action. She had pushed the ring away and cried loudly. "Jim are you out of your *mind*? I don't want to marry you. I don't want to date you. I never have."

He had stared at her blankly, then me-thodically closed the tiny box and hid it back in his pocket again. "You don't get it, do you?"

"No, *you* don't get it! You've hung around

long enough that I consider you a friend. Not a great friend. Not even a good friend. But I have never given you the impression that what we have is more than a casual friendship."

Jim's face reflected the pain her words had caused him. But almost instantly his expression had changed and a wicked grin broke across his face. His eyes boldly roamed the length of her. "Don't you see, Jade? You're nothing. Nobody. Your father's an alcoholic; you have no friends. What're you going to do? Live alone for the rest of your life?" He shrugged as if she'd done little more than turn down an offer of dinner and a movie. "Have it your way. But one day you'll come to your senses. I'm the best thing that ever happened to you, Jade Conner. And don't you forget it. Give me a call when you change your mind."

Jim still called now and then, but Jade had the feeling he was giving up on her. He wasn't a bad guy, really. Just shallow and self-centered, and the thought of being married to him made Jade nauseous.

She stretched and forced Jim's face from her mind.

No, Tanner hadn't looked at her the way Jim Rudolph had. Tanner saw straight into her soul. But he was also attending one of the finest universities in the country with plans to be elected to public office. He had a wonderful family, more money than she would ever see, and a future brimming with possibilities.

Whatever came of them this summer, it would not amount to more than friendship. Tanner deserved someone like himself.

And she . . . well, maybe her father was right. Maybe she deserved someone like . . . like Jim.

If that were true, Jim had been right that day in the sporting goods store. Because she would rather live alone till the day she died than marry Jim Rudolph.

SEVEN

It started with evening walks along the Cowlitz River and up the trails through Tam O'Ashanter Park and quickly progressed to dinner every night that week. They ordered pizza and watched a baseball game at Tanner's apartment. Another time they ate at a Chinese restaurant and flew kites on a bluff overlooking the banks of the Cowlitz River.

By the end of that first week, Jade hoped the summer would never end.

Most couples spending this kind of time together would have considered themselves dating. But Tanner had not looked at her again the way he had that first night, after the town meeting. He did phone her every day when he was finished at the office and seemed happy to spend time with her. But then, she was the only person in town he knew. Nothing in his manner or words gave her any indication that he desired more than friendship from her. He didn't seem to think

90

of her in a romantic sense, and Jade was glad. What could possibly come of it?

They lived in worlds separated by three thousand miles and a chasm of time too great to bridge.

Even so, Jade was enjoying herself immensely. She was surprised at how freeing it felt to spend evenings away from home. By the time she got home each night, her father was asleep, and she would creep to her room unnoticed. No yelling or threatening or accusations.

No one telling her she was an idiot.

It was Friday evening, and again Jade and Tanner had plans to be together after work. They met in front of his apartment just after six. Tanner greeted her with a hug and a bag of sub sandwiches. "Joe's Deli?"

"Mmm. Good choice."

"The supervisors said I couldn't go wrong at Joe's."

Jade followed him inside. "The supervisors . . . ah, yes. My favorite people. At least they're good for something."

He flipped on a light, pulled out two paper plates, and set them on the table. "How's Shaunie?"

Jade wasn't used to someone asking about her day. Three days ago the question would have made her suspicious, but now she smiled as she sat down at the table. "The infection's gone. So far her tests look good. She might be able to go home tomorrow."

Tanner sat down across from her and peeled the wrappers off two subs. "Pray?"

Jade nodded and quickly bowed her head. Tanner had prayed often that week — over every meal and sometimes after spending an evening talking. Just to let God in on the conversation, he'd told her.

When he was done, he caught her gaze. "You care about her, don't you?"

"Shaunie?" It was wonderful talking with someone who so easily read her mind. "Yes . . . like she was my own daughter."

Tanner took a bite. "Think you'll have a daughter one day? Kids?"

"I don't know." She glanced down at her plate where the sandwich looked suddenly wilted.

Tanner set his food down and leaned back in his chair. He studied her in silence for a moment then tilted his head. "Every time I bring up relationships you shut down." His voice was soft, and Jade could hear how much he cared for her, how much he wanted her to open up to him. But how could he understand what her life had been like? How it felt to have your mother leave and be raised by an alcoholic father?

She sighed. "I'm sorry."

Tanner pushed his plate aside and rested his forearms on the table. He leaned toward her when he spoke. "No, *I'm* sorry. I don't mean to make you uncomfortable. I just want to know you, Jade . . . what you're thinking behind those beautiful eyes."

Her heart skipped a beat, and she wanted to bolt from the table, escape back to the private solitude of her cluttered home and stuffy bedroom. She forced herself to remain seated, studying her plate.

"It's about your mama, isn't it?" Tanner inched his chair near hers, then reached out with gentle fingers to take her hand in his. "I'm here. If you want to talk about it."

Jade had hidden her feelings about her mother for so long, she'd become expert at it. But being around Tanner that week had weakened more walls than she cared to admit. Right now, with Tanner stroking her hand and questions about her mother dangling in the air like so many skeletons, Jade felt the dam breaking.

She still hadn't looked up, and as the tears gathered they spilled freely onto her plate.

Tanner must have seen them. He moved closer still, put an arm around her shoulders and hugged her close. "It's okay, Jade. I'm here."

She had never cried about her mother's leaving, preferring denial at first and anger after that. But here, with Tanner's breath against her face and her father miles away, she no longer had the desire to fight the pain that welled within her. Instead she slumped against Tanner's shoulder and gave in to a torrent of grief. He stroked her hair and turned so that his other arm embraced her also. In hushed tones he uttered caring words, calming words until her sobbing eased.

"I'm so sorry." Tanner was still stroking her hair and her back, comforting a place in Jade where the child still lived. A child who had spent too many years alone.

Tanner pulled away, found a tissue, and handed it to her. "It must have been awful."

Jade blew her nose and leaned back, settling her gaze on his. She stayed that way a while, and Tanner waited, letting her decide when she was ready to talk. Like the tears, there had never been any place for words regarding her mother. Now finally she was ready. Tanner cared how she felt, what had happened to her after she moved from Williamsburg.

Jade drew a shaky, deep breath. "She never even said good-bye."

Tanner kept his eyes trained on her.

"I still don't know exactly what happened. Something . . . someone must have caught her attention. Whatever it was, she left and never looked back."

"Did you ever ask your dad?"

Jade closed her eyes. "A hundred times. The answer was always the same. 'Your mother's a whore. Don't bring her up again in this house.' " Jade's voice echoed with anger as she recalled her father's words. When it came to the disappearance of her mother, anger was the only emotion Jade's father had ever displayed.

"So you still don't know what happened?"

She shook her head, then hesitated. Tanner eased closer again, his arm around her shoulders once more. She struggled to find the right words. "There must have been some other man. Otherwise Daddy wouldn't have called her a whore."

Tanner stroked her arm, and Jade pulled slightly away so she could see his eyes. "You asked me if I want a daughter someday." She blinked back fresh tears. "Probably not. Because that would mean getting married, and I've seen what marriage does to people." A picture of her father passed out in his vomit came to mind, and she dismissed it. "I would only want a child if I could provide her the home I never had. A mom and a dad and security. A place where she would be loved."

Tanner stroked her cheek again. Still he remained silent, and Jade knew he was giving her the space to say everything she'd never said. She sighed. "What kind of mother leaves her child and never looks back? She never called me or visited me or remembered my birthday. Didn't she love me, Tanner? Didn't she care about what I might feel when I was old enough to realize what she'd done? To realize she didn't want me?"

She began crying again and through her tears her voice rose. She hated her mother for what she'd done, and it felt good to be able to finally say so. "Other little girls talked about their mamas . . . how they baked or shopped for them, how they curled their hair or helped them with their homework.

"Every time someone asked me about my mother I felt like a piece of my heart was being strangled."

Jade relaxed against Tanner's chest and stared at a picture on the wall. The image of Tanner and his parents outside their home in Virginia smiled back at her. She closed her eyes. How could Tanner relate to this sorry picture of her adolescence?

Jade clung to Tanner. It didn't matter if he couldn't relate. She felt utterly safe and cared for, and now that she had begun, she wanted him to know everything.

"I was thirteen when I got my period. We'd seen the film in school, but I wasn't ready. When I saw how much I was bleeding, I hid in my backyard behind a trash pile. I cried and cried, scared about what was happening to me."

She craned her head and found his eyes again. "Do you know what I thought? I thought I was dying, Tanner. Because I didn't have a mother to tell me . . . I had to sneak into my dad's wallet and steal five dollars so I could buy pads at the corner store. I wasn't even sure how to use them or where the blood was coming from."

The memory churned in her stomach. She faced Tanner. "I could never, ever in a million years do that to a child. If I had a child I'd want him to have two parents, so he would know he was loved by a mother and a father."

Tanner was silent, listening, watching her. Jade felt more tears and she blinked them back. "I'd cherish everything about him. The baby years, the toddler years. Kindergarten and grade school. I'd volunteer in his classroom and take him with me on walks. I'd make scrapbooks of his life so he could see where he came from and know where he was going. I would be his closest friend in the world, and we'd love each other forever." Jade paused. "Maybe that's why I feel so strongly about the children's unit at Kelso General."

Tanner placed his finger under her chin and Jade could see in his eyes that he understood. When he spoke his voice was filled with compassion. "Those are your children. You don't want me or the board or anyone else taking them away from you."

Jade nodded. "I can't tell you how many times my dad has told me I'm nothing, a nobody without a future. . . . But when I'm with those sick babies, I know what I'm supposed to do with my life. That's why I was so mad that day at the meeting."

Tanner still cupped her face with his hand, tracing her jaw and staring deeply into her eyes. "Your father says that to you?"

He was clearly horrified, obviously unable to fathom a father like hers, and again Jade felt their differences. "All the time."

"You don't need that, Jade. The man isn't good enough for a daughter like you. You should leave home. Get a place of your own."

Jade nodded. "I will. As soon as I finish

my nurse's training."

Tanner stood then and moved across the room. When he returned, he held what looked like a Bible. "I want to show you something."

"In the Bible?" What did this have to do with her sordid life? Jade watched as Tanner flipped his way through the pages. She noticed highlighted areas throughout and tiny scribbling in the margins. Apparently Tanner was a man who took the Bible seriously. He quickly found what he was looking for.

"Here it is. In Jeremiah. God was reassuring the people through the prophet Jeremiah that if they turned their hearts toward him, he would be faithful with them for all times."

Jade nodded, still not sure what this had to do with her.

"I want to read you something from Jeremiah twenty-nine." He put his finger on the section of text, and Jade saw it was already highlighted. " 'I know the plans I have for you,' declares the LORD, 'plans to prosper you and not to harm you, plans to give you hope and a future.' "

Tanner passed the Bible to Jade. "Here, read it again."

Jade read it to herself and then looked at

him. "What does it mean?"

He angled his head back thoughtfully and considered her question. As he did, a feeling, a hot sensation spread across her cheeks, and again their differences seemed glaringly obvious. "I uh . . . well . . . we didn't read the Bible much."

There was nothing condescending in Tanner's expression, but Jade had the sense he could see into her soul, as if he knew her heart long before she was willing to frame her thoughts with words. She hung her head slightly. "Okay, never . . . We, well, we weren't exactly church-goers." She hesitated. "I talk to God sometimes, though. When there's no one else to talk to."

Tanner's eyes lit up. "Good. That's all this is, really. God's way of talking back to us." He pointed to the verse in Jeremiah again. "So what you see there is a promise that applies to anyone who puts their trust in the Lord, just like it applied to God's people back then. Because that's how God feels about those who love him." Tanner ran his finger under the words again. " 'I know the plans I have for you . . . plans to give you hope and a future.' "

It sounded nice, Jade had to admit. But had she ever put her trust in the Lord? She didn't think so, but she wasn't willing to discuss it with Tanner. Not now. She tried to imagine how different her life might be if the Bible verse were true. Almighty God? A plan for her life? She didn't think so, but it was comforting to think about. "Thanks, Tanner."

"Do you believe it?"

She shrugged. "Hasn't happened so far."

Tanner's shoulders dropped. "That's why it's so important that you accept him as your . . ." Something in his eyes withdrew. "Never mind . . . I'm not trying to confuse you, Jade. But you've got to believe God loves you. Your life's just beginning. Don't you see?"

"I see that our sandwiches are wilting."

He eyed the partially eaten subs and smiled. "I get the point. Topic closed."

They finished eating and watched the movie — a comedy Jade had seen twice before. But watching it with Tanner made every line new, and she laughed until she could barely breathe. When it was over, they sat facing each other on his rented sofa.

"I have an idea." Tanner laid his arm across the back of the sofa so that it was nearly touching Jade's shoulder.

"I'm listening."

"Come with me Sunday to Portland. I've been so busy I haven't called my mother in days. I promised I'd see her this weekend —" he leaned closer and his eyes clouded with doubt, as though he was sure she'd say no before he finished asking — "we could go to church in the morning and spend the afternoon with my mom. Have dinner at her house, something like that."

Panic coursed through Jade's veins. She'd barely known Tanner's mother back when they were children. Even though she hung out at his house, his mother rarely made herself available or went out of her way to be kind to Jade. "Do you think she'd want me to come?"

Tanner moved closer so that his arm rested against her, and there was a flicker of something deeply intimate in his eyes. Once more he drew nearer to her, then — as though he'd changed his mind — he stood and leaned casually against the wall. He looked down at her, and for an instant his eyes darted along the length of her. Then just as quickly they connected with her eyes again. What was that look on his face? Almost as if she could see a piece of his soul, a piece she couldn't quite read. Was he nervous? Afraid of saying something wrong? Whatever it was, he was trying to hide it.

"Of course she would. You're a familiar face from the old neighborhood. She'll be thrilled that we ran into each other again after all these years."

Jade imagined dinner with a cultured woman like Doris Eastman. She was proper, a regular churchgoer — and Jade was terrified at the thought of trying to meet the woman's approval.

But it might be nice . . . spending a day at church with Tanner, then the two of us being with his mother. . . .

Tanner was waiting for her answer. "Do it, Jade. It'll be great. I know this amazing church ten minutes from my mom's house. Crossroads. Lots of people, great music, incredible preaching. You'll love it."

Jade drew a deep breath. "Promise she'll like me?"

He laughed. "My mother? Be serious. What in the world's not to like?"

"Okay. Want the truth?"

Tanner nodded.

"The church thing has me interested."

"Good." He broke into a grin. "I'll call Mom tomorrow and let her know."

Jade stood and moved closer to him. "I should get going. I've got to be at the hospital early —"

She paused when he shifted away from her. Confused, she looked at him — and frowned. There it was again. The strange

103

fear thing in his eyes. Like she'd caught him thinking something he wasn't supposed to be thinking. He moved away abruptly and crossed the room to get a drink of water. When she followed, he moved with his glass to a lone chair in the corner of the room.

Stopping in her tracks, Jade planted her hands on her hips and shook her head at him. "Are you trying to avoid me?" She was teasing, not sure what to make of his nervous behavior.

For a moment, Tanner opened his mouth but no words came out. Then he smiled the smile that Jade was sure would one day win him thousands of votes in public office. "Yes, in fact I am." He waved his hand near his face and wrinkled his nose. "Onion breath. I don't want to knock you over. I should have known better than to order onions on the subs."

Jade laughed and collected her purse and car keys. "Mine can't be much better. Hey, thanks again for dinner." She grinned, still caught up in the laughter. "Especially the onions."

Tanner walked her to the door and watched her go. When she was halfway down the sidewalk he yelled out to her, "Talk to you tomorrow."

Her car was parked just outside his front

door, and he watched her until she had climbed inside and drove off. As she made her way through town toward the city dump, she had the unusual feeling that all was right with her world. She had laughed more that night than the past five years combined.

It was Tanner, of course. He made her heart feel light as the summer breeze dancing over the Cowlitz River, as though she were normal for the first time in her life. As though she didn't have a mother who'd abandoned her and an alcoholic father at home.

As though the only friend she had in the world weren't only passing through her life for one golden summer.

Tanner watched her drive away. Then he closed the door, sank against it, and blew out the air that had been collecting in his lungs all night. His voice was a frustrated moan. "Jade . . . You're killing me."

Onion breath. That was believable enough. He sure couldn't tell her the truth: that every time she got close, his flesh was being assaulted by incredible feelings he'd never imagined existed. He could hardly tell her that after the movie, with the two of them so close on the sofa, all he'd wanted to do was take her in his arms and . . . and . . .

He closed his eyes. *Lord, I'm struggling here. Why does she make me feel this way? I can't even be near her without wanting to kiss her, to hold her, to . . . Lord help me. What I really want is for Jade to come to know you. I should be leading her to you, not . . . well, you know."*

It was a feeble prayer, but it was all he could manage.

No temptation has seized you except that which is common to man. . . .

The words echoed deep in his soul, and he felt a wave of reassurance. God was with him. He heard Tanner's prayers and he understood. Tanner recalled the rest of the Scripture and knew that God would not let him be tempted beyond what he could bear. And that when he was tempted, the Lord himself would provide a way out.

Tonight, without a doubt, God had done exactly that.

EIGHT

It wasn't that Jade had ever suffered a bad experience in church. Rather it was simply that her father hated the place. He insisted it was some church back in Virginia that had forced them out of town, across the country to Kelso.

"Church folk are hypocrites," her father would say when Sunday rolled around each week. "They like pointing fingers at ya. They'd recognize you as the daughter of a whore and make you leave the building."

Jade had heard that a hundred times, and as she drove with Tanner south on I–5 she heard it again and again in her mind.

"What are you thinking about?" They passed Ridgefield and were heading toward Vancouver. According to Tanner's calculations they'd be at Crossroads Church in fifteen minutes.

Jade stared out her side window. The rain of the week before had disappeared, and the past few days had been brilliantly sunny. With the blue sky as a backdrop, the layered brush and trees along the freeway looked vibrantly green. She turned to Tanner. "Whether they'll like me."

"Jade, they won't even know you. Crossroads is a big church. We'll just be two more people sitting in the pews."

Still she had the feeling someone would know. Someone would spot her and recognize her for what she was and ask her to leave the building, just like her father had always said.

The parking lot was full, and traffic attendants directed the flow of cars leaving the earlier service as well as those arriving for the next one. Jade had never seen this kind of crowd at any church gathering. The thought of being among so large a sea of people made her relax. Maybe she'd be safe after all.

Tanner walked alongside her, and for an instant Jade wished he would take her hand. He'd been careful not to since she'd pulled away that first day after the meeting. Of course, he'd held her hand that night at his apartment when she told him about her mother. But that was only for comfort. Now, even though it would never be true, she wished he'd hold her hand for different reasons: to show the world she belonged to him.

The church was filling up quickly, and they found seats near the back. Jade saw how comfortable Tanner was, reading the bulletin, filling in the blanks on the sermon outline form inside. She clutched her papers tightly and sat low in her seat. People greeted each other, hugging and smiling, and Jade took in all of it. In one of the pews, a cluster of people bent their heads together in what Jade assumed was prayer. She couldn't hear what they were saying, only that they were saying it quietly, out loud.

Okay, God, I'm here. I'm finally in a church. Help me last through the hour without getting kicked out.

Jade's conversations with God were always very simple and to the point. She talked to him like she would a friend, as if he was always with her ready to hear what she had to say. This other prayer, this thing these people were doing, was not something she understood. She sat stone still, uncomfortable around so many good people.

The music started, and Jade was struck at how it filled the building. Full and professional sounding, the band up front included a piano, several guitars, drums, and a keyboard. The music filled Jade's heart with peace, and again she felt the tension ease from her body.

She had figured church music would be like she'd heard it on television. Somber, sullen, sung in soprano with little emotion. The music at Crossroads was vastly different. The worship leader played the piano like no one Jade had ever heard. She listened carefully to the words. It was a song about how the Lord had torn down the walls around the hearts of his people and loved them through every step of their lives. And it was a commitment in turn to walk beside God and speak his truth as long as breath could be drawn.

The music built to a crescendo, and Jade was taken aback by what was happening around her. Scattered throughout the church, a number of people were closing their eyes, raising their hands while they sang. *What is this, God? What are they doing?* She glanced at the bulletin, somehow embarrassed by their strange actions. Near the printed words to the music was an invitation to join in the singing — *worship* they called it. There it also said that occasionally people might raise their hands while worshiping. It went on to explain that this was merely a spontaneous act of love toward God.

The band was repeating the song, and this time Jade felt herself humming along. The tune was catchy, the music enjoyable, and the words . . . Jade felt like she could have written them herself. They filled her heart to overflowing.

From you, Lord, I won't part. . . . You've torn down walls around my heart. . . .

It was that part, the walls around the heart part, that sent chills down Jade's arms and caused tears to well up in her eyes. *Is that what I've done, God? Put walls around my heart?* She closed her eyes. *Tear them down, God. I can't breathe inside these walls.*

The third time through, she sang along and meant every word. She caught Tanner smiling at her and smiled back. And somewhere inside her heart she felt a rush of fresh air. There were two more songs, and they, too, seemed to be written for Jade alone. But it was the fourth song that made her tears spill onto the bulletin in her hands. It talked about having a father who knew his children by name, one who was proud to call them his own, one who would never leave her no matter what.

One who didn't think she was an idiot.

Jade sat, unmoving, ignoring the tears. Was this what it felt like to have walls torn down? Walls that had stood around her heart for

111

more than ten years?

The music was over and a man stood to talk. Tanner had told her that the pastor, Bill Ritchie, could be heard on the radio across the country and that his sermons were powerful. Jade wasn't sure what Tanner meant.

All she knew was that she wasn't looking forward to the message.

This would be the part where he would get in their faces, condemn them and criticize them. He would shout and tell them they were terrible sinners and warn them about hell fire and brimstone. Then would come the part where he would demand they give money otherwise God couldn't possibly have mercy on their souls.

Instead, Pastor Ritchie smiled. "Isn't it a glorious day in the Lord? Let's rise and give him thanks."

The crowd was on its feet, and Pastor Ritchie was reading something from the Bible. It had a poetic ring to it, something about how God had known them from the beginning, how he had formed them in their mother's wombs, and how all of their days were planned from the beginning.

Was it true, God? Had he really formed her in her mother's womb with plans for her from the start? Jade made a note to ask

Tanner later where the Bible really said that.

For the next half hour the pastor talked about choices that face all people at one time or another. The first choice, he told them, was whether or not to believe God's claims about himself and his son, Jesus Christ. Rather than a lecture, Pastor Ritchie's sermon was more like a fireside chat. He strolled from one side of the stage to the other, making eye contact with individuals and holding the audience captive in the process. Occasionally he'd chuckle out loud or smile fondly when giving examples about how people often worked all their lives to keep God out, only to give in when crisis hit.

"And let's face it, folks," Pastor Ritchie said. "We're all going to have to deal with crisis at some point."

Jade listened intently. The second choice, the pastor said, was whether people were willing to give their lives to the Lord and let him do with them what he wished. He talked about the futility of holding tightly to a life lived without Christ when there was such freedom in living alongside him.

The time flew by, and soon the pastor was winding up. Jade was mesmerized, spellbound by the way the man's words made sense. She hadn't glanced at Tanner once

113

through the pastor's sermon. She hadn't looked anywhere but straight ahead, soaking in what the man was saying, amazed at how completely it applied to her.

Pastor Ritchie paused and studied the group of people before him. "The thing is, folks —" he held his arm up and pretended to stage an arm wrestling contest with an invisible opponent — "God won't wrestle with you forever." He let his arm fall forward. "Eventually he'll let you have your way." He hesitated again. "Let's not let that happen. If you've never made a decision for Christ, isn't it time? Shall we pray?"

Jade closed her eyes and felt the tears again. She had talked to God, but never tried to live for him. Tanner's words from that night in her apartment came back to her — *the promises are for anyone who loves the Lord, anyone who has given their life to God.* She'd kept him at arm's length, not wanting to get close to him any more than she'd wanted to get close to anyone else. He wasn't her Lord — he was another of her many acquaintances.

Pastor Ritchie was praying. "Father God, I know there are some here today who've never made you Lord, never given their lives completely to you. You brought them here today so they could finally make the right choice, take advantage of this opportunity so that not another day would go by without their names being written in the Lamb's book of life.

"Oh, maybe they think they're here because it was something to do on a Sunday morning, maybe a friend asked them here and that's why they came —"

Jade wondered if someone had told him. How come everything he said seemed to apply directly to her? Had Tanner planned this? The pastor was finishing the prayer. "Of course we know the truth, Lord. You brought them here today so you could meet them where they are." He paused and it was as though Jade could physically feel the walls around her heart crumbling. "With everyone in prayer, eyes closed, if you are one who wants to make Jesus the Lord of your life right here, right now, raise your hand, would you? Raise it high so I can see it."

Jade squirmed in her seat, tears streaming down her face. She was tired of fighting through life on her own. And though she had no solid reason to believe the things Pastor Ritchie had said that morning, somehow she was desperate to do so. More than she'd ever wanted anything.

The pastor's voice was kind, beckoning.

"Anyone else. Please, don't let another day go by. Believe me, there's nothing outside those doors that matters more than meeting Jesus Christ for the first time right here, right now, before another minute goes by . . . anyone else?"

And in that moment, as though her arm had a mind of its own, Jade's hand was up.

It was true. She wanted to give her life completely to the savior that Pastor Ritchie had shared about, and she wanted to do it now, before another minute passed.

Eyes still closed, hand raised, Jade heard the pastor finishing his prayer, thanking God for those who had taken that first step of faith. The pastor paused. "Now, will those of you with hands raised please stand up. Come on, stand up. No one's watching."

Terror ran through Jade. She couldn't stand up! Not here, among this sea of churchgoers. They would know she was different and ask her to leave. No, she wanted only to fade into the pew and treasure this decision quietly in her heart.

Stand, my daughter.

She heard the voice deep within her soul and recognized it the way a child recognizes the voice of her daddy. God wanted her to stand, and with that knowledge she did so without hesitating.

Pastor Ritchie continued. "All right, now will those of you who are standing please make your way up here to the front. We have guys and gals who want to pray with you, help you nail down what a new life in Christ really looks like. It is absolutely essential that you do this. Come on, right up here."

Jade leaned down and whispered to Tanner. "Come with me?"

He opened his eyes and she saw his unshed tears. Somehow he must have known the way God had been calling her. Maybe he had even prayed for her. He rose and walked with her toward the front of the church. From upstairs and other areas, a handful of people — most of them with tearstained faces — were also making their way to the front where two men with kind eyes stood waiting.

"Let's praise the Lord for what he has done here today among us," he said. And then the pews of churchgoers, the people Jade had feared since she was a young girl, did something that nearly brought Jade to her knees.

They applauded.

Her father was wrong. They hadn't looked on her with disdain, hadn't asked her to leave. Instead they had shown her what it was to worship the Lord in song, they had listened alongside her to Pastor Ritchie's amazing message.

And now . . . now they were clapping because of her decision.

NINE

Tanner held her hand as they walked across the church parking lot, and she enjoyed the feel of his fingers intertwined with hers. Her soul felt remarkably light, and she was filled with an overwhelming sense of hope. Once they climbed inside Tanner's car, he turned to her, his eyes glistening.

"Is it what you really want, Jade?"

She studied his face and remembered that he had always been like this — concerned for her. She drew a deep breath. "All my life something has been missing. Now I know what it was."

"I remember when I gave my life to the Lord. . . ." Tanner leaned against the car door, facing her. He was in no hurry to leave and Jade was glad. They hadn't been able to talk yet, and she still had so many questions.

"When was that?"

Tanner's gaze shifted to the distant mountains and the shimmering white peak of Mt. Hood. "I was in high school. A bunch of us went to a Young Life gathering, and for the first time I realized God wasn't a program or a club or a part of my heritage. He was a living God, waiting for me to turn my heart to him."

"Exactly." Jade leaned forward, remembering the meeting they'd just had with one of the associate pastors in the church prayer room. "That's how I felt in there. Like God was waiting for me to make a decision for him."

Tanner nodded. "Back then our family attended Williamsburg Community Church. Same as your folks, I think."

Jade nodded, and for a moment she started to hear her father's bitter words. *You're nothing but the daughter of a —*

She shut them out and focused her attention on Tanner instead.

"Anyway, I'd never thought about having a personal relationship with God. That night I opened my heart and asked Jesus inside. I studied the Bible daily over the next few weeks, and at the end of the month I got baptized."

Jade sighed. "Yeah, that's another thing. I think I want to do that, too, but what is it?"

Tanner smiled and focused on her. As he

did he leaned closer, taking her hands in his. "Baptism is part of giving your life to Christ." His eyes lit up. "Hey, I have an idea. I have a beginner's Bible study. I keep the notes written in the back of my Bible. We could go over it together. Tomorrow, maybe."

Jade watched him, and her heart soared. She'd never allowed herself to feel so deeply about anyone, but something about Tanner was unquestionably safe. Despite all the reasons a relationship between them couldn't possibly work, she felt herself falling hard. "I'd like that."

Jade had once heard love described by one of her nine-year-old patients. *It's like an avalanche,* he'd said. *When it happens to you, the best thing to do is run for your life.* Jade thought about that and knew it was too late. She was already in over her head.

Tanner's eyes remained locked on hers. "You're going to love getting to know God better, Jade. No matter what else happens in life, you'll always have Jesus with you." He paused. "I can't imagine life any other way."

She drew a deep breath, and her grip on Tanner's hands tightened slightly. It was time to bring the walls down all the way. "Remember that first day after the meeting?

You asked me if I trusted you. . . ."

A knowing look filled Tanner's eyes, but he stayed quiet.

Help me open up to him, Lord. She closed her eyes for a moment and when she opened them again she felt a new strength she hadn't had before. "You told me the question wasn't whether you trusted my driving or not. It was whether I trusted you."

Tanner's voice was quiet. "You never answered me."

Jade leaned closer and placed one of her hands on Tanner's upper arm. "I trust you, Tanner. I always have. I trust you now more than ever." She felt her eyes fill with tears and saw that he was listening intently to every word she said. Her hand fell back to her side. "That's all . . . I just wanted you to know."

His borrowed car wasn't very large — a four-door sedan in which Tanner was already close. But as she finished speaking, he moved closer still and took her face in his hands. "Now it's my turn. . . ."

Jade searched his eyes, wondering what he was going to say. Whatever it was, she had a strong sense that it would change things between them forever. He raised his hand gently as she waited, tracing her cheekbones with his fingertips. When he finally spoke it caused feelings in her that were almost more than she could bear.

"I love you, Jade." His voice was mesmerizing, and she felt herself sucked into his gaze. She might live a hundred years, but the memory of this single moment, this day, would remain alive forever. "As long as I live, I'll never love anyone the way I love you right now."

Tears blurred Jade's vision, and she blinked them back as Tanner pulled her into an embrace. She didn't cry because she doubted Tanner's words or feared them. Rather, she cried because she believed them with all her heart. And though she couldn't quite yet voice the words back to him, she felt the same way. She loved him; truly she did.

Even if they only had this summer, she knew one thing for certain: She would never love any man like she loved Tanner Eastman.

TEN

Doris looked at her watch and tapped her foot nervously. One-fifteen. They had four o'clock reservations at Beaches — a steak house on the river. That would give them plenty of time to talk first.

Something about Tanner's elusiveness bothered her. He had called and made plans to spend the afternoon with her, but when she asked him why he hadn't called much, he hesitated and blamed it on work. But how much work could a summer intern have the first week on the job? Certainly not so much that he couldn't find time to call. Then Tanner had done the strangest thing. He'd told her he wanted to bring a friend.

"A friend?"

"Yes, mother. I'm not a social outcast. I do make friends on occasion."

"I know that, dear." Who could he possibly want to bring to meet her? Who could matter so much to him in such a short time? "Definitely, I think it'd be lovely if you brought a friend."

Doris had been too taken aback to ask further questions, too afraid of his answer. It couldn't be the girl. There was no way he would have run into her so quickly. Probably someone on the board of supervisors, a fellow intern, maybe.

But why hadn't he said that?

She glanced about, satisfied that the condominium was impeccable as always. The cleaning woman came twice a week, and now that Hap was gone it wasn't much of a cleanup. Doris heard a car door outside and walked to the front window. There was Tanner and a girl, a beautiful, brown-haired girl. Doris couldn't quite make out her face. . . .

She gasped out loud, filled with sudden, desperate panic. *It was her.* It couldn't be, but it was. Doris was positive. The girl was older, taller, more womanly. But the resemblance to her mother at that age was uncanny. The couple moved closer, and Doris saw the girl's emerald eyes. Yes, indeed. *Same seductive eyes as her mother.*

Doris wanted to lock the door, pretend that she'd gone out for the day and forgotten their visit. But it was too late. Tanner

125

had spotted her and he waved in her direction. That's when Doris saw something that made her stomach turn.

Tanner and the girl were holding hands.

She drew two deep breaths and steadied herself. This was no time to faint. She would have to put on a good show for Tanner's sake. He would never understand her feelings about Jade Conner, and the last thing Doris wanted to do was turn her own son against her.

Calm. Be calm. She exhaled slowly as she reached for the doorknob. There was nothing to get worked up about. Jade was not the type of girl Tanner would be serious about. Besides, he would go home at the end of the summer. Eleven more weeks. Then he'd forget about her.

"Hello, Tanner." She stood stiffly, waiting for him to approach her. When he did, he pulled her into a loose hug, gently kissing her on the cheek.

"Good afternoon, Mother." He turned to the girl who stood beside him. How was it possible? *Wretched girl.* It was all Doris could do to maintain her composure. She hated Jade for trying to look shy and demure, like a blushing virgin. *Exactly the way her mother had looked so many years ago when Hap —*

"Mother, I'd like you to meet an old friend of mine." He put a protective arm around Jade, and Doris had to fight the bile that rose in her throat. "This is Jade Conner; remember her mother? From Williamsburg."

Tanner searched his mother's face, obviously looking for her reaction. Doris summoned all the theatrical ability she could muster. "My goodness, you don't mean little Jade, the pixie from across the street, do you?"

"How do you do, ma'am?" Jade looked nervous, and Doris wondered what she had to hide. *Are they already sleeping together?*

She banished the thought and nodded politely toward Jade. "Well, you certainly have grown up since last I saw you." Doris forced a smile. "You're a mirror image of your mother, Jade."

Doris searched the girl's face for a reaction, and sure enough, her slim shoulders fell slightly and her smile faded. Tanner seemed to sense an awkwardness between them, and he took the initiative, his hand still firmly clasping Jade's. "Let's go inside. Mom, maybe you can whip up some of your famous iced tea."

"I've got a pitcher chilling in the refrigerator." Doris trailed behind them. *This can't*

127

be happening. This couldn't be Jade Conner walking into Doris's very own living room, holding Tanner's hand, and having the nerve of looking exactly like her temptress mother? Doris steadied herself as she made her way to the kitchen and poured three glasses of tea.

It's just for the summer. She served the drinks and took a seat across from Tanner and Jade. She hated how they looked so comfortable together. Jade had obviously wasted no time getting close to Tanner. *Like mother, like daughter.*

"So tell me, Jade, how ever did the two of you meet up again after such a long time?" Doris hated having to play friendly with the girl, but Tanner was watching her, so she had no choice. She refused to let the girl come between her and her son.

"I live in Kelso, ma'am. Lived there since we left Williamsburg."

Tanner smiled fondly at Jade, and Doris felt as if someone had kicked her in the stomach. Why was he looking at Jade that way? What had gone on this past week? Doris forced herself to listen to what her son was saying.

"Jade works in the children's unit at the hospital. The board of supervisors had a meeting Monday night to discuss the possibility of closing that wing." He nudged Jade playfully with his elbow. "I had the good folks of Kelso just about convinced until Jade, here, took over. Next thing we knew the idea was tabled, and Jade was sounding more like a legal intern than a nurse."

Jade smiled shyly but said nothing. Rather than validate anything about the girl, Doris changed the subject.

"So, Tanner, you must have been busy with work this week. I thought I'd hear from you more often." She was prying, hoping to find out how close the two had become.

Tanner looked at Jade again and the two exchanged a look that terrified Doris. It was the look of two people in love.

"The work's been okay. Mostly I've been with Jade. May I tell her?" He looked at Jade, and Doris saw the girl nod her approval. *Dear heaven, what is this? What terrible announcement are they going to make?* For a moment, Doris felt her heart stop. *Don't tell me they're considering . . .*

Tanner beamed as he spoke. "Jade gave her life to the Lord today at church."

Doris's heart resumed beating. So that was all. Tanner had spent a week with the girl and already he had converted her. *Naturally.* Doris resisted the urge to roll her eyes in the wake of Tanner's announcement. *Whatever happened to old-fashioned denominational Christianity? The kind you didn't wear on your sleeves or try to spread among your friends?* "I suppose I should say congratulations." Doris nodded a brief smile in Jade's direction.

Tanner was apparently too excited to notice Doris's lack of enthusiasm. "We went to Crossroads . . . that church I like over in Vancouver. At the end of the service Jade made a decision for Christ." Tanner turned to his mother, and she was hurt by the joy she saw there. It wasn't right that a girl like Jade Conner could make her son feel so happy. *Get away from him before I —*

"Isn't that great, Mom?"

Doris paused. What could she say? "Didn't you have a faith before, Jade?" She knew she sounded abrupt, and she hoped Tanner wouldn't think she was being rude. She wanted to tear the girl apart, ask her about her background and how many young men had fallen prey to her the way . . . well, the way young men had fallen prey to her mother so many years ago.

Jade's voice was barely audible. "No, ma'am. We weren't churchgoing folk."

Doris nodded once. This was her opportunity. "Ah, yes. Now I remember. Your mama ran off, didn't she? With the Stevens man, wasn't it? Back before you and your daddy moved away."

A crimson blush spread across Jade's face. *Good. You deserve to suffer embarrassment. It's a small enough price compared to what Tanner will suffer if he stays with you for long.*

Jade struggled for a moment as though she wasn't sure what to say. "Uh, yes, ma'am . . . I . . . I'm sorry. Which way is the restroom?" The girl's face was filled with alarm, and Doris thought she almost looked shocked. As though this were new information to her. . . .

Jade stood and Doris pointed down the hall.

When the young woman was out of earshot, Tanner hissed at her. "Mother! That was completely uncalled for."

Doris remained calm. "What, dear?"

"That bit about her mother running off. Don't you think that's hard enough on her without you bringing it up now? When we've only been here five minutes?"

Doris waved a hand at her strapping son. "Tanner, don't be silly. A girl like Jade isn't bothered by hearing the truth about her mother. After all, she's lived with it all her life."

"What do you mean, 'a girl like Jade'?"

131

Tanner was getting angrier by the moment, and Doris searched for a way to defuse the situation.

"I mean nothing by it, dear. Don't get excited."

Tanner's eyes narrowed as he set his jaw. "Listen, Mother, don't bring it up again. It's not an easy thing for her." His voice was still a whisper. "She's my guest, and I want you to make her feel comfortable — not force her out of the room."

Doris rose and patted her son on the shoulder. "Fine, I won't let it happen again. I didn't know your friend was so sensitive."

"Don't you like her, mother? I mean, you could have said something nice. She just gave her life to the Lord an hour ago."

"Of course I like her, Tanner. I meant no ill will by what I said." She leaned down and kissed her son on the top of his head. "Forgive me?"

Tanner sighed. "Yes. But please be more careful. I care a lot about her."

Doris smiled, hiding her alarm as she strode into the kitchen to refill their glasses. There was no place in Tanner's life for a girl like Jade Conner. He was going to be a senator, a congressman. He was headed for the Oval Office, and he would need a wife as cultured and well bred as he.

Doris considered the exchange she'd just had with Jade. She had come close, but she hadn't quite crossed the line, and she congratulated herself for making the comment seem like an innocent mistake. After all, it was the single detail from Jade's past that Williamsburg people would obviously remember about her.

And the reality was that Doris had struck first blood. If there was going to be a battle for Tanner, she hoped Jade would remember this moment.

Because she wasn't going to lose him to the daughter of a harlot without a fight.

ELEVEN

Scripture was like a miracle salve on wounds Jade had long since thought would never heal. As the days of summer wore on, she and Tanner spent as much time in God's Word as they did sharing walks along the shores of the river and late-night conversations on his apartment patio.

She was falling in love, but not just with Tanner — with life itself and most of all with God's promises.

Tanner was incredible, a walking encyclopedia of Scripture references. No matter what the conversation, he was always ready with a verse.

If she grew sad over his impending departure: *All things work to the good for those who love God. . . .*

When they discussed how a long-distance relationship might work: *Nothing is impossible with God. . . .*

The times when she fretted over the

children's unit at the hospital: *Cast your cares on him for he cares for you.* . . .

If she got ahead of herself and wondered who would take care of her father once she moved out: *Do not worry about tomorrow for tomorrow will take care of itself.* . . .

And of course her favorite: *I know the plans I have for you . . . plans to give you hope and a future.*

Scripture really was alive and active. It worked in her heart and changed her perspective so that every day was bursting with hope and promise. She and Tanner had found a church in Kelso where the Bible was preached and people seemed to care about each other the way they had at Crossroads.

By July, the two of them were regulars and had joined a Bible study class. The second Sunday of that month, Jade was baptized — like the preacher had quoted from Scripture, "for the forgiveness of her sins and the gift of the Holy Spirit."

Each day she listened to praise music while she got ready for school. The words spoke of the wealth of feelings that filled her heart. One evening in late July while she was humming a song about how nothing could compare to the love she had in Christ, her father shoved open her bedroom door and scowled at her.

"What's that garbage you're listenin' to?"

Jade turned down the music and silently uttered a prayer for her father. "Christian praise music. Was it too loud?"

Her father rubbed his temples, muttered a string of expletives, and squinted. "No. It's too religious. God this and God that. Since when did you start believing all that trash?"

"Tanner and I bought it at church a few weeks ago. I'm sorry you don't like it, Daddy." Jade took a step closer, studying her father's eyes and wondering how he became such a miserable man. "Anyway, I like it. I'll turn it down so you can't hear —"

"Tanner?" Her father bellowed. "You're still seeing that snobby kid?"

Jade sighed. "He's a man, Daddy. And yes, I'm still seeing him."

"He's using you, Jade. You know that, right? His kind don't associate with our kind but for one reason only."

"Daddy! It's not like that!" Tears filled Jade's eyes, and she smelled stale alcohol on her father's breath. *Why can't he be happy for me? Just this once.*

Her father studied the CD cover in her hands. "This Tanner guy's got you converted, is that it?"

Jade felt her face grow hot. Her father would never understand her precious faith. But still, maybe this was an opportunity to share some of the gospel with him. "Yes, Daddy. But it isn't Tanner's doing. It's God's. He'd been calling me for a long time. I finally listened, that's all." She paused. "He's calling you, too, Daddy."

"Shut up!" Her father all but snarled, his eyes angry. "You might be a holy roller, but don't go preaching to your old man. I know all about church people and if you're one of them now, maybe you better pack your things."

Later that night she related the encounter to Tanner as they sat side by side on his sofa, listening to Steven Curtis Chapman.

"It scares me, Tanner." They held hands and sat close enough so the bare skin on their arms was touching. "I have two more years before I finish nurse's training. If he kicks me out —"

"Shhh . . ." Tanner held a finger up to her lips and gently brushed a lock of hair off her forehead. "Keep your focus, Jade. God has a plan, even if you wind up on your own."

She was quiet for a moment as they studied each other. Every day she felt more comfortable with him, and even though they

137

hadn't done more than hold hands, something deep inside her had started to stir whenever he was near. She knew by the look in his eyes that he felt the same way, but . . .

"What are you thinking?" His voice was tender, patient.

She let go of his hand and drew her knees up to her chest. "How weird I am."

Tanner grinned. "But then, we already knew that."

Jade's heart was heavy and she didn't return his smile. "I'm serious, Tanner. I'm the strangest girl in the world."

"How so?"

Maybe it was time. She'd never talked about this part of her life, but she couldn't hide behind her aloofness forever, pretending she didn't have an aversion to attachment. At some point she would need to talk about why she never allowed herself to get closer to him. "Okay. But I've never told this to anyone before. It might take a while."

Tanner took her hand in his, leaned back against the sofa and waited.

Should I be telling him this, Lord? She heard no answer and finally she steadied herself. Now that she'd started she would have to finish. She only hoped he would understand. "I know there are times when you want to

. . . to kiss me." She paused. "Right?"

His eyes softened and he nodded slowly. "But I can tell you don't want to. So I've kept my distance."

Jade drew a shaky breath, her eyes locked on his. "It isn't that I don't want to. I care about you." She was struggling, searching for the strength to continue. "It's just . . . well, I've never kissed anyone before. I've always thought it was repulsive."

Tanner raised an eyebrow. "Kissing?"

Jade's eyes filled, and she could barely make him out through the cloud of tears. "That's where it gets complicated. It was something that happened a long time ago. I was eleven or twelve, I think . . ."

Tanner's eyes filled with concern, but he held his silence. Still, she saw the alarm in his eyes and knew what he was thinking. She shook her head. "I wasn't raped or anything. But still . . ."

He tightened his grip on her hand. "Tell me."

"Okay." She hated thinking about that night, but maybe talking about it would help. "Well, that night my dad had been drinking, only instead of coming home by himself he brought a friend."

"A guy?"

"Yes. Just as drunk as he was." Jade pulled

her hand from Tanner and hugged her knees again. She stared at her feet and saw that even they were trembling. Why couldn't she have had a normal childhood like Tanner? As if he could read her mind, Tanner put his hand on her arm and massaged it. If only he could rub away the memories of her past. *Lord, give me strength, please.*

She drew a shaky breath. "Anyway, I was in the living room, watching television when I heard them. The guy made some comment about me, and then I heard my dad laugh. He told the guy to give me a try if he wanted. Daddy told him I was probably loose like my mother so it didn't matter to him what the guy did."

Tanner slumped forward like he'd been hit. "He said that?"

Jade nodded.

"What happened?"

"I tried to leave, but they heard me and blocked my way." Jade hung her head. How could Tanner care for her after hearing this? "My dad was laughing, and the guy, his friend, came toward me and grabbed my hair."

She looked up and saw that Tanner's eyes were moist as he silently encouraged her to continue.

"He smashed his face against mine and

. . . and kissed me." She felt tears running down her face, and she desperately wanted to finish the story, to move past it. She forced herself to regain composure. "After that he and my dad left. They were both laughing like it was the funniest thing they'd ever seen." She hesitated and looked at Tanner, searching his eyes. "That's the only time I've ever been kissed."

Tanner released the hold he had on her arm and angrily combed his fingers through his hair. Slowly he blew the air from his lungs. "That man is no father, Jade. Why didn't you tell me?"

Her voice was choked with emotion. "I — I couldn't."

Tanner groaned and leaned toward her, taking her in his arms and stroking her back. "I'm so sorry, Jade. I wish . . ."

The tears came again, and she collapsed willingly into Tanner's comforting arms. She felt safe and loved there. *What was this? Why did Tanner make her feel like she never wanted to be anywhere but in his arms?* "It's okay." She muttered the words against his chest. "It could have been worse."

"But look how it's hurt you. No wonder you've kept your distance."

Jade pulled back and uttered a short laugh. "You've kept your distance, too.

Remember the onions?"

A strange expression crossed Tanner's face, almost as though there was something he wanted to tell her but couldn't quite bring himself to do it.

"What are you thinking?" Jade wanted to know. She wanted to know everything about him.

The curious look disappeared from his eyes. He pulled back slightly and put his hands on either side of her face. "Nothing. You're right. I've prayed a lot about you . . . us. I haven't wanted to make you uncomfortable. It's okay that we haven't kissed."

"I've prayed about it, too." Jade rested her hands on his shoulders as she studied him, savoring the closeness of their faces, his sweet breath and day-old cologne. They stayed that way a while until finally she whispered. "I'm not repulsed now."

Tanner searched her eyes, clearly questioning the intent of her statement. In response, she moved closer, her gaze unwavering. He ran his fingers down her neck and traced her collarbone. When he spoke, it felt like his words were aimed directly at her heart.

"A kiss . . . between two people who care about each other . . . should be something beautiful . . . something you remember."

Jade nodded. For the first time in her life,

she wasn't afraid of love. She loved Tanner with everything she was about, even if she hadn't been willing to tell him. And now . . . now all she wanted was . . .

She could feel his fingers trembling as he slowly traced her lips. "Jade, would it be all right —" he moved closer — "if I kissed you?" His voice was barely audible, his eyes still locked on hers.

She swallowed and nodded. As she did, he lowered his face the remaining distance to hers and tenderly kissed her jaw, her chin, her cheek, until finally his lips found hers. Jade heard him moan softly as she returned his kiss and her fingers worked their way up his neck to his face.

The feelings that ravaged her body in that moment were so great she feared she might die of pure pleasure. But they did something else. They brought about a strange aching that caused her upper body to move more closely against him. Their kiss continued, and Tanner parted his lips ever so slightly. As he did, the feeling in Jade grew stronger, almost urgent.

Tanner pulled away first, breathless, his eyes searching Jade's. His body was on fire with desire so strong it had been all he could do to tear himself from her.

Lord, what have I done? Douse the fires that rage within me, please! He felt his body relax. Jade was watching him, and he didn't want her to feel guilty in any way.

He framed her face with his fingertips once more. "That's the way a kiss is supposed to be."

Jade's eyes grew troubled. "Is it wrong? In God's eyes, I mean?"

Tanner drew a deep breath. How could anything that felt so right be wrong? *Okay, God, help me on this one.* He steadied himself. "Did you feel anything? While we were kissing, I mean?" They had gotten close enough over the summer that he felt comfortable asking.

Jade nodded and a pretty blush crossed her face. "I felt . . ." Her gaze dropped to her hands. "I didn't want to stop."

Tanner leaned forward and set his forearms on his knees, close to Jade but not touching her. "Me, too."

"And that's bad?" Jade's question was genuine, and Tanner was struck at how inexperienced she was. In many ways she was like an orphan who'd never had the chance to grow up.

Woe to anyone who causes one of these little ones to sin. . . .

The Scripture sent a wave of alarm

through Tanner, and he stared at his shoes. Jade was waiting for an answer. *Help me, Lord.* He looked up and met her gaze. "Well, those feelings are kind of like a warning. You know where they lead, right?"

Jade nodded. "I knew girls in school who slept with their boyfriends. It was so foreign to me, though, I guess I never really understood what the big deal was." She looked at him, her soul laid bare before him. "Until now."

"It's a big deal to God. Sometimes a kiss like . . ." he let his eyes drop briefly to her lips . . . "a kiss like that one takes people to a place where they can't stop. Do you understand?"

"I think so . . ." Her voice trailed off and Tanner saw she was struggling with something. "Have you ever . . . you know?" The blush on her cheeks darkened.

"Slept with a woman?" Tanner was glad for their conversation, glad to be honest with his feelings after hiding them for so many weeks. "No. I've done some dating, some kissing. But God's Word is really clear on the issue."

"What's it say?"

Tanner reached over and grabbed his Bible from the end-table. He flipped to Galatians and found the verse he was looking for. With the Scriptures in his hands, he felt his body cooling, but still there was a tremble in his voice. "It says here that the sexually immoral will not inherit the kingdom of God. There's other verses about sex outside marriage being sinful."

"So that's why you've never done it?"

"I believe God has a plan for me." He studied her eyes, wondering if she could see how badly he wanted her to be part of that plan. "A plan for you, too, Jade."

"Like that first Scripture you showed me, the one from Jeremiah?"

"Right. I don't want to mess up that plan by acting outside God's will. Make sense?"

He set the Bible down and took her hands in his. She still looked puzzled. "So is . . . is kissing like that a sin, too?"

Tanner sighed. *It couldn't be, could it, Lord?*

He didn't wait for a response. Instead he leaned toward her, wove his fingers firmly through her hair, and kissed her again. Immediately the fire returned, and Tanner forced himself to come up for air.

Desire, once it's conceived, leads to sin, and sin when it's full-grown leads to —

The answer was clear. But Tanner shook his head. "No. Kissing like that isn't a sin . . ." They'd done nothing wrong. A kiss, after all, was only a kiss. His eyes were trained on hers, and he kissed her more slowly this time, speaking to her only when he needed to breathe. "It's what . . . it leads to . . ."

He felt her nod, and the fire in him raged hotter when she brought her lips to his. After a while she tipped her head so she could see his eyes. "We can't let it go further."

"I know." He raked both hands through her hair, angling her face, kissing her closer. "We'll have to . . . be very careful. . . ."

Jade closed her eyes, her lips moving on his. When she pulled away she stared at him, her face shadowed by concern. "Promise?"

Tanner pulled her close and kissed her again. She was addicting. . . . But there was no harm in this. He would never let it go further. No matter how his body screamed for more, he could never hurt Jade that way. Never hurt his Lord that way.

Finally, breathlessly, between kisses that grew more and more urgent, Tanner whispered the one word he meant with all his heart.

"Promise. . . ."

TWELVE

The heavenly, hot days of August raced by with Jade and Tanner spending as much time together as their schedules would allow. Tanner had taken his promise to her seriously, and they spent more time outside and in public than before. When they wound up at his apartment, she set herself a curfew and went home by ten o'clock.

Tanner's work with the board of supervisors had turned out to be productive. Although there was still a chance the board might close the children's unit at Kelso General, Tanner had found a dozen alternatives that would balance the budget and keep the unit open.

Jade loved hearing about his work. He was bright and articulate, and she knew he would make a brilliant politician one day. She had long since given up her earlier efforts to maintain some emotional distance with Tanner. He had worked his way into the very core of her heart, and no matter what their futures held his presence there would remain.

Although there were more questions than answers, they often sat in folding chairs on his apartment patio and talked about the future.

"Move to the East Coast, Jade. You could finish school there, do your nursing just like you planned." Tanner would take her hand and squeeze it gently, his eyes imploring her to agree.

But Jade knew that wasn't the answer. Tanner still had a year of school left, and then he could take an entry level political position anywhere in the country. It didn't make sense for her to relocate. Not yet. Besides, Tanner had talked about marriage, but he hadn't asked her to marry him. Jade wanted to know his intentions before she made any life-changing decisions.

"I'm going to miss you, Tanner. . . ." She wasn't afraid to say it, and although she'd never told him she loved him, she was convinced he knew.

"I'll be back. . . . I promise." Tanner told her that nearly every time they were to-gether. "On breaks and three-day weekends. I'll fly out, and we'll figure out what we're going to do."

Jade would study him, wondering what the future really held for them.

"I let you go once, Jade Conner. But I won't let you go again. I want to marry you one day."

Many times, when there were no answers in the discussion about their future, they talked about religious freedom and the fact that many of the privileges Americans had long taken for granted were being undermined by liberal political groups. Tanner was strongly opinionated on the topic.

"We need a group who'll fight for the rest of us. Someone who can step in and take charge when a student is told he can't bring his Bible to school, or a child is forbidden to talk about the nativity at Christmas."

Jade was impressed with how well read he was on the topic. He was familiar with landmark cases and had a very clear grasp on what he considered the eroding of religious rights in America.

She couldn't help but be struck by the fact that he lacked that energy when he talked about becoming a politician. But when she would pry further, he would change the subject. Often they talked about her spiritual growth and how hungrily she sought God's word for every situation. And many times she asked about his mother, how she was doing and whether she was making progress in packing up her condominium.

She and Tanner had been back to visit his mother twice, and, in Jade's dreams, she imagined staying in close contact with the woman after Tanner returned to school. Although Mrs. Eastman was never quite warm, Jade could picture getting phone calls from her and spending Sunday afternoons with her until the woman moved back to Williamsburg.

Then, several weeks ago, Tanner had stopped taking Jade along when he visited his mother. It had seemed odd to Jade, but she hadn't wanted to bring it up, hadn't wanted to ask why he no longer included her. She was afraid of what Tanner would say if she did.

One day, a week before Tanner's internship was up, they were on his patio, side by side soaking in the steady summer sun and talking about the memories they'd made those past months when there was a break in the conversation.

"I'm going to spend Saturday at my mother's."

Tanner looked uncomfortable as he spoke, and Jade understood. If they talked about the weekend, they would have to acknowledge that Tanner was going back to school. "So you'll leave Saturday."

Tanner nodded. "We can be together Friday night, but Mom wants me to help her go through a few more things before I leave."

Jade was quiet. She felt the sting of tears but she refused to cry. Not yet. "What time's your flight?"

"Three-forty-five Saturday afternoon."

Why didn't he ask her to come with him to Portland? She could drive her own car and make her way back without him. Why was Tanner's mother so off-limits lately? In the quiet, Jade found the courage to voice the question. "She doesn't like me, does she?"

"Who?" Tanner's blank expression made Jade wonder if maybe she was only imagining his mother's dislike.

"Your mother. I get the feeling she doesn't approve of me."

A momentary sadness appeared in Tanner's eyes; then he hooked her neck playfully in the crook of his arm and drew her near, kissing her tenderly on her forehead. "Of course she likes you. She's just . . . stiff, I guess."

Jade pondered the thought. *Is that really all it is?* "I don't know."

"No, really, Jade. She's told me herself. She thinks you're great."

"Then why haven't you invited me to Portland with you lately?"

Tanner looked frustrated. "My mother asked me to come alone. She said she felt more comfortable talking about my father when I was by myself."

Jade thought about that for a moment and decided it was a plausible explanation. Still . . .

"Have you told her about us?" Jade leaned toward him and kissed him on the mouth, a kiss that lasted longer than she intended. She finally pulled away and eyed Tanner. "Have you told her how we are now? How . . . serious we are?" She was trying to sound lighthearted, teasing even. But deep inside she wondered. If he were proud of her, wouldn't he want his mother to know how serious they'd become?

Tanner squirmed uncomfortably. "Not exactly."

Jade withdrew her arms from Tanner's neck and sighed. "Why not?"

For the first time, Tanner sounded impatient with her. "You don't know what it's like to have a mother like mine."

The moment he said it, regret flashed in his eyes. Jade looked away. *No, Tanner. I don't know what it's like to have any sort of mother at all.*

He sighed. "I'm sorry. It's just . . . ever since I was a kid my mother has planned my life for me."

Jade knew that. This past summer there had been many times when Tanner shared the ways his mother had organized his childhood so that when he went to college he would study politics and one day be ready for a position in public office. She exhaled slowly and placed her hand on his knee. "I know. I just wish you'd tell her."

"I will eventually. See —" he hung his head and stared at his feet for a moment before looking up again — "she has this idea that I should finish college, take a position in government somewhere, and then get married once I'm established. She's told me a hundred times how a girl can be the undoing of a man. Especially a man who might one day find himself in the White House."

Jade stood, pacing the patio area with her arms crossed firmly in front of her. "And you believe that? That I might be your undoing?" She was angry and didn't try to hide it.

"No, of course not." He rose and was at her side instantly. "Jade . . . you can't think that. It's just —"

154

"What?" Jade felt the tears well up, but she didn't care. Let them spill over onto her face. Tanner was making it sound like he was ashamed of her, and for an instant she could hear her father.

"You're a waste, an idiot, Jade. Jim Rudolph is the best thing that ever happened to you."

She turned her back to Tanner and tried to work through her anger. He was at her side instantly, putting his hands on her shoulders and holding her close, but she remained stiff in his arms. "Why do I feel like you're embarrassed about us?"

He gently turned her so she faced him, and she saw nothing but sincerity in his eyes. "You have to trust me, Jade. It isn't the right time. She'll think I'm throwing away my political chances."

"Is that what you think?"

"Of course not."

"Then why are you so afraid of her?"

Tanner was silent. He stuffed his hands into his shorts pockets.

Jade quietly fumed. *Stand up for me, Tanner.* She positioned herself so she could make eye contact with him. When she spoke she was careful to hide her frustration. "Your mother is a good woman, but she can't run your life forever."

"She expects so much of me." He seemed

155

to be speaking to himself as much as to Jade. "She wants me to be the president, for heaven's sake. Do you know what kind of pressure that is?"

Tanner moved back to his chair. He sat down, set his head in his hands, and stared at the cement beneath him. Jade waited a moment then moved nearer, crouching on the ground beside him, her hand on his knee as she searched his face. "What about you? What do *you* want?"

Tanner shook his head. "I don't know anymore."

Jade considered what she was about to say. She'd wanted to say it many times before, whenever he got excited about religious freedom, but she hadn't wanted to seem pushy. Now she felt she had no choice. "You don't really want to be a politician, do you?"

Tanner kept his eyes trained on the ground, but Jade saw them fill with tears. For a long while he stayed that way, considering her words, silently mulling over them. Then finally he shook his head again. "No."

Jade sighed and rose to her knees, circling her arms around his neck. They stayed that way as Tanner drew a deep breath.

"I have the gift for it, the total package like my mother's always said. She's probably right. One day I could wind up in the

White House if God were willing."

"I'd vote for you." Jade felt Tanner chuckle at her soft comment.

"Thanks." He pulled away and met her eyes straight on. "I must be crazy."

Jade smiled, allowing herself to get lost in his eyes. "How come?"

"I'm about to leave the only woman I've ever loved to finish an education I'm not sure I care about that will lead me into a job I know I don't want to do. It doesn't make sense."

She ran a finger over his brow. It felt so good to hear him being honest with himself.

"You know what I'd really like to do?" Tanner's expression was somber. Their arms were still locked around each other, their faces inches apart.

"Kiss me?" She smiled. He was leaving too soon for them to be so serious. She wanted to enjoy these last days.

He tousled her hair and grinned. "That, too. But besides that —" his smile faded — "when I think of spending the rest of my life in a job, there's only one thing I'd really love to do." He paused. "Fight for —"

"— religious freedom." She finished his sentence and saw his eyes widen in surprise.

"How did you know?"

"I've been with you every day lately, remember?"

Tanner was quiet, and Jade knew he was thinking of his mother again.

"She'd think I'd flipped for sure."

"Does it matter what she thinks? God gave you this desire for a reason, Tanner."

"I don't know, I can't change directions overnight when I've been planning my life one way all these years."

"Why not?" His mother would understand eventually, even if she didn't right now. "You're young, Tanner. At least think about it. Pray about it. Please?"

He nodded. "Okay." He drew her nearer still and lowered his face to hers. Jade's body responded to his closeness, and she was thankful they were outside in broad daylight. He kissed her neck and whispered in her ear. "Now, about that other thing I'd like to do . . ."

Jade had gone home, but Tanner was still feeling the effects of her presence. They had kept their promise, limiting their physical contact to kisses only. But some of the kisses they shared . . . It was a good thing they'd taken to ending their evenings in prayer. Talking to God had a way of dousing inappropriate desire in an instant.

Tanner moved into his bedroom and

flopped onto the comforter. *Lord, I don't want to be president of the United States. I want to marry Jade and stay here with her forever. Help me know what I'm supposed to do.*

He thought about their conversation earlier, and Jade's words challenged him. Why was he studying to be a politician if that wasn't where he felt God was leading him? And how in the world would he break the news to his mother?

He stood up and wandered toward a desk in his bedroom. Immediately his eyes fell on the file he sought and he pulled it out, thumbing through it until he found what he was looking for. It was a flyer announcing a trip that would take place in mid-September — just three weeks away. The trip was to Hungary and would be led by Youth with a Mission. Tanner's eyes scanned the information until he found the line that mattered most: "Trip objective: To study religious freedom and the consequences of what happens when those freedoms are taken away."

Do this, my son.

The voice was clear and Tanner closed his eyes. *Lord, is this what you want? Is this where you're leading me?*

It would mean taking extra courses in the summer so he could still graduate with his class, but suddenly it was the single thing he wanted most in life. Jade was right. He could see religious freedom being stripped away all around him, and now he was being called to do something about it. He would take the trip, graduate, and marry Jade. Then he would enroll in law school and after that, he'd open shop. He would take on the liberal special interest groups bent on destroying religious freedom, and he would rely on the Lord's strength every step of the way.

He would make the phone call in the morning.

His mother would simply have to understand.

THIRTEEN

The days dissolved like so many hours until finally it was Friday. Their last day together.

Tanner presented Lang and the others on the board with a stack of briefs detailing the conclusions he'd reached on the budget issue and several other items he'd been involved with. Good-byes were exchanged and Lang patted him firmly on the back.

"I expect to see your name on a ballot one day, my boy."

Tanner smiled. The two had enjoyed a friendship that complimented their working relationship. But a twinge of guilt tugged at Tanner's conscience. His name would never be on a ballot if things went as he hoped they would. He thought about the phone calls he'd made that week — everything was in order, but he had yet to tell anyone about his decision. Not Lang, not his mother. Not even Jade. He would do that tonight when they were together.

He nodded to Lang as he finished packing up his cubicle. "You never know. Maybe it'll be the other way around."

They made small talk until finally Tanner heaved his box of belongings into his arms and left. On the way home he picked up a Hawaiian pizza with olives — something he and Jade had shared every Friday night since they had run into each other back in June.

She was waiting outside his apartment for him, and when he approached her he could see she'd been crying. "Jade . . ." He set the pizza box down on the roof of her car and drew her into a full embrace. They remained that way until he felt the flames of desire begin to dart through his body.

Be careful, my son. . . .

Yes, tonight especially. Tanner knew he would have to be especially cautious if this was the way his body was going to react to a sympathetic hug.

Jade pulled away and sniffed, wiping a hand under one eye. "I don't want to talk about it. Not yet. I can't."

Tanner understood. It would be hard enough to say good-bye without starting the process now. He held the pizza against his body with one hand and took her arm with the other. They were both tired of looking for ways to spend time together in public. Tonight they had given themselves permission to visit at his apartment. Just the two of them for the last time in what might be months.

Neither of them was hungry, so they talked about work and school and church news — anything but the fact that in twenty-four hours he'd be gone. They watched a sitcom, and when it was over they turned off the television and played three games of backgammon, all the while pretending summer would stretch on forever and that this wasn't the last night they'd have together.

Finally, sometime after nine o'clock, Tanner heated up the pizza, and they sat down to eat. The mood between them had changed and neither was willing to make small talk. The night was drawing to a close, and sooner or later they would have to find a way to say good-bye.

They ate their pizza in silence, allowing a somberness to fall over the meal despite Tanner's intention to avoid the sadness until the last possible moment. Finally, Jade pushed her half-eaten pizza aside and turned toward him.

He contorted his face into different shapes as he ate, trying desperately to make her smile. "All right, come on. You'd better smile or I'll have to call in the tickle police."

Jade shook her head and her eyes filled with tears. "I'm sorry, Tanner. I can't."

He sighed and set the rest of his pizza back on his plate. Her eyes were so green when she was sad. He ran his thumb over her left brow and smoothed her hair back behind her ear. It was hard to believe that by the following night, three thousand miles would separate them. "I won't be gone forever. . . . I told you I'll visit."

She nodded and blinked, sending two tears spiraling down her cheeks. "It won't be the same. I want you to stay. . . ."

"Me, too. But I can't."

"I know." She blew a loose strand of hair off her forehead. Her eyes grew distant and her tone hard. "Your political career awaits you."

It was time to tell her. No point in making her wait until the end of the evening to know what he'd done, how she had caused him to change the direction of his entire life's plan. He lifted her chin so that their eyes met again. "I have something to tell you."

Jade did not look enthused. "What?"

"Ah, come on, Jade. You can sound more excited than that." He grinned at her, but still the sorrow on her face remained, and

Jade said nothing.

"All right, then. Time to call in the tickle police." He wiggled his fingers up into her armpits and jabbed twice at her ribs.

"Don't!" Jade laughed, and the sound of it made Tanner's heart soar. He continued, poking her, tickling her mercilessly until she leapt from the chair and placed it between them. "Stay back!"

Tanner tried a few more jabs but she kept her distance. "Here I come." He stood up and started for her as she uttered a short scream.

"Stop!"

"Okay, okay, relax." He raised his hands in surrender and grinned breathlessly. "I'm done. No more tickling."

She waited, and when Tanner kept his promise, she pushed away the chair that separated them and placed her hands on her hips. "That's better. Now, what news were you going to tell me?"

"News?" He was having trouble thinking with her standing so near, breathing hard from being tickled. He pulled her to him instead and kissed her. "I love your smile, Jade. Don't stop smiling just because summer's over."

She kissed him back and then whispered, "Okay."

He found her mouth again and moved his lips over hers, massaging her jaw gently with his thumb. "Remember what Scripture says in Jeremiah. 'I know the plans I have for you . . .' "

" '. . . plans to give you hope and a future.' " Her voice was barely audible, and they remained in each other's arms, their eyes locked. "Now . . . what were you going to tell me?"

Tanner struggled to control the feelings that welled up inside him. There was no end to the longing her nearness caused him. Reluctantly he pulled away. "Okay . . . come on. I'll show you."

She looked around. "What?" Her eyes scanned the room.

"Come on, it's back here." He motioned for her to follow. He had planned on leaving her in the living room. He'd go get what he was after and bring it back to show her. But he didn't want to miss a moment with her.

Be careful, my son . . . be careful.

Don't worry, I will. He wasn't a fool. He had no intention of letting things get out of hand tonight with Jade. There was no reason to worry, just because the flyer and the gifts he had for Jade were in his bedroom. It was merely a matter of convenience.

She followed him through the living room, then hesitated. He turned around and laughed. "Come on, don't worry. I won't bite."

She raised a doubtful eyebrow, but he laughed again. "Jade, you have to trust me. . . . Come on, silly. This'll just take a minute. Besides, it's almost time for your curfew."

Sadness fell over her face at the thought, but she followed him in silence. When they were in his bedroom, he directed her to sit on the foot of the bed.

"What's going on?"

"You'll see." He went to the desk, opened a drawer, and pulled out a single long-stem red rose, an envelope, and the flyer regarding the trip to Hungary. Then he turned around and joined her on the foot of the bed. "Here. These are for you."

Tears filled her eyes again and she tilted her head, looking from him to the rose and back again. She was clearly too choked up to speak.

"Read it." Tanner leaned toward her and braced an arm behind her so their sides were touching.

Jade dabbed at a tear as she opened the envelope and pulled out a greeting card with a picture of a breathtaking rainbow across the front. She opened it, and over her shoulder Tanner read the words he'd written earlier that day. "My sweetest Jade . . . from beginning to end, this has been the summer of my dreams. God has used you in so many ways to draw me closer to him, closer to everything he has wanted for me. One day soon I want to marry you. But not yet. I have some planning to do first. In the meantime, know that I am thinking of you always, wherever I am, whatever I'm doing. I love you, Jade. Thank you for opening my eyes. All my love, all the time, Tanner."

Scribbled underneath he had written the verse that had come to represent everything they shared. The verse he had spoken to her only minutes earlier. "I know the plans I have for you . . . plans to give you hope and a future."

Jade finished reading and closed the card. Her arms moved slowly around his neck, and as she held him, he could feel her beginning to sob.

He ran his hand softly down the back of her head. "It's okay, Jade, honey. I love you. I'm not going away for good. Hey —" he pulled back — "there's something else I have to show you."

She drew three quick, convulsive breaths, and Tanner could see she was trying to compose herself, trying to keep a flood of tears from letting go. She waited while he presented her with the flyer. "What's . . . what's this?"

"Open it." Tanner grinned and watched as Jade unfolded the paper. A moment passed as she read over the details, and when she looked up at him, her eyes were filled with questions. "I don't get it."

"I found that flyer almost a year ago. Think about it, Jade . . . what better place than Hungary to study what happens when religious freedom is taken away?"

"Hungary?" Her voice was quiet.

"Yes. I picked up the flyer and carried it with me because I wanted so badly to go." He hesitated. "Only there was no way I ever would. Not as long as my goal was public office. But after our talk the other day I knew I had to go. I wouldn't be happy unless I did."

"But . . . what about your classes?" She ran a trembling hand through her hair.

"I called the university and made arrangements, then I contacted Youth with a Mission. They had room for me so I paid in full. I leave in two weeks for Hungary."

"How long will you be gone?" Jade searched the flyer.

"Two months." Tanner grinned, proud of himself for finally making this decision.

"But I'll write."

"Two months in Hungary?" Jade looked bewildered, almost fearful. "What about . . ."

Suddenly Tanner understood her fears. She thought he was cutting her out of the picture, and he rushed to explain himself. "Don't you see, Jade? I'll take the trip, work extra hard to graduate in May, and then next summer I want us to get married. After that I'll be going to law school for a few years, and when I'm finished, I'll take my place in the fight for religious freedom. It's my life and I'm going to do what I want with it, what God has planned for me."

Jade scanned the flyer again. "Wow. I can't believe it."

Tanner studied her and a sliver of doubt pierced his heart. Why wasn't she excited about his plans? *She loves me, doesn't she, God?* He believed her feelings for him were sincere, and yet she'd never said the words. Never declared her love. He took her hands in his. It was time to find out.

"Jade, you know how much I love you. . . ." She nodded, a faint smile curving the corners of her lips. He paused. "But . . . but you've never told me if you feel the same way." He kissed her once, tenderly. "You've never told me you loved me."

Tears came to her eyes again, and he

forced himself to continue. "Do you?"

She circled her arms around his neck once more and hugged him, resting her face against his chest. When she spoke, she pulled away and looked into his soul. "You're the only one I've ever loved."

"Really?"

She nodded and traced his lips with her finger. "I used to imagine I'd marry you one day, even back when we were kids."

He was flooded with relief. "Me, too."

"I think I loved you even back then, Tanner."

He moved his lips against hers as he ran his hands along her back and the sides of her neck. "I love you, Jade. Marry me. . . ."

She was crying openly now, and when he kissed her again he tasted her tears. Her sobs made it difficult to hear her answer but he heard it all the same. "Yes. Yes, I'll marry you, Tanner."

His mouth covered hers and he held her closer.

Get out of the bedroom!

The warning sounded clearly in his mind, but he brushed it off. What difference did it make what room they were in? It was their last night together, after all. Tanner stroked the back of her head and drew her to him again. "God brought us together . . . and

171

when I leave tomorrow, I'll take you with me in here." He touched the area over his heart. Then he placed his hands on her shoulders and searched her eyes. "We'll be together again, Jade. I promise." Their kiss was longer this time. "I'll never, ever leave you."

He took her hands in his and felt a strong reaction to the contact. But this time he didn't hear any warnings. Instead, he pulled her close, nestling her against him. Softly, near her ear, he whispered the truth: "I never could have done this if it hadn't been for you." He drew back and saw that Jade's eyes glistened with happy tears.

"Does your mother know?"

"I'll tell her tomorrow."

Their kiss was more urgent this time, and after a few minutes he felt her stiffen in his arms. She pulled away and caught her breath. "I should go. You have to get up early."

"Okay, soon." Tanner studied her eyes, memorizing her. He would never forget how she looked, sitting beside him in her sleeveless denim shirt and cutoffs. Eyes as green as they'd been back when she was a child. She would always be the most beautiful woman he'd ever seen.

He knew he should let her go, walk her

out and tell her good-bye. But in that instant he couldn't bear the thought. His lips moved up her cheekbone toward her earlobe. His body shook from the flames that shot through him, and he wondered if she could sense the depth of his passion. "Jade . . ." The word came out low and breathless. "Oh, Jade, what you do to me."

He lowered his lips to hers, savoring their closeness, savoring her.

Leave the bedroom! Go! Flee!

The warnings were distant, easily dismissed. God would not let him be tempted beyond what he could bear. He wasn't really losing control; his body only felt that way. He ran his fingers lightly down the length of her bare arms and felt her skin chill under his touch.

"Tanner . . ."

"It's okay." He pressed his lips to hers, stopping her questions before she could ask them. Ignoring the dim warnings, he moved his lips down the curve of her neck.

She moaned softly, and reaction jolted through him. Was this how it felt to lose control? To be so drawn in that there was no human way out? He banished the thought. He could stop if he wanted to. They were just saying good-bye, sharing a memory that would help them endure their long separation. His breathing came faster, and he gave himself permission to kiss her shoulders, her throat. Permission to continue.

Finally, Tanner knew he'd gone too far. Desire drove him, and it was far more powerful than he'd ever imagined. He couldn't stop it.

In that instant, despite everything he knew to be true and right, regardless of the promises and plans of a mighty God, Tanner knew something else.

He no longer wanted to.

Warnings echoed loudly in Jade's mind as well, rattling her heart and making it difficult to breathe. Verses about the sexually immoral and adultery and desire leading to death. But Tanner knew what he was doing, didn't he? He wouldn't let things go too far. He would stop before it was too late

She could trust him.

Flee, my daughter. Flee!

She heard the silent voice and was filled with alarm at the heat coursing through her. *Come on, Tanner, stop.* She needed to leave, needed to be anywhere but in his bedroom, kissing him, wrapped in his arms on the foot of his bed.

He'll be gone tomorrow. We're just kissing.

Can't we have this one moment to say good-bye? Eventually the warnings grew dim.

Tanner moved his mouth down her neck toward the hollow of her throat, and she tipped her head back, shocked to hear herself moan. Her body ached with a need she knew could be met only one way.

Never, Lord. We'll stop. I promise. This is only because he's leaving. Help us, Lord.

Flee!

She closed her eyes and refused. Things were under control. They were two grown adults, after all. Slowly she drew closer to Tanner until her mouth was on his neck, tasting the saltiness of his skin, the stubble of his day-old shave. She gripped his arms and felt him flex beneath her fingers. He was strong and good and right. His very presence felt like a dream come true.

Gently, tenderly, ever so slowly they fell back onto the bed, still locked together, their kisses hungrier than before.

Tanner moved so that his chest lay partially over hers, and his kisses became longer, deeper. Another wave of alarm washed over her. "Tanner . . . we can't . . ."

For a moment he stopped, breathless, and held a finger to her lips. "It's okay. . . ." He brushed back her hair with tender fingers. "Don't worry, Jade." Another kiss. "Just

175

relax. . . . We'll stop in a minute. . . ."

Her body blazed with desire, and she knew deep in her heart that Tanner was wrong. God would not be okay with this. But, then they were still only kissing, weren't they? Certainly he would forgive them for being together like this longer than usual. Just this once.

Jade ran her hands over the muscles in his lower back, pulling him closer to her. "We have to stop. We have to . . ."

Tanner moved his mouth along her throat again and brought his knee over hers. "We will." He looked at her then, and she saw he was trembling, his eyes filled with wanting her. "We won't be together again for so long." His lips traveled up her neck as he made his way to her mouth. "We'll stop. . . . Don't worry."

Ten minutes passed and then twenty. All the while she assured herself they could stop, they would stop. She was safe here in Tanner's arms, a princess being loved by her one and only prince.

But as the evening grew later they kept on, trapped in a moment of weakness stronger than anything either of them had ever known. And sometime after midnight, when they dressed in silence and Tanner walked Jade to her car to kiss her good-bye,

she was no longer a princess.
She was a whore, just like her mother.

FOURTEEN

She was tired almost immediately, and on the twelfth day the nausea kicked in. That night, Jade clutched her sides as she lay on her bed, weeping. Over and over she told herself it was nothing more than the obvious. She hadn't been eating well since Tanner left for Portland, and her father seemed to be shouting at her constantly.

Most of all, she had become shameful in the sight of God.

A sick stomach was understandable.

It was two days before Tanner would leave for Hungary, and she was an emotional basket case. Since Tanner had gone back to school, she'd done her best to avoid her father, choosing instead to spend the hours locked in her bedroom. Penance, she told herself. For committing the unpardonable sin.

Summer classes were over, and the fall schedule would begin at the end of the month. She increased her hours at Kelso General, thinking she might somehow show God the sincerity of her sorrow, how much she wanted him to think her good again.

She brought her knees up nearly to her chin, curled up under the covers, sobbing alone in the night. *I'm sorry, Lord. Forgive me. What have I done? Why did we go against your plan?*

She heard no response. As though the Lord had utterly and completely abandoned her.

Maybe her constant weeping could explain the tiredness and this strange nausea that had come upon her. That had to be the reason. It had to be. She shut her eyes, forced out her fears, and focused on surviving.

"I miss you, Tanner." She whispered into her pillow. Almost as though he'd somehow heard her, the telephone rang. Jade answered it quickly so her father wouldn't pick it up in the other room.

"Jade, it's me. . . ." Tanner's voice sounded tinny and hollow. *A payphone,* she thought. And instantly he felt a million miles away.

She tried to speak but a single sob escaped before she could say anything.

"Jade, you're crying . . . talk to me. . . ."

She heard people laughing in the background.

"Where . . . where are you?" Her voice was thick with tears. She knew Tanner wouldn't want her crying, but she couldn't change how she felt.

"Cafeteria. The pay phones in the dorm were busy." Tanner sounded rushed, and Jade was having trouble feeling close to him. Everything about their conversation felt strained, and the realization brought another wave of tears.

"Jade, baby, stop crying. Everything's going to be okay." He sounded so far away, and in two days he would be thousands of miles farther. Once he left for Hungary, there would be no contact between them for two months. He had told her he'd write, but mail delivery could take two weeks or longer. Since his group would move from place to place, there was no way she could write to him. Their contact — however limited — would be completely one-sided.

A minute had passed and still Jade quietly cried, unable to answer.

"Jade, what's wrong with you? Why won't you talk to me?"

She sought desperately for something to say, but there was nothing.

Tanner's voice grew impatient. "I feel bad,

too, you know. I never meant for . . . oh, you know what I mean."

She stifled her sobs. "I know."

"I'm sorry. How many times do I have to tell you."

She choked out her response. "I told you . . . I'm not mad at you. I just feel bad. Like we blew it."

"I know." He lowered his voice. "I said I'm sorry. What else can I say?"

She continued weeping, struggling to speak. Nothing felt right anymore. "It . . . it feels like things are different between us."

"Come on, Jade. That's your imagination. Satan wants you to be buried under guilt so you'll never be happy again."

"I should have stopped it, Tanner. I had a choice and I didn't." She tried to compose herself. "Besides, we haven't come to the Lord together and asked for forgiveness."

He fell silent, and Jade wondered why. Didn't his heart seek repentance over this? Didn't he think they should come before the Lord as a couple? Maybe his faith wasn't what it had seemed to be all summer. Jade felt even more sick at the thought.

When he finally answered, the impatience was back. "Listen, I have to get going. I have a lot to do before I leave. I didn't call to hear you cry for thirty minutes. I already got that earlier when I talked to my mother. Naturally she thinks I'm crazy, throwing away my future and all." He paused. "I was kind of hoping you might be able to cheer me up."

Jade stared at the phone, open mouthed. *Is it so easy for him to dismiss what we've done, how it's changed things between us?* "I'm sorry. I don't feel very cheery."

"What *do* you feel, Jade? Do you still love me?"

She felt her anger rising. "Of *course* I love you. But I feel all messed up inside. Like we've turned God against us and like . . . no matter what we do now our plans won't succeed." She wept more loudly. "Right now I feel too ashamed to even talk to you, and you want me to be cheery?"

He sighed slowly, and she could hear more voices in the background. He was obviously in a busy part of the cafeteria, and it gave her the feeling he wasn't paying attention. "Okay, we were wrong. *I've* said that. *You've* said that. I'm sure we've both admitted it to God. We're both sorry. Now we pick up the pieces and go on. You can't let what happened change things between us."

She was silent for a moment, trying desperately to fight off the nausea that passed over her. "It's too late." She drew a deep, steadying breath.

"What's too late?" He sounded tired.

"Things have changed already."

"Well, then maybe you and I have some thinking to do over the next two months."

Fear ripped through Jade's heart. *What are you saying, Tanner? Are you breaking up with me?* "I'm not sure what you mean by that . . . but I love you, Tanner. I just can't pretend things are the same."

Tanner paused. "Fine. Listen, I gotta go, Jade. I love you. I'll be praying for you. Just because we made a mistake doesn't mean God's forgotten about us. Jeremiah 29:11 is still true. Okay?"

His words sounded hollow, forced . . . and Jade swallowed the lump in her throat. "Okay. 'Bye . . . I'll miss you."

"I'll miss you, too. And I'll write."

They hung up, and Jade flopped onto her stomach, sobbing as if her heart would break. *Two months.* There would be no conversation between them for two months. He hadn't been gone two weeks, and already their relationship was strained. *What'll happen in two months?*

She turned onto her side. A collage of Kelso General's sick children hung on the wall, and she stared at it. When was her last period, anyway? She calculated the dates as she'd done a dozen times since August thirty-first. . . .

What she and Tanner did hadn't been planned, so they hadn't used birth control. And now she realized that she'd been smack in the middle of her cycle. Her period was due tomorrow: September fourteenth. Ever since she was thirteen they'd come every twenty-eight days without fail. As predictable as her father's drinking.

God, what'll I do? What if I'm pregnant?

But instead of the Savior's kind prompting, she heard unholy voices, voices that had haunted her since that Friday night at Tanner's apartment.

Whore! Your father was right! You should have run off with Jim Rudolph. Tanner deserves better than a piece of trash like you.

She closed her eyes, trying desperately to shut out the voices. For a moment she glanced at her Bible and considered looking through it for help. But she hadn't been able to open it since Tanner left. She felt too dirty, too much a hypocrite to hold God's perfect word in her filthy hands.

Her period did not come the next day or the next, and by Friday, three weeks after that night at Tanner's apartment, Jade did not need a pregnancy kit to tell her she was with child. Nevertheless it was time to take the test. Otherwise she might never really accept the truth.

A few days later she drove to a remote part of town and found a drug store she'd never been to before. There she paid for a test that promised accurate results just one day after a missed period. She took the test home and performed it in the bathroom, careful to hide the packaging in a brown paper bag. Three minutes later two pink lines appeared in the test-tube window, and she had her answer.

She was pregnant.

The next day she skipped classes and stayed in bed, suffocating beneath her warring emotions. At times she wept, thrashing about under her covers, wondering what had gone so wrong in their plans and why they'd been so weak that final night together.

Other times she was overcome with fear. What would she do? Where would she live? How quickly could she get word to Tanner? What kind of mother would she be?

The last question was easy. She would be everything her mother hadn't been. Nothing and no one would ever separate her from the infant she carried. Regardless of the cost — and she was sure their choice that night would cost them much — she would love her child unconditionally as long as she drew breath.

If this were two years from now, Tanner and I would be celebrating. Nothing could have contained what she knew would be their mutual excitement. And even in the midst of her turmoil, the reality of what had happened to her filled her with awe. Tanner's child was within her . . . a baby created out of their love for each other. *Only we didn't wait for God's perfect plan, and now everything is wrong.*

She wanted desperately to talk to Tanner, get his reaction. He'd been in Hungary for a week and she had hoped to receive a letter from him but so far there had been nothing, no word at all. Would he want her to move out to New Jersey and marry him immediately? Would he send her away, sickened by the sight of her? She thought she knew the answer, but she wasn't sure anymore. Everything had changed.

Should she tell her father? She would have to let him know eventually. But how would he take the news? What names would he call her? Jade wept again because she knew the answer. The weeping and wondering and wishing she could go back in time continued until late in the evening, when finally she arrived at a plan. She would call and see if

Tanner's mother knew a way to get a message to him. He had explained to Jade that the group leaders allowed only emergency phone calls back to the U.S. Surely this would qualify. After all, it was his baby, too. Between the two of them, they could figure out what to do.

She made the call the next morning and waited. Tanner's mother answered on the second ring.

"Hello, Mrs. Eastman, this is Jade." She waited but there was no happy greeting, no words of acknowledgment. Jade started to tremble, and a wave of nausea forced her to sit down. "Mrs. Eastman? Are you there?"

"Jade . . ." the woman sounded as though she were trying to place her, almost as if they'd never met. *How come she doesn't know who I am?* Hadn't Tanner been talking about her during his visits? An alarm rang deep within her.

"Ma'am, this is Jade Conner . . . Tanner's friend from Williamsburg. Remember? We visited your house together a few times back in June?"

"Oh! That Jade. Yes, I'm sorry. Forgive me. I must have been distracted." Mrs. Eastman sounded friendlier, and Jade breathed a sigh of relief. "How are you, dear?"

"Uh . . . fine, thanks. And you?"

"Well, I must admit my arthritis has been acting up. But otherwise I'm just fine. Getting ready for the move back to Williamsburg and missing Tanner, of course. But otherwise good."

"That's what I'm calling about." Jade waited a beat and then plunged ahead. "I was wondering if you knew some way to get a message to Tanner?" She crossed her arms against her stomach and closed her eyes. She felt like she was going to throw up but now was not the time. She held a piece of notepaper in her hand and prepared to jot down whatever numbers Tanner's mother might give her.

"In Hungary?"

Jade exhaled slowly and breathed in again, forcing herself to continue the conversation. "Yes. I thought you might know who to call."

"Why, dear, surely you know he can't receive calls. He's on a missionary trip." The woman sounded pleased with her son, and Jade wondered if she'd had a change of heart. Tanner had said his mother had been furious when she learned of his intentions to change career paths and spend two months in Hungary.

"Yes, ma'am, I know he can't. This . . . well, this is kind of an emergency. I really need to talk to him."

"An emergency? Why, Jade, are you okay?" The woman's voice was filled with warmth and concern, and Jade felt tears sting at her eyes. If only her own mother had been there to comfort her and give her direction.

She swallowed hard. "I'm fine. It's . . . well, it's very important that I talk to him."

"I'm sorry, dear. I'm fairly certain I don't have any numbers." The woman sounded worried for Jade. "Of course, we could always call Youth with a Mission. They might know how to reach him." She hesitated. "If you don't mind, Jade, what's the emergency?"

Jade almost wanted to tell her. Maybe Tanner's mother would know what to do next, maybe even find the right words to assure her everything would be okay. "It's . . . personal, ma'am."

Mrs. Eastman hesitated. "Personal?"

Jade paused. "Yes. I really don't want to talk about it until I've had a chance to speak to Tanner."

For several moments Mrs. Eastman said nothing, and Jade assumed she was searching for numbers. She was completely unprepared for the serenity in the woman's voice — or for what she said next. "Are you pregnant, Jade?"

Jade's vision grew blurred and she thought she would faint. What was this? How had Tanner's mother known? Jade blinked and tried to focus on her surroundings. Maybe she hadn't heard the woman correctly. "Excuse me?"

"I'm sorry if I'm prying, but . . . Tanner told me what happened. That the two of you slept together. He was quite honest about it."

Jade's head swam in a sea of unanswered questions. Why had Tanner told his mother? He'd been afraid to tell her they were dating, but now he'd told her they'd slept together? She gulped and searched for something to say. "He . . . he told you that?"

"Why yes, dear. He tells me everything. We're quite close, you know."

"I . . . I know. I just didn't think . . ."

"Well, dear, are you pregnant?"

Jade began crying. "Yes . . . I am." She struggled to speak. "That's why Tanner and I have to talk. I don't know what to do, Mrs. Eastman. Please . . . help me."

The woman's voice was soothing and reassuring. "Tomorrow is Sunday. Why don't you drive down, and we'll spend the afternoon together. I'm sure we can figure something out."

"Okay." She thought about attending

Crossroads on the way down, but then changed her mind. They hadn't recognized the fact that she came from tainted parents, but surely they would recognize what she had become since then. She would avoid church until she had a plan and knew what to do. "Would two o'clock be fine?"

"Yes, dear. I'll look for you then. Drive safely."

Jade's heart soared with hope as she hung up. Tanner's mother liked her! She had been warm and kind and understanding in the wake of what had to have been the most shocking news she'd ever received. Maybe Tanner had told his mother about his intentions to marry her.

Jade lay back on her bed, her mind racing ahead to a host of possibilities. Maybe Mrs. Eastman would ask her to come around more often, offer to attend doctor appointments with her. Perhaps she would be the mother Jade had always wanted and everything would fall in place.

If Mrs. Eastman could love her, then life was suddenly filled with promise. Maybe things really would turn out all right.

She ignored her father that evening, skipped dinner, and for the first time since Tanner left, she slept soundly. The morning couldn't come soon enough, and when it did she hummed happily to herself as she got ready. Whether they figured out a way to contact Tanner or not, Jade knew that with Mrs. Eastman on her side everything was going to be okay. The plans she and Tanner had made were shaky, but they were still intact. God had forgiven her.

And he had blessed her with a friend like Mrs. Eastman in the process.

FIFTEEN

Doris Eastman paced the plush carpet of her uptown condominium, fuming. She had been right, of course. On every account. Jade Conner was a loose, good-for-nothing seductress just like her mother.

The nerve of the girl, calling her for information about how to reach Tanner.

Doris replayed the conversation over and over. The moment Jade mentioned that there was an emergency, bells began sounding in her mind. She knew what kind of girl Jade was. The emergency could be one thing only.

When Jade mentioned it was personal, Doris had taken a chance. Tanner hadn't told her anything about his relationship with Jade. Through July and August she'd asked him to stop bringing the girl to her house and he'd agreed. He hadn't even put up a fight. How important could the girl be to him, really?

Doris considered herself a Christian woman, but she'd had no trouble lying to Jade earlier. Nor would she hesitate to do what she planned when Jade arrived. She would lie a hundred times if it meant protecting Tanner from a girl like Jade. Besides, if she hadn't lied, Jade would never have opened up to her in the first place, never planned to visit that afternoon. Doris wondered what other dark secrets she could extract from the girl.

Not that it mattered.

Doris planned to do most of the talking. She tapped her foot anxiously and looked at her watch. Her plan was perfect, and she congratulated herself for being so cunning in her old age.

Woe to you, woman . . . remember the height from which you have fallen. . . .

The thought interrupted her plotting, and she scowled. Where had *that* come from? She hadn't read a Bible in twenty years. For a moment she thought of Tanner and the hours he'd spent preaching to her, warning her to get right with God again. Huh! What a hypocrite he turned out to be.

Perhaps she should have told him long ago what had happened with his father. How during her engagement to Hap, that Conner woman had shown up on his doorstep one night . . . how she'd wormed her way inside, just like the women in Proverbs. And how she'd . . .

Doris couldn't bear the thought.

But at least if she'd told Tanner, he might have made better choices that summer. She considered her son's decisions over the past months and shook her head angrily. The boy was crazy. First he'd given up his political future. Then he'd decided to spend two months on a missionary trip to God-forsaken Hungary. And finally he'd bedded the daughter of a . . . a woman like Angela Conner. Obviously Tanner had suffered some sort of mental breakdown or emotional collapse over the summer. Perhaps a delayed reaction to his father's death.

Whatever it was, it was all Jade's fault.

She looked at her watch again.

Hurry up, Jade. She smiled. *The web's ready and the spider's waiting.*

Jade parked her car outside the Eastman condominium, grabbed the bouquet of fall flowers from the front seat, and headed up the sidewalk. She had eaten a few saltine crackers on the drive over to stave off any nausea. Although pregnancy was completely foreign to her, she thought it must have been early to be experiencing so strong an

195

upset stomach. Maybe Tanner's mother would help her know what to do, and what to expect in the coming weeks and months.

She hoped Mrs. Eastman would enjoy the flowers. She was filled with peace at the thought of knowing she could talk about her pregnancy and that Tanner's mother truly cared about what happened to her. She rang the doorbell and waited.

Doris Eastman was always dressed impeccably and today was no exception. She wore an eggshell knit skirt, a sweater with a pearl snap, and handsome, low-healed shoes. She welcomed Jade with a warm smile and ushered her inside. "Come in, Jade. You look well."

They moved into the front room, and Mrs. Eastman directed her to a comfortable oversized sofa chair. "Make yourself at home. . . . I'll get us something to drink."

"Thank you, ma'am." A sense of warmth came over her at the woman's words, and Jade played them again in her mind. *Make yourself at home . . . at home . . . at home.*

Tanner's mother returned with two glasses of water. When they were both situated, Doris cocked her head, her eyes filled with concern. "Now, dear. Tell me what happened?"

Jade drew a deep breath and pressed her

hand to her flat stomach. "I can't really believe it myself."

"You're sure though? You took a test?"

Jade nodded. "I'm already feeling sick. It'll probably be a strong baby."

Tanner's mother slipped one leg daintily over the other. "Have you told anyone else?"

Jade took a sip of water and shook her head. "Just you." She let loose a brief laugh. "Never in a million years did I think Tanner would have told you about us."

Mrs. Eastman smiled. "Tanner and I talk about everything." She paused and dabbed her lips with a napkin. "Whenever he gets in trouble, I'm the first person he turns to."

What a wonderful mother she is. Jade relaxed back into the chair and noticed that her nausea was gone. She was perfectly at ease in Mrs. Eastman's home, struck again by her gracious concern and kindness. Why had she ever doubted this woman's intentions? She was gentle and serene and warm as the recent Indian summer days. Jade imagined her offering support every time Tanner . . .

Every time he got into trouble? She hesitated. "That can't have been too often, knowing Tanner. His getting in trouble, I mean." She grinned, enjoying the easy banter of their conversation.

197

Mrs. Eastman leaned slightly forward and took another sip of water. "Not as a boy, no. But ever since the girls discovered him —" the woman made a face that indicated the severity of the problem — "he's gotten in trouble more times than I care to count."

Tanner? In trouble with girls? The pointed blade of alarm stabbed at Jade, and she felt the smile fade from her face. "Is that right?"

The woman looked surprised. "Oh, didn't he tell you, dear?"

Jade had the strange sensation that something bad was about to happen. "Tell me what?"

"Tanner has two children on the East Coast." Mrs. Eastman folded her hands comfortably. "Of course, he doesn't talk about them often. I send their mothers a check every month, and that's about the extent of it."

Jade's vision grew blurred again and her head was swimming. What was this woman saying? Tanner had no other children. He'd never even been with a . . . "I . . . I didn't know."

Doris angled her head sadly. "I'm sorry, dear. I thought you knew." She spanned the distance between them and reached for Jade's hand. "Tanner can be an awfully convincing storyteller, I'm afraid."

"How . . . how old are the children?" Jade felt like she was having an out-of-body experience. She was talking, desperate to know the truth about the man she thought she loved. But her breathing seemed to have stopped, and she was certain she was going to faint.

"Amy is three. Tanner met her mother his senior year in high school. They were very physical, very fast, but Tanner never cared for her. He offered to pay for an abortion, but the girl wouldn't hear of it. Now she gets her monthly check like clockwork."

The nausea was back with a vengeance, and Jade knew she needed a bathroom. She forced herself to wait, to hear the sickening news. "The other child?"

"Justin. Almost two." Mrs. Eastman paused. "Tanner had three women between the mothers of the children. Two of them took him up on his offer and had abortions. The other one must have gotten smart and used birth control. There's been at least five women that I know of. What I mean is, this certainly isn't the first time I've helped him out of trouble." Mrs. Eastman's eyes softened, and she gently squeezed Jade's hand. "I guess you're number six."

"Will you excuse me?" Jade rushed out of the room and barely reached the bathroom in time. There she vomited until there was nothing left inside her.

Until her stomach was as empty as her breaking heart.

It couldn't be true! It was a nightmare, and any moment she was going to wake up and start the day over again. Her stomach convulsed again and nothing came up. *Dear God, is it true? Was everything he told me a lie?* Had he manipulated their time together that summer so that she'd sleep with him? Her heart raced and once more her stomach convulsed, as if her body were trying to rid itself of everything about Tanner Eastman.

When she was finally finished, she stood and wiped her face. Her legs were wobbly and her head pounded. It couldn't be true, could it? Tanner loved her. He had wanted to marry her, to wait until then before they . . . She made her way slowly back to the living room and sat down.

"Are you all right, dear? You look pale." Tanner's mother extended her hand and Jade took it. After all, it wasn't her fault Tanner had lied.

"I'll be okay."

The woman paused and presented two separate snapshots. "I found these while you were gone. This is Amy and this . . . is Justin."

Jade stared at the photographs, and she was blindsided by another wave of nausea. There was no mistaking the resemblance. The children had Tanner's piercing blue eyes, his strong jawline. They were gorgeous — and very much without a father.

The shock was wearing off. The pictures were proof — no question about it. Tanner had lied to her from the beginning. And like numerous other women before her, she had believed him willingly.

Anger began to replace her shock. "He doesn't stay in touch with them?"

Mrs. Eastman shook her head sadly. "I'm afraid not. He isn't very fatherly, actually. Doesn't even send presents on their birthdays."

Jade felt whatever color remained drain from her face, and again Tanner's mother leaned closer. "You don't look well, dear. Can I get you anything?"

"I'm sorry . . . I feel faint, I guess. This is all such a shock. He . . . he never told me any of it."

The woman huffed in frustration. "I really thought he'd outgrown this irresponsible behavior. Especially what with his decision to work for the governor's office next year."

Jade's head spun faster. "What?"

"Certainly he told you that much."

Jade shook her head. "He's going to law school. He wants to fight for religious freedom."

Mrs. Eastman released a sad laugh. "He loves to talk about religious freedom. That was something his father and I always wanted for Tanner. That he might pursue a career in law, fighting for his faith. Despite his failings, he's still a very religious young man, you know. But last week he accepted an entry-level position in the governor's office. The governor of Virginia."

Jade drew three quick breaths. She felt sick again, and her body shook uncontrollably. No matter how hard she tried she couldn't get warm, couldn't stop the trembling. "What about Hungary?"

"Tanner's such a thrill seeker, he just couldn't resist the challenge. It will look good on his resume, of course, that he spent a semester helping the people of Hungary restore their rights. And you can be sure that's how it'll appear on his resume."

"I'm sorry, I . . ." Jade spread her knees and hung her head, desperately trying to stave off the fainting spell that had suddenly engulfed her.

"Here, dear. Have some water." Mrs. Eastman was by her side, offering the drink.

Jade took two sips and then slowly returned to an upright position. There was something she wanted to know. "Tell me one thing, Mrs. Eastman. . . ."

"Yes?" The woman returned to her chair and smiled sympathetically.

"Did Tanner love any of those other women? Did he talk about marrying them?"

"Tanner has a double standard that way. He considers marrying a girl until she gives in to his advances. Once a girl has slept with him, he has no further interest. Wouldn't look good on his political resume."

Jade thought about Hungary. Was it true what Tanner's mother said? Was Tanner not at all interested in fighting for religious freedom? Had he lied about that, too? Her body was seized with cramps, and she shook from the overload of shock. "But he told me politics were *your* idea."

For a moment the woman's eyes hardened, but then almost instantly they were kind again. "No, no, dear. Tanner's wanted to be a politician as far back as I can remember. Oh, his father and I would have loved him to be a lawyer, helping the religious among us. But Tanner is very single-minded. When he wants something, he gets it . . . when he doesn't, well . . ."

Jade thought of little Amy and Justin. He hadn't wanted them or their mothers, and now he lived his life completely separate from them. It was the same thing he'd do to her.

Mrs. Eastman was watching her, and Jade was overcome with a sense of loss. How could she have been so wrong about Tanner? After being his best friend so many years earlier. . . .

"Jade, dear, I'm afraid Tanner can be very irresponsible. But he's my son and I love him. One day the whole world will love him."

Jade's eyes filled with tears. Shock and anger were giving way to repulsion. She had been used and made to feel like a whore at the hands of a man who had lied about everything. Certainly he had lied about his love for her. No wonder he sounded so short-tempered during their last telephone conversation.

"Here, dear —" Mrs. Eastman handed Jade a tissue — "I see you're upset. Should we see if we can find an emergency number for Tanner?"

Jade clenched her jaw and gritted her teeth. "No, thank you. I have no interest in calling him now."

"Oh, dear, I'm so sorry. I shouldn't have said anything."

Jade felt the steady stream of tears on her

cheeks, but she was not filled with grief. No, what filled her to overflowing was much more direct, more simple. Hatred. That's what she felt. If she hadn't seen the pictures of the children, she wouldn't have believed a word of it. She had thought she knew Tanner better than she even knew herself. But now . . . "No, Mrs. Eastman. I'm glad you told me. You spared me from making a fool out of myself."

"Now, now, child. How could you have known?" The woman reached for her purse, opened it, and pulled something out. "You're planning to keep the baby, is that right?"

Jade nodded fiercely. "Definitely."

"Well, I'll treat your child the same way I treat Amy and Justin. But there are a few stipulations I'd like to discuss."

Stipulations? What in the world was she talking about? This wasn't a business transaction. Jade stared at Tanner's mother and noticed something she hadn't before: The kindness was gone.

Mrs. Eastman cleared her throat and continued. "You will not put Tanner's name on the birth certificate. He'll not want anything to do with the child anyway, and it will only complicate things. Also, you will not mention the identity of the baby's father to anyone." The woman crossed her legs again and smiled through hard eyes. "Tanner will be a household name one day, and he and I will deny to the death that he ever had anything to do with you. Is that understood?"

"I thought . . . you seemed like you wanted to help. Like you wanted to be a part of my baby's life. You've been so . . ."

"Friendly? Do I have a choice?" Mrs. Eastman cast her a look of disdain. "As long as Tanner keeps getting girls like you pregnant, it'll be up to me to cover his tracks. There will be no room for scandal in the White House. Tanner will be remembered for his high standards, his moral character. I've told the same thing to the other women."

"So you're in charge of cleaning up after him, is that it?" Jade forced herself to breathe, to remain seated even though everything in her wanted to walk over and choke this woman. How dare she place demands on Jade and her unborn child? "What if I don't agree? What if I choose to put his name on the birth certificate anyway?"

The woman made an exaggerated shrug of her shoulders while her eyes shot daggers at Jade. "That will be your choice. But the moment you do, you will be cut off from any financial assistance I might otherwise give. Also, I will hire a batch of attorneys to sue you for child endangerment and complete custody of that brat you're carrying. And then you'll lose the child for good." Mrs. Eastman uttered a short, mocking laugh. "Girls like you would never win a court battle against the Eastman estate. If you know what's good for you, and you want to be a mother to that baby, you'll take the money I'm about to offer and any other money I send you, and once in a while you'll send me a photograph." Mrs. Eastman smiled wickedly. "I like to be kept apprised of my grandchildren."

Jade was on her feet, grabbing her purse and keys. "I don't want your money." She glared at the woman, sickened at how hateful and evil she was. Just like her son. "You and Tanner don't have to worry. My baby won't have anybody's name but mine." She paused. "And I'll never tell a soul as long as I live who the baby's father is."

Tanner's mother settled back in her chair. "I thought you'd see it my way." She held out what looked like a check. "It's a cashier's check. I never send Tanner's children money any other way. Wouldn't want it to be traced, you know."

Jade stared at the woman in shock. She was every bit as good a liar as Tanner. To think she had spent nearly an hour believing the woman cared about her! A sickening shudder coursed through her veins. She needed air. "Keep your money. I said I don't want it."

Mrs. Eastman raised an eyebrow and continued to hold the check in Jade's direction. "Are you sure? It's ten thousand dollars."

Jade's eyes widened and she hesitated. She was about to set out on the world pregnant, single, and penniless. She could live with her father for a while, but once he found out about the baby . . .

Anxiety wrapped its arms around her, and even her teeth chattered from the shock. How could this be happening? Her body trembled with rage, furious at the way Tanner had tricked her, betrayed her. Maybe he did owe her something after all. It wasn't much. It wouldn't replace the fact that her child would be without a father, but it would help. It would mean that her baby wouldn't starve while she figured out how to find a job.

"I'm not sending you pictures." Jade held her ground, too angry and proud to approach the woman.

Mrs. Eastman nodded. "Very well, then I won't be sending you monthly support."

Jade hesitated. She desperately wanted to take the check and rip it in half. But the truth was, she had no other means of existence. She had to think of the baby. "So you give me ten thousand dollars and that's it? Neither of us ever looks back?"

"I told you, Jade, I like you." The woman's eyes were hateful as she came near, the check clutched in her outstretched hand. "Consider the money a gift."

Everything in Jade was repulsed at the thought of taking this woman's check. *Think of the baby. Tanner should be responsible for something.* Jade snapped the check from the woman's hand. "One thing . . ."

Mrs. Eastman waited.

"Don't tell Tanner." She had made up her mind in the last few minutes. If he hadn't been a father to the other children, he'd never be one to this baby either.

The woman's mouth curled into a smile that looked practically evil. "Very well, dear. You have my promise. I'll not mention a word of your . . . this situation . . . to anyone. Not even Tanner."

Jade's heart fell at what she'd just done. Tanner would never know about the baby now, never know what had become of Jade and the child she bore. She wanted to spit at Tanner's mother for being so obviously glad about the fact. "I'm leaving now, Mrs. Eastman. You'll never hear from me again."

"Very well." Tanner's mother ushered her to the front door and glanced anxiously at her watch. "You'd best get going."

Jade's head was spinning, and she thought she might need a bathroom again. None of it mattered. She had to get away from this woman, had to find a place to get her bearings. Feeling unsteady on her feet, Jade moved as quickly as she could down the sidewalk toward her car. Mrs. Eastman raised her voice so Jade could hear her. "I'm sorry things didn't work out like you thought they would. You know, I think Tanner really liked you, Jade."

She spun around. *He loved me! Even if he lied, he loved me!* She wanted to tell Tanner's mother how great her son's feelings had been, but it was too late. Mrs. Eastman saw Jade's hesitation and cast one final dagger her way.

"But you weren't the marrying type, were you? Just a tramp like all the rest."

With that, Tanner's mother disappeared behind her door.

Inside the house, Doris Eastman peered

through the window and watched until Jade's car disappeared from sight. *It worked! That stupid girl believed everything I said.*

It had been the pictures, of course. Jade was having trouble believing the lies about Tanner until she saw the pictures of Amy and Justin. Doris felt utterly satisfied with herself as she moved into the living room and found the framed photographs of the children on the coffee table where she'd left them.

Her oldest son had never been much of a business man, never gifted with the social graces and heady future that awaited Tanner. But Doris would say this for him: He always remembered to send pictures of his children.

Jade felt like she'd been trampled by a herd of wild horses.

As she pulled away from Doris Eastman's home, she tucked the cashier's check into her glove box and started the engine. Three blocks down the road, she pulled over, and for the next hour she wept until she thought she would die from the pain.

Tanner had loved her, hadn't he? She sobbed and struck the steering wheel with her fists. He had told her the Lord had plans for her, that she was a precious child of

God, and that next summer he would marry her. Jade shook from the weight of it all. So many lies. No wonder he hadn't written to her since he left. He was finished with her.

She thought about all the ways Tanner had fooled her. Pictures of little Amy and Justin came to mind again, and she felt another wave of nausea. What kind of man would call himself a Christian and turn his back on his own children? If she'd had any doubts about the awful things Mrs. Eastman had told her, the pictures of Amy and Justin dissolved them. Those were Tanner's children. She had no doubt whatsoever.

After an hour, she pulled back onto the road. She needed to get home and face her father. *Help me, God. I can't do this alone.* The prayer seemed to bring a sense of peace in her heart. She would survive. She had her baby to think about now. As she headed north on I-5, she was struck by the fact that only two things had been true about that summer.

First, she had become a Christian. She might be the very worst one of all, but the fact remained that God had called her his own. No litany of lies from Tanner could mean her salvation wasn't true. She had a long way to go before things were right with the Lord, but one day they would be good again. He was her everlasting father, and nothing could change that.

Second, as long as she lived she would never, ever love any man the way she had allowed herself to love Tanner Eastman. All the earthly love she had to give from now on would be showered on one alone.

Her unborn child.

Sixteen

After decades of oppression and government bans on Bibles, the Hungarians were hungry for God's Word. Knowledge of that fact kept Tanner going even on days when he missed Jade so badly he felt physically ill.

The trip had been a whirlwind such that had there been the opportunity for phone calls back home there certainly would not have been the time. Since the trip was equally devoted to research and outreach, Tanner and seventeen college seniors from the East Coast spent their mornings going from school to school with a local translator.

The truths they were allowed to share to public school children would have sent the ACLU into a tailspin of lawsuits and outrage.

They kept their message simple. God was creator of all, sovereign and eternal, compassionate and full of love. His son, Jesus Christ, had come to the world, laid down his life for the sins of all so that any who believed in him might live forever. His word was truth. Period. And faith in him was the only hope for the world.

When Tanner wasn't speaking, he watched in amazement as the wide-eyed Hungarian children eagerly — almost desperately — soaked in the gospel message. Even more stunning were the public school administrators who welcomed Tanner's group and their message with open arms.

Back home students were not allowed to mention Jesus' name, even during the week before Christmas. Easter break had become spring break, and prayer was often forbidden at graduation ceremonies. Schools permitted rock lyrics with a message of hatred, but a student dare not sing a song of praise to God. Children with the freedom to purchase guns opened fire in schools, killing their classmates, particularly Christian classmates. And the ACLU defended those same students' right to brandish symbols of death, swastikas, and hate slogans on their notebooks and T-shirts.

Tanner wondered how long it would be before the United States government banned Bibles? Before Christians were hunted down and thrown into jail for being 'conspirators against the government'? Tanner feared the answer, and it motivated him to learn all he could during his time in Hungary.

From before sunup to late in the night, Tanner was absorbed in the process. He and his peers studied archives, interviewed former government officials, taught children, and made home visits to the families of school children who had requested additional information. Everyone wanted a Bible, and by the ninth day the Youth with a Mission leader had run out and wired back to the states for additional supplies.

They heard horrendous stories from the recent past, stories of people being jailed, tormented, and beheaded for their faith. Early in the trip, Tanner met a teenage boy named Peter. He was a ward of the state, and when Tanner brought the gospel message to the boy's classroom, he began filling in details for his classmates, quoting Scripture in the process.

Tanner asked the boy how he knew the Bible so well.

"My parents were Christians," Peter said through the translator. The boy's faith shone through strong eyes. "They taught us the Scriptures late at night, when police could not hear. We all committed to memory books of the Bible. Letters from St. Paul about suffering for the faith."

Peter hesitated. "Before the change in government, police found out what my parents were doing. They came one night, broke into the house, and shot my parents in the head. My parents were holding their Bibles when they died."

Tanner learned from Peter that he and his two sisters were forced to watch their parents' execution. Afterward, they were separated and sent to different parts of the nation to be raised as wards of the state. Peter had not heard from his sisters since.

After more than a week of hearing similar stories, Tanner was motivated like never before. The United States would not go the way of Hungary if he had anything to do with it. And God had showed Tanner that he would, indeed, have much to do with it.

In the quiet moments — moments scheduled for devotion, reflection, and Bible study — Tanner was more certain than ever that this was his calling. He would be a warrior for religious freedom in a country desperate for someone to take on the cause.

He memorized Romans 10:14–15, repeating it to himself when he became discouraged. *How, then, can they call on the one they have not believed in? And how can they believe in the one of whom they have not heard? And how can they hear without someone preaching to them? And how can they preach unless they are sent?*

He would carry the message back home where God would use him to expose the ways religious freedom was fading in America. He prayed God might use him in an amazing way so that no American child would ever be ripped away from his parents because of his or her faith.

No, he would never forget Peter or the people of Hungary.

His determination drove him to continue even when he missed Jade so much he couldn't sleep, couldn't eat. With her half a world away, he realized for the first time how long a week could be — or a day. Or, for that matter, even an hour.

Tanner's bed was a worn-out, government-issued cot, and he shared a room in a decaying school dormitory with three students from East Coast universities. On the first day of the fourth week, Tanner lay awake, wishing he could toss and turn, but knowing he would fall on the floor if he did.

I miss her, Lord. Let her know how much.

He shifted slightly and winced. The foam

rubber mattress was supported by bars that dug into his ribs whenever he moved.

Sleep did not come easily in Hungary, but the quiet hours allowed him to reflect on his summer with Jade, especially the days before his trip. He had been impatient with her, and he wished desperately for the chance to call and apologize. If only Jade weren't so deeply depressed about the way they'd fallen that night.

Tanner flipped onto his back and gazed out the dusty, double-paned window. What he and Jade had done was wrong. He would give anything to go back in time and heed the Lord's warning that night. But there was no going back. The way they'd gone against God was something they could never undo, and Tanner realized they would suffer consequences as a result.

One of which was the way Jade had felt worthless about herself since that night.

Before leaving, Tanner had assured her several times that God still loved her, still had her name in the Book of Life. He promised her they would set more stringent boundaries next time they were together. He would not make the same mistake twice.

But at some point, Tanner believed they needed to move on, and he'd shared that thought in their final phone conversation.

Tanner's eyes adjusted to the dark, and he could see his roommates sleeping soundly. He sighed, lifted his head, and turned his pillow over. Of course they were sleeping. None of them had let God down in the weeks before taking this trip. None of them had a troubled fiancée a million miles away. He lifted his head again and folded the pillow in half.

He thought of the Scripture about temptation and God providing a way out. No doubt, God had given him ways of escape that night. Tanner had simply ignored the warnings.

He sighed and tried to think of something else. It wasn't always a good thing to dwell too long on Jade. Feelings of repentance tended to give way to feelings far less pure.

He was counting down the days until next summer. Two-hundred and seventy-two, come morning. As far as he was concerned, the school year couldn't go by quickly enough, because then Jade would be his wife. Once that happened, the feelings that plagued him now would be a blessing.

On the first day of the trip, he had written her a lengthy letter apologizing for being impatient with her when they last talked. He missed her, loved her, couldn't wait to see her, couldn't wait for the day — not far off — when he could marry her. His letters since then spoke everything he felt in his heart; . . . he hoped she had received them by now.

Tanner prayed for Jade often and thought of her throughout the day. But as he turned onto his side again, in the early morning hours of his tenth day in the field, he couldn't get the image of her out of his mind. It wasn't desire he felt, but concern, alarm.

Tanner flipped onto his stomach and stared out the dirty windowpane to the swaying silhouette of maple trees outside. *What is this, God? What's wrong? Why is she so heavily on my heart?*

Jade's in trouble, my son. Pray. Pray quickly.

He heard the urging in his heart and felt a sense of terrifying alarm. Without hesitation he closed his eyes, bowed his head and for the next hour — sometimes in tears — he prayed for the woman he loved with all his heart.

The rains had started again, helping to wash away the memories of summer that haunted Jade. It was Monday afternoon, and she sat on the familiar box under the covered front porch praying for wisdom and waiting for her father to come home. She had to tell him soon; her health coverage was provided through her father's job at the garage. But how would he ever understand? What would he do to her once he found out? And how was it that forty-eight hours earlier everything had seemed like it was going to work out?

No matter how the facts shouted the truth, she still found herself wanting to believe Tanner. If she thought it might change the truth, she would have called Mrs. Eastman and told her how badly mistaken she must have been about Tanner, how Tanner had never been with any woman before and how he would always love her more than life itself.

But every time she reached for the telephone, she remembered the photographs. And the fact that she'd still not received even a single letter from Tanner. Then the reality — as impossible as it was — would set in.

There was a rumbling at the end of the street, and Jade knew it was her father's pickup. She glanced at her watch. Four o'clock. That meant he'd run out of work early and spent the hours since lunch at the bar. Jade clenched her jaw. *Lord, give me the words. Help him understand.*

She watched her father swing the pickup

into the driveway and squarely hit a rain-filled rut before jerking the truck to a stop. He staggered out of the truck, and Jade was seized with a fear she'd felt hundreds of time. *Dad . . . you're going to kill someone driving like that.*

He walked slowly, tripping over his feet and very nearly falling on the porch steps before he stopped, lurched slightly, and spotted her.

"Whatcha doin' home? Aren't ya supposed ta be with them sick kids?"

Jade's heart pounded. Maybe she should wait and tell him some other time, when he hadn't been drinking. She swallowed and stepped toward him, and the alcohol on his breath assaulted her sense. If she waited until he was sober, she might never have the chance. It was now or never.

"I'm not working today, Daddy." There was disgust on his face as he studied her. Then he shrugged and turned away. She took another step in his direction. "I have something to tell you."

Her father spun slowly back around and scowled in a way that made Jade's insides shrivel. He waited a moment and then shouted at her. "Well . . . spit it out!"

"Daddy, let's go inside."

Her father did not look happy, but he

moved into the house and flung himself into his recliner. Jade followed and sat on the sofa across from him. She picked at the foam rubber sticking out from holes in the cushion. *Help me, God. Please.*

"Daddy, something's happened and you need to know. I want you to know."

A strange, angry look filled her father's eyes, and he pushed himself up straighter in his chair as he glared at Jade. "What'd you do?"

Her response came quickly. "Nothing . . . I mean . . ." She was filled with shame. "Tanner and I . . ." She paused. "Daddy, I'm pregnant. I have to see a doctor."

Her father leaned back slowly in his chair, his mouth twisted into a sneer. "So, I was right all these years. You turned into a slut jus' like your dear old mother."

"Daddy, I'm not a —"

"Ah, shut up!" Her father narrowed his eyes, his face flushed. Jade wondered how much he'd had to drink, and she was suddenly afraid of him. He snarled when he spoke again. "You don't need a doctor for an abortion. Clinics do that kinda thing."

Jade shook her head. "No, Daddy, I'm not getting an abortion. I want this baby. But I need to see a doctor."

Her father eyed her as if she were worthless. "Where's the won'erful neighbor boy who got the goods from you? If you're havin' his baby, why don't you go live with him?"

"He's gone. He's . . . he's not in the picture anymore."

Her father came out of his chair so suddenly that Jade gasped. In seconds he was towering over her, glaring at her. "He's not in the picture because you're a no-good whore —" he raised his hand over her — "like your *mother*." As he said the last word, his hand came down and slapped her, hard, across the face.

The stinging force took Jade by surprise, and she cried out as her head rocked back from the impact. She brought her arms up, cowering behind them in an effort to stave off any more blows.

Her father's hand was still raised, but he lowered it slowly. He looked less angry and more shocked at what he had done, but his eyes still glistened with contempt. "I always told you Jim Rudolph was the best thing that ever happened to you. He'd a married you. But now that you're knocked up he won't want you, either. No one'll want you."

Jade tried desperately to stop the tears, but they came anyway. *What can I say to make him understand?* "Daddy, I'm an adult now. I'll get a place of my own, and I won't be in your way. But I need your help. I can't go through this alone."

Her father sneered at her. "You'll get no help from me. You made your bed . . . now you can lay in it. Just like a pig in its slop. I won't be respo'sible for your brat."

Jade stared at her father, stunned. She had expected him to be angry, but this . . . There was no way around what he was telling her now. He wanted nothing to do with her. "Daddy, I'll —"

"Get out! Get your things and leave. You've got yourself in grown-up trouble, Jade." Her father was shouting, shaking in anger, and Jade feared he might hit her again. "Now be a grown-up and get out!"

Jade considered ignoring her father's command, writing it off as something crazy spoken in a moment of intoxication. But then her father's eyes locked onto hers, and in them she saw that no amount of time or circumstances could change the truth. He didn't love her.

But I love you, my child. I know the plans I have for you. . . .

Jade blinked back the voice. If God loved her, he had a strange way of showing it. As for his plans . . . they had disappeared weeks ago in Tanner Eastman's bedroom.

Her father took a step toward her, his fist raised again. "Get out!"

Jade wondered how she had lived with him this long. If he wanted her out, then she would leave. And whatever happened, she would not look back. Not ever.

She turned and went to her bedroom. In an hour she had stuffed all her worldly possessions into three pillowcases and an old suitcase. There wasn't much. She hadn't saved scrapbooks from high school or photo albums of days gone by. There were a dozen mystery novels, a photograph of her in her mother's arms when she was two, and a dozen journals and diaries. She had barely enough clothes and shoes to fill the suitcase. A few posters and knickknacks.

Everything Tanner had given her she placed in a small box. A dried rose, several cards including the one he'd given her their last night together. Two teddy bears, a gold bracelet, and a framed photograph of the two of them taken by a passerby one afternoon when they were at the river.

She looked over the collection and thought ahead fifteen years to a time when her child might treasure them — the only reminder of a father who never existed. But then she pictured Mrs. Eastman and her sickly sweet smile threatening to steal her child with a team of powerful lawyers if she dared tell the truth about who the baby's father was.

She wasn't afraid of her child's eventual questions, but she was terrified of Mrs. Eastman's threats and the hatred behind them. No one would ever find out Tanner was this baby's father, even if she had to eradicate all signs of him from her life. Trash day was tomorrow. Folding the container so the contents would stay put, she carried it outside and pushed it deep inside the trash can.

Exactly where her box of dreams — and everything associated with Tanner Eastman — belonged.

When she was finished packing and loading her car, she found her father snoring on the sofa, two empty beer cans lying on the carpet below him. She studied him for a long moment and wondered if she should wake him and tell him good-bye. This would, in all likelihood, be the last time she stood in this living room, the last time she saw him.

But she was strangely unaffected.

She studied him one final time, his undershirt riding up on his belly, his workpants covered with week-old grease stains. She could hear his accusations as clearly as if he were still shouting at her. *You're an idiot,*

Jade . . . worthless, just like your mother. . . .

Jade felt no connection whatsoever to the man lying before her. *He never loved me. Even in his sober moments.* He had felt guilt and remorse and inadequacy. But never love, Jade was sure of it. And she would not tell him good-bye. If this was how it felt to have a father, she was thankful her child would be spared.

Jade turned and without looking back she left, walking away from the house where she'd spent eleven years, and leaving all the sordid, sad memories that went along with it.

Later that evening, Buddy Conner woke up, belched loudly and rubbed his bare belly. *Stupid undershirt never stayed put.* He stood, moved his tongue along the inside of his pasty mouth, and tried to remember if there were any beers left in the refrigerator.

"Jade, get me a beer." He waited but there was no response. "Jade!"

Then he remembered. She was pregnant and he'd told her to leave. He hadn't really meant it. The girl could live here for a while, anyway. She was his daughter, after all. And he hadn't exactly been surprised by her announcement: he'd always known she would wind up like her mother. He raised his voice. "Jade, get in here."

His words echoed through the house, but there was no response. Buddy scratched his armpit and shuffled down the hall to Jade's room. Posters were gone from the walls, and her closet was empty.

He shrugged. She was gone, but she'd be back when she figured out how hard it was living on the streets with a baby on the way. They could live with him, but if Jade thought he was going to raise the kid, she was in for a rude awakening. *No, sir, not Buddy Conner.* He was a busy man, and he had no intentions of raising some fatherless brat.

He huffed as he moved back down the hallway. He was a generous man, but he had to draw a line somewhere. The effects of a perpetual hangover pulsed at Buddy's temples and he thought about getting a drink. But there was something he had to do first. Now that he was sober enough to concentrate and Jade wasn't around.

He lumbered into his bedroom, pulled out his top dresser drawer and took out a bundle of three envelopes. Letters from that snobby neighbor boy, postmarked Hungary. Buddy carried the letters into the kitchen and ripped them into a dozen pieces. He may not have been a very good father — he may not have been a lot of things — but at least he'd kept these letters from Jade. Uppity kid like Tanner Eastman wanted one thing and only one thing from a girl like Jade. Well, he'd gotten what he wanted, but he wasn't getting anymore. Buddy simply wasn't going to stand by and watch the guy break his little girl's heart.

He wadded up the torn pieces of the boy's letters and tossed them in the kitchen trashcan where they settled unceremoniously on a pile of rotting spaghetti and beer-soaked cigarette ashes.

Jade would never know the difference.

Seventeen

Driving seemed to be the answer at first. She headed toward I-5. "Where do I go, Lord? Where would you have me set up a home for this child? How can I ever make it alone?"

Tears streamed down her face as she drove, making it difficult to see. The windshield wipers swished out a rhythm, and the rhythm became taunting words in her head: *Whore, whore, whore, whore . . .*

Every movement was another reminder. Jade blinked back her tears so she could see the road more clearly, but they continued to come. She had lost everything except the one thing no one would ever take away from her.

Jade placed her hand over her abdomen and massaged the area gently. *Stay safe, little one. Mommy's here. Mommy'll never, ever leave you, baby.* She realized that she would have to withdraw from fall classes at the

232

college. She had more to think about than school. On her way out of town she stopped at Kelso General, and when she had collected herself, she went inside and informed the head nurse on the children's unit that she was going to be gone for a while.

"Everything okay, Jade?" The woman looked concerned. "You look like you've been crying."

For a moment she wanted to tell the old nurse everything, but then she stopped herself. There was no point making the staff at Kelso General think poorly of her. They would know soon enough. "I'll be all right. I'll let you know when I can come back."

Before she left, she checked on Shaunie, who was back in the hospital with more kidney problems. But the child had been discharged earlier that day. It was fitting. There wasn't anything keeping her in Kelso anymore.

She drove to the freeway, heading south toward Portland. Without realizing her plan, she exited west Highway 26, and two hours later she was at the beach. The rain came down in heavy sheets, and she pulled into the parking lot of a motel with a neon-lit sign that promised color TV and vacancies. The paint was peeling on the office door. She paid forty-two dollars cash and took her room.

A small table and chair sat by a narrow glass door overlooking a deserted highway and beyond that the ocean. She was too frightened to cry, too painfully aware of the truth. She was twenty years old, pregnant, without a friend in the world or medical benefits, and with barely enough money to get her through her pregnancy. What would she do then?

She thought about praying but changed her mind. It hadn't helped her so far. If anything, it had brought her bad luck. Jade chastised herself for thinking that way. It wasn't bad luck, just a lack of connection with the Lord. God had saved her, but like her earthly father, he no longer seemed to want anything to do with her.

For I know the plans I have for you. . . .

Jade disregarded the thought. No, if she was going to find hope and a future out of this problem, she was going to have to find it herself. She sat back in the chair, motionless, allowing herself to sort through the possibilities. There were relatively few, really, and each of them involved single parenting, full-time daycare, state-provided medical treatment, welfare, and low-income housing. There were children who managed to do well under such circumstances.

Jade began to shiver. *Not my baby.*

The sun disappeared beyond the water and hours passed. Ten o'clock. Ten-thirty. Eleven. Still Jade sat, unmoving, desperately trying to think of a solution.

Then, just after midnight, the answer came. It was so obvious she didn't know why she hadn't thought about it before. As soon as she formulated the plan, she began to cry, her heart sinking like sand in an hourglass. *Is this it, Lord? My hope and future?*

She didn't wait for a response. *I don't care; I'm doing this. It's the only choice I have.*

The cost will be high.

Jade squeezed her eyes shut, willing away the holy whispers that ricocheted about in the corners of her mind. *It's my life.*

You were bought with a price.

Jade's crying grew harder, and she felt herself losing control. This time she answered out loud. "Stop! I have no choice. . . ."

No, my daughter, you do have a choice. I know the plans I have for you . . . plans to give you hope and a future.

Jade covered her ears with her hands. *I have no hope, no future.* She wrapped her arms around her midsection. *I have to do this. Now, leave me alone!*

Silence.

Jade waited, but the voice had stopped. God may not have wanted her to do the thing she was about to do. But he hadn't provided any alternative, either. She thought about the plan and realized it was true, the cost would be high. Nothing less than her heart and soul. But if it meant protecting her child, it was a price she was willing to pay.

In return, her baby would never lack anything. There would be food and a warm bed and a mommy and daddy. What more could a child need? She fell asleep then, dreaming of the infant inside her and whether he or she would have Tanner's eyes or his tall, athletic frame.

The next day she checked out of the motel, drove to Portland, and got the directions she needed. At five o'clock she stood on the porch of a man she had never intended to track down.

"Well, well, well . . ." Jim Rudolph allowed his eyes to wander lazily over the length of Jade. "What a pleasant surprise. I always knew you'd come to your senses one day." He leaned against the doorframe. "Tell me . . . have you changed your mind about my offer?"

Jade wanted to turn and run back to her car. *There's no choice now. Think of the baby.* The voice didn't seem like God's, but it was the only one she could hear. She closed her eyes briefly. "Yes. May I come in?"

Jim opened the door wider, and without hesitation Jade walked inside. She would do anything for the child she carried. Even this. It didn't matter. What she was about to do would never involve her heart. She would be kind, dutiful, pleasant. Grateful she had someplace to turn.

In exchange, Jade knew Jim would provide for her, shower her with attention, and treat her well. He would give her child a home and a name. Yes, Jim lacked the depth of character to ever love her the way Tanner had seemed to love her. No, she would never love this man. But she would be indebted to him forever.

That Saturday the two of them stood before a justice of the peace. And in ten minutes, Jade Conner became Jade Rudolph.

EIGHTEEN

The Virginia sky stretched like blue canvas over the Richmond Airport as Doris Eastman waited for her son to return from Hungary. She had missed Tanner. He was such a good, idealistic, young man, just what the country needed, perfect for public office. The way Doris saw it, she was willing to forgive him and move forward. Tanner had sowed his wild oats — first with the Conner girl and then with this trip to Hungary. There was still time between now and graduation to line up a political job. Still time for Tanner to come to his senses.

His connecting flight from New York was scheduled to arrive in five minutes, and Doris had to admit she was nervous. The issue with Jade would have to be handled delicately; Tanner must never know that his mother lied to protect him. Even so, Doris was worried about how Tanner would react when he heard the news about Jade.

Thoughts of the girl and her sudden wedding brought a smile to Doris's face. When she'd first learned about it, she'd been unable to contain her elation. At least she didn't have to lie to Tanner. Jade had taken care of the problem herself.

To think she had almost avoided making the phone call.

It had been two weeks after Jade's visit, and Doris was bothered by the girl's anger. What if she tried to find out the truth about Tanner's background? Doris was plagued by such questions. She knew she'd done a brilliant job of lying that day; Tanner's older brother's children looked just like their uncle. Jade had believed every word.

Still, Doris had been uneasy and so she called.

An airplane taxied slowly up to the gate, and Doris breathed a sigh of relief. She hated Tanner being in the air. Too uncertain. Too many risks. Now he was here and he was safe — safer than he knew now that Jade was out of his life.

She remembered the phone call like it was yesterday.

A man Doris assumed was Jade's father answered and spoke in short, gruff sentences.

"What do you want?"

Doris had been taken aback. "Well . . . I need to speak to Jade, please."

"Jade don't live here no more."

A flicker of concern had rattled through Doris's bones. "Is that right? Well, would you have a forwarding number for her?"

"I ain't plannin' on keeping in touch with her."

Doris struggled to think of the right questions. "All right, then. Could you tell me where she moved? Maybe I can look her up myself."

"Listen, I don't know who you are, lady, but I'll tell you why Jade left. She got herself pregnant, and now she's run off and got herself married. They live in Portland somewhere, I think."

Doris had been stunned by the man's revelation. Jade . . . married? With Tanner in Hungary? Then there had been someone else the whole time. Instantly, Doris regretted giving the girl the money. The brat probably wasn't even Tanner's. "Did you say she was married?"

"What'sa matter, lady? Ya deaf?" *Rude, belligerent clod.* Doris felt tarnished for even speaking with him.

"I'm surprised, that's all. I thought . . . I didn't know Jade had planned to marry."

"Listen, lady, she's married, okay? She's

240

knocked up and she's married. Married a guy named Rudolph. Jim Rudolph, okay? Listen, who are you, anyway?"

Jim Rudoloph. Doris had never heard the name before. "Uh . . . never mind. I'll try to contact her another way."

The man had hung up on her, and in disbelief Doris marveled at her good fortune. She had planned to tell Tanner a lie. Something about how Jade had never really loved him and how she'd disappeared without a trace while he was gone.

Doris hadn't perfected the story and was working frantically on making it sound truthful until she'd placed the call to Jade's home. After the conversation with the girl's father, Doris's problems felt as if they'd disappeared completely.

In the weeks that followed, Doris moved back to Virginia, set up house in a retirement condominium in Williamsburg, and made time for old friends. She was no longer worried about what she'd tell Tanner when he got home. The story was simple. Jade had gotten pregnant and married a man while Tanner was off witnessing to the Hungarian people about God's love. There was nothing more to say. Once Tanner was able to grasp the truth about the girl he assumed he loved, he would disregard her as a bad seed and be thankful he hadn't wasted more time on her.

She stood and stretched and watched the stream of people until she spotted Tanner.

God, help me sound believable.

It had been a while since she'd prayed, and the silent words felt strange in her heart — stranger still when they were not followed by any measure of peace or assurance. It didn't matter. She had the perfect story and was certain Tanner would believe it. If God didn't want to help her, so be it. She was only acting in her son's best interests.

Tanner made his way slowly off the plane, searching for Jade, hoping that she'd gotten his letter and the money he'd sent for a plane ticket. He shook his head. What was he worrying about? Of course she'd be there to meet him. He had so much to tell her, so many stories to share.

He scanned the faces of those waiting for passengers and saw his mother's among them. He waved and continued searching until finally he was at his mother's side.

"Hey, Mom, have you seen Jade?"

His mother put her hands on her hips and cocked her head, smiling slightly. "You're gone to Hungary for two months, and the first thing you say to your mother is, *'Hey,*

Mom, have you seen Jade?' " She leaned up, pecking him on the cheek and hugging him.

"I'm sorry. . . ." *Where was she? Why wasn't she here?*

His mother searched his eyes and looked him over the way she'd done after football games back when he was a teenager. "So, son, you look like you survived. Did you figure out how to save the world?"

Tanner's eyes roved the perimeter of the airport. *She should be here by now.* Could something have happened to her? A plane delay or something. Ignoring his mother's question, he met her gaze straight on. "I'll tell you about the trip later. But I'm serious about Jade. Have you seen her?"

Tanner watched and thought his mother was acting strangely uncomfortable. She cleared her throat as if she didn't want to speak her next words. "I don't think Jade's coming to Virginia, son."

Tanner felt his insides unwind, and he was flooded with disappointed. He sighed. "I asked her to come."

His mother raised an eyebrow. "You . . . you talked to Jade?"

What was that in his mother's eyes? If Tanner hadn't known better, he'd think it was fear, but that was impossible. His mother had never been afraid of anything. "Of course not. I couldn't make calls from Hungary, Mother. You know that."

Doris uttered what sounded like a forced laugh. "I know, dear. It's just that you said you told her . . ."

"I wrote to her. Many times. And I figured based on my last letter that she'd be here."

His mother sighed and stared sadly at her hands. It was a dramatic pose, one she often assumed when she was about to be the bearer of bad news. Seeing his mother that way sent a shiver of terror down Tanner's spine. "What is it, Mother?" He knew he sounded impatient and he felt bad. He'd only been off the plane a few minutes, and already his mother had him on edge.

Doris linked elbows with him and gently led him toward the baggage pickup area. "Son, I'm afraid we have a lot to talk about." She hesitated and Tanner saw contempt in her eyes. "Jade wasn't the person you thought she was."

Tanner stopped in his tracks, forcing his mother to stop as well. "What's that supposed to mean?"

Doris looked uncomfortably at the passersby, some of whom were forced to walk around them. "This isn't the time, dear. I'll tell you everything when we get home. Besides, I have a nice lasagn—"

"I want to know now, Mother." A building panic was causing his head to swim. *What does she mean Jade isn't the person I thought? And where is she, anyway? Why isn't she here so she can help me make sense of this craziness?* He ushered his mother to the nearest seating area and directed her to a seat. He took one next to her and stared at her. "Talk to me, Mother."

She licked her lips nervously, and the sense of panic began to spread to the pit of his stomach. "I said, *talk* to me, Mother. What's going on?"

"You're yelling." His mother clasped her fingers together tightly and did her best to look proper.

Tanner lowered his voice, but the anger remained. "I'm waiting. Now, tell me."

"I really don't think this is the place to have such conversations, son."

"Mother —"

"All right, all right." She put a hand on Tanner's knee and tilted her nose a degree higher. "I'm sorry to have to tell you this. Especially now . . . here." She looked around as though she were afraid someone might be listening. "Jade got married while you were gone."

For the briefest moment, he wanted to slap his mother for saying something so cruel. Jade? His Jade? Of course she hadn't gotten married. Whatever his mother had heard was a big mistake. "Mother, are you trying to say Jade Conner married someone else while I was in Hungary?"

Doris nodded, her chin tilted, nose higher still. "She was a two-timer. A loose girl, Tanner. She was only after your name . . . our money."

A hundred voices were shouting in Tanner's head. It was impossible. Jade loved him fully. She had never loved anyone, never kissed anyone before him. His mother must be losing her mind. "Listen, I don't know where you heard this, Mother, but you're wrong. Jade's going to marry me."

His mother's face grew several shades paler. "Well . . . I had no idea, Tanner. . . ."

"We were going to tell you together. This week, now that I'm home. I haven't even bought her a ring yet."

Gradually his mother's color returned. "Well . . . it seems it's best you saved your money." She looked sadly into his eyes. "It's true, Tanner. She married someone else."

Tanner's heart was racing, and he tried to think of a way he could stop this nonsense. He stood, pulled out his billfold, and began searching for his phone card.

"What are you doing? Sit down and let

me finish." His mother remained seated, her voice ripe with chastisement.

"I'm going to call her. Right now. Before you say another word." He took his mother gently by the shoulders. "Jade Conner is in love with me. There's no way in the world she would have married someone else."

At his insistence, his mother stood with an exaggerated sigh. "Very well. Where's the telephone?"

"What are you doing?" Tanner felt another wave of fear. If his mother was willing to let him make a phone call . . .

"I'm coming, too. I want to be there when you see for yourself. Everything I've told you is true, Tanner."

A volcano of anger erupted in Tanner's heart, and he silently fumed. He would not let his mother get the better of him. She was mistaken somehow, and he would prove it. He turned without saying another word and made his way to a row of pay telephones. Swiping his card through, he did what he'd longed to do for two months.

He dialed Jade's number.

His mother stood beside him, watching him, studying him confidently, making him feel five years old again. The phone rang three times, and Tanner glanced at his watch. It was Saturday, ten o'clock in the morning in Kelso. Someone should be home.

The phone rang three more times, and finally Tanner hung up. "No one's home." He did not look at his mother, didn't want to see her smug expression, the surety in her eyes. She would owe him an apology when he got to the truth of the matter. He stared at the phone and racked his brain, thinking who would know where he could find Jade.

The hospital. Of course. He dialed information and got the number for Kelso General.

His mother tapped her foot impatiently. "Now who're you calling?"

Tanner glared at her but didn't answer. The phone was ringing at the hospital.

"Kelso General, how may I direct your call?"

"Children's unit, please." Tanner's heart was racing faster now. *Come on, please. Someone pick up.*

"Children's unit."

"Yes, I'm . . . may I speak to Jade Conner, please."

The woman hesitated. "She doesn't work here anymore."

Tanner's panic increased and he struggled to speak. "Do . . . you know where I can reach her?"

"Who is this, please?"

Tanner gulped. *What is this? Why is everyone acting so strange?* "I'm a friend."

"Oh. Well, I'm sorry I can't help you. Jade got married about a month ago. We haven't heard from her since then."

The air around him turned to quicksand, and Tanner felt himself being sucked into a cavernous abyss. *My God, why? What's happened? I loved her, Lord. I thought she wanted to marry me.*

He felt as though his heart might explode. He heard himself thank the girl and watched his hand slowly hang up the phone. His mother's expression was the picture of arrogance and pity, and Tanner walked past her to the nearest chair. There he sat down, dropped his belongings, planted his elbows on his knees, and hung his head in his hands.

"I'm sorry, Tanner. I tried to tell you. . . . Her father doesn't know where she's living now. No one does."

Tanner wasn't ready to talk, didn't want to look at his mother. *How had this happened? What had Jade been thinking?* As one minute and then two passed, tears filled Tanner's eyes and began dropping to the floor.

Why would she marry someone else? Who

would she marry? Tanner felt as if he'd been run over by a 747, and though the tears came more quickly, he had only one answer: His mother was wrong. Jade was not a two-timer; she had not been seeing someone else while they were together that past summer. And she definitely was not after his name or their family money.

Somehow, something had gone terribly wrong, and she had married someone else. Tanner would have to find a way to accept the truth. But he had not been wrong about who Jade was. He knew that much.

His mother's voice interrupted his thoughts. "Come on, son. We need to get home." Doris patted his knee, and Tanner knew she was unaware of his tears. She had never seen him cry and wouldn't think it a sign of strength. But he didn't care. Jade had taught him to be his own person, and now she was gone.

He stood like a man who had aged forty years in a single instant, and he realized a part of him had died with the news about Jade. *So, Lord, this is what it feels like to have a broken heart. A broken life.*

As he and his mother left the airport, he remembered something he'd said as a young boy the first time Jade had disappeared from his life. The words were as true now as they had been back then. He and Jade would be together again one day — even if for only a moment so she could explain what had happened. He would find her. Even if he had to search the world over.

With that thought firmly in place, he collected his things and took the first step toward a future that was suddenly darker than the winter skies in Kelso.

■ ■ ■ ■

PART II

■ ■ ■ ■

"You will seek me and find me when you
seek me with all your heart.
I will be found by you," declares the LORD,
"and will bring you back from captivity."
Jeremiah 29:13–14A

NINETEEN

Eleven years later

The rain had been relentless, and Wednesday, February 9 was no different from a dozen previous Wednesdays. At nine that morning, the women from the Bible study group shed raincoats, umbrellas, and muddy shoes at the door and filed into Jade Rudolph's living room, where the atmosphere was considerably warmer and brighter. Coffee and fresh-baked brownies filled the table, and a glowing fire crackled in the brick fireplace.

The women took their seats, and Jade poured coffee as several moms set their toddlers in the next room with a variety of toys. Jade loved the sounds of the little ones. It made her remember when Ty was a baby.

The Bible study, made up entirely of mothers, had been meeting at Jade's house for the past year, and she'd gotten close to many of the women. They had students of all ages who attended Portland public schools — specifically three schools on the city's northeastern boundary: Shamrock Elementary, Woodbridge Junior High, and Riverview High School.

They met each week and discussed education-related issues, keeping each other apprised about problems that might affect their children. For the most part, they spent the hour in prayer. Deep, heartfelt, fervent prayer. Public schools had taken a violent beating over the past few years. If there was one thing their children needed, it was prayer.

Jackie Conley was among the women in the group. Her husband was a teacher alongside Jade's husband, Jim, at Woodbridge Junior and the two women had become friends when Ty was a baby. Jackie had invited her to a Bible study, and by the end of the eight-week session, Jade's strained relationship with the Lord had been restored.

She thanked God daily for Jackie and trusted her like a sister.

The current discussion involved an issue at Woodbridge. The junior high had adapted as part of its curriculum a government-sponsored program called Channel One. Jackie's husband had expressed concern over the programming content, and Jackie and Jade agreed to research the matter.

The women were alarmed at what they learned. The program provided public classrooms with free televisions along with considerable grant money in exchange for a commitment from the administration: Each day students would watch a fifteen-minute program titled "Channel One." Jade and Jackie had chosen this morning to inform the Bible study group of their findings.

"Explain the problem again. . . ." Susan looked confused. Her daughter was in kindergarten, and she'd told the group that free televisions in every classroom seemed like a good idea. Kids might learn something from the documentaries.

Jade understood. At first glance it sounded like a situation where everyone might win.

"The televisions come with strings attached." Jade fidgeted with her fingernails and thought about how to say it simply. "The school gets the televisions and money as long as the kids watch the Channel One program."

The other women sipped coffee and looked concerned. If Jade and Jackie were bothered, there was probably trouble brewing. Susan shook her head and looked from one woman to the next. "I'm still not seeing the problem."

Jade drew a deep breath. *Help me explain this, God. Please.* "The problem is Channel One has questionable content. Unchecked news programs, two-minute documentaries on the proper use of condoms, open discussions of sex, and at least four minutes each day of advertising."

Susan's eyes were wide, and Jade felt a wave of relief. Channel One was a big mistake, and she was glad the group was finally seeing the problem.

"And they show it every day?" Susan sounded angry.

"Yes. Every day. Classrooms give up fifteen minutes of instruction in exchange for the Channel One time."

Jackie leaned forward and checked her notes. "The corporate sponsors — fast food restaurants, clothing companies — support the programming with commercial money — part of which goes back to the U.S. Department of Education."

Susan tapped her pencil on her paper. "So what you're saying is, the U.S. Department of Education is making a profit on televised commercials being shown to our children each day while they're supposed to be learning at school." She paused. "And our schools have agreed to this garbage because they want free televisions?"

"And grant money." Jade searched the faces in the group. "The government makes the package attractive so the schools buy in on the idea."

Jackie nodded. "Not only are the kids subjected to commercials when they should be learning, but they're exposed to whatever programming the government agrees to. Generally, that can be a fairly liberal, slanted dose of documentaries. Politically correct items about alternative lifestyles and insensitive religious right-wingers along with stories — like Jade said — about the importance of condom distribution in schools."

The women were stunned, and Jade knew they finally understood.

Susan spoke first. "We need to get those televisions out."

Jade nodded. "That's the first thing we want to pray about today." She looked at Jackie. "As some of you know, I've spoken to the school board about this already, and they'll be discussing it at a public forum in a few weeks. Apparently, they're not convinced that commercials and provocative programming warrants the removal of the TVs. So I've done a little digging and found something else. . . ."

Jade explained how she'd seen a Web site

advertised continuously at the bottom of the screen throughout the Channel One programming.

"Last week Jackie and I looked into the site and found an entire Channel One menu. Among other things, it had a chat room where people who I presume were junior high and high school students — although they could have been forty-year-old predators — were discussing sex in vulgar and explicit language." She hesitated. "We also found links to documentaries already featured on Channel One."

Jackie sorted through a stack of papers until she found a wrinkled page of hand-written notes. "Many of the programs have been objectionable, but one was a special on a rock singer we've talked about before. He is a favorite among hate groups and has songs with lyrics instructing kids to kill and commit suicide. He is openly, violently hateful toward God and things of God. Once when an interviewer asked him how he pictured his own funeral, this singer said he wanted everyone he ever knew and anyone who had ever attended any of his concerts in attendance. Then, when they were all assembled, bombs would go off and kill everyone."

"That's terrible!" Susan's face was red. "I

guess my kids are too young to know about that stuff. . . . Thank God. . . . I can't believe anyone that awful would get air time in our public schools!"

"I agree." Jade sighed. "Remember that high school in Denver where the boys killed a dozen classmates and a teacher and hurt about twenty other kids?"

Faces grew troubled as everyone nodded, thinking back on the tragedy. Jackie drew a deep breath. "Those trench-coat gothic kids listened to this singer constantly, quoted from his songs, and apparently bought into his message." She paused. "And Channel One carried a special on the guy that ran into the classrooms of every school that has made free televisions and grant money more important than our children."

"The televisions need to go. Immediately." Susan looked at the other moms for approval, and Jade was glad when she saw them nodding in agreement.

"What's your husband think about this, Jade?" It was Beth, a quiet mother with twin daughters at the junior high. The women knew each other well enough to know that Jade's husband was not a Christian. More, that he was adamantly against Jade interfering with the ways of the school.

"Jim and I are struggling, Beth. . . ." Jade

261

was pierced with sadness. The issue had been a thorn in their marriage for the past month. Not that their marriage had been without thorns prior to Channel One.

There had been numerous issues over the years, times when Jim disagreed with her. Still, Jade had been wrong about what she was capable of feeling for him. Jim proved kinder than she'd thought possible, a good provider and often fun to be with. Although they never connected the way she and Tanner had, she grew to love him in her own way. For a while, she even considered having more children — laughing, sweet faces to fill the house and be brothers or sisters for Ty. But for all the attention Jim gave Jade, he was often disinterested in their son and expressed no interest in having another child.

Three years after Ty's birth, Jim had pulled her aside one evening and shared his feelings about parenthood. "The truth is, I never pictured myself as a father, Jade." His shoulders sagged and his expression was defeated. "All I ever wanted was you and me. Together. Kids . . . well, they were never part of the picture, you know?"

Jade knew only too well. Nothing about her life was how she had pictured it.

"What I'm trying to say," Jim had continued, "is . . . I want a vasectomy, just so we don't take any chances."

Jade had been sad at first, but she eventually agreed. She could lavish all the love bottled up in her heart on Ty. She had no need for other children, especially when Jim had no interest in being a father.

He'd gotten the vasectomy weeks later, but in the years since, Jade always thought Jim had been lying about the surgery somehow. Since then on several occasions she'd been plagued with questions. Why hadn't she gotten pregnant in the years after having Ty, especially since they hadn't used birth control? If Jim was so set against having more children, why hadn't he insisted on the vasectomy sooner? And how come there hadn't been any downtime associated with his surgery? The procedure was done in the afternoon, and Jim was back to work the next day without taking so much as a single aspirin.

Somehow there seemed to be a missing piece to the story, and occasionally — when she would note the lack of bonding between Ty and Jim — she would wonder if Jim had been sterile all along. And because of that, perhaps even known the truth.

That Ty wasn't really his son.

There had been other issues over the

years, and once, after a particularly rough evening, Jim shouted at her in frustration. "What do I have to do to win your love, Jade? All my life I've loved you, whether I wanted to or not. It's like you're some kind of . . . of disease that worked its way into my blood." He waved his hand toward Ty's room. "I've seen you love *him.* You love that boy more than anything, but what about me, huh? What sort of curse am I under, driven to love you when all your life you've never, not once, loved me back?"

Jade could still feel how her face had flushed from Jim's accusation. She had never meant to hurt him, but clearly he had been suffering. Her heart had softened as she crossed the room toward him. "That's not true, Jim . . . I love you. I've said it a —"

"Stop!" He held up his hand, preventing her from coming closer. "I understand. . . ." His body had been trembling, and he struggled to regain control. "You love me in your own way, on your terms. But I don't care what you say, Jade. This relationship has always been one-sided, and there's nothing either of us can do to change that." He let his arm drop and disappeared up the stairs into their bedroom.

Jade remembered the outburst like it was

yesterday.

Jim had been right then, and he was right now. But through the years they had stayed together longer than many of their friends, and Jade knew she would never leave him. God wanted her where she was. And maybe, if she prayed diligently, one day she could love Jim the way she knew he longed to be loved.

Lately, their biggest disagreements came whenever she took a stand on issues that affected Woodbridge. For the past two years, when Jade was busy fighting the school board on whatever issue she was involved in, Jim would grow distant and spend his evenings meeting with colleagues or having drinks with friends. There were times when Jade wondered if maybe he was trying to distance himself from her, finally rid her from his system. When she felt that way, she tried harder to pay him attention, listen to him, be available for him. But she could not stop herself from being involved at Woodbridge and no matter how hard she tried, she felt Jim growing away from her.

Especially now. Her attack on Channel One seemed to make him angrier than all the other issues combined.

She exhaled slowly, and her thoughts returned to the Bible study group and the meeting they were having. "Jim's upset about my involvement, no question about it. He wants the televisions to stay. He says the school gets precious little grant money at Woodbridge, and the kids need the funds."

"What's he think about the government using the kids to make money on those commercials?" Susan raised an eyebrow. "Doesn't that bother him?"

They don't know the half of it. Lord, help me be careful how I talk about Jim. "Truthfully . . . Channel One doesn't bother him nearly as much as I do, Susan." Jade hung her head. "You can pray about that, too. . . . Sometimes I don't know if my marriage can take it."

A knowing look crossed Jackie's face. "Jade, we need to talk. Later, okay?"

A ripple of alarm disturbed the waters of Jade's mind. Scott and Jim talked at work, and there were times when Jackie knew what was troubling Jim long before Jade. She nodded to her friend. "Okay, later. Let's pray now."

The women near Jade reached toward her, placing their hands on her shoulders and gripping her knees. While their toddlers continued playing unaware, the group of moms bowed their heads and prayed that

Channel One be taken out of Woodbridge Junior High.

And that Jade's marriage might have the strength to withstand the fight.

Meat loaf simmered in the oven, and Jade busied herself with a broom, sweeping the kitchen floor and in general tidying the place before Jim arrived. If there was one thing that upset him, it was coming home to a messy house.

At times like this Jade was thankful she'd stayed in shape and in general had the same strength and energy she'd had ten years earlier. Otherwise she would have been too tired to balance her schedule. When she thought about all she managed to do in a day, the sum of it was almost dizzying.

She had finished her nursing training when Ty started kindergarten and now was one of the most requested nurses with Portland Home Health Care. She worked four to six hours each day traveling from house to house caring for homebound patients. She loved her job and had no complaints about her schedule. As long as she was home when Ty got home.

Ty was in fifth grade — one year away from attending Woodbridge. Twice a week she made time in her schedule to volunteer in his classroom, helping students learn word processing. Ty was proud of her, and she wouldn't have missed the opportunity for the world.

"You're the prettiest mom at school," he'd told her the day before. It was something he mentioned often. "All the guys say so."

"Is that right?"

"Yep. Jack says you're a babe."

Jade had smiled and tickled Ty in the ribs. "This babe wants you to get your homework done, okay?"

They shared the relationship Jade had always dreamed of sharing with her child. The boy was lanky with an easy smile, gifted both athletically and academically. People liked to say he must have gotten these gifts from her since Jim had long since lost his football physique and allowed himself to grow soft.

But Jade knew the truth.

Ty was exactly like his father.

She swept the floor and mentally calculated that by this hour of the evening Ty would be finished with basketball practice. Jim would be picking him up, and the two of them would be home in fifteen minutes. That was another area of concern. Jim thought they were babying Ty by giving him rides home from school.

"He's a big boy, Jade. He can walk home."

"It's not safe. A boy that young shouldn't have to walk a mile in the dark."

"Sure he should. It'll make him tough."

Jade could have picked him up, of course. She would have walked barefoot in the snow to greet her son after basketball practice. But then she wouldn't be home to have the house clean and dinner on the table. And there was something to be said for keeping peace in their home. Besides, the ride home was the only time Ty and Jim had alone together. Especially now that Jim preferred coming home, eating dinner, and then going back out again.

"It's stressful teaching kids that age." He complained whenever she balked at his evening ritual. "Teachers need to spend time together after school. Deal with it, Jade."

Deal with it, Jade.

His words ran through her mind again and again. Until two years ago, Jim never would have spoken to her that way. He might not have appreciated her viewpoint, but he never mocked her. Not until lately.

She sighed and ran a dishrag once more over the kitchen counter. She had the uneasy feeling that their marriage was falling apart. *Help me, Lord. What can I do to make things better?*

As far as it depends on you, live at peace with one another. . . .

It was the same Scripture that came to mind whenever she doubted her marriage. But there were times when she wished for more than peace. Times when she wanted only to be loved the way she'd felt loved that summer with Tanner. No matter how she prayed and tried to see Jim in a different light, she was never physically attracted to him. She tolerated him and allowed him to have his way whenever he felt the need, but their unions were brief and filled with a sense of hurried desperation. Jim did not concern himself with whether she enjoyed their time together. In that sense, things hadn't changed much since high school. Jim was too concerned with himself. Even in his kindest moments, he genuinely believed Jade was lucky to be married to him, and he reminded her of the fact regularly — especially at night, after they'd been together.

Jade knew it was wrong to compare him to Tanner. But their marriage had never been anything like the magic she'd felt with Tanner that summer. She and Tanner had been wrong their last night together at his apartment, and they would spend their lives dealing with the consequences. But her heart and body had never felt so right. Not before or since.

She wrung out the dishrag and draped it over the faucet. *Tanner.* The memory of him still caused an ache in her heart. It had been many years since she'd seen him, but she thought of him every day, wondering if he'd married or if he was still getting girls into trouble.

Even now, with all the time that had passed and all the miles between them, she struggled with the image of a conniving, womanizing Tanner. Maybe because Ty was so like Tanner had been at that age, or maybe because her son's gentle heart reminded her so much of how Tanner had been that summer. Either way, when she remembered Tanner, it wasn't as an evil, self-centered monster. Rather she thought of him as she would always think of him: pure and wonderful and kind. The only man she had ever truly loved.

Except for Ty, of course.

Jade thought about how fast his childhood had gone and how even now he was like a brilliant comet arcing his way out of her life and into that of his own. She had not pigeonholed him into a career like Tanner's mother had done to her son. Nor had she considered deserting him like her mother had done to her. Rather she treasured every moment, knowing time was both precious and fleeting.

She surveyed the clean kitchen and thought about the Moms in Touch group. Jackie had wanted to talk to her about something, but they'd never connected after the meeting. She crossed the kitchen and reached for the telephone just as the door opened. *Jackie would have to wait.* Jade put away the broom and headed for the front door.

"Mom! You won't believe what happened!" Ty was all legs and wide-eyed excitement as he tossed his gym bag on the recliner and wrapped his arms around her in a hug.

"Tell me." She smoothed back a lock of sweaty hair from his forehead and wrinkled her nose. "Hmm. Shower time right after dinner."

Ty laughed. "Pretty slimy, huh?"

"I'd say." She laughed, too, as she wiped her hand on her jeans.

Ty flopped to the ground and ripped off his shoes and ankle braces, scattering them about on the floor. As he did, Jim rounded the corner, briefcase in hand, and stopped, taking in the mess. A scowl spread across his face.

"Haven't I told you not to throw your stuff around the minute you get in?" His voice was loud. Not angry, like Jade had heard it get lately, but heading that way fast.

Ty's smile fell, and immediately he jumped up and collected his things. "Sorry."

Jim turned and began stomping up the stairs. "You're always sorry. Let's see some action behind it."

"Yes, Dad."

Jade craned her neck and saw that Jim was out of earshot. Then she pulled Ty close again and rubbed a hand over his damp back. "Don't let him get you down, buddy. He's just had a hard day."

Ty nodded and Jade saw the sadness in his eyes. "He always has a hard day."

"I know. But give him a few minutes, and he'll come around."

"Okay." Ty carried his shoes and bag toward the stairs.

"Wait a minute." Jade was careful to keep her voice low so Jim wouldn't think she was contradicting him. "Tell me what happened first."

Her son's eyes filled with adoration, and Jade knew that whatever else she had to do, whatever sacrifices she had to make, they paled in comparison with the joy this boy brought her. Theirs was a good life, and maybe one day things between her and Jim would change, and they could have the marriage she longed for. Until then, she would never go to sleep feeling sorry for herself. She had Ty and a precious relationship with God. In all the ways that mattered, it was more than Jade had ever hoped for.

Ty talked fast when he was excited, and he was reeling off sentences one after another. Whatever had happened it was important to Ty, and Jade listened intently, keeping her eyes glued to his.

"And so I made five rebounds and six inside shots, and no one on the team's ever done that in practice, and Coach Benson said I'd be starting forward at the next game, and —" he took a breath — "next year I know I'll be a starter at Woodbridge and then for Riverview. We're gonna be state champs, and then I'll go to Arizona or Kansas or Duke, and after that probably fourth, maybe fifth round in the draft, and then . . ."

Ty was breathless from the story and Jade smiled. *He's so full of life, so like his* —

"The draft?" She was playing with him.

"Come on, Mom, you know: *The draft.* The NBA draft. As in pros . . . professional basketball . . ." Ty rolled his eyes and flashed a heart-rending grin at her. He headed toward the stairs again and shrugged. "Girls! What do *they* know. But I still love you, Mom."

"Love you more." She watched him disappear and uttered a silent prayer that Jim's recent moodiness wouldn't harm her son.

Ty was upstairs changing when Jim came down. Something about his clean jeans, new navy pullover, and the fresh splash of cologne he wore caused a tremor of anxiety that shook Jade's soul. He came to her, looking up and down her body but never once making eye contact. Then he pulled her to him, nuzzling her neck with his mouth. As he did, he grabbed her bottom and worked his hands up.

"Jim!" Jade pulled away and turned to stir the vegetables on the stovetop. "Ty's on his way down."

"So. When's that ever stopped me?"

What was wrong with him? Was Channel One really the only problem they were facing?

She pushed away her thoughts as he came up behind her, moving his hands wherever he wished. Jade kept her eyes on the dinner and hoped Jim would lose interest. She wasn't worried about what Ty thought. He'd seen his parents kiss before, and certainly

Jim could move his hands in an instant if they heard Ty on the stairs. But something had changed in Jim, and she was almost afraid to find out what.

"Feeling prudish, are we?" Jim sneered at her and grabbed a pop from the refrigerator.

Jade could feel her cheeks growing hot. *Lord, why can't he ask me about my day like he used to?* "No, it's just that . . ."

Jim narrowed his eyes at her. "It's a real shame, Jade. Such a waste." Jim walked away and popped the top on the can.

She glanced at him over her shoulder and opened the oven to check on the meat loaf. "What?"

"God gives you the body of a goddess —" he took a swig of the drink — "and all the desire of a cold fish."

Desire wasn't a problem when Tanner and I —

Immediately Jade banished the thought. *I'm sorry, Lord. That wasn't right. But I won't have Jim talk to me that way, not now or ever.* She pulled the meat loaf from the oven, set it on the stove, and spun around to face her husband.

"What's with you lately? It's like . . ." she struggled to contain her frustration. "It's like you've turned into someone else."

They locked eyes, and his were filled with meanness. He shrugged. "Maybe I'm finally letting you see the real me, Jade. Or maybe I'm tired of playing games for your attention." He tossed her a sarcastic glance. "Besides, it's your loss."

"I've never been cold to you and you know it." Jade didn't want to fight, but Jim's comment wasn't fair. She made herself available as often as Jim wished. But here, now, in the kitchen while she was cooking dinner, she wanted to be treated with respect. *Help me, God. Is that too much to ask? What's happening to us?*

As far as it depends on you live at peace with everyone. . . .

The Scripture came to mind again and Jade mentally agreed. She moved closer to Jim, put her arms around his neck and kissed him long and slow, desperate to make things right between them again. "Is that better?"

Jim smiled at her and studied her a moment. "Much better." He kissed her back and his voice softened. "You're so beautiful, Jade. I'm sorry. . . . I know I haven't been myself lately."

Jade nodded and silently thanked God for the guidance he'd given her.

"Hey . . ." Jim nuzzled her neck more

gently. "How 'bout a quickie before we eat? The bathroom, maybe, or the hall closet?"

She heard Ty galloping down the stairs, and Jade raised an eyebrow as she wriggled from Jim's grasp. "How 'bout we eat while the dinner's still hot."

Jim pulled away, took another swig of his drink and made his way to the table. "Don't run on the stairs, Ty. I've told you that before."

Ty rounded the corner, slowed to a screeching halt and walked to the table. "Sorry, Dad."

" 'Sorry, Dad,' " Jim mimicked. " 'Sorry, Dad . . . sorry, Dad.' Is that all you can say? You need to remember the rules, boy, is that clear?"

Ty took his spot at the table, and Jade's heart broke for him. He was probably dying to talk about basketball, and he was just a boy, after all. He'd been so excited he probably could have flown down the stairs and not realized it.

Dinner was strained despite Jim's earlier apology, and Jade prayed her husband would lighten up so the evening wouldn't be completely ruined. Times like this she wondered what deep thoughts Jim was thinking. Why hadn't she gotten pregnant those early years of marriage? And could he possibly know Ty wasn't his. . . .

No, it wasn't possible. Jim would never have kept that kind of suspicion from her. He would have found some way to use it against her. Jade stared at her plate. The meat loaf was dry, and she chewed a piece until it felt like rubber in her mouth. The meal passed without a question or comment from Jim to Ty, and Jade silently grieved for her son. She knew he craved his father's attention, but there was nothing she could do to change Jim's shortcomings as a father.

For the most part, it was the same way Jim treated her or anyone in his life for that matter. The problem was simple: No one was as important to Jim Rudolph as he was to himself. Especially lately.

When Jim was finished, he pushed his plate back and exhaled loudly. "Best meat loaf in town." He patted his stomach and smiled at Jade. "Hey, how did your meeting go today?"

She shifted and moved her food around on her plate with her fork. He seemed so content right now, she hated to answer him. She was sure he wasn't going to like what she had to say. "It was fine. We talked and we prayed."

His smile faded a notch. "Well, you always do that, right? What did you ladies talk abo—" His smile disappeared. "Jade? What was your meeting about today?"

Lord, help me say this right. She looked up and met his gaze, knowing she couldn't lie. "Channel One."

She saw how hard he was working to stay neutral. He didn't seem to want to fight any more than she did. With a sigh, he looked down at the table. "Who brought that up?"

"Well, Jackie . . ."

His eyes came back to meet hers. "And you?"

She didn't answer. Instead she begged him silently to let it drop, to try to understand. . . .

"So you joined the discussion."

She nodded at the flat statement.

"And I'm guessing you didn't stick up for Channel One."

Swallowing hard, she fingered her fork. "No."

The disappointment in his eyes pierced her. "Jade, I thought we talked about this. I thought you were going to drop it like I asked you to?"

Jade stared at her nearly full plate and remembered several times in the past month when Jim had made a point of asking her to stay out of the Channel One situation. "No . . . we've, uh, done a lot of research. . . ."

She looked up, willing him to understand, to hear her out. "It's not a good thing, Jim. I could tell you —"

He cut her off when he slowly pushed his chair back from the table. His tone was low — and full of hurt — when he spoke. "Do you know what's happening at work? The teachers are practically plotting your downfall. And they keep asking me what's wrong with you, why you're so focused on destroying education in our community."

"I'm not —"

He shook his head, stopping her. "You know what I keep asking myself, Jade?"

She sat in troubled silence, staring down at her clenched hands in her lap. Finally she shook her head and whispered, "What?"

"Why you're so focused on destroying me."

Before she could reply, he stood and moved across the dining room. Grabbing his keys from the countertop, he glanced back at her. "I haven't asked that much of you, Jade. Just that you support me, as my wife. That you show me I'm as important to you as one of your little crusades. That's all." His face twitched, and she had the horrible feeling that he was fighting tears. But that was ridiculous. Jim didn't cry. He never cried.

He gave a heavy sigh, his fingers clenching and unclenching on his keys waving his hand at her. "Instead, you seem determined to humiliate me. To make me look like a fool."

Jade glanced at Ty. The boy hung his head and kept his eyes trained on his plate as he dragged his fork back and forth through his vegetables. *Protect him, Lord. Don't let him be the victim in this.* "I'm sorry, Jim. It isn't about you or your job at Woodridge. It's about keeping our kids safe."

"Safe! Fifteen minutes of television each day isn't going to harm those kids. They watch five hours at home. What's the difference?"

Jade was desperate to diffuse the situation.

"Let's not talk about it right now, okay?" She met his eyes and then glanced toward Ty. The boy seemed to understand his mother's unspoken message, and he excused himself from the table. When they heard him close his bedroom door, Jim leaned back against the counter.

"How do you think it makes me feel, Jade? I spend my day defending evolution and teaching kids to think for themselves, and the other teachers snicker because they think I'm married to the most extreme religious fanatic this side of the Columbia River."

"I'm sorry, okay. I'll see what I can do." Jade forced a smile, anything to keep their argument from escalating. Lately when Jim got angry, she sensed a near violence beneath the surface. As though he wanted to throw something or smash his fist into a wall. The anger was further proof that something was very wrong with Jim.

Is he sick, Lord? Frightened? Or is it me? Have I really humiliated him? I never meant to. . . .

Whatever was happening with Jim, it scared Ty, and Jade knew later that night she would need to console the boy before he would feel secure enough to get to sleep.

Jim stared at her, and she saw something in his face she couldn't ever remember seeing there before: hopelessness. "You'll *see* what you can do?" He shook his head. "Don't make empty promises, Jade. I think you've given me enough of those, don't you? We both know what you'll do. You'll get your oh-so-righteous and oh-so-worried group together and get Channel One removed from the school. You have a way with these things, Jade. But this time you're going too far. I'm warning you . . ."

Jade wasn't worried about his threat; she

was worried about their marriage. Her fight against Channel One came from deep inside her. Something in her soul would shrivel and die if she were to pull out of the battle now. She was driven to be involved, make a difference. It had been the same way anytime she witnessed an injustice. She thought of Shaunie and Kelso General Hospital and how her passionate plea had saved the children's wing.

If only her husband could understand what moved her. . . .

Tanner would have understood perfectly. He'd have been fighting alongside her. Just like he'd wanted to fight for religious freedom back when . . .

Jade shook her head to clear her mind. *Where were all the memories of Tanner coming from, and why now?* With all that was happening between Jim and her, the last person in the world she should be thinking of was Tanner. She said nothing as Jim flung his jacket over his shoulders.

"I'll be late."

"Where are you going?" For the first time, Jade didn't care what his answer was. If Jim was determined to keep leaving like this, then she would spend a quiet evening alone with Ty. But the pattern stirred an anxiety that had been building in Jade for weeks.

"The Sports Page . . . that okay with you? Maybe you'd like to start a sidewalk boycott against the place. They serve alcohol, you know."

Jim's tone was still angry, but he had lost interest in arguing with her. Now it was obvious all he wanted was to leave.

Warning bells rang in Jade's mind. *What if he isn't meeting teacher friends? What if the signs have been there all along and I've refused to see them?* "Meeting anyone special?" She tried to keep her voice casual, but inside she felt another stab of fear.

Jim smiled sarcastically at her, and Jade's heart grew heavier. *This isn't how you want our marriage, Lord. Loveless, faithless. . . .* I'm losing him, Father. Help me, please.

"Why on earth would I want to meet anyone *special* when I have such a loving, tender wife at home?" He uttered a short, harsh laugh, and the sound of it made Jade feel sick to her stomach. "You're such a good little Christian wife. Don't you worry about a thing, Jade; I'll come home tonight like I'm supposed to."

With that, he disappeared out the front door.

When the sound of his car grew faint, Jade picked up the phone and dialed Jackie Conley. "Hi. I only have a minute . . ." Jade kept her voice low. She didn't want Ty to hear her conversation. "About what you said earlier . . . what did you want to tell me?"

Jade heard Jackie sigh on the other end. "This isn't easy, Jade. But I think you should know."

The fear in Jade's gut grew. "What? Is it about Jim?"

"Yes." Jackie hesitated. "Scott thinks he may know why Jim's taking this Channel One thing so hard."

"I'm listening." Jade began clearing the dinner dishes, hoping they would cover up the sound of her voice since Ty was still in the next room.

Jackie hesitated. "Jade . . . I wish I could be there to tell you in person. . . ." She paused again. "Scott says Jim's been spending a lot of time with Kathy Wittenberg. She's new on staff — assistant administrator and part-time health teacher."

Relief made its way over Jade. "That's nothing new, Jackie. Jim spends time with a lot of teachers."

There was a moment of silence, and instantly Jade had the feeling there was more to the story. Jackie drew a deep breath. "Kathy's the one who wrote the grant for Channel One. It was her idea, her project from the get-go."

A clearer picture was taking shape in Jade's mind. "So Scott thinks Jim could be trying to discourage me from getting in Kathy's way."

"Well, there's something else. . . ."

"What?"

"Kathy and Jim are on a committee — not sponsored by the school, mind you — whose primary goal is to stomp out the voice of the religious right in our schools. They literally earmark parents like you and me and do their best to thwart our efforts."

Jade thought of the time her husband had been spending away. "Does the committee meet after hours?"

"Yes."

A cloud of desperation descended on her, and she made her way to the nearest chair. Nausea rose up in her stomach as she considered Jackie's words. *A committee designed to stomp out the voice of the religious right in public schools?* It sounded like something from a science fiction novel or a third-world country. *And Jim is involved?*

"Jade, one more thing . . ."

"I'm listening." Jade was leaning over the table, struggling to regain her bearings.

"When I say Jim's spending a lot of time with Kathy, I mean a *lot* of time. An awful lot of time."

Another realization came over Jade. "You don't think . . ."

"Well, Scott didn't come out and say they were having an affair, but . . ."

"Kathy's married, isn't she?" Jade pictured the blond at Jim's office. She was intelligent and sophisticated, a bit hard around the edges. Not pretty enough for Jim. Jade couldn't picture her husband falling for her.

"They split up two months ago. The divorce is in process."

Jade felt her heart plummet. "So you think there's something going on?"

Jackie paused. "Well, Jade, let's just say the signs are all there." She exhaled slowly. "I thought you should know."

No, Lord, don't let it be true!

Jade's mind raced. Kathy Wittenberg had brought in Channel One and found her primary support in Jim. The two had hit it off and joined a committee to eliminate the Christian influence that classrooms were feeling from certain parents in the district. More time together meant more time for indiscretion. It made perfect sense, and Jade could feel the ground beneath her feet beginning to shift.

"Listen, Jackie, I have to go. Ty's waiting for me."

288

"I'm sorry, Jade. . . . I didn't want to tell you."

"No, don't be. I needed to know." Jade closed her eyes. *Give me wisdom, God. Please.* "Pray for me, will you?"

"Always."

Jade closed her eyes. She knew Jackie would keep her word, and she was thankful again for her friendship. "I want God to show me the truth . . . so I don't have to go out looking for it."

"I will."

Jade's heart was racing, and she felt herself being buried beneath an avalanche of panic. "Jackie . . . I'm not feeling right. . . ."

"Remember what you always say, Jade. God must have a plan in all this."

Yes, that was it. There must be a reason this was happening. "Could . . . could you do me a favor?"

"Anything."

"Please, Jackie, pray I'll know the reason soon."

TWENTY

Tanner Eastman had fifteen minutes before meeting with his next client, and he intended to use the time to clear his desk. Neatness was not his strong suit. Generally there were a dozen things that seemed more important than tidying his work space, but if he didn't spend some time organizing soon, Tanner knew he'd have to start over with a second desk.

Office upkeep had been easier back when all he had was a ten-by-ten, rented space with nothing but his name on the door to prove he'd arrived. Now he had ten attorneys working for him, all dedicated to preserving religious freedom. Center for the Preservation of Religious Rights, he called his firm, and it had taken on the moniker CPRR.

As he had been shown during his days in Hungary, God was using him in a mighty way to preserve freedom in the United

States. When citizens found themselves in a fight with the ACLU over religious rights, the first group they called was Tanner's. It was no accident that the two groups' initials were so closely linked. Tanner liked it that way. The battle had been one-sided until the CPRR came along, and now Tanner felt confident they had successfully slowed the erosion of rights taking place across America. In many instances they had actually restored them.

He collected two files spread across his workspace and placed them back in his cabinet. As he did, his eyes fell on the elegantly framed picture adorning his desk. *Leslie Barlow. Daughter of California Supreme Court Justice Ben Barlow. Graduated Harvard, 1997. Accomplished pianist. Mean tennis player.* And about to become Tanner's wife in July — just five months away.

Tanner tried to smile at the thought but felt strangely overwhelmed instead. Which made no sense. Leslie was beautiful and cultured and the perfect adornment for the arm of any prestigious man. His mother had reminded him often how blessed he was that Leslie had come into his life.

Tanner chuckled. His mother used words like *blessed* for his benefit. Regardless of his devotion to God, she had grown increasingly far from things of the Lord. Tanner knew she only tolerated his choice to start the CPRR and defend cases where people were persecuted for their faith. But she hadn't approved of it until he became a household name.

Tanner would never forget the incident that put his firm on the legal map.

School officials at Jefferson High, south of Salem, Oregon, had asked a girl to sing for graduation ceremonies and merely to inform them of the artist and song ahead of time. The girl chose a song by Christian artist Steven Curtis Chapman. When the officials realized the song contained Christian lyrics, they cancelled her performance.

The girl's father was a reporter at the local newspaper, and almost overnight the story took on national public interest. Tanner represented the girl in a lawsuit against the school, and three days before graduation he won the case. The girl was allowed to maintain both her freedom of speech and freedom of religion. In the end a host of reporters covered the ceremony, and the girl sang the song she'd chosen — not just for those in attendance but for a television audience of more than a million.

The aftermath of media attention was both positive and overwhelming.

The program *20/20* did a special on Tanner's law firm — which at the time included him and a part-time paralegal and operated heavily on donations from churches. Next came *60 Minutes,* then *Larry King Live.* Everyone wanted to know why Tanner Eastman — a brilliant young attorney — had devoted his life to fighting for religious freedom.

The attention drew dozens of cases and then hundreds. Tanner began receiving tremendous donations from mainstream churches and organizations. Many times checks were accompanied by notes of encouragement.

"We've allowed the ACLU to tell us their definition of separation of church and state for too long. We'll support you each month. Godspeed and keep up the good work."

"I had begun to fear for my safety each time I prayed before lunch," one high school student wrote. *"Thank you and know that now I pray without fear. And when I do pray, I remember you and your law firm."*

Within the month, Tanner was overwhelmed with business. He had to hire a staff of attorneys and move to new offices, which he did in the San Fernando Valley on one of the top floors of a high rise located in the prestigious Warner Center Business Park.

Meeting Leslie was a direct result of his success. They had been introduced two years ago when he gave a presentation to the California Supreme Court. When the session ended, Justice Barlow and his daughter engaged Tanner in conversation. Leslie was stunning, and that night she suggested Tanner take her out to dinner. He gladly obliged, and they had dated ever since.

Tanner's mother had been thrilled to learn her son was dating the daughter of Ben Barlow. In fact, everyone seemed to agree that she was perfect for Tanner.

On the whole, Tanner agreed with them. He enjoyed himself with Leslie and figured they would be happy together. Only one thing troubled Tanner. Leslie wasn't a Christian, not in the sold-out sense of the word. She claimed a knowledge of Jesus Christ, but she wasn't a strong believer.

And she wasn't Jade Conner.

Tanner sighed as he straightened Leslie's picture. He had done what he could to find Jade and had turned up nothing. Not that it mattered. She was married and obviously not interested in finding him. Certainly at some time in the past five years she had heard his name mentioned, knew of his organization, perhaps read something in the paper about him.

But not once had she called or made contact.

He ran a hand over his desk, scattering a fine layer of dust. He could hear footsteps in the hall, and he knew his next client had arrived. But before he switched gears, before he devoted his entire attention to the next pressing legal matter, Tanner allowed himself to miss her one more time.

Where is she, God? And how long will I ache for her?

TWENTY-ONE

The meeting was underway, and by the mixed looks on the faces of the school board members, it was going to be a night to remember. Jade ran through her notes one more time. *God, help me make sense. Help them understand what children are exposed to because of this program.*

Jackie leaned over and squeezed her arm. "No sign of Jim yet."

Jade felt somewhat relieved. They had argued again before she left. He told her he was staying home, and if she cared at all about what was good for them, she'd forget the meeting. Jade told him she was sorry. Some things simply had to be done and this was one of them. She had taken Ty with her and dropped him off at a baby-sitter's house.

School board president Bo Hepler began the meeting and summarized the argument from Jade's Bible study group. Parents were concerned that the programming on Channel One was questionable and exposed children to subject matter that needed parental approval, at best. Then there was the question of the Web site. By following the directions at the bottom of the Channel One screen, children could tap into a world with meeting places that, according to the moms in Jade's group, would appall most parents in the room. Including those on the school board.

"At this point we'll open the floor to anyone who'd like to comment on Channel One." Mr. Hepler scanned the room.

Jade sat near the front of the auditorium and turned and looked over the audience. Her Bible study was there in full force. Joining them this night were more than a hundred members of the PTSA. Jade and Jackie had made a presentation to the group on Monday, imploring them to take an active interest at Wednesday's meeting. The turnout was more than Jade had hoped for.

Five parents, including an attorney, took turns debating the issue while Jade sat tight, her stack of notes ready for the moment they might be needed. Three of the parents were in favor of pulling the televisions and canceling Channel One. The attorney wanted to keep it.

"Program content should not be an issue where our children are concerned." He slipped a hand in his coat pocket and strolled in front of the school board. Jade wanted to remind him this wasn't a trial, but she sat tight.

Tell me when, God. I'm ready if you'll only give me the words.

The attorney continued about freedom of speech and freedom of opinion and how it did children no good to live sheltered lives when real life was so hard these days.

"Wait a minute. . . ." One of the parents stopped him with her comment. Jade recognized her from the PTSA meeting. "You're saying it's okay to watch a government-sponsored program that — at least once — featured a rock singer whose hate lyrics may have inspired two teenagers to open fire on their classmates in Colorado? You're saying that kind of person ought to hold our children captive for the first fifteen minutes of a school day?"

"I have a document right here wherein the U.S. Department of Education promises not to feature that singer again. It was an oversight."

"And what about documentaries where students learn the proper way to use a condom? Was that an oversight also? I send my child to school for an education, not to be spoon-fed whatever material the government determines politically correct. Don't you think I have a right as a parent to decide what television programming my child watches?"

The debate grew more heated until finally Jade felt it was time. She stood up and waited to be recognized.

". . . and as for the Internet problem. I've logged onto that Web site and never seen anything remotely objectionable."

Jade's hand was up. "Excuse me." The attention of the board and everyone else in the room was directed to her. She held up her notes. "I have a copy of several items I've pulled off that site. I can pass them out if you'd like to see for yourself the types of information our kids are being exposed to."

Mr. Hepler nodded and leaned toward the microphone. "Yes, Mrs. Rudolph. Why don't you hand them out to the board members." He looked to the audience. "If there aren't enough, please share with your neighbor."

Jade did as he asked and then began reading through a few of the most shocking items. In one case a chat conversation included dialogue between two people who called themselves students and members of a neo-Nazi group. Their discussion, caught in print and now in the hands of most of the people in the room, involved advice on how to make bombs and stockpile ammunition so one of the students could "take care of business" at his local school. There were several exchanges that contained blatantly graphic sexual material.

As she was finishing, there was a sound near the back door. Jade turned and saw Jim walk in. She paused midsentence and — along with everyone in the room — watched him walk past her without so much as a glance and take a seat next to Kathy Wittenberg.

Jade felt her face grow hot. Jim had never ignored her in public before. A ruffling of whispers began to build until Mr. Hepler leaned into the microphone and said, "Go ahead, Ms. Rudolph." The school board president seemed flustered, though whether by the interruption or by Jim's choice of seats, Jade wasn't sure. Either way Mr. Hepler was obviously determined to keep the meeting on track.

Jade's knees knocked and she felt her convictions waver. Was anything worth the humiliation she was enduring over Channel One? The answer was swift: *If I don't step up, who's going to fight for freedom in this country once our rights get taken from us?*

They were Tanner's words, and Jade felt a rush of strength at their memory. Tanner had been right. She would fight this battle no matter the cost.

Consider it pure joy whenever you face trials of many kinds, for you know that the testing of your faith . . .

The Scripture filled her mind and gave her something concrete to stand on. *Okay, Lord, but you'll have to hold me up.* She drew a deep breath and faced the board squarely. "That's all. I thought you'd like to know the full extent of Channel One before we make a decision on whether to keep it." Jade nodded to them and took her seat.

"Are there any other comments?" Mr. Hepler looked directly at Jade's husband, and she watched Kathy squeeze Jim's arm. They exchanged a glance, and he rose slowly.

"Just a few, if it's all right." Jim's tone was friendly and appealing, and Jade was taken aback. This was the Jim she had married, the one she hadn't seen at home for months.

"Go ahead." Mr. Hepler sat back, and Jade had the feeling he sided with her and the Bible study group. *Please, Lord, let justice prevail.*

Jim turned to face the crowd. "I'm sorry

301

for interrupting the meeting." He smiled and Jade saw him for the first time through the eyes of strangers. Jim Rudolph could be charming and persuasive, everyone's favorite teacher. The boy voted most popular at Kelso High so many years ago. "I wanted to go on record as saying that I am in favor of keeping Channel One." A few people shot backward glances at Jade.

"And one more thing. Many of the moms in favor of pulling Channel One aren't here tonight for the kids, folks. They're here with their own political agenda. The agenda of the religious right."

Jade's embarrassment evaporated, and she fumed silently, hoping the school board would remember the documents they'd just seen.

Jim went on. "I think it's time we stop listening to these radical parents and remember the importance of separation of church and state. There's no place in our schools for religious fanaticism, whether it's teachers who lead prayer groups during class or parents —" he looked pointedly at Jade — "who think they can force their religion on everyone else."

He held up a copy of the note Jade had passed out earlier. What? Had he gotten into her file and taken it when she wasn't looking? Why hadn't he asked her for a copy? Jade felt a wave of dizziness wash over her. What was he trying to do?

Jim pointed to the notes. "You'll notice a list of links the Bible study group finds objectionable. These in particular: 'Why prayer must stay out of the schools.' And 'Celebration of Evolution' along with 'Abortion, Every Woman's Choice.' Look past the righteous indignation here, folks, and see that these women are simply trying to stop schools from teaching truth to our kids. If it goes against their religious viewpoint, these mothers don't want it."

Jade glanced around the room and saw several members of the audience nodding and exchanging whispered conversations. . . .

"I, for one, say we can't do that. Not today when we are finally understanding the issue of separation of church and state. Let our children decide. Let them have the benefit of a television set in every classroom. And if parents object, let them sign a note that forbids their student from watching."

Jim looked at Jade once more, and she wished she could stand and fight him face to face on the issue. But she feared she would sound like a fanatic pitted against him. Besides, he was her husband, and a public debate with him would have the entire room gossiping about their private life for weeks to come.

Her conversation with Jackie two weeks earlier came to mind. Was Jim so invested in Channel One because of his friendship with Kathy? She glanced again at the woman sitting beside her husband. Kathy was barely containing a smile, beaming her support for Jim and everything he was saying. The woman had an unmistakable glow about her, and Jade felt a gut instinct, a woman's intuition.

Kathy was in love with her husband. She watched Jim make eye contact with Kathy and wink.

This can't be happening, Lord. Is he really having an affair?

She thought of how Jim had been gone four of the last five nights, and the reality of what was probably happening was finally clear. She could no longer hide from the facts.

Her husband was having an affair with Kathy Wittenberg.

The audience had their eyes glued on Jim as he finished. "Please let our children keep their televisions and the grant money. We have plans to use that money to buy a dozen new computers for the library. Our children deserve the very best in education today. Not a handful of right-wing adults censoring their every thought." He looked at Mr. Hepler. "Thank you."

Jade studied the audience and guessed there were probably twenty-five teachers in attendance. When Jim was finished speaking, Kathy rose to her feet in applause, and a majority of the teachers joined her.

As the applause increased, several members of the PTSA — parents who hadn't been at Monday's meeting — joined in. Jade knew there were at least twenty PTSA members who supported her, friends and acquaintances who were most definitely appalled by Jim's statements and behavior that night. Jade watched as many of them began talking amongst each other so that finally Mr. Hepler had to rap his microphone to regain order.

"That will be all. We'll postpone making a decision on this issue until the board has had time to consider both sides. Thank you."

With that Mr. Hepler moved on to other matters. Jade watched as Jim patted Kathy's knee, whispered something in her ear, and then stood and left the room.

Jade waited a moment so she wouldn't make a scene, and then quietly, she rose and followed him out the same door. Jim was waiting for her, and when she was outside, he turned on her, his voice an angry hiss.

"I warned you, Jade. I will not let you make a mockery of this school's decision to have Channel One or any other program." He motioned toward the still-full auditorium. "They knew what I was saying made sense." His face was inches from hers. "Back off, Jade. You and your friends, back off. Keep it up and you'll really be sorry."

"What's that supposed to mean?" Was he this defensive because Channel One was Kathy's project? Or because he and Kathy had an agenda?

He pulled away and took two steps back toward his car. "One of these days you just might find out."

Jade was tired of being patient with him, tired of walking on eggshells to keep him from being angry with her. "Is that a threat?"

"Listen, Jade, I don't have time for your games." A couple exited the auditorium, and Jim lowered his voice. "I'm leaving town this weekend, going camping with a few teachers. You need some time to think about what you're doing."

A weekend camping trip with a few teachers? She crossed her arms. "What's wrong with you, Jim? You acted like you didn't even know me in there. Now you're going camping without me and Ty?" She knew she was pushing him, but she wanted him to admit the truth. "Why don't you take us with you? Make it a family trip. Give us a chance to figure things out."

Jim stared at her, his eyes cold. "You've always had some sort of twisted hold on me, Jade, but you know what? Not anymore. I'm finally feeling free from you . . . and I like what I'm feeling."

She studied his eyes and was shocked to find hatred there.

"You can't come on the trip. I don't want you there. Besides, you wouldn't be interested. Someone might have a drink or say something unkind about your God. Believe me, you wouldn't fit in."

Jade felt the sting of his comments. *What do I do, God? Help me.*

As far as it depends on you, live at peace with everyone. . . .

She drew a deep breath and resisted making a comment about Kathy. "All right. You go. But when you get back, we need to talk. I'm not fighting Channel One as some kind of attack on you and the teachers at Woodbridge. You've got to know that, Jim."

"Right. Neither was the abortion protest you and your group staged at the Women's

Care Clinic."

Jade was stunned. *The abortion protest? Had that bothered him, too?* "What do you mean? That wasn't —"

"Don't waste your time, Jade. Or mine." He glanced over his shoulder, watching carefully as people left the meeting. "You know the students at Woodbridge and Riverview use that clinic. You might as well have targeted my students. You can't begin to know the heat I took for that one. *'Hey, Jim, how's your preacher wife?'* I get things like that all day long, and I'm fed up to here with it." He made a cutting motion against the top of his forehead. "And what about the Wal-Mart thing? You and that busybody group of yours getting magazines you don't like pulled from the shelves? Like Portland needs that type of censorship."

"Those magazines were —"

"Spare me your religious drivel, Jade. I've heard it all. You're the pushiest religious do-gooder in the community, and I've tried to be tolerant with you. But now . . . now you're moving in on my territory."

"As long as Ty is in the public school system, it's my territory, too." She was shaking, not sure what was going to happen next but certain her life was falling apart quickly.

Jim turned and walked toward his car.

Before climbing in, he called back, "Don't wait up. I'll be late."

A lump formed in Jade's throat as she watched him leave. Was this what their years of marriage had come to? Fighting and cheating and being angry with each other? Kathy Wittenberg exited the auditorium, glanced at Jade with a look that shouted disapproval, and then headed for her car. She left the parking lot, driving away in the same direction as Jim.

Jade stood alone in the damp, wet night, darkness surrounding her, and all she could hear was Tanner's voice. Soothing, calm, confident as the summer sun. Full of what she had once thought was love.

Remember, Jade, God has a plan for your life. Jeremiah 29:11 . . . "I know the plans I have for you . . . plans to prosper you and not harm you, plans to give you hope and a future."

She closed her eyes and felt two tears trickle down her cheeks. Then, like all the plans and hopes that had ever mattered, Tanner's voice faded into the darkness.

Twenty-Two

The phone rang at three-fifteen Sunday morning, and Jade sat up in bed, alarmed and bewildered. She made a mental checklist and knew that Ty was safe in bed, Jim out with his friends camping. Who would be calling at this hour?

The room was pitch dark as she reached for the phone, knocking over a glass of water in the process. She brushed the water off the dresser and grabbed the receiver on the third ring. "Hello?" Her heart pounded in her ears.

"Mrs. Rudolph?"

"Yes, who is this?" She was trying to clear her head, and she leaned over and flipped on the light.

"This is Dr. Bryce Cleary at Emmanuel Hospital. Your husband's been in an accident."

Jade's eyes were still trying to adjust to the light, and she shook her head. Jim? In an accident? *Please, God, let him be okay. Please.* She felt her fingers beginning to tremble. "Is he . . . is he all right."

"He's suffered a spinal injury. I'm afraid he's in pretty bad shape. The girl was luckier; she has a broken leg but she'll be fine."

For an instant, Jade wasn't sure how to place that last comment. *What girl? Jim had been with a girl?* "I'm not sure I understand." She wondered if the doctor knew he was revealing something unknown to her.

"Your husband was riding an ATV in the off-road area of the Columbia Gorge. He had a girl with him, a twenty-nine-year-old woman named Kathy. We think they must have been drinking, and your husband lost control of the ATV. They hit a tree." The doctor paused. "They're both lucky to be alive."

Jade's head was swimming. Kathy Wittenberg had been with Jim on the back of an ATV? Drinking?

Nausea swept her and clutched her stomach. This couldn't be happening. Not again. Not with Jim, too. It had been enough that Tanner was a liar and a cheat. She had married Jim to give her child security. She had tolerated his latest behavior because it seemed best for her son, the godly thing to

311

do. Jim had never wanted anyone but her, and back when they got married Jade had been sure he'd be faithful.

But now . . . now he'd been caught with another woman. Jade felt as though her worst fears were coming true.

She exhaled slowly and heard the doctor clear his throat. "The woman also suffered a concussion. She's still pretty groggy." He hesitated. "Is she a friend of yours? A family member?"

Jade released a short laugh. "No . . . she works with my husband."

Dr. Cleary paused. "I'm sorry, Mrs. Rudolph. You might want to come down to the hospital. They're still checking to make sure your husband has mobility. There's a possibility . . ."

No, not Jim. "You mean he could be paralyzed?" Jade shuddered with alarm. Would God really ask her to care for an unfaithful man who didn't love her? Were these the plans he had for her? Tears filled her eyes. *Surely not, Lord.*

"We won't know for a day or so. But there is a chance. Like I said . . . he's pretty banged up. Lacerations and lots of stitches. He's semiconscious so he hasn't been able to help us much. We found your phone number in his personal belongings."

Jade sighed. "I'll be there. Thank you, Doctor."

"Mrs. Rudolph . . . I'm sorry about all this. I'll be here through the night if you have any questions."

She thanked him and hung up. She wanted to creep into Ty's room, curl up next to him, fall asleep, and forget the phone had ever rung. But that wasn't possible. No amount of pretending would erase the truth: Jim was having an affair and he'd been caught. For that matter, he might be paralyzed.

She bowed her head and clenched her fists. After learning the truth about Tanner ten years ago, Jade had nearly suffocated from grief and anger and loss. This time with Jim she was frightened about how she and Ty would get by. But she'd seen it coming, and somehow she knew they would survive. Even if she and Ty had to live alone the rest of their lives.

Whatever else happened, she was not turning her back on the Lord. Not this time. *Lord, I want to do your will. Give me the words to say, the way to act so that I can glorify you in this. Help me know how to cross this great ocean of anger and fear inside me. You know me, Lord. I'll sink if I try to swim it alone.*

She started crying as she telephoned

Jackie Conley. Between sobs she explained the situation.

"I'm so sorry, Jade." Jackie offered to watch Ty, and in ten minutes she pulled into the drive. The women hugged, and again Jade was thankful for her friendship. At least the Lord had given her that.

"I'll be okay. Pray for me. For God's will, whatever that is."

They held hands and prayed in quiet whispers. Thirty minutes later she was sitting in a cold chair adjacent to Jim's hospital bed. Dr. Cleary had been right. Jim's face was swollen, his eyes black and blue. His right hand was in a cast, and there were bandages covering numerous leg wounds which Jade presumed had required stitches.

She prayed over him, prayed that perhaps this would be a turning point in his life, a chance to give his heart to the Lord and come clean with his past.

Sometime before six that morning she fell asleep, still praying over him. She stayed that way until she heard voices. Her eyes opened and she found Jim sitting up in bed, sipping orange juice. Relief swept over her. He wasn't paralyzed, at least not in his upper body. She sat up straighter, and her movement caught his attention.

"You didn't have to come." Jim didn't

make eye contact. He reached for a piece of dry toast and gingerly took a bite.

Jade had no idea what to say. She leaned back in the chair and pulled a blanket around her shoulder. Someone must have covered her up after she fell asleep. She watched her husband, wondering how he could eat when their marriage was falling apart.

"Why don't you go home and get some sleep." Still no eye contact.

"Can you move your legs?" Jade's voice was void of emotion. It seemed important that they get past that issue before talking about anything else.

Jim moved the bed sheet with his toes and winced. "I'm fine."

He was nearly paralyzed, nearly killed, and he acts like nothing's happened. Had they told him about the severity of the accident? Did he know how his poor decision to lie and drink and cheat had nearly cost him and Kathy their lives? Jade studied him and saw no signs of remorse.

"I guess they told you what happened." Jim's voice was gruff and his hand trembled as he lifted a bite of scrambled eggs to his mouth.

"About Kathy, you mean?"

Jim showed no reaction. "So you know?"

315

"I'm not a fool, Jim." Jade could hear the resignation in her voice, and she made an effort not to cry. "I've known for a while now."

He released an exaggerated sigh. "Here we go."

He's become a complete stranger. The man before her was her husband, the one she'd shared the last ten years with. But he had been unfaithful for who knew how long, and now he had the nerve to sound angry about being caught. Her eyes were dry. She had cried enough last night. It was time to face the truth about their future.

"How long has it been going on?"

For the first time, he looked up and stared at her. His eyes held no fear, no anger. Just cold, calculated emptiness. "I won't lie to you anymore." His voice was as cold as his eyes. "Things . . . well, they haven't been good between us for a long time. You know that."

Her heart responded by skipping a beat, but she said nothing.

"Jade . . . I want a divorce."

Her fingers wrapped tightly around the arms of the chair, and she steadied herself. This couldn't be happening. He had no intention of working things out. She would be alone again, she and Ty. The thought of it terrified her.

"Because of her? Is that what this is all about?" Jade forced herself to sound calm. Jim hated when she got upset.

"Yes . . . no . . . I don't know. It just isn't working between us anymore."

No, this can't be happening. . . . He's already made up his mind. "People make mistakes, Jim. We can get past this . . . make it work. People do it all the time."

Jade's heart pounded erratically. She hated having to beg Jim, but how could she support Ty on her own? And Ty needed a father, didn't he? Jim might not have been the most responsive and loving dad, but he was still a real presence in her child's life. Ty's world would be set upside down if they divorced now. Just like hers had been when her mother —

"Jade, I've made up my mind. I don't want a sermon." He spat the words, and with his bruised and battered face she almost didn't recognize him. *He really is a stranger. I don't even know him anymore.* Jim interrupted her thoughts. "I'm in love with Kathy. I want out."

Jade felt the sting of tears. "What about Ty? Have you thought about him."

Jim was silent. He focused on his breakfast again.

"Are you listening to me?" Jade raised her voice and moved to the edge of her chair.

Jim slammed his toast back to his plate and glared at her. "To tell you the truth, I'm worried about the boy."

"Meaning what?"

"Meaning what chance does he have growing up with a mother who's a religious fanatic? You're brainwashing him, Jade. A little more every day." He paused and Jade's heartbeat quickened. *What was he talking about?* "I've hired an attorney."

"When? The accident just happened."

"Nothing just happened, Jade. Who are you kidding?" Jim looked at her like she was a dimwitted child. "I was going to tell you later this week."

"You're serious? You really want a divorce?" Jade felt her foundations shake, and she prayed God would give her the strength to stand. *You are my rock, my God, my strong tower —*

"I want more than the divorce." Jim leveled his gaze at her, and Jade felt a chill run down her arms. "I want Ty, too."

"Joint custody?" Maybe she was in a nightmare? Maybe the whole thing — starting with the phone call — was only a bad dream.

Wake up! she told herself. *Wake up, now!*

"No, Jade. Full-time, permanent custody."
He pushed away his tray. "I want the boy.
My attorney thinks I can get him."

Jade had the impulse to run from the
room, find Ty, and escape with him to some
remote Swiss mountaintop. He was *her*
child, not Jim's! Besides, why would Jim
want him? He had provided for Ty, but
certainly he had never shown any fatherly
interest. Why would he fight her for permanent custody of a son he'd never cared to
get to know? She closed her eyes for a moment and decided he must be playing with
her. *This can't be happening. . . . Help me,
Lord.* "You're not serious."

Jim leaned back against the hospital pillows. "Yes, in fact, I am. Dead serious." His
eyes were like daggers, slicing to the core of
her heart and that place where everything
safe and secure had lived until now. "I told
you, Jade. I've had it with your religious
craziness. I don't want my son raised in that
kind of environment. You'll turn him against
me, against any hope of free thinking.
Personally, I think Kathy and I could do a
better job. We don't want to share him with
you. Or your extreme beliefs."

Jade uttered an astonished laugh. "*We?*
Kathy Wittenberg has no claim on my son."
She realized she was on her feet. "You don't

319

have a chance of winning full custody of Ty.
No judge in America would grant that."

"You'd be surprised." Jim's hand was
steadier as he took another bite of eggs.
"Courts aren't happy with people like you,
people who tell their kids what to think and
who to agree with and how they should act."

"You're crazy if you —"

"No, Jade, you're crazy. Crazy like a fool.
I'm telling you, no son of mine —"

She took a step toward him, her voice raising. "He's not your —"

Her hand flew to her mouth and she
stopped herself. *Dear God, help me get a
grip here.* Her heart raced and she felt
perspiration gathering on her forehead.
*What if he's right? He and Kathy will try to
make an example of me and then . . . Could it
actually happen? Could a court actually take
Ty away from me because of my faith?*

Jim leveled his gaze at her, and again Jade
wondered if he knew the truth about Ty.
"He's not my what?" Jade saw the accusation in Jim's eyes. *He couldn't know. The
dates had lined up perfectly.* He could never
have known what led her to his doorstep
that day so many years ago.

She thought quickly. "He's not your
responsibility. I'm there when he gets home,
when he goes to school. I volunteer in his

classroom. He needs *me*, Jim, not you. You don't even like giving him a ride home after practice. Why would you want custody of him now?"

"To save him from a wretch like you!" Jim spat the words and then waved his hand at her. "Get out of my room, Jade. You make me sick."

Jade stood up and realized she was light-headed. She braced herself on the arm of the chair and stared at Jim. *Who was this man? What had happened to the Jim I'd longed to love, the man I'd hoped would one day share my heart?* She'd heard enough. Maybe Jim was out of his mind, under the effects of medication or a concussion. Her heart raced and her hands trembled. She needed to get home and check on Ty.

Jade made her way out of the hospital and into the parking lot. *He can't be serious, God. He wouldn't want custody of Ty. And if he did, there's no way he could win. Right, Lord? Please tell me I'm right.*

Trust in me and lean not on your own understanding. . . .

The verse brought a rush of peace and Jade exhaled slowly. As she did, her hands stopped shaking so she could unlock her car door. There was no way he would fight her for full custody. And if he did, there was no way he'd win.

It was impossible.

But as Jade drove home, the trembling returned and she was consumed by fear. She prayed with the intensity of someone clinging to life, and that night in church she held Ty's hand tightly.

This can't be real, Lord. It can't be. Tell me there's nothing to worry about, that I don't have to fear losing Ty to Jim because of my faith. Please, God.

In this world you will have tribulation, but be of good cheer . . . I have overcome the world.

What did that mean? Why had that Scripture come to mind now? She closed her eyes and knew she was on the verge of crying. Ty squeezed her hand and leaned near. "What's wrong, Mom?"

She opened her eyes and smiled at him. "Nothing, honey, Mommy's just praying."

"About Dad?" Ty knew his father had been in an accident, but that was all. She would spare him the other details until later.

"Yes, dear. I'm praying for Daddy."

A calm came over Ty's face, as if all was right with the world. He wrapped his arms around Jade and held her tight while she fought off a torrent of tears.

The fear didn't return until the next day. At just after four, Jade saw a sheriff's deputy pull up in front of her house and make his way up her sidewalk. She felt her heart stop, and then tumble into an erratic beat as she wiped her hands and opened the door. "Yes?"

"Mrs. Rudolph?"

"That's me."

"I've got a summons for you. I need you to sign here." He pointed to the piece of paper in his hand and held it up for her to read. The document stated that she was acknowledging receipt of divorce papers. She was officially being served. Jade felt a crushing fear, one that wove itself between her ribs and permeated her lung tissue. Her breathing grew labored as she moved the pen across the page.

The deputy turned to leave, taking his portion of the document and leaving Jade standing in the doorway, her eyes frozen on the papers in her hands. She moved slowly into the house, closed the door, and sat at the foot of the stairs where she began sifting through the pages, occasionally reminding herself to exhale.

They were divorce papers, all right, requesting her presence at a hearing set for mid-March.

Their marriage had begun in a small courtroom, and now it would end that way.

Jade closed her eyes. *God, I know you hate divorce. . . . I'm so sorry. Please don't let it happen, Lord.*

In that instant, Jade knew she would have done whatever she could to reconcile with her husband, but she also knew Jim was beyond that point. With her eyes still closed, she reminded herself that with God all things were possible. Jim could wake up tomorrow, repent of his arrogance and pride, and turn his life to the Lord. She could apologize for letting her fight against Channel One take precedence over her marriage. And with God's help she could take him back and somehow save their marriage. With God it was all possible.

Two tears slipped out from the corners of Jade's eyes, but still she kept her eyes shut, not willing to look at the destructive papers in her hands. "Forgive me for my part in this, Lord. I'll pray for Jim every day." She whispered the promise out loud but heard no response. Minutes passed while terrifying thoughts made their way across the canvas of Jade's mind. Eventually she opened her eyes and stared at the documents in her hands.

It must be here somewhere. She began flipping through the pages looking for the section that dealt with custody. Jim had made threats in the hospital, but certainly he didn't really want full custody. The documents were loaded with legalese, but Jade quickly found the area marked "custody." She scanned the words and felt herself grow faint.

"Mr. Rudolph seeks permanent, full-time custody of minor child, Ty Robert Rudolph. Mr. Rudolph cites that Mrs. Rudolph is guilty of mental abuse and brainwashing where the minor child is concerned. He also states that Mrs. Rudolph's views are highly unstable and extremely intolerant. She is mean-spirited, overbearing, and completely lacking in judgment according to Mr. Rudolph."

Jade read the words again. *Highly unstable . . . extremely intolerant.* Jim's attorney was trying to make her look crazy. As if it had nothing to do with her faith in God. *Mean-spirited, overbearing, and completely lacking in judgment.*

It was the most inaccurate thing anyone could have said about her, and after she'd read it three times through, Jade dropped to her knees.

"No, God! Can't you hear me? Can't you help me? Ty is *my* son, not his." Jade knew she would not survive if she lost custody of Ty. "Help me, Lord. I don't know what to do!"

In this world you will have tribulation, but be of good cheer . . . I have overcome the —

"No!" She didn't want to suffer tribulation or trials or any such thing where Ty was concerned. "I can't."

You can do all things through Christ.

Jade caught her breath and closed her eyes. Her body shook from the sobs that wracked her soul. It dawned on her that Kathy — and not Jim — was probably behind this. Kathy had no children and had mentioned on occasion at staff parties that she and her husband were trying to have a family. Now that she was making plans to be with Jim, she apparently thought she could gain a son and save a child from religious fanaticism all in one move.

No, Jim was not using this issue as a weapon against Jade. He was using it to win over Kathy Wittenberg. For that reason, he had made up his mind to make an example out of Jade. He wanted her to look like a freak, someone who was crazy and could certainly not maintain custody of her child.

"Why, Lord?" She cried until her tears became sobs and still she remained on the floor, hunched over her knees, begging God for help and understanding.

Once more the feeling came over her that she needed to get Ty and run away with him, to never look back even if it meant living undercover the rest of her life. Why had she trusted her son to a man like Jim Rudolph in the first place? Certainly welfare and food stamps would have been better for Ty than a father who never loved him and now wanted to use him to make an example of her.

She was not going to let it happen. The date of their hearing had been somewhere in the court papers, and Jade sorted through them frantically. There it was. Mid-March. Ten days away.

Jade leaned against the wall. Her mind raced, thinking of a solution, a way out. First she needed an attorney, someone who understood the nature of custody battles, someone who knew the importance of religious values and freedom of religion. . . .

One name came to mind, and Jade caught her breath. *No, Lord, not him. He'd take one look at Ty and know for sure the boy was his. Please!*

Once several years earlier Jade had been washing dishes while Jim flipped through the channels. He settled on one station long enough for her to hear Tanner's name. Her heart beat wildly as she set down the soapy dish, wiped her hands on her jeans, and joined Jim in the TV room.

There was Tanner, and Jade remembered how she drank in the sight of him for the first time in too many years.

He'd been more handsome than ever, confident, and genuine as a summer breeze. Jade had watched for several minutes, making herself appear busy so Jim wouldn't be suspicious. He had never known about her relationship with Tanner, but she didn't want to make him curious.

As Tanner spoke that day, she found herself carried back in time. Apparently, Mrs. Eastman had been wrong. Tanner hadn't wanted to be a politician, after all. Instead he had followed his dream and become a fighter for religious freedom. He had a firm called the CPRR with a number of attorneys working for him. Despite her bitterness toward the man, she couldn't help but feel proud of him.

She could still picture his face on her television screen. Jade's heart stopped racing and slowed to a steady thump. She could try to prove Tanner was Ty's father, but she might lose the child for good. Any mention to Tanner or anyone else that Ty was his son would mean Doris Eastman might make good on her promise. She could still hear the woman's hateful words that awful day: *I will hire a batch of attorneys to sue you for defamation. And I will get custody of that child, mark my words. Girls like you would never win a court battle against the Eastman estate.*

Jade sighed and knew she would have to keep Tanner's place in Ty's life a secret until the day she died. Otherwise it would cause too much public attention, and Ty would be the loser. Tanner hadn't wanted his son, anyway. Just as he hadn't wanted his other two children.

She rose up off the floor, straightened the papers, and set them on her desk. If Jim planned to sue her for full custody of Ty, if he intended to punish her for her beliefs, then she was faced with one undeniable fact: In all the world, only one man could help her now; the one man she must never contact again.

Call him, my daughter.

Jade heard the voice and hesitated. What could possibly come from it?

Call him.

There had been few moments since Jade had become a Christian that she had willfully gone against the still small voice of God. She drew a steadying breath. This was not going to be one of those times.

Walking across the room, she picked up the telephone and began to dial.

TWENTY-THREE

One of the benefits of working in the Los
Angeles area was the number of cases that
crossed the desks of the CPRR. Of course,
they could also be a curse. Tanner studied
the mass of humanity seated around him at
Tony Roma's. Most of them were blissfully
unaware of the desperate battle waged by
the CPRR to preserve freedoms long taken
for granted by many in the United States.

For all the time and energy he and his staff
had put into the battle, Tanner had the sense
lately that things were not getting better. If
anything, they were heating up. Many times
instead of gaining ground, they seemed to
be treading water: clinging to basic freedoms
while watching others erode with case precedence.

He took a swig of water and glanced at
the restaurant's entrance. Matt Bronzan
would be there in five minutes. He'd told
Tanner he had an urgent issue to discuss.

Something about a case that needed their immediate attention.

The cases they handled now would have been unthinkable five years ago. Churches whose tax-exempt status was being called into question, private business owners forbidden by city council from bearing a Christian fish on their store sign, teachers fired on the spot for mentioning God in a public classroom.

The CPRR won nearly all their cases, but not before much money and time was devoted to the matter. Tanner ran his fingers over the water drops on the side of his glass. Fired for mentioning God? He still couldn't believe the case had actually made it to court. Tanner and Matt had won the decision, but barely. How far had they come from the days when teachers were directed to lead prayer in school, how far from the days of even setting aside a moment of silence?

He sighed and stared through his water to the blurry images on the other side. The problem was public opinion. More often than not, his cases made their way into national headlines leaving people with the impression that — in the case of the dry cleaner operator — a Christian fish symbol was somehow illegal. Regardless of the fact that they'd won the case.

The attack by the liberal left and the ACLU was relentless and had served to erode the way the public viewed religious freedom as a whole. Anymore, churches felt thankful that they still had the privilege to meet on Sundays. Forget the freedoms they'd lost in the process.

Tanner spotted Matt heading for the table. At least he had this one friend. Matt had been with him since their first big case — the one with the student who wanted to sing at graduation. A former district attorney, Matt had once prosecuted mainly drunk-driving cases.

Then he met a widow, a Christian woman named Hannah Ryan, whose husband and daughter were killed by a man driving under the influence. Matt took the case and wound up winning a first-degree murder conviction. The drunk driver was given twenty-five to life, and Matt earned national attention overnight.

But something else happened.

Matt fell in love with Hannah. One year after the case was resolved — two years after the accident — the couple married. They had one daughter, Jenny, a sixteen-year-old who was the only survivor from the accident. Shortly after the wedding, Matt decided he'd spent enough of his life convicting drunk drivers. It was time to branch out. He had heard of Tanner's law firm and contacted him, looking to help.

Tanner liked him immediately. Matt was sharp and sincere and devoted to the Lord. He had won numerous cases since joining forces with Tanner and was, without a doubt, as great a fighter in the cause as anyone at the firm. Occasionally, Leslie and Tanner shared dinner with the Bronzans, and Tanner had always been impressed with Hannah's quiet strength. Whatever nightmare she'd been through, she'd made it to the other side by God's grace. Clearly she and Matt shared a bond that spoke volumes.

The kind of bond he couldn't imagine sharing with Leslie, no matter how wonderful she was. The kind of bond he once thought he'd share with —

"Hey, did you order?" Matt was breathless. He'd probably kept four appointments back-to-back before arriving at the restaurant.

Tanner shook his head. "Just the loaf." Once a month he and Matt met at Tony Roma's for lunch, and the onion loaf was a given. The men were both in exceptional physical shape and knew their monthly indulgence would not make a difference.

"How'd the meeting with Swires go?"

"Good." Matt gulped down half his glass of water. "I think I convinced him to give up. Showed him documentation, precedence."

"Good. We might live in a tolerant town, but even Los Angeles isn't ready for the 'Mother God Transvestite Club' to march in the Boy Scouts' Easter Parade."

Matt set his water down. "I told him they didn't stand a chance. Even if they *did* wear merit badges on their dresses."

Tanner laughed. Matt was the only one at the firm he could lighten up with. They played basketball at Racquetball World and on Saturdays met at seven in the morning for tennis. Time had earned them the right to joke with each other, even when the matters were utterly serious and close to their heart. "Is it just me, or is it getting crazier all the time out there?"

Matt rested his forearms on the table and leaned forward. "That reminds me."

Tanner rocked back in his chair. "The case you mentioned earlier?"

"Right. It's a doozy. Don't know if it's legit, but it has the earmark of a national headline grabber. And then some."

They were all worthy of such attention, but Matt had always had a keen sense for knowing when a case had the potential to shake Americans.

The waitress appeared with the onion loaf, took their order, and made a hasty exit.

"Gotta love these onions." Matt dug his fork into the loaf as Tanner raked a section onto his plate.

After a few bites, Tanner wiped his mouth and exhaled loudly. "Okay, I'm listening. Tell me about this case of the century you've discovered."

"Might be nothing." Matt shrugged. "But if it's true . . ." He took two more forkfuls of onion rings and then leaned back in his chair. "It's a custody case."

"Custody? As in divorce?" Tanner had handled only a few cases that involved divorce. Usually battles over which church a child would attend or whether the mother or father could force attendance if the child wasn't interested. That kind of thing. "How'd you hear about it again?"

"I got a call yesterday afternoon." Matt hesitated. "Anyway it's this woman, and she's terribly nervous. Says she doesn't want to give her name, but her husband is divorcing her and suing her for complete custody of their son."

Tanner finished the plate of onions and cocked his head. "Where do we fit in?"

Matt wiped his mouth. "He wants custody because he thinks she's an unfit mother."

"Unfit because . . . ?" Tanner was struggling to see the connection.

"Because she's a Christian."

Tanner felt the winds of outrage blow against him. "Are you kidding? He wants custody because of his wife's faith?"

"I'm serious. She told me her husband hasn't been involved in their son's life. The marriage fell apart when she discovered her husband was having an affair. Apparently there's more to it. The caller said she's fairly vocal on the school board or something. Hasn't kept her beliefs a secret."

Tanner was beginning to see the picture. "Now her husband wants to make an example of her. . . ."

Matt raised an eyebrow. "According to the divorce papers, he's out to prove the woman brainwashed the boy into believing and that she's an unfit mother because of her extreme religious beliefs."

Tanner anchored his elbows on the table and brought his fists together. He had feared it would come to this one day but never dreamed with the ushering in of a new century that they were there. If the man were to win this case, parents across the country would have to fear losing their children because of their faith. "What's her name?"

Matt sighed. "That's just it. She wouldn't give it to me."

"Why not?" Tanner was suspicious of people who called anonymously. If they needed help, if the situation was what they said it was, why not be honest about the facts. Including revealing their identity?

"Didn't say. Apparently she called for advice."

"What did you tell her?"

"The truth. No one could take her son away from her because of her faith. I asked her if she wanted someone from our office to help her, maybe represent her at the hearing."

"And . . ."

"She said no. Real adamant about it, too."

"Is it a financial concern?" Tanner thought it strange the woman would call but then refuse help.

"I told her there was financial assistance available, but she said she wasn't interested. Just wanted our advice."

Tanner sighed. "Strange. How did you leave it with her?"

"She said she'd get an attorney right away and she thanked me. I think she was relieved when I said her husband didn't stand a chance."

"Hmm. When's the hearing?"

"A week or so, apparently."

Tanner thought about the missing details. "We might never hear from her again, but you never know. Did she tell you where she lived."

"Yeah, I got that much. She lives in Portland."

"Why don't you put someone on it. Have them scan *The Oregonian* for the next few weeks, see if anything comes up. If she loses custody of the boy at the hearing, the paper will definitely cover it."

They changed the subject then, but Tanner's mind was stuck on the strange case Matt had shared. His heart ached for the woman — whoever she was — who was living in terror somewhere for fear that she would lose custody of her son.

All because she had chosen to identify herself with Jesus Christ.

TWENTY-FOUR

The north annex of the Clackamas County Courthouse was not an impressive structure. It consisted of a single hallway with various offices and courtrooms on either side. Jade arrived thirty minutes early so she could read the Bible. Matthew, chapters 5 and 6 and part of 7. Jesus' Sermon on the Mount always soothed her fears, no matter what she was facing.

She had read it by herself in a hotel room on the Oregon coast more than a decade ago, and again while waiting for Jim to regain consciousness after his accident.

And she read it now, as the hearing to decide whether she would lose custody of Ty was about to begin.

If ever there was a time she needed a reminder from Jesus it was now.

Therefore I tell you, do not worry about your life. . . .

Jade stopped reading and closed her eyes.

I'm trying not to worry, Lord. Help me believe what that man from Tanner's office said. No way can they take Ty because of my faith. Please, Lord, help me trust you.

She had survived the previous weeks by telling herself there was nothing to worry about. It was craziness. Pure craziness. No judge in his right mind would penalize a parent for her faith. She was sure of it. The man from Tanner's office had made her confident of the fact.

The day after Jade received the divorce papers, Jim had moved out. He and Kathy shared an apartment now, unabashedly driving to school together. From what she'd heard, Jim was still treated with utmost respect, though several staff members apparently didn't approve of his leaving his wife and moving in with another woman. But then, Kathy was one of them. And she wasn't a religious fanatic.

In the wake of Jim's decision to sue for complete custody, he had become the devoted father. He was suddenly attentive to Ty's needs, showing up on weekends to take him out for ice cream, engaging him in conversations about basketball and evolution, the professional football draft and alternative lifestyles. Kathy was often present.

340

Almost daily Jade found herself putting out fires Jim had started in the child's mind.

One night after spending an evening with Jim and Kathy, Ty had come home and approached her curiously. "Mom, did you know scientists have found the missing links that prove evolution is true?"

She had taken Ty in her arms and held him tight. "Honey, where'd you hear that? There's a lot about evolution that has never been proven. A lot of very smart scientists have actually stopped believing in it altogether."

Ty scrunched his handsome face sadly. "Dad and Kathy said you'd say that. . . ."

There had been several similar incidents, and Jade wished she could forbid Ty from leaving the house with Jim. But her attorney had advised her to cooperate. Otherwise she would only support Jim's accusations and come across fearful and fanatical. Jim's discussions about evolution and other hot topics were probably only intended to bait her.

"Do whatever you can to get along." Her attorney had repeated that just last week, and Jade knew she had no choice.

Jim's relentless attention toward Ty continued, and Jade was helpless to do anything to stop it. Clearly her son was torn by the situation and had been moody and sensitive as a result. Jade understood. Ty wanted to maintain his fierce loyalty to Jade, but there was no denying how much he enjoyed his father's sudden attention.

Jade glanced at her watch. Fifteen minutes had passed. She heard voices from the other end of the courthouse, and she stared down the hall. Nothing. No one headed her way. Jade twisted her fingers nervously. Her attorney should have been there by now. He hadn't been good about returning phone calls, and Jade feared he might show up late.

Her thoughts drifted back to Ty. Most recently, over the weekend, Ty came home from Jim's almost belligerent toward her.

"Daddy and Kathy say you're intolerant of people, is that right, Mom?" They had been to the Oregon Museum of Science and Industry, and Jade wondered how such a discussion could possibly have related to their visit.

"What people?"

Ty shrugged. "Different people. Like when two guys fall in love and get married."

Jade had to lean back against the kitchen counter for support. Why was Jim doing this? The boy was too young for such discussions. "Well, sweetheart, it's not that I have anything against those people. But God has something against the way they act."

"You mean God doesn't like it when two men fall in love?" Ty seemed genuinely confused, and Jade was sick about it. Jim was turning the child into a pawn for his own interests.

"Right, dear. God says it's a sin."

Ty studied her. "Daddy and Kathy said you'd say that."

Jade struggled to maintain her composure. "Daddy and Kathy aren't Christians, Ty." Jade had pulled her son close and hugged him. "We still love people who live like that, and we pray for them. But it isn't something God likes, and that's the truth, Ty."

"Daddy says truth is different for different people."

The comments continued until Jade practically looked forward to the hearing. At least then they could come to some kind of agreement and move on. Her attorney was hoping to win 80 percent custody for Jade.

Once he lost his battle for full custody, Jade was sure Jim would give up.

Unless Kathy had convinced him she wanted to be Ty's second mother. Jade's stomach hurt at the thought. *Please, no, Lord.*

Until her attorney arrived — just three minutes before the hearing — Jade remained alone, silent, absorbed in an urgent conversation with the only One who could set her son free.

The hearing was underway, and the Honorable Judge Arthur Goldberg presided. So far Jade was having trouble keeping up. Issues of material goods and financial support and joint bank accounts were discussed and considered. Generally, their possessions were split down the middle, and the attorneys handled the details. Meanwhile, Jade sat on one side of the courtroom; Jim, the other.

Occasionally, she would glance in his direction and wonder again why she had married him. Why hadn't she trusted God to give her the strength to be a single mother? Jim kept his gaze straight ahead and seemed almost unaware that she was in the room.

Judge Goldberg was speaking. "And now, we will decide the custody matter. First we will hear from the plaintiff."

Jim made his way to the witness stand, and Jade watched him smile warmly at the judge.

"Mr. Rudolph, this court understands you are seeking full and permanent custody of your minor child, Ty Robert Rudolph, is that correct?"

"Yes, your honor." Jim looked the picture of professionalism. Only someone like Jade, someone who knew him well, could detect the steel-hard hatred that lurked deep in his dark eyes. "That is correct."

"Would you please explain to the court your reason for this?"

Jim drew a deep breath and began. He talked about Jade's determination to convert everyone to her way of thinking. It was enough that Jade did this with strangers and merchants and school board members, he said. But now she was doing it with their son. One by one, he rattled off detailed accounts of the battles she'd fought, battles to maintain religious values and overt parental control in areas that concerned her son.

Jade's hands began to tremble as Jim continued. She clasped them tightly and worked to draw a deep breath.

Do not be anxious about anything. . . .

Somehow, when Jim was finished speaking, Jade realized her efforts didn't seem altruistic. They seemed extreme and paranoid and one-sided, a distraction to the job of raising a child. *What's happening here, God? It isn't supposed to be like this.* Jade struggled to breathe under the weight of her fear.

By the time she was allowed to speak, Jade had trouble keeping her head up. She felt like a terrible mother, a criminal almost, and she struggled to make eye contact with the judge.

"Is it true you told your son it was wrong for two men to love each other?" Judge Goldberg's question caught Jade off guard. *What? How did the judge know that? Ty must have innocently passed her comments onto Jim and . . .*

"Yes, your honor. But only because that's what God's Word teaches." Jade studied the judge's face and saw that clearly he did not approve of this.

"So you're raising your son by the standard of the Bible, is that right?" The judge said the word Bible like it shouldn't be spoken in public places, and Jade looked to her attorney for help. He was sorting through a stack of documents and seemed unconcerned with the dialogue taking place.

Jade continued to answer questions until finally the judge called for a brief recess. Five minutes later he was back with his decision.

"This court finds Mr. Rudolph to be of sound mind and accurate opinion when he states his concern for his son. Indeed, the boy is at great risk for being converted to his mother's way of thinking. I believe he is being forced to adapt her views of intolerance at an age that is too young to make those types of decisions. Intolerant children will only spread hate in our world, and when presented this type of opportunity, I must act the way few judges have acted before."

Jade shot a desperate look toward her attorney, but again he was preoccupied with paperwork and seemed unaware of the proceedings taking place. What did the judge mean that he must "act the way few judges have acted before"? What was happening here? Where had this judge come from anyway? Didn't her attorney know the judge and what his opinions would be about the case?

Judge Goldberg glanced at Jim, and then Jade. "For that reason, I do hereby award full custody of minor child, Ty Robert Rudolph, to Mr. Jim Rudolph. Supervised visits for Mrs. Jade Rudolph will begin one week after the custody exchange takes place."

Jade stared at the judge and blinked. It was impossible. This couldn't be happening. A cold clamminess came over her, and spots danced wildly before her eyes. This wasn't Judge Goldberg's decision to make. It couldn't be. She was Ty's mother, after all, and Jim . . . he wasn't even . . .

"Wait a minute!" She was on her feet, her voice ringing through the courtroom. "You can't do this. My son needs me; we need each other."

The judge looked at her over the rim of his glasses. "You had your chance, Mrs. Rudolph. Even over the past few weeks you've been given an opportunity to soften your views. But you've insisted on leaning so far to the religious right that this court no longer feels you to be a safe and responsible parent for your son."

"But you can't!"

"Order!" Judge Goldberg rose from his chair, his face twisted in a scowl as he banged his gavel twice. "If you speak again, I will hold you in contempt of court. Is that understood?"

Jade sat weakly down in her chair and felt the tears begin to flow. *Why, God? What can I do to stop this?* She looked at Jim and saw he was smiling and whispering with his attorney. Jade felt as if her heart had been ripped out and thrown on the floor for everyone to step on and laugh at.

Jim and his attorney had actually done it. They'd won Ty because they had the correct viewpoint and she did not. *I'll get him back; I have to. But until then . . . Oh, God, please help me. . . . How will I live without him?*

"Mrs. Rudolph, you will have forty-eight hours. At that point a deputy will arrive at your door, along with Mr. Rudolph and his attorney, and custody will be handed over. If you do not cooperate or do not make yourself available for the transfer, you will be in contempt of court, and a warrant will be issued for your arrest. Is that understood?"

Jade had to force herself to respond. "Yes, your honor." She looked at her attorney once more, but still he seemed like an indifferent bystander watching the proceedings without a single interjection or show of concern.

Feeling helpless, Jade spoke out. "Please make a note that I will be finding a new attorney. . . ." Her lawyer cast her a look and then shrugged. The man didn't care about her pain or whether she won the case. He was merely going through the motions, earning a paycheck. Jade struggled to remain standing and thought she might faint or die from heart failure. Her chest ached from the blow of the judge's decision. She cleared her throat. "And please make a note that I will be appealing this decision."

The judge looked at her, and Jade had the

feeling he was mocking her. "That will be noted. You have sixty days to file an appeal, or the decision will stand."

Jade did not talk to anyone, including the reporter from *The Oregonian* who sat in the back row. Why bother? He had a story that would, Jade guessed, make the front page. She needed a new attorney, needed a plan. But right now none of it mattered. As she stumbled to her car, weak from shock and pain, terrified about the future, there was only one thing she wanted: to get home and explain the situation to Ty, help him understand that for a little while — and only a little while — they would have to be separated.

Then she would spend the next forty-eight hours telling him good-bye.

TWENTY-FIVE

The wedding plans were far more extrava-
gant than Tanner had pictured, and by the
third week of March they were becoming
overwhelming. Leslie showed amazing attention to detail, and Tanner was growing
increasingly tired of her twice daily calls
updating him on the progress.

He had her on the phone now, and Tanner tapped his pencil against the edge of his
desk as he listened to the latest bit of wedding information. Leslie's voice sounded
shrill and demanding. Funny how it hadn't
seemed that way at first. *What's wrong with
me, Lord? I should be thrilled to marry a
woman like Leslie. . . .*

Do not be unequally yoked, my son.

The verse caught Tanner square in his gut.
Leslie continued to ramble, but he wasn't
listening. If God hadn't wanted him to be
unequally yoked, why hadn't he pointed it
out earlier?

Tanner thought of the Bible, and a sinking feeling settled in his heart. He had known from the beginning that Leslie wasn't a strong believer. In fact, there had been many times when the fact had haunted him late into the night. God had indeed pointed it out earlier. *But she does believe, Lord.*

I know the plans I have for you. . . .

There it was, that Jeremiah verse again. Ever since Jade had married someone else, Tanner had been unsure about the plans God had for him. Leslie had brought him new perspective. She might not have been a dynamic believer, but she had potential. Certainly she was the plan God had intended for him, wasn't she? Doubts nibbled at him like so many bats in a dark cave.

Tanner forced himself to concentrate on what Leslie was saying.

"There is simply no way we can sign the current caterer. Mother checked his background, and he's only had three years of professional experience. Ours would be the largest wedding he's serviced, and that won't do. We need someone with experience; there's no other way around it."

Tanner stared at the crystal blue sky and wished for a moment he was outside walking somewhere. Between Leslie's wedding

352

plans and the workload he was facing that day, he needed a moment by himself to clear his thoughts. Or maybe his workload had nothing to do with it. Maybe it was the wedding itself making his thoughts foggy. *What am I feeling, Lord? Why am I confused?* He loved Leslie, didn't he? Of course he did. He was only tired of the details. Color schemes, bridesmaids' dresses, tuxedos, flowers.

Leslie was still stuck on the caterer. He tuned back in and tried to feel interested.

"Anyway, Mother says she knows someone in the Bay Area who could fly in, but then I thought we should check into that famous chef, what's his name? The one who creates meals for the stars?"

Stars. For an instant he thought of a night long ago when he and Jade sat alongside the Cowlitz River and counted the constellations. He had seen more stars that night than at any time before or since. Or was that just the way Jade made him feel? Tanner drew a deep breath.

Fine time to be thinking of Jade.

". . . of fish and veal, and anyway, it's got to be the right man, don't you agree, Tanner?"

He felt a rush of panic. He had no idea what Leslie was talking about. "Right.

Definitely. The right man."

"Tanner!" Leslie's voice was half whine, half reprimand. "You're not listening are you? You never listen when we talk about the wedding. I hope you're planning to show up."

Tanner forced a laugh, but it sounded hollow even to him. "Honey, it's just that you're so much better at making these decisions than I am. I'll be happy with whatever you choose. Really."

"It would be nice if you were interested, even just a little bit." For a woman with a Harvard English degree and a resume littered with accomplishments, Leslie sometimes acted like a child demanding attention. Tanner shook his head and tried again to clear his thoughts.

Leslie's wonderful. Why am I sabotaging my feelings toward the woman I'm about to marry? The woman I'll spend the rest of my life with?

"I'm listening and I'm interested. I'm sorry, honey, go ahead. Have you called anyone about the catering."

Leslie released an exaggerated sigh. "I already told you, I called him yesterday. I'm waiting to hear back later today whether . . ."

Matt Bronzan entered his office. He held

a newspaper clipping, and he looked stricken. Tanner raised his eyebrows in response, and Matt mouthed the word, "Emergency."

Tanner motioned for Matt to sit down and he pointed at the phone, signaling that he would be off in a moment. He waited for Leslie to take a breath. "Honey, something's come up. I gotta run." He hesitated. Why was he feeling so uncomfortable with her? Maybe they needed a day away, time to talk about something other than the wedding.

"As usual. Something always comes up. I'll figure it out by myself." She was gifted at playing the role of persecuted martyr. "I'll let you know what time to be at the church."

"I'm sorry, Leslie. I'll call you back. . . . I love you." But the words sounded forced. He did, didn't he? If he didn't love her, what was he doing marrying her? And where were these feelings of doubt coming from? He tried to remember all the reasons he'd asked her to marry him in the first place.

Be careful, my son. Fools rush in where angels fear to tread.

The warning flashed through his mind and hit him like a physical blow. First the verse about being unequally yoked and now this. Was the Lord trying to warn him? He stored the possibility in the back pocket of his mind and turned his attention to Matt. "What's up?"

Matt set the news clipping on the desk and turned it so it faced Tanner. He glanced at the headline. "Woman Loses Custody of Son Because of Religious Fanaticism."

Tanner's eyes grew wide. It was the case Matt had told him about. It had really happened. The woman had been genuine, and now she had lost possession of her son. "Is it her?"

Matt nodded. "Definitely. Portland. Press makes her out to be a freak, just like the guy's attorney and the judge. One of those cases where everything lined up against her."

"Have you read it?"

"Yep. Woman says she's going to appeal, says she's going to need a new attorney."

"Yeah, I guess." How could her first attorney have blown such an obvious case? Religious freedom was a protection guaranteed by the Constitution, pure and simple. Was the entire country losing its collective mind? He reached for the article and scanned the first few paragraphs while Matt waited.

"A Portland woman lost custody of her only son today because of her extreme religious views in what will no doubt become a landmark case. Municipal Court Judge Arthur Goldberg made his decision based on the complaint by the woman's husband. His complaint stated that their son was being forced to believe the same way as his mother. Goldberg cited the boy's age as a leading factor in his decision against the child's mother, Jade Rudolph, 31, of north Portland."

Tanner's eyes froze on the woman's name. *Jade Rudolph. Age thirty-one. No, it wasn't possible.* There had to be other women named Jade living in the Northwest. Besides, his Jade could have moved anywhere by now. It couldn't be her. Not after all these years.

"You with me, Tanner? You look like you saw a burning bush or something." Matt lowered his face and tried to make eye contact with Tanner. "Did I miss something?"

Tanner shook his head slowly. "It's just the . . ." He met Matt's questioning stare. "I knew a girl named Jade once."

Matt's expression went blank. "How 'bout that. Me, too. In first grade, I think."

"No . . ." He didn't expect Matt to understand. He'd never told Matt or anyone else about Jade and their summer and all she

357

had meant to him. All she still meant to him. "I . . . I loved a girl named Jade once."

"Oh." Matt tried to look sympathetic, but it was obvious he wanted to return to the matter at hand. "You never mentioned her before."

"It was a long time ago. I was going to marry her, but then . . ." Tanner gazed back at the article, at the woman's name. "She married someone else."

Matt leaned back in his chair, eyebrows raised. "You think it's her?"

Tanner shrugged. "Could be, I suppose. It'd be a long shot." He had never learned her married name. "I'm sure it's not her. She's probably back living on the East Coast by now."

Matt hesitated. "Anyway, we need to get on this right away. It's the biggest issue this country's faced yet. A mother losing custody of her child because of her religious beliefs."

Tanner tried desperately to put thoughts of Jade out of his head. "Right. We need to contact her." He thought about his schedule over the coming week. "Why don't you see if she's free this Thursday? I have appointments Wednesday and Friday, but if she's all right with it, arrange to meet her. We'll fly up Wednesday evening and meet with her Thursday morning."

Matt nodded. "Done. I'll go track her down." He made his way toward the door. "I'll let you know what I find, whether she's open or not and if she's interested in meeting. Last time I talked to her, she didn't want our help."

Tanner's heart felt heavy as he considered the woman's situation. "She's lost her son, Matt." He took the news clipping and folded it, tucking it into a fresh folder. "She'll want our help now."

There was no point sending Ty to school, not with deputies about to arrive at her house and escort her son away. She had explained it several times, but still Ty had spent much of the past thirty-six hours crying.

"Why, Mom? I don't want to live with him and Kathy." Ty had finished breakfast and was sitting across the table from her, desperate to understand why his world had just been turned upside down. "Tell them I don't want to do it, Mommy, please."

Jade leaned toward her son, pulling him close. Tears filled her eyes, but she held them back. She didn't want Ty to see her crying. There would be time for that later.

"I'm sorry, honey. I'm trying hard as I can to change this. We need to pray, okay? God will help us be together again."

Jade believed it with every fiber in her being. If she had doubted it for a moment, she would collapse with grief. Instead, she viewed this as a stunning mistake, an oversight that would be corrected soon. It had to be. A person didn't lose custody of her child because of her faith. Not in the United States.

She ran her hand over Ty's back and felt him shaking. "It's okay, honey. Mommy's going to pray, okay?"

Ty nodded, sobbing quietly against her sweater. Jade closed her eyes and lowered her voice so that it sounded soothing, even to her. "Dear Jesus, we are so sad at what's happened. Please help me get Ty back soon, and please be with him as he goes to live with his dad for a while. Amen."

Ty pulled away and studied her. "How come God let this happen to me, Mom?"

Jade had no answers. She smoothed a lock of hair off Ty's forehead and kissed his cheek. "God has a plan in this, Ty. Things are going to work out. I promise."

For a moment she could picture Tanner whispering those same words to her so long ago. Things hadn't worked out then. Jade sighed. *Help me, Lord. My faith is so weak.*

Her prayer was interrupted by a phone

call. "I'll be right back, sweetheart." She tousled Ty's hair, moved into the kitchen, and answered the phone. "Hello?"

"Mrs. Rudolph?"

Jade recognized the voice on the other end, but she wasn't sure from where. "Yes. This is she."

The man sighed in what sounded like relief. "I found you. This is Matt Bronzan with CPRR, the Center for Preserving Religious Rights. I believe we spoke last week, am I right?"

Panic coursed through Jade. "Uh, yes. I called about my divorce."

"Mrs. Rudolph, I saw the article in *The Oregonian.* You lost custody of your son two days ago, is that right?"

Jade struggled to speak past the lump in her throat. If this man knew who she was and the problem she was facing, did Tanner know, too? And if he knew, was it possible he realized who she was? "I . . . yes, at the . . ."

The man seemed to understand her sorrow. "It's all right. Take your time." He hesitated. "We'd like to represent you, Mrs. Rudolph. If that would work for you. We feel confident we can win back your custody rights."

Tears streamed down Jade's face, and a

sob made its way to the surface. "I'm sorry. This is . . . very hard."

"I understand." The man paused. "Have you heard of our firm, Mrs. Rudolph?"

Jade's crying subsided and she uttered a shaky sigh. "Yes."

"Then you've heard of Tanner Eastman, the man who founded it."

Heard of him? There was no way to hide from him. Jade remembered that day at Doris Eastman's house, the day she learned the truth about Tanner. She had intended to leave everything about him behind her. She had taken complicated detours in life and done her best to lose track of him. Instead, his was the first face she saw every night while she slept. And in the morning, he was sitting at her breakfast table, smiling at her through the eyes of the little boy that meant everything to her.

"Yes, I've heard of him."

Matt Bronzan sounded relieved. "He's the best in cases like this. He and I would like to handle it together." He paused, and Jade wondered if she could stand the shock of seeing Tanner again. Certainly his mother had kept her promise and told him nothing of her pregnancy. He would never guess that Ty was his son. Or would he?

"I'm not sure . . ." Her head was swimming. If Tanner found out, would he seek custody rights, too? Would he refuse to represent her case because the child was really his? Would he bring out a team of lawyers to sue her for defamation?

"Mrs. Rudolph," the man's voice was suddenly filled with concern. "It is not easy to overturn a decision. Especially one such as this. I think you should consider —"

"I'm sorry." Jade interrupted. What was she thinking? So what if Tanner found out the truth? If he could help her win back custody of Ty, however that might happen, then she needed to agree. There was no other choice. "Please forgive me, Mr. Bronzan. Yes . . . I'd like your help very much."

For a moment she considered telling this man that she knew Tanner. That way there would be no surprises. But she couldn't bring herself to say the words. It had been too many years.

"We'd like to fly up and meet with you Thursday if possible. That way we can get to know you and the case a bit better."

Jade managed a short laugh. "You mean see if I'm really a religious fanatic, like the paper says?"

The man did not laugh in response. "After our talk the other day, I'm confident you're not a fanatic or a freak. But still, we need to talk."

Jade squeezed her eyes shut. "Okay. Thursday is fine." How could this be happening? After all these years she would actually see Tanner face to face in just a few days. What would she say to him? Would she hate him for pretending to love her all those years ago?

They finished making plans, and Jade hung up the phone. Her heart raced for fear of the future — especially the immediate future when she would turn her son over to deputies. But somehow, as she made her way back to Ty, she found the courage to believe God was working.

And that seeing Tanner again might actually be part of the solution.

Four hours passed while Jade and Ty sat curled on the sofa, taking turns reading aloud from Michael Jordan's biography. Two suitcases sat nearby, packed with her son's favorite clothes and books and his basketball. When they grew tired of reading, they talked about his season and how quickly the years would pass before he'd play ball in high school.

"You're still going to come to my games, right, Mom?" Ty's eyes were dry and Jade was thankful. She'd prayed constantly throughout the afternoon, aware that her darkest moment was approaching. She owed it to Ty to be strong, and she was pleased to see he was not as frightened as he had been earlier.

"I wouldn't miss 'em." She kissed the top of his forehead. "I'm your biggest fan."

"Do the police have to be there?"

Jade felt her heart sink. "No, Ty, why would you think that?"

"They have to be there when we spend time together, right?"

She felt her shoulders slump, and regardless of her resolve, her eyes grew wet again. "Yes." She hugged him close. "But only for a while."

"But why, Mom? You didn't do anything wrong."

"I know, sweetheart, but the courts are afraid I might take you and run away with you."

Ty's eyes lit up. "Hey, that's a great idea! We could pack our bags and head for the woods or something. Kinda like a movie. The Wilderness Family, maybe."

Jade studied her son, and her heart swelled with love for him. "Does sound sort of fun, doesn't it?"

"I'm serious!" Ty was on his feet. "My stuff's ready. We could have yours packed in a few minutes and be gone before the police get here." He started for the stairs, but she took his hand gently in hers and pulled him back.

"Sweetie, it wouldn't work. God wouldn't want us running away like that." She framed his small face with her fingers. "We just need to believe, Ty. God's in control, and he'll help us through this. In the meantime, I'm here. Any time you want to call me, just ask your dad. The judge said phone calls were okay whenever you wanted. Even if . . ."

Their conversation was interrupted by a sharp knock at the door. *The police.* Jade's breathing came in short, desperate gasps. *This isn't happening. It isn't possible.* How long could she keep up the front for Ty? Jade forced herself to speak. "Come on, buddy, time to go."

Ty hung his head and clutched her sweater as she lifted the suitcases and carried them to the door. They heard a second knock, and Jade caught the fearful look in her son's eyes. She stooped down and met him at his level. Her throat was swollen with emotion and her voice was barely audible. "It's okay. You'll be back before you know it."

She stood and forced herself to open the door. Two somber deputies stood there, and beyond them Jade could see Jim and his attorney waiting near Jim's vehicle. None of this made sense. Why didn't they trust her? She would have handed Ty over to Jim without the presence of officers and attorneys. Did Jim honestly think a police force was necessary to be sure she complied with court orders?

"Mrs. Rudolph, we've come for the boy." The larger of the two officers stepped forward, and Jade wanted to push him off her porch. She felt like a criminal, and she could see Ty was starting to cry as he hovered beside her.

"If you don't mind waiting down the walk a bit." Jade studied the man through her tears. "I need to say good-bye."

The deputies nodded, took Ty's suitcases, and retreated ten paces. When they were out of earshot, Jade stooped once more to Ty's level. He flung his arms around her neck and spoke in a muffled voice Jade knew she'd remember forever. "I love you."

Jade swallowed hard. "Love you more." She stroked the back of his head, clinging to him as if by doing so she could make the deputies outside disappear, make everything right, the way it had been before. "Ty, whatever happens, however long this takes, you know that Mommy loves you, right?"

Ty nodded. She could see he was trying to be strong. His cheeks were wet with tears, but he stood proudly, his back tall.

"Okay, then, come here." Jade pulled her son close and held him, soaked in the warmth of his little body, and tried to memorize the feeling. She would miss him so much she wondered if she'd survive. The part of her that was moving and breathing and making decisions knew that through Christ she could do all things.

But right now she felt like a blind person balancing on a tightrope strung a thousand feet above shark-infested waters.

"I don't want to go." Ty's voice broke, and it brought another wave of tears in Jade.

"Honey . . ." She looked at him, searching his eyes, willing him to understand.

His gaze fell and he nodded. "Okay. Bye . . ."

"Bye, honey. Call me." She pulled him close once more. "And pray. We have to pray for each other, okay?"

One of the deputies shifted positions. "Ma'am, we need to take custody now. Your husband is waiting."

Jade wanted to scream at the officer. Let Jim wait. Let him watch how Ty clung to her and hated to say good-bye. Let him see that he was using this child as a pawn and very nearly destroying him in the process.

She closed her eyes and willed the entire scene to disappear. *Why, Lord? Why are you letting this happen?*

Trust in the Lord with all your heart and lean not on your own understanding.

The Scripture flooded her with enough strength to open her eyes, to let her precious son go. She glanced at the officer. "He's coming."

She rested her hands on Ty's shoulders and smiled through her tears. "You gotta go, Ty. I love you."

"I love you, Mom." Ty hung his head and pulled away. The separation was as painful as if someone had sliced her arms off. She stayed stooped down, sobbing quietly, watching as Ty walked four steps and then five. Then as one of the officers held out his hand, her son stopped and spun around.

"*No!* I won't go!" He raced back to her and flung his arms around her neck. Jade clutched him and covered the back of his head with her open hand, stroking his hair, holding him close as he sobbed out loud. Ty had never cried like this before, and for a moment, Jade wished she had acted on her earlier impulse to run away with him. She should have taken him to Canada or Mexico. Some place where she could love the Lord and not lose her son because of it. At least then she could have spared him this pain. Spared them both.

At least until they were caught. And then she'd never have seen him again.

She sighed. No, this was the only option. She would work with Tanner and his law firm, and they would win Ty back. It had to happen. She held her son and let him cry until he had calmed down. "Honey, you have to go. I'm sorry, baby."

Ty nodded. "I'll be back, right? Soon?" His eyes were filled with uncertainty, his face red and puffy, streaked from so many tears.

"Soon. I promise."

Ty swallowed hard, kissed her on the cheek once more, and then turned and walked to the waiting officer. He kept his gaze downward as the officers handed him over to Jim. He would go, but not gently, not willingly. Jade wondered if the officers could see how ludicrous the situation was.

Ty climbed into Jim's backseat and turned to face her. She kept her eyes locked on his and saw that he was crying hard again. Sobbing. Probably out loud. *Why, God? What good can come from this?* The last thing she saw before Jim and his attorney drove out of sight was the tormented face of her only son, his hand up against the glass of the rear window, and the single word he repeated over and over again: "Mom!"

With visions of him threatening to suffocate her, Jade limped inside, grabbed a jacket Ty had forgotten, and collapsed on the tiled floor. She lay there, sobbing and clutching the jacket, savoring the smell of her little boy until she had no more tears left to cry. Finally, when she could find the strength, she pulled herself up and forced herself toward the bedroom.

With Ty gone she was empty, dead inside. Everything hurt and nothing mattered. That night as she tossed on her bed, God made one thing painfully clear:

Whatever it might cost her personally, she was ready to face Tanner.

TWENTY-SIX

Tanner arranged for the meeting to take place in an empty classroom at a large church in downtown Portland. According to Matt, the woman hadn't wanted to meet at her house, and certainly a diner would be too distracting. The classroom would be quiet and neutral, and hopefully set the woman at ease so they could get to know her and the story behind her loss of custody. He and Matt arrived at nine-thirty, half an hour early. They spread an assortment of briefs over the table and studied them one last time.

Over the past week they had requested the help of nearly everyone in the office, making certain every case regarding parental custody and issues of faith was researched and summarized. The summaries were contained in the briefs that now filled the table.

"There's enough precedence here to win

an appeal without even making an appe.
ance." Matt tossed the last of the cases o.
the table, folded his arms, and stared at Tanner. "I still can't believe we're doing this."

"Believe it."

"I mean, who'd have thought it?"

Tanner remembered Peter and the people
of Hungary. "I have a feeling it'll get worse
before it gets better." He ran his fingers over
the assorted documents, recalling the high-
lights of each case. "Bottom line is Jade Rudolph. What kind of mother is she?"

Matt shrugged. "Hard to tell from our
conversations."

"But she's not a cult member draped in
white linen refusing her son medical treatment and encouraging him to drink cyanide
Kool-Aid. We know that much."

"She's definitely not that."

Tanner straightened the documents and
pulled out a single sheet, a retainer that the
woman needed to sign if she wanted the
CPRR to represent her appeal. "The only
problem here is the local judges."

"A bit liberal?" A grin spread across
Matt's face.

"They define the word."

"Still, it's crazy. We'll win the appeal hands
down."

"I'm worried about it."

"Why?"

"Because these days certain judges enjoy going against precedence. Charting their own course in history."

Matt grew pensive. "I hadn't thought of that."

"Before too long, everyone in America will know about this case. Last week it was played on wire stories across the country. Soon the talking heads will get hold of it, and long before the appeal, public opinion will be set — or at least the media's view of public opinion. Jade Rudolph will be dragged through the gutter before this is said and done. She'll be accused of being intolerant, hateful, extreme. . . ."

"Taking Jade Rudolph's son from her is hardly a way of eliminating hate."

Tanner nodded slowly. "You and I know that. But the media wields a fickle finger at times. When I first took on religious freedom cases, they applauded me as a hero, a voice where once there had only been silence. My practice exploded overnight because of the media's positive attention. . . . But Jade's story is something else entirely."

"The Channel One thing?"

"The media has long supported Channel One as an educational tool. By taking a stand against it, Jade's put herself in a tough spot."

"So you think public opinion could hurt the case?" Matt shifted positions and eyed Tanner curiously.

"It could. In some ways the timing is perfect for a precedent case that would send a message to everyone: Watch yourself. Too much faith might be a bad thing."

"You really think so?"

Tanner remembered the feelings he'd had recently, warnings, almost as if God was trying to tell him something about this case. He had long since dismissed the idea that this woman could be his Jade. But still he felt for her. "All we can do is feed the public a vivid picture of the kind of mother Jade Rudolph really is. Then we cite our case precedence and, of course, the protection offered by the constitution."

Matt glanced at his watch. "She should be here soon. You have the tape recorder ready?"

Tanner tapped his briefcase. "I'm not bringing it out unless she's willing to give me a deposition today, and even then —" There was a knock. Tanner glanced across the room. "I'll get it."

He stood, reached for the door, and pulled it open. As he did, the woman came into view — and the shock was like a sucker punch to his gut, leaving him struggling for breath. . . .

God, Father, it's her.

He stood frozen in place. It was like seeing a ghost, an image lifted from some long ago memory. How long had he searched for her? How many times had he imagined this, wondered what he would say, how he would react?

"Jade . . ." It came out low and ragged.

"Hello, Tanner." She wasn't surprised. She had known he'd be here. The truth of that hit, and it was like a physical blow. She'd known he would be here, and still she hadn't called him.

He composed himself and stilled his trembling hands. "Why didn't you tell me?" His voice was a whisper, and he felt tears in his eyes. It didn't matter that she didn't love him anymore, maybe never had. She was here, inches from him, and no matter what had gone wrong so many years ago, she was still the only woman he had ever truly loved.

"I couldn't." She looked the same. Her face was unlined and, though he wouldn't have believed it were possible, even more beautiful. But something was different about her eyes. They were still green, but they didn't sparkle. Instead they held a dense layer of fog, a cloak protecting h[...] from anyone who might try and see into he[...] soul.

Whatever life had dealt Jade, it had left her unwilling to share it with anyone. Especially him. Tanner guessed the barrier harbored an ocean of sadness. *What are you thinking, Jade? What happened a decade ago that drove you into another man's arms?*

He was trapped in her gaze, studying her, a million questions fighting for position when he heard Matt laugh behind him. "Aren't you going to let her in?"

Tanner broke the lock he held on Jade's eyes and stepped aside. "I'm sorry. Come in, Jade."

Matt looked from Tanner to Jade and back. "Did I miss something?"

Tanner searched Jade's face again and shivered. She was cold as ice. "Uh . . . Jade and I were friends. A long time ago."

A knowing look crossed Matt's face as Jade took a seat next to him and clutched her purse tightly in her lap.

She hates me, Lord. What did I ever do to her?

He cleared his throat. The last thing he wanted to do was talk about Jade's custody battle. He wanted to excuse Matt and not let her out of the room until she told him what happened.

"Do you still think you can win my son back for me?" As cold as she was toward Tanner, her eyes were filled with hope, and he remembered a conversation they'd shared over pizza once during that long ago summer. If there had been one thing Jade was determined to do in life, it was to stand by her child. She'd been so determined, that she'd told him she'd rather not have children at all if she couldn't offer them a stable home. Again Tanner wondered what went wrong.

"It isn't a clear-cut case. We've done some research on custody cases involving issues of faith. On the surface . . ."

The words faded to a halt. Tanner couldn't think, let alone talk. He couldn't make sense if he tried. Not with Jade Conner in the same room and a lifetime of unanswered questions dying on the table between them.

He shot a look at his partner and Matt cut in. "On the surface your case looks like an easy win. There's no way a mother should lose custody of her child because of her belief in God. But what we're seeing lately is a shift in public opinion. It's okay to believe in God. Not okay to take a public stand on issues of faith, on areas where morality might be perceived as intolerance."

Jade drew a shaky breath and stared Matt. "If there's some kind of law these day, stating that *I* have to be tolerant of their views, don't they also have to be tolerant of *mine?*"

Matt cocked his head. "Depends. Tolerance is a one-way street. The social definition is to have a viewpoint that is politically, morally correct. The courts and government and media tell us we should accept all faiths, all lifestyles. What you've done is crossed a line. You've taken a stand against Channel One and apparently several other issues that the mainstream is choosing to accept."

"Isn't that my choice?" Jade's voice rose.

Tanner leaned back in his chair and watched her. So some things hadn't changed. She was still a fighter.

"Yes and no. If you were a single parent, no one would have a problem with your decisions to defend your faith. But . . ."

Jade's face fell and Tanner could see the regret. "Since I'm married it's different, right?"

"Right." Matt crossed his arms. "Now two parents are involved. Your husband was able to convince the judge that his tolerant, accepting mind-set made him a better parent than you."

"So why not force us to split custody? Why take him away from me?"

Tanner stepped back into the conversation. "Because parents like you have become a danger to the system. You teach your child biblical truths and clear-cut lessons on right and wrong, and suddenly, in their eyes, you've brought up a clone, another voter among the masses who isn't politically correct." He rested his elbows on the table and looked at Jade. He'd had time to catch his breath. They could talk about their past later. "At the same time, you deny your husband the chance to raise the boy with a liberal mind-set."

Jade shifted her gaze back to Matt's. "Why is his way better than mine?"

Tanner answered, forcing Jade to look at him again. "Because, like Matt said, public opinion has it that people strong in faith are dangerous, that we're hateful."

Jade's eyes locked on his. *"We're?"*

Tanner felt as if he'd been slapped by the challenge in her tone. "Yes. You and Matt and I. Everyone at the CPRR has a deep and devoted faith."

Her gaze fell to her hands. "I wasn't sure."

What is she saying, Lord? What's happened to her?

Trust in the Lord with all your heart and lean

380

not on your own understanding. . . .

Tanner felt himself relax. Jade obviously had something against him, but there would be time later to talk about that. Now they needed to get through the interview.

The look in Tanner's eyes told Jade he was upset, and she found that disturbing. He hadn't cared for her anymore than he cared for the other women he'd been with. Why had he looked so pained since she opened the door?

He was asking her questions about Ty, about their relationship and daily routine. "How old did you say he was?"

Jade felt her heart rate double. Clearly Doris Eastman had kept her promise and told Tanner nothing about her pregnancy. Still, the answers to these questions were bound to make him wonder. "Ty's nine. He'll be ten in a few months."

Tanner started writing down the information, then his pen slowed. Stopped. He looked up at her, his gaze intent. "When's his birthday?"

Jade knew he was looking for more than a date. He wanted to know when she got pregnant. She considered making up her answer, but the dates had always convinced Jim. No point in lying about a detail that would eventually come out in court. "June 14. Almost nine months after Jim and I married." She hesitated, hating the look in Tanner's eyes. What right did he have to look so upset? It was his fault, after all. He was the one who had used her and lied to her. "Ty was three weeks early."

For a moment Tanner stared at her, and Jade could see the questions in his eyes. She could almost hear him asking her why, what had happened. If only he knew that his mother had told Jade everything about his sordid past and the children he cared nothing for. Tanner's heart was cold as stone, and Jade shivered at his nearness.

Tanner broke the lock they held on each other and scribbled something on the paper. *What was he doing? Calculating dates? Does he know, Lord?* She studied him, looking for any hint that he might doubt her story and think he was the child's father.

"Why don't you tell us about your community involvement. Start with the Channel One thing, since that's been most recent."

At Tanner's change of subject, Jade was caught off guard. So, he believed her. For some reason she felt herself growing angry with him. Did he really think she could leave his arms and so quickly sleep with another man if she hadn't been absolutely desperate? Didn't he for even a moment think Ty might be his son?

She could come up with just one answer: Tanner truly didn't care.

At the end of two hours, Matt suggested they break for lunch. "We can share the case precedents with you after we eat." He stood up and stretched.

Tanner looked at his calendar. "We need to schedule a press conference as soon as possible. The buzz in legal circles is that Judge Susan Wilder might hear the case."

"Is that good or bad?" Despite the emotional strain of being near Tanner, Jade was thankful for him and his staff. She would never have been able to fight this battle without them.

"Very bad. She's a blatantly liberal judge who enjoys making examples out of conservative Christians. I'll tell you more about her later, but pray we get someone else. In the meantime, like I said, we need a press conference so we can give the media a chance to hear your side."

"The press?" Jade felt a wave of alarm. What if they hated her? What if they found out the truth about Ty?

Tanner rocked back in his chair. "They already know about the story. If we ignore them, they'll assume you have deep, dark secrets in your closet."

Oh, Tanner, if you only knew. . . .

Matt was talking now. "Since you don't have anything to hide, this case is a prime example of religious persecution. If we want the media on our side, we need a press conference." Jade watched as Matt looked to Tanner, and she realized how highly Tanner's associate regarded him. Tanner took the cue. "We have to fly home tonight, but I could be back Monday."

"Monday's booked for me." Matt tilted his head thoughtfully. "But I could help from Los Angeles. Work the fax machines, send out data to the media, that kind of thing."

Tanner nodded and looked at Jade with a lopsided grin that caused her heart to skip a beat. The resemblance between Tanner and his son was uncanny, and Jade looked down nervously at her ringless fingers. "Well, Jade, it's up to you. We could set it for Monday afternoon. Then we'd have the morning to go over the questions you'll get that day. Does that work for you?"

It sounded like a nightmare. A picture formed in Jade's mind . . . Ty weeping and calling for her from the back of Jim's car, reaching for her as the car drove away. She gulped twice and the image disappeared.

"Yes," she said quietly. "It works for me."

Tanner stood and straightened his things. "Okay, then, let's head for lunch."

They worked through the meal and late into the afternoon until Tanner and Matt had to leave for the airport. As the hours passed, Jade had the increasing feeling Tanner wanted to talk to her alone. By the day's end, Matt must have picked up on it, too. When they were finished, he excused himself. "We have about five minutes, Tanner. I'll be out in the car."

There was no wink or grin, nothing inappropriate. But clearly he was giving them time alone together. Jade and Tanner stood uncomfortably near the door, their arms crossed.

God, help me. What will I say to him? How can I face him alone after so many years, so many of his lies?

Tanner spoke first. "It's been a long time, Jade." His eyes searched hers, and she looked away again.

"Yes."

"Are you well, other than the obvious trouble?"

"I'm fine." She looked at him quickly. "You?"

"Good. Lots of work, doing what I love."

He hesitated. "I'm getting married this summer."

Something like an arrow pierced her heart and stuck there. Her gaze dropped briefly as she struggled for the right words. *Why, Lord? Why does he affect me like this after all he did to me?* She steadied herself. "I'm . . . happy for you, Tanner. Really." She glanced at him but refused to maintain eye contact.

Jade had taken a dozen detours on the path of life where Tanner was concerned so that he might never find her and Ty. But the path went both ways. Now, looking at him, she knew that even if for some reason she wanted to find a way back to him, she couldn't have. Not then, when they were living on opposite sides of the country, and not now, with him inches from her. She had driven out his memory, and she had no intention of allowing it to haunt her again.

Tanner studied her and for a moment he was silent. "Why'd you do it, Jade?" When he spoke, there was something different in his voice, something that made her hurt inside despite her convictions. Tanner reached out and gently lifted her chin so she had no choice but to look in his eyes.

Tears stung at hers and she felt a lump gathering in her throat. How could any man be such a good liar? Even now he refused to be honest with her. Clearly he did not think she knew about his past, the children he'd fathered and the others he'd helped get rid of.

"Answer me, Jade. Why?"

"It's a long story."

Tanner's eyes shone, and Jade wasn't sure if he was about to cry or to yell at her. "I was coming back for you. Didn't you believe me?"

Jade had the impulse to lean over and slap him. Didn't she *believe* him? If only he knew. She didn't believe anything he said. "I guess not."

"By the time I got home you were gone." Tanner exhaled slowly. "I looked, called around. But no one had any idea who you'd married. Your father wouldn't tell me a thing."

Jade's head was spinning. What was he talking about? Her father had never mentioned Tanner's phone call. She had always believed he'd never tried to find her, all of which had only verified everything his mother had told her in the first place. They had slept together and so he was through with her. He hadn't called once since he returned to the United States. At least that's what she'd always thought. "My dad never told me. . . ."

Tanner raked his fingers through his hair, his eyes angrier than she'd ever seen them before. "You could have called *me*, Jade, told me what happened. You knew where to find me."

"But . . ." Jade felt her resolve melting, and she steeled herself against him. She would not tell him. There was no point telling him the truth — that she knew about the other women. What would it prove now? They had their own lives, and this meeting was about her son, not the relationship they shared that long ago summer.

"But what?" Tanner took a step closer, and Jade saw how desperately he wanted answers.

"Nothing. You need to go. Matt'll be waiting."

Tanner's eyes were damp, searching hers, and for a moment Jade thought he might break down and cry. Instead he turned and collected his things. Before walking out of the room, he stopped and studied her one last time. "We'll be spending a lot of time together on this case, and I don't want our past to get in the way."

Jade shook her head, again unable to meet his gaze.

"But sometime, when you're ready . . . I want to know what happened. You owe me at least that much."

She hung her head and said nothing.

"Hey . . ." Tanner's tone was softer and she finally met his gaze. "I'm sorry about all this. I'm going to do whatever I can to get your little boy back for you."

"I know." She whispered the words and stared at Tanner a moment longer. "Thanks."

"Monday?"

Jade nodded. Tanner reached out and gently squeezed her arm. A show of support, the same one he'd given her the day before he left, just before they started kissing and . . .

She forced her mind to stop. He was not the person he seemed to be. He never had been. Besides, he was engaged to someone else now. Whoever the woman was, let her deal with his past.

His hand remained on her arm, and she felt herself stiffen under his touch. He seemed to notice and let go, taking one step backward, then heading for the door. "Bye . . ."

"Bye."

She stood there long after she heard his car pull away, paralyzed by the nearness of him, furious and flustered all at the same time. Saturday would be her first supervised visit with Ty, and if she found a way to get through that, she would have Monday to deal with. First, a private meeting with Tanner, and then a press conference to show the nation that despite previous reports she really was a fit mother. Even if she was a Christian.

Help me, Lord. Help me.

In that moment she was overwhelmed by the sum of it, and slowly, like a sandcastle giving way to one relentless wave after another, she sank to the floor. When her body was little more than a heap of broken dreams, gasping for direction in a world that had gone utterly dark, she did the only thing she could do. The only thing she had left.

She prayed.

Twenty-Seven

The tortillas were warm and moist, the chicken tender, and the strolling mariachi singers brought a festive atmosphere to the dining room. Clearly the women in Tanner's life were having a wonderful time, running over details of the coming wedding and predicting the number of guests who would attend.

Invitations were set to go out in two months.

Tanner bit into a rolled up fajita and wondered why — if everything were so wonderful — he was unable to get Jade's face from his mind. Why he had been unable to pay attention to the conversation?

"Are you listening, Tanner? Your mother wondered if you were going to invite any friends from law school." Leslie set her fork down and stared at him. She was the only person he knew whose lipstick could withstand Mexican food. Her expression was quizzical. "You're not listening, are you?"

Tanner wiped his mouth with a linen napkin. "I'm sorry. I have a lot on my mind."

Leslie rolled her eyes. "What else is new?"

Tanner's mother clucked her tongue. "What could be more important than the concerns of your beautiful fiancée?" She smiled at Leslie, and Tanner was struck again by how quickly they'd become friends. "Men can be so dense sometimes."

Leslie laughed, but Tanner could see she didn't think his lack of attention was funny. She directed her gaze at Tanner. "Really, don't you think you could listen for just a few minutes? Are your cases so important that you can't give me that?"

Images of Jade crowded his mind, and he blinked them back. "I said I'm sorry." Tanner reached for Leslie's hand and squeezed it. "Go easy on me, huh? I'll try to listen."

Both women looked at him, and eventually Leslie's expression softened. "Okay. Maybe it's my fault. I haven't asked you about your trip to Portland. Did you meet with the woman?"

Tanner's mother frowned. "What woman?"

"Jade Rudolph. She's the woman being sued for complete custody of her child. All because of her faith."

"Jade Rudolph?" Tanner watched his mother's color change and noticed her weathered hands begin to tremble. "You mean Jade Conner? From our old neighborhood?"

Tanner was confused. "Wait a minute . . . how did you know?" Back when he had first returned from Hungary his mother had sworn she did not know who Jade married or her new last name.

Leslie crossed her legs impatiently. "What girl from the old neighborhood?"

Tanner held up a hand to Leslie. "Hold on." He turned to his mother. "Answer me. How did you know her last name?"

His mother gave a small shrug and took a small bite of salad. When she had finished chewing, she set down her fork and spoke in a calm voice. "You can't expect me to remember that, Tanner. I have no idea. Someone must have told me." She paused. The color was returning to her face. "I do keep in touch with people in Virginia, you know."

Tanner shot his mother a look that said they would discuss the matter later. She had known how desperately he wanted to find Jade. She should have told him the moment she knew. He glanced at his fiancée and saw she was still waiting for an explanation. "Jade was a friend of mine growing up. We . . . spent time together one summer about ten years ago."

Leslie raised one perfectly arched eyebrow. "What exactly does that mean."

"Nothing." His mother waved her hand as if she was shooing away a fly. "The girl up and married someone else the minute Tanner left. They were just friends."

Tanner felt his blood beginning to boil. He did not need his mother answering for him. He leveled his gaze at her, hoping she could read the message in his eyes. "If you don't mind, mother, I'll explain the situation."

"There was no situation —"

"Mother!" The musicians strolled past their table singing a cheery rendition of "La Bamba."

"Fine. You tell it." His mother cast a glance at Leslie and returned to her salad.

Tanner looked at Leslie. How could he explain Jade to a woman he wasn't even sure he loved? How could she possibly understand what had happened that summer between him and Jade when he didn't understand it himself. "Jade and I were very close that summer."

Leslie's other eyebrow lifted in surprise.

"Is that right? And she's the woman you're representing in this big Portland case?"

"Her husband is suing her for complete custody of their child. It's a national case, bound to set precedence for years to come. Yes, she's the woman being sued."

"That's nice." Leslie tried to keep her tone light, but Tanner could see the concern in her eyes. "I'm here making wedding plans while you'll be running back and forth to some old girlfriend. Does she know you're engaged?"

Tanner met Leslie's stare straight on. "I told her about us, and don't worry. Jade is not interested in me. If she were, she would have called me years ago. She knew where to find me."

His mother had finished her salad. She pushed her bowl carefully to the side. "How many children does Jade have these days?"

Tanner thought the question strange. "One. Why?"

Again his mother's color paled considerably. "How old?"

Why was she suddenly interested in Jade? Just moments ago she was busy convincing Leslie that he and Jade had never been more than friends. "She has a boy. He's going to be ten this year."

His mother coughed hard and was forced

to take a drink of water to settle her throat. "Ten?"

"Yes, Mother. Why do you ask?"

His mother took another sip of water, and her nerves seemed to settle considerably. "Seems a child that old should be able to decide for himself which parent he wants to live with."

"That's not the way the courts see it."

Leslie sighed impatiently. "Can we stop talking about Miss Portland and get back to the planning? Neither of you seems to have any idea how much goes into a wedding. We're only a few months away here and still we haven't . . ."

Jade and her son and whatever importance the case held in his life were forgotten as the two women in his life resumed chattering about florists and videographers and the correct layout of the ballroom where the reception would be held. Tanner watched Leslie, the way she appeared to be including him and his mother in the discussion when in truth she was *telling* them the plans. Her plans.

But that wasn't unusual. Leslie usually found a way to get what she wanted.

He remembered the early days of their relationship. Leslie was funny and charming and witty. She understood his place in the public eye and would work to enhance his image at every turn. Tanner was sure she was a believer, even if he wasn't completely convinced of her commitment to God. His feelings for her weren't what they had been for Jade, but then nothing would ever feel like that. He was older now, and the timing was right. Leslie had his best interest at heart. That was enough, wasn't it?

Tanner thought back to the night they'd gotten engaged. Hadn't that been Leslie's doing, also? He remembered driving her to dinner at the Charthouse in Malibu and thinking that one day, perhaps, he'd like to marry her. Not that night; not anytime soon. But someday. Somehow, though, through the course of conversation at dinner, they'd wound up engaged. In the hours afterward he hadn't been sure exactly how it had happened. They had started talking about the future, and before the conversation was finished, they were engaged.

Tanner had been happy enough about the arrangement. It was what he wanted, too. At least that's what he'd told himself a hundred times since.

But watching Leslie now he realized she had probably come to the Charthouse that night determined to advance their relationship. In many ways Leslie didn't need him.

She would host the reception, welcome the guests. Of all the roles she played, she was most excited about being Mrs. Tanner Eastman. That was good, wasn't it? A woman should be proud of the man she was about to marry.

Tanner stared at his plate, pushed his fork around in his fajita and drifted back in time. He couldn't get Jade's face out of his mind, the distance in her eyes and the way she had avoided making eye contact with him. What had he done to make her hate him so?

As the women continued their discussion, agreeing on elements of the wedding that Tanner wasn't even aware of, he was lost in a sea of memories. He and Jade finding each other again at the supervisor's meeting, he and Jade walking along the Cowlitz River, he and Jade sitting on the edge of his bed . . .

A strange sensation coursed through his veins, and he felt his face grow hot. His heart remembered, but that wasn't all. Clearly his body remembered, also.

Lord, I need your help here. Make me forget her. What we did was wrong. She's changed, moved on. Help me love the woman before me, the woman you've given me.

Tanner said the prayer silently, but his

tone was desperate all the same.

Because no matter what Leslie said, no matter how many plans were decided, regardless of how soon the wedding was, there was one undeniable fact.

He was still in love with Jade.

Doris Eastman had no trouble doing two things at once. And so she continued her conversation with Leslie, agreeing and keeping in step as Tanner's gorgeous fiancée chattered on about the wedding. But at the same time — without anyone at the table realizing it — she watched her son.

He was with them in body only. His mind, his heart were three-thousand miles away in Portland, Oregon. Just as they'd been for years after Jade got married.

How was it possible? How had the Conner girl found a way back into his life after so many years? And the child . . . ?

Doris had been having chest pains lately, and though she hadn't told anyone, she had a feeling they were brought on by stress. She wanted Tanner's wedding to be perfect. Fitting for a man of his public stature. Naturally, the preparations could be stressful, especially when they were already so short of time.

Doris had grown accustomed to dismissing the pains. Stress was curable. A little change of diet would work wonders.

But the news Tanner had just revealed brought new meaning to the word stress. The moment Tanner mentioned Jade Rudolph, Doris's heart responded by seizing. She'd almost blown it by giving away the fact that she knew Jade's married name. Her father had known that much, and the second time she called him she caught him sober. Doris knew Jade was married to a man named Jim Rudolph, a school teacher in Portland, Oregon.

But she'd never let the fact slip until tonight.

Nitroglycerin. That was all she needed. A little medicine for the heart pains.

Remember the height from which you have fallen. Repent! Or I will come and remove your lampstand. . . .

Doris massaged her eyebrows. There it was again. Another strange verse from the Bible resounding in her mind for no apparent reason at all. Verses like that had been assaulting her with almost the same regularity as the chest pains. Verses about getting right with God and repenting and asking God to give her a clean heart.

Doris was sick of such verses. Nothing but hogwash! She had no need of repentance.

The lies she'd told Jade and Tanner she'd told for their own good. They didn't belong together. Certainly God didn't want her to repent of looking out for her son. And what if God *did* want that? Doris had always done things her own way. Including the manner in which she exercised her faith.

God would simply have to understand.

She forced herself to listen to Leslie's ramblings, tried to appear interested. But her chest was so tight she could barely catch her breath. Rays of pain radiated up her neck into the fleshy underneath portion of her jaw. *Calm down. Get ahold of yourself.*

The mandate did not work. Her heart began racing, and she felt a thin layer of perspiration break out on her forehead. She could pretend all evening, but the truth demanded her attention like a relentless, barking dog.

Jade had one child — a boy, ten years old. Tanner's son. Apparently she had kept her promise and told Tanner nothing about the boy's identity. Doris could hardly believe it had come to this. Tanner was representing Jade in a custody battle wherein Jade's husband wanted full custody because of Jade's faith. And all along the child wasn't even related to Jade's husband.

The child was Tanner's.

She studied her son and saw he was distraught. Oh, he put on a good face, and he knew how to respond to Leslie in a way that kept her from noticing. But Doris knew. Tanner was thinking about Jade, wondering why she'd never called. Doris would have done anything to take the pain from her son's eyes. If only he could get through this dreadful case and forget about her. Didn't he understand how much better his life was without her, how good Leslie was for him?

Doris held her breath and willed the chest pains away. What if Tanner asked Jade the next time they were together? What if they compared stories?

She could barely tolerate the thought. Again the chest pains increased, and Doris understood why. Despite her son's deep faith and strong convictions, if Tanner found out the truth about what had happened ten years ago, he might never forgive her.

In fact, he might actually hate her.

Twenty-Eight

Jade spent Saturday morning reading the first chapter of James from the Bible, verses about considering it joy when facing trials and how the testing of one's faith develops perseverance. She knew the Scriptures were true. They had pulled her through when she and Jim first married.

For much of the past decade she had tried to forget what had happened when she showed up on Jim Rudolph's doorstep that day. But now, with her life falling apart and her husband living with another woman, Jade wanted to remember. As though recalling her every move might help her realize where she'd gone wrong.

Every part of her body had been shaking while she waited for Jim to answer the door that day. His shock lasted only a moment before a lazy grin spread across his face. "I always knew you'd come to your senses one day, Jade Conner. . . . Tell me, have you changed your mind about my offer?"

Jade could still hear his words echoing in the hallways of her mind. Going against everything she knew to be true and right and good, she entered Jim's house that day. He didn't ask for an explanation; didn't seem to want one. He'd been eating a tuna fish sandwich, and his breath was heavy but that didn't stop him. The moment the door shut behind them, he pulled Jade close and kissed her. It was a kiss that brought tears to Jade's eyes for want of Tanner and his kisses. But Tanner had lied to her; Jim was all she had left.

"You're not kissing me back." Jim had stared at her. "Why'd you come if you weren't sure about me, Jade?"

She remembered nearly every detail of that first afternoon. She had apologized and forced herself to return his kiss. Jim did most of the talking after that. Jade recognized his desire, and when he suggested a quick wedding, she agreed.

On her honeymoon night, as Jim undressed her, Jade had felt disgusted, worthless, a shell of the woman she'd been only a week earlier. Jim had whispered, "You're so beautiful, Jade, I can't believe you're finally mine." And while he spoke, Jade packed what was left of her heart and hid it away so that all Jim took from her that night was her body.

When they were finished, he turned to her and studied her. "I always knew you'd come to me one day, Jade. I've wanted you since the first day I saw you, and deep down I know you've always felt the same way." He kissed her again. "I promise to make you happy."

There were other times in their marriage when Jim uttered similar promises to her, and Jade believed he had intended to keep them. But she'd never been comforted by his words. She remembered being over-whelmed by the deepest sense of grief. Almost as if someone had died. . . .

Only now did the feeling make sense. The death had been her own.

Jade drew a deep breath and remembered that though she'd been suffering morning sickness the day after her wedding, she had managed to hide it from her new husband. After that, they settled into a routine. He worked; she looked for a job, and when she didn't greet him with a smile or seem to enjoy their time in bed, he would look at her, an odd sadness in his eyes.

So Jade worked harder. After a month, she was so good at acting, Jim seemed to believe her when she told him she was happy. About that time, she broke the news about being pregnant.

A strange look had crossed Jim's face, something hard and a bit frightening. For a moment, Jade was sure he knew the truth. Instead he just smiled. "Any baby of yours is bound to be beautiful, Jade. Let's make sure we keep an eye on your weight."

The subtle attacks on her faith began about a month later.

She could see him still, shaking his head at her for reading her Bible.

"Myths and fables, Jade. Surely you know that. . . ." He put his hands on her shoulders, massaging them. "Of course, some of it makes sense. Doesn't the Bible say something about the wife's body belonging to her husband?"

She didn't think Jim meant harm with his comments. Not really. Faith in God was simply foreign to him. Since she didn't want to argue, Jade had never known what to say, how to answer him. Usually he didn't give her enough time anyway. He'd tug the Bible from her hands, smiling at her. "How about focusing less time on this little book and more on your husband?"

She grew frustrated with herself at the memory. Why had she rushed into marriage in the first place? So that Ty would have a father, a real home with two parents, and dinner that wasn't provided by the government? In light of the crisis she was facing now, the reasons seemed ridiculously unimportant.

Why was I so dense, Lord? Why didn't I see how poorly matched we were. How far apart we were? And how much those differences would hurt us? She stretched her legs across her bed and eased down into the pillows. There was no denying what had happened. She had known Jim wasn't right for her, recognized it all along. That's why she turned down Jim's proposal. But when Tanner betrayed her, she listened to her own reasoning rather than listening to the Lord. In the process, she had hurried into the marriage with Jim. *Why didn't I wait on you, God?*

She felt tears form as the question hung in her mind. There were other times, moments that made being married to Jim tolerable. They had quiet nights with rented movies and popcorn and conversations about his students. Those had ended in the last few years . . . a fact Jade hadn't understood until now.

One thing she did know; God hated divorce. It was his will that they remain married and that somehow, through some miracle, Jim might turn his heart to God and change his ways.

Even now Jade desperately wished Jim would hear God's voice and change his mind. The Lord could breathe man into existence. Surely, he could heal her hurt and Jim's betrayal and change him into a believing, godly husband.

Jade set her Bible down and slipped her hands behind her head. Now that she'd had time to think about it, Jade realized he'd probably been having an affair with Kathy for more than a year. Before that, she was sure he'd been faithful. Whatever the reason, she'd held some sort of spell over Jim since their teenage days.

"Sometimes I hate your faith, Jade," he told her once. "But there's something about you, something I've always wanted to call my own. And now that I have you, I won't let you go. Not ever."

It was Kathy Wittenberg who'd put him over the edge. Whatever he felt for Kathy had served to break the spell. In that woman's company, Jim had begun seeing Jade's community involvement as more than an annoyance.

She wanted to believe there was still hope for their marriage. But lately, especially during her quiet times with God, Jade had begun to accept her situation for what it was. Jim wasn't coming back; and if she didn't get significant help from Tanner and the CPRR, Jim and Kathy could wind up with Ty.

Jade turned and gazed out her bedroom window. The pain she felt wasn't about Jim; it was about missing Ty, missing the stable life she had always wanted for him. Jim's affair hadn't hurt her the way it might have. After all, he had never owned even a small piece of her heart, and he couldn't break what he didn't have.

Not like Tanner had.

She pulled on a pair of new jeans, a white turtleneck, and a sweatshirt with the words Shamrock Elementary printed on the front. Jim had taken an apartment across town near the high school. Ty had called each night during the past week and informed her that he had his own bedroom and spent much of his time there.

"Dad's girlfriend is here all the time. They sit on the couch and do all this mushy stuff, so I just go to my bedroom every night and read and talk to you. Mom, I hate this so much."

In many ways, Jade felt like they were both in prison, unable to be together, at the mercy of a man who did not love Ty and a legal system that no longer valued faith. A system that, in fact, rebelled against it. Jade sprayed her favorite perfume and ran a brush through her hair. She always took care of herself, and today would be no exception. Even if her world was crashing in all around her.

She was tired of thinking about Jim and what had gone wrong in their marriage. With an hour left before her scheduled visit, she curled up in a comfortable chair nestled in the corner of her bedroom and gazed out the window. The tulips were making their way out of the ground, and in a few weeks they would dot the Northwest with a brilliance that seemed almost artificial.

The landscape faded, and suddenly Jade's mind drifted back to the classroom, remembering Tanner the way he'd looked a few days earlier. Why had he acted so strangely? He was the one who'd lied, the one who'd gotten other women pregnant and shunned his responsibility as a father. How could he question the fact that she hadn't called him?

She sighed and watched a hawk drift over the makeshift baseball field across the street. His flight lasted less than a minute before he swept down, grabbed a mouse in his talons, and soared back to his perch in the trees.

That was her. The helpless field mouse. There for the taking for whatever hawk might choose to sweep overhead. Last week the hawk had been Jim and his attorney, then the judge, and now Tanner. It didn't really matter. Now that she'd lost Ty, Jade would gladly take a ride in the talons of any bird of prey. If it meant getting Ty back, she'd do whatever God asked of her. Even spending time with Tanner.

Lord, if only you'll help me survive it all.

There was only silence.

Are you there, God? Jade closed her eyes and tried to hear his voice. Finally, faintly a single Scripture ran through her mind: *I know the plans I have for you . . . plans to give you hope and a future.* Jade sighed and felt her eyes fill with tears. That wasn't the voice of God. It was memories of her past. Seeing Tanner had brought them to mind again, but clearly they did not apply to her situation now. Her future plans had evaporated like rain on an August afternoon. Life was nothing without Ty.

Jade stood and wiped her eyes dry. It was time. She was about to spend an hour with her son, and at that moment she didn't care that it would be in the presence of deputies. Before now, she and Ty had never been apart longer than a night, and no matter the circumstances all she wanted was to hold him and feel him in her arms again.

She made the drive quickly and saw that the officers were waiting. One of them rolled down the squad car window and motioned for her to join them. She parked and did as they asked.

"We don't think the boy's in any danger, ma'am." The older deputy did the talking. "Crazy case, if you ask me."

Jade shifted positions. "What are you saying? Can I visit with him alone?"

The deputy shook his head. "Nope. 'Fraid not. But how about we wait right here? Catch up on our paperwork. You and the boy can sit in your car or on the grass here. Wherever you like. We'll stay out of your way."

Jade's heart swelled. These men were on her side. They saw how ridiculous the situation was. She smiled at them through eyes clouded with tears. "Thank you."

The older officer tipped his head and leaned back in his seat, directing his attention to the paperwork on his lap. Drawing a deep breath, Jade turned, walked up to the apartment, and rang the doorbell. It took Ty just seconds to fling the door open and run into Jade's arms.

"Mom!" Her son's arms flew around her neck.

"Oh, honey, I've missed you so much." She forced herself not to cry. Ty was so happy to see her she didn't want to give him a reason to be sad.

They sat together on the porch step, Jade with her arm around Ty as he told her about school and basketball and his father's girlfriend. "She's not even pretty, Mom."

"Is that right?" Jade grinned at her son.

"Oh, man, you should see her. Big nose. Big teeth. I think she teaches biology or something. Probably spends her days mopping up frog guts."

Jade laughed. It felt so good to be with Ty again, and it made her more determined than ever. She would work with Tanner, and very soon she would regain custody of her son. For now, Jim was paying the mortgage and sending her enough money to survive. But eventually — after she won the case — she and Ty would move to another state, and she would have to get a job. That way she wouldn't have to rely on Jim, and after a year or two he was bound to give up the custody issue. Then she could have Ty all to herself.

The hour flew by, and long before she was ready to leave, Jim poked his head out.

"Time's up."

Jade wanted to ask him when he'd become such an attentive father that he might actually miss an hour of Ty's time. She wanted to shout a dozen retorts at him and kick the door shut. Instead, she just nodded.

Give me the right words, Lord. Everything I say he'll write down and pass along to his attorney. Help me, please.

She felt a peace wash over her. "Thank you, Jim." She smiled at her husband and turned to Ty. "I'm sorry, honey, what were you saying?"

Her composure seemed to irritate Jim, and he raised his voice. "I said time's up. Now get out of here before I have the deputies haul you out in handcuffs."

Ty began crying, and he stood up, facing Jim. His fists were clenched, and his face was red with anger. "Leave her alone!"

Jim opened the door wider and raised his hand threateningly over Ty. Just as he was about to strike the boy, he realized the deputies were watching him. Easing back into the house, Jim hissed at Ty from a place just out of view of the patrol car. "Don't you sass off to me, boy, you hear?"

Ty was sobbing harder, and he said nothing as Jim disappeared back into the house. Instead, he turned to Jade and wrapped his arms around her neck. "Don't leave me here, please, Mom."

Jade tried to speak, but a lump had formed in her throat. She blinked back tears and struggled to find her voice. "It's okay, honey." She ran a hand over his back and thought about the last time they'd said good-bye. Was this how it was going to be every Saturday until she got him back? And what if Tanner couldn't make it happen? What if she didn't get her son back? She closed her eyes tightly and held him close. "You can come home soon, Ty. I promise."

The boy was still crying, but he pulled away, his eyes pleading with her. "Dad said I can't ever go home. He said he was going to take you apart for the whole world to see."

A flicker of anger became a hot, burning flame in Jade's heart. "He has no right telling you that, honey. It isn't true."

Ty hung his head. "He says a lot of bad things about you, Mom."

Jade felt like she was suffocating. *Help me, God. This is your problem, not mine. I can't deal with it alone.* She drew a deep breath. "I'm sorry he's doing that. But you know the truth, right?"

Ty wiped his eyes and seemed to catch his breath. "Don't worry, Mom. I know you a lot better than that."

"Okay. Let's pray before I go, huh?"

Ty sat beside her again and held her hand as Jade led them in prayer, begging God to end their separation and to let the truth be known. When they were finished, Ty hugged her, kissed her, and promised to call each night.

"Hurry, Mom, please. I want to come home."

Ty kissed her one last time and then vanished behind the apartment door. Jade walked back to her car, waved to the officers, and slipped behind the wheel. There, safely away from Jim and Kathy and Ty and the deputies, Jade cried as if her heart would break.

Ty's pained expression and the way he'd begged her not to leave haunted her as she drove home. If Jim wanted to fight, then she was going to have to be a worthy opponent. Especially when the stakes were so high. As she parked the car and went inside she begged God to give her a way out, show her a way in which she might be more effective.

Pray, my daughter. Bring it to me in prayer.

Of course. Jade pulled out her Bible study list and began making phone calls. They would have to meet the following evening because Jade would be busy the rest of the week. Any other time they might have postponed the gathering altogether. But the group hadn't met since she'd lost custody of Ty. These were faithful women, friends who would jump to her assistance and pray without ceasing until the matter was resolved and Ty was home where he belonged. If ever she needed the prayers of her friends, it was now.

One by one the women in the Bible study group arrived at her house until finally Jade was ready to begin. When they were all arranged in a circle, she drew a shallow breath and began speaking. "You've all seen the newspapers?" She looked at the faces around her and saw compassion there.

"So it's all true . . . ?" Susan leaned forward, her elbows on her knees. "They took Ty because you're a Christian?"

"That's not what they're saying. The judge said my extreme views were unhealthy for a young child and that he'd be safer with his father."

Jackie sat across from Jade, and tears filled her eyes. "That means they took Ty because of your faith. It's the same thing. What they're basically saying is that the courts feel it's okay to take our children away if we choose to stand up for what we believe in."

Jade nodded. "That's right."

"Are you doing okay financially?" Jackie hadn't asked before, but Jade didn't mind discussing the issue with these women.

"I'm fine. Jim's paying the mortgage and sending me enough money to survive. Maybe just to make himself look good, but at least I'm okay that way." She wanted to ask them to pray about the situation with Tanner, but she wasn't sure what to say. None of the women knew about Tanner and the role he'd played in her life ten years ago. Still, she needed their prayers on every side, and she thought quickly how best to ask.

"There's going to be a press conference tomorrow, is that right?" Jackie's face was tear streaked, masked with concern.

"Right. And there's something else. The man who's going to represent me is Tanner Eastman."

Lydia perked up. "I've heard of him. He's perfect for this kind of case."

Jackie nodded. "A Christian man, brilliant and full of integrity. Sounds like an answer to prayer."

"He's the perfect guy if you ask me." Susan smiled. She was a single mother and often commented on how few unmarried Christian men there were. "Single, gorgeous, and sold out to God. Maybe you could introduce me."

Jade knew Susan was joking, but she couldn't bring herself to laugh. If only they knew the truth. . . . "Tanner and I were friends a long time ago, and, well, just pray about that, too. That I'll have the strength to get through it."

Susan squirmed uncomfortably in her chair and seemed to be fighting herself to keep from asking a question. In a matter of seconds she lost the battle and spoke out. "Were you and Tanner . . . you know . . . did you date him?"

Jade shook her head quickly. "Nothing like that. But there were some hard feelings. I don't want what happened in the past to play a part in this situation." She hung her head, and tears spilled from her eyes onto the legs of her jeans. "The only thing that matters is Ty. That's what the press conference is all about."

Jade saw that Susan wasn't convinced about the role Tanner had played in her life. Either way the discussion about Tanner was closed. Jade shifted her gaze to the other women and reached for a tissue from a nearby endtable. "Also please pray I say the right things in front of the cameras tomorrow. I need to maintain my stance on morality and faith and somehow avoid coming across as weird or different because of it."

The ladies nodded, and after a brief discussion they bowed their heads, joined hands, and prayed for Jade. That she would have comfort in the temporary loss of Ty, wisdom to speak with the reporters the next day, and strength to face Tanner.

They prayed for nearly an hour, and then the women went home, leaving Jade alone with her thoughts. In twelve hours she and Tanner would be together again, and she realized there was one thing the women hadn't prayed for that night. Because in light of everything that was happening so quickly around her, there was no way she could ask the Bible study group to pray for something she shouldn't have been struggling with in the first place. . . .

The feelings she still had for Tanner Eastman.

TWENTY-NINE

Tanner called that morning, and they agreed to meet at Starbucks at Jantzen Beach — an outdoor shopping mall in northwest Portland along the Columbia River. Jade wasn't hungry, and Starbucks had quiet tables so that she and Tanner could talk without being interrupted.

Jade arrived first and ordered a decaffeinated latte. Her heart was racing badly enough without adding caffeine to the mix. She chose a table situated in a windowless corner of the café. Starbucks was adjacent to a large bookstore, and customers were encouraged to browse through the shelves while sipping their coffee. Jade was certain no one would bother them there. The few customers who sat at tables generally stayed near the windows.

She took a sip of her coffee and stared at the front door. All morning she'd been plagued by a sense of impending doom.

Several times an hour this feeling had driven her to pray, seeking God's protection in whatever the day would bring. Still, she was tempted with the notion of finding Ty at school and heading for the Canadian border.

It was raining steadily outside, and Tanner swept into the coffeehouse wearing a business suit and a long, sleek raincoat. The girl behind the counter watched him and nudged her coworker. Jade rolled her eyes. Yes, Tanner still turned heads. Was he carrying on with a handful of women despite his engagement, or had he finally learned to be faithful? Either way she pitied his fiancée. If Tanner could abandon his own children, he was bound to bring her nothing but heartache.

Tanner spotted her and quickly ordered a coffee. When he had his drink, he joined her at the table. Again his eyes looked troubled.

"Hi."

"Hi." Jade glanced at her coffee and felt her stomach begin to churn.

"How'd the visit with Ty go?"

Jade felt a stab of fear at the sound of Ty's name on Tanner's lips. *Get me through this, God, please.* "It was okay. Too fast. Too impersonal . . . deputies watching us the whole time."

Tanner sighed. "Did you write down anything Ty said?"

Jade pulled a typed sheet of notes from her purse. "Right here."

A smile lit Tanner's face, and Jade's heart skipped a beat. Why did he still have that effect on her? "That was fast."

"My son's at stake. It's not like I have anything else to do."

Tanner stared at her solemnly. "We'll do everything we can to get it admitted during the hearing." He reached across the table to take the notes from her. As he did, their fingers brushed against each other, and Jade jerked back, dropping the paper on the table. Tanner studied her for a moment, and then reached for the paper, opening it and reading slowly. When he was finished he said, "This is great, Jade. Pray they'll let us use it."

She hung her head. *He's reading things his own son said. This is too close, Lord. Help me.*

When Jade said nothing, Tanner moved the paper to his pocket. "I have good news and bad news."

Jade sat up straighter. "I can't take any more bad news. Give me the bad news first."

Tanner frowned. "I found out this morning. Judge Susan Wilder has been assigned the case. It's a done deal."

Jade felt the sting of fresh tears. "Great. What else can go wrong?"

Tanner nodded. "She's not good for the case, but you've got to remember, Jade, God is in control here, not Judge Wilder."

Oh, please, Tanner, stop the hypocritical religious drivel. Jade was irritated with him. A man who'd abandoned his own children had little room to talk about God being in control. "What's the good news?"

"The press conference is set. CNN's covering the whole thing. All the networks, too."

Jade looked up and felt her pulse quicken. "It's that big?"

Tanner slid his chair in closer and leaned his elbows on the table. "Jade, this is national news. A mother's never lost custody of her child because of her faith."

"What are they going to ask me?"

"They know about your involvement in community and school issues. How you had magazines removed from store shelves and books eliminated from the library."

"The magazines had pictures of some evil guy sacrificing animals on stage."

"I know."

"And the books had story lines about kids

killing their teachers and classmates." Jade had done the right thing by taking on those battles, and she would do it again if the opportunity arose. If someone didn't take a stand, the children would pay the price. Jade wasn't about to let that happen.

Tanner's expression softened. "I know all that, Jade. I'm just telling you the media knows, too." He hesitated. "I might think you're a hero for doing those things. But for the most part, the media thinks in terms of freedoms. Freedom of speech, freedom of expression, that kind of thing. They see pulling magazines and books off shelves as censorship."

Jade sighed. "And that makes me look extreme."

"Right."

"So what do I do?"

Tanner leaned back in his chair and sipped his coffee. "You remain calm and pleasant. Discuss everything from the perspective of Ty and your intention to protect him. We want the press to see you as a concerned mother, one who cares deeply for her son. Not some angry radical Christian who next week might organize a hit on an abortion clinic."

Jade stirred her coffee. The only thing that angered her was losing Ty. Certainly she could do what Tanner asked, remain calm and pleasant and avoid sounding defensive. "What if they try to trick me?"

Tanner uttered a laugh. "You can count on that much. They're looking for a snappy sound bite they can play and replay on the news tonight. Something where you fly off the handle and declare them all ACLU-card-carrying liberals bent on the destruction of family values and churches in general."

Jade couldn't help but smile at his example. "So whatever I do, don't get angry."

"Whatever you do, don't say something that could be taken out of context. No long pauses or lengthy explanations. They'll cut what you say and use it to fit their storyboard."

Jade wondered if she could remember it all. "Nothing extreme; no lengthy pauses."

"Exactly."

"What about my faith? If they ask me, should I quote the Bible, or is that off limits?"

"Everyone knows you're a Christian. The story has been discussed and replayed in newspapers across the country all week. There's no point in backing down now." He paused. "Besides, I don't think that would please the Lord."

Jade wanted to laugh at him. Here was a man whose children were growing up without their father. Who was he to remind her of what it meant to please the Lord? She forced herself to remember that whatever Tanner's personal shortcomings, he was the expert when it came to these types of legal matters. "I never intended to back down." She met his gaze straight on. "I only wanted to know if there were things I should avoid saying."

Tanner studied her and set down his coffee. "Jade, can I ask you something?"

For the first time since seeing Tanner again she didn't want to run from him. She wanted to take him on face to face and find out why he had lied to her all those years ago. "Anything."

"Why are you angry with me?"

She set her drink down and crossed her arms. "I'm struggling with a lot of things, here, Tanner." *Don't cry. Whatever you do, don't cry.*

He sighed and raked his fingers through his hair, a gesture he'd done since he was a boy back in Williamsburg.

"What did I ever do to you?" He sounded sad, and he kept his eyes locked on hers. When she could stand it no longer, she looked away.

"I don't want to talk about it."

"I loved you, Jade. I wanted to marry you. I go off to Hungary for a few months, and when I come home my mother tells me you married someone else. And now *you're* mad at *me?*"

"I said I don't want to talk about it." If he pushed much more, she would tell him the truth: that she knew everything there was to know about his past.

"I don't care what you want, Jade. We need to talk." Tanner set his cup down hard, and Jade looked up at him. "I got off the plane from Hungary, and you know what I did?"

Jade waited.

"I looked all over that airport for you. I sent you a ticket, and I thought you'd be there."

More lies. "There was no ticket, Tanner. My father would have told me."

"Oh sure, just like he told you about my phone calls."

Jade considered that. "Why would you send me a ticket? You hadn't written the whole time you were there. You expected me to look for a ticket in the mail when I hadn't heard from you in two months?"

Tanner's face twisted. "I wrote you. Every other day I mailed off another letter to you."

"And I'm supposed to believe they all got lost in the mail?"

"No, try asking your father. Maybe he never gave them to you."

A strange sensation began working its way from the back of Jade's head down her spine. *It doesn't matter if he wrote, he still lied to me about his past.* "That's not the point."

"What's that supposed to mean? I'm there at the airport, looking for you, expecting you to be there, and all I see is my mother. She tells me she has bad news. I was wrong about you, she says; you've married someone else."

Tears flooded Jade's vision, and she shaded her eyes with one hand.

"Do you know something, Jade; I didn't believe her. I had to call Kelso General to see if she was telling the truth. I didn't believe it until I talked to one of your coworkers, and she told me it was true; you'd married someone in Portland."

"That's my business, Tanner." Jade uncovered her eyes, her voice little more than a whisper.

His eyes blazed with angry frustration. "Okay, so it's your business, but couldn't you have called me, told me what happened? I thought you loved me, Jade. I'm gone three weeks, and you marry someone else? I didn't understand it then, and I still don't."

"Can we talk about something else?" Jade wiped her eyes and searched Tanner's face. She didn't want to tell him why she'd left. There was no point going back to that time in her life and risking the relationship she and Ty shared. If he ever found out about Ty, she'd be the loser. Mrs. Eastman had made that more than clear.

Tanner exhaled slowly and massaged his eyebrows. "Fine. But give me this."

"What?"

"After the press conference let me take you back to your house."

Jade took another sip of her coffee and noticed her hands were trembling. She didn't want to spend more time suffering in Tanner's presence than necessary. "What for?"

"So we can talk. I want to know what happened, Jade. I'm going on with my life, getting married, putting you behind me. But it's taken a long time, and I think you owe me an explanation. At least that much."

Jade sighed. Maybe if she could tell him the truth about what she knew, without telling him why she was at Doris Eastman's that afternoon in the first place. Maybe then he'd come clean about his past, never make the connection about Ty being his son, and leave her alone. "Fine. What time do you fly out?"

"Not till midnight. I'm taking the redeye back to Los Angeles."

Jade nodded. "Okay. But let's get through the press conference first."

They finished their cold coffees in silence and headed for the door. The media was set to meet them in the lobby of the Clackamas County Courthouse in two hours.

Forty-five members of the press showed up for the conference, and Tanner wished he could watch from a distance. He couldn't stop thinking about Jade and his hunch that there was something she wasn't telling him. Whatever it was it would have to wait. The media event was crucial to their case, and Tanner would have to maintain his concentration.

Tanner took his spot in front of the podium. He thanked them for coming and introduced the case by comparing it to conditions in the former Soviet Union.

"People in this country have never had to fear the government because of their faith. Religious freedom is something guaranteed each of us in the constitution. But here in Portland, in this very courthouse, a woman dedicated to her son has been stripped of her rights as a parent because of her faith."

Tanner made eye contact with each of the reporters, careful to keep his face at just the right distance from the dozen microphones taped to the podium. He still thrived in public situations, and he felt confident as he continued. "If we allow this case to stand, then I'll tell you where we're headed. Ten years from now this kind of custody arrangement will be commonplace, and the people who make up the backbone of this great nation will find themselves being rounded up and arrested for attending church on Sunday."

He paused and saw that eight national news cameras were focused on him. "We are here today to tell the people of this country that we will not stand by idly and watch our rights be stripped away. Mrs. Rudolph will win back custody of her son, and men and women who make up the heart of our nation will be able to sleep better at night. We will fight to maintain the rights promised us by our forefathers. And we will pray, as they did, that the United States courts wake up and recognize the error of their ways."

Tanner finished his opening comments and introduced Jade. He stepped away from the podium and watched her take his place. She looked innocent and utterly beautiful. But most of all she looked sincere. Tanner knew it wasn't an act. Jade — the Jade he remembered — was the genuine article.

He studied her and watched her make a few opening remarks, informing the press that she had gotten involved in community affairs as a way of protecting her son. She hit on each of the issues upon which she'd taken a public stand and explained simply that if she hadn't acted, the problem of immorality and violence among teenagers would only increase. Finally she showed them a few snapshots of her and Ty on various outings, sailing boats in a pond, singing together around a campfire.

The photos were something she hadn't showed Tanner, and he watched her in amazement. First the detailed notes, now the photos. He should have realized she'd do everything she could to help her case. He fought for religious freedom on a national level, but in many ways she'd been doing the same thing in her community.

When she finished speaking, the press pounced with questions about her beliefs and about whether she was in favor of censorship.

"Sometimes censorship is necessary. . . ."

From his position several feet away, Tanner cringed. She had done the very thing he had warned her not to do. *Sometimes censorship is necessary. . . .* He could hear the line played over the networks later that evening, and he wanted nothing more than to stop the cameras and give Jade a chance to answer the question again.

Her comment certainly wouldn't make many people sympathetic.

"But that doesn't mean I'm in favor of censorship across the board. Americans must maintain our right to free speech if we are to remain a strong nation. We wouldn't have Bibles if it weren't for freedom of speech." Jade was calm, but passionate at the same time. Tanner studied the reporters and saw they were still suspicious of her. Tanner wondered if they would get past her remark about censorship being necessary sometimes. By the hard looks on their faces, he doubted it.

"However, when magazines release unfit material on our children for their own financial gain, someone needs to stand up and fight against them. We must care more about our kids than to let them fall prey to the whims of consumerism masking itself in freedom of speech."

Tanner was awestruck. Jade's understanding of religious freedom was strong enough that she could easily take her place alongside him at the CPRR offices. *Way to go, Jade.* If only she hadn't slipped up that one time early on.

The press conference wound down, and when the last reporter left, Jade turned to Tanner. She was flushed and breathless. "Well?"

"You did great."

A look of panic flashed in her eyes. "How come you sound worried?"

Nearly everything Jade said had been brilliant. But that one line, the comment Jade had made about censorship, gnawed at Tanner's confidence.

"I sound worried because I am."

THIRTY

They stopped for pizza, and Jade waited in the car while Tanner picked up their order. The evening was beginning to feel too familiar, too much like it had felt when she and Tanner were together that summer. She wanted to be alone, turn on the television, see how the media would play up her interview.

But she figured she owed Tanner this one night to explain herself. Then he could admit his lies, make his apologies, and go back to Los Angeles where his fiancée waited. After that, they would have an easier time remaining on business terms throughout the proceedings, and Tanner wouldn't feel compelled to ask questions about their past.

He returned with the pizza, and Jade didn't have to ask what kind it was. It would be Hawaiian with olives. Just like the pizzas back in Kelso that summer. She stared out the passenger window and remained silent as they drove to Jantzen Beach where her car was still parked.

"I get the feeling you don't want me coming over." Tanner turned toward her and shut off his engine.

Jade shrugged and opened the car door. "We might as well get it over with."

"Look, if you don't want to —"

"No, I'm sorry." They'd come this far. Now she almost wanted to tell him the truth about what she knew. "I have a lot on my mind, but you're right. I think we should talk."

Tanner shrugged and started his engine again. "Okay. I'll follow you."

She climbed out, shut the door, and headed for her car. Fifteen minutes later they pulled up outside her home in Clackamas, a suburb in southeast Portland. They entered the house in silence.

"Nice." Tanner was making small talk, and Jade could tell he was uncomfortable. It was just before six, and Jade had no interest in making him feel at home. The news was about to come on.

"Thanks." She set out paper plates and napkins and moved into the TV room. "The news should be on in a minute."

Tanner helped himself to pizza and joined

her. "Try ABC first."

She turned the channel until she found it. A serious-looking anchor told viewers that there was more trouble in Yugoslavia. "But first, we'll update you on a story that is sweeping the nation. Last week Jade Rudolph lost custody of her only son because a Portland judge deemed her viewpoints too religious, too narrow and possibly damaging to the boy. Today, Ms. Rudolph staged a press conference in the Portland Municipal Court Building alongside her attorney, religious rights fighter Tanner Eastman."

The network cut to a live shot of Tanner and his opening remarks. While a reporter shared the voice-over summary, cameras moved on to a shot of Jade responding to the question about censorship.

"Sometimes censorship is necessary. . . ." They cut Jade's remarks there, and Tanner groaned. The reporter picked up with narrative that explained some of Jade's attempts to censor local markets and libraries. The anchor bridged to the next story by telling viewers that maybe the time had come to consider this type of thinking dangerous. Especially where children were concerned.

Jade felt her face grow hot. "How could

438

she? They took that completely out of context."

Tanner sighed and situated himself so he could see her better. "I was afraid they'd do that. The minute you said it, I wanted to jump in and tell them what you meant."

"I told them what I meant." Jade didn't need Tanner explaining her to the press.

"Okay, but you paused." Tanner set his pizza down. "Pauses are deadly in this type situation because it gives them the perfect opportunity to cut."

The television remote shook in Jade's hand, and she flicked the channel. There she was, saying the same thing on the competing network. Only CNN included several of her statements as well as her comment on censorship. But even they were quick to say that this case might have enough merit to stand an appeal.

Why, God? Why, when you've always been so faithful to me?

She felt sick to her stomach as she prayed. Another flip through the channels showed that the other networks presented similar stories. By six-thirty, Jade flicked off the television.

For a moment there was silence. Waves of nausea battered Jade's insides, and she felt dizzy. "Well?"

"It's not good. But I don't think it'll hurt us too badly."

Jade stood up and paced away from Tanner. "What do you mean, you don't think it'll hurt us *too* badly? They made me look like a fundamentalist freak! Of *course* that'll hurt us." She whirled around and stared at him.

"Public opinion is a tricky thing, Jade. Some people might side with you because . . . well, because you're beautiful. No matter what you said."

He still thinks I'm —

Jade felt her face growing hot, and she was silently thankful he couldn't read her mind. "But they'll probably turn against me because of what I said, isn't that what's worrying you?"

"People might watch and think if you're pro-censorship, then maybe you *are* too extreme to raise a little boy."

Jade sat back down again, dropped her head in her hands and massaged her temples with her thumbs. "This whole thing is crazy!"

"You and I know that, but not the viewing audience." She felt Tanner's hand on her arm, and she changed positions so that it fell to his side once more. Tanner hesitated, and Jade wondered if he was going to say something about her moving away. Instead he sighed and said, "They only get what they see. And what they hear."

Jade tried not to think about what she had said, the line that had made her look like a fanatic. "So we've already lost." She could feel herself beginning to shake. She'd had one chance to face the public and tell them something that would help win back Ty. And now she'd blown it. If she didn't get him back, it would be her own fault.

"No, there's still time. Like I said, it's possible some of the people will agree with you. There's an undercurrent of thinking among many circles that perhaps our country has too much freedom of speech."

"What good will that do?" Jade hugged herself, willing her body to stop trembling.

"It depends. The judge will be swayed by public opinion. Whether that's in our favor or not will make all the difference in the world."

"So what can we do?"

Tanner leaned over his knees and met her eyes so intently Jade felt forced to look away. "Pray that people see it your way."

Jade fell back into the sofa and hung her head as tears fell to her knees. From the corner of her eye she saw Tanner move toward her and then hesitate, as if he'd changed his mind. Three feet separated them, and Jade saw pride in his eyes as he studied her. "Who cares what people think. You did great, Jade. Look at the bright side . . . When you get Ty back you can come work for me."

Jade glanced up, and through her tears she felt herself smile. From somewhere deep in her heart a warning sounded: *Don't let him charm you again.* "What's that supposed to mean?"

"I could use an attorney like you. Get your law degree, and who knows." Tanner grinned, but Jade could see sadness in his eyes.

Jade was no longer smiling. *Come on, Tanner, don't play with me. Not after all we've been through, all the lies you've told me.* She crossed her arms and waited for him to be serious again.

In the wake of Jade's silence, Tanner shifted uncomfortably and changed the subject. "Really, Jade, you did great. That press conference was amazing."

Jade relaxed her shoulders and felt her defenses drop. There were still tears in her eyes, and she said, "I'm so worried about it. You do think we'll get Ty back still, don't you?"

Tanner's face clouded. "It all depends on

the judge."

Jade thought about losing Ty for several months, even years, and she felt herself grow faint. It was impossible. Ty wanted to be with her; didn't that count for something?

"Lawyers, people in legal circles, they talk about this kind of case." He hesitated. "There are a few judges who might handle the hearing, but like I said before, word is we'll get Judge Wilder. If that's the case, it could mean serious trouble. She doesn't exactly broadcast her opinions, but people in the business know how she thinks. I'm afraid she might want to make an example out of this case."

"What?" Jade felt the room closing in on her. "She can't do that."

Again Tanner started to move closer and changed his mind. "If she's the judge, she can do whatever she wants. I could ask for a different judge, but like I said, she doesn't make her opinions public. Technically there wouldn't be any grounds to grant a change."

Jade's throat was suddenly dry. "I can't believe this is happening."

"There's still a chance we'll get someone else." Tanner's gaze fell to his hands, and he sighed.

More warnings sounded on the panel in

Jade's heart. Judge Wilder would take Ty away forever and then — *God, why aren't you helping us?* "Isn't there anything we can do?"

Tanner nodded and met her eyes once more. "Yes. That's why we needed this press conference."

Jade hadn't expected Tanner to have any doubts. But with Judge Wilder . . . Her body trembled with panic. "If we lose the hearing, then what happens?"

"We appeal it again. All the way to the Supreme Court if we have to."

Jade let her head fall back against the sofa. "That could take a year. Two years, even. Maybe three." She thought of Ty and the way he'd begged her to take him home. "I don't have three years."

Moving slowly, cautiously, Tanner made his way closer to Jade and gently squeezed her knee. "I know that, Jade. Pray for a different judge. If we get Wilder, I'll do everything I can. I'm just trying to be honest with you."

Don't touch me. Jade adjusted herself once more so Tanner's hand fell away again.

"I guess that brings us —" Tanner took in the distance between them and drew a deep breath — "to the reason we're here tonight."

Jade sat up straight and turned so she

could see him. "I guess."

"You're angry with me, aren't you?"

Jade remembered how it felt when Doris Eastman told her about Tanner's children — little Amy and Justin. She thought about how Tanner had left her alone and how he'd lied to her that summer. "Yeah, I guess you could say that."

Tanner seemed to struggle for a moment, as if his own anger were bubbling just beneath the surface. She waited. The house was silent except for the subtle whirring of the refrigerator and the persistent ticking of Jade's grandfather clock in the next room. Tanner trained his eyes on hers and appeared to search for the right words. Finally he drew a deep breath.

"All day I've been thinking about this moment, wondering why in the world you'd be mad at me. And I have to tell you, Jade, I'm still in the dark."

"Come on, Tanner. . . ." Jade was tired of playing games.

"I'm serious. I come back from Hungary, and you've married someone else." His eyes flashed, and Jade wondered how he could maintain his act so well. Did he really think he could keep the truth about his past a secret from her? "I'm sure you must have had your reasons, but really . . . I think you owe me an explanation, and whatever it is, I don't think it gives you the right to be mad."

That was it. Jade had heard all she could take. "Is that right?"

"Yes. You hurt me, Jade. I still don't know why you did it."

Jade cocked her head and leveled her gaze at him. "Do the names Amy and Justin mean anything to you, Tanner?"

Tanner thought a moment and his brow creased. "Yes . . . so? What do they have to do with us?"

She wanted to slap him. "They have *everything* to do with us. Did you really think I could go on with my plans to marry you after I found out about them?"

Tanner released a frustrated sigh and leaned closer to Jade, his face a web of confusion. "You're losing me, here. Who told you about Amy and Justin?"

"Your mother." Jade had to force herself to lower her voice. *How could he sit there and —*

"My mother? When did you talk to her?" Tanner leaned forward and dug his elbows into his thighs. His face was contorted in what seemed like genuine and utter confusion.

At that instant a thought dawned on Jade, a thought so terrible it caused a churning

terror deep in her gut. What if Doris Eastman had lied? What if that was why Tanner
was so calm about her knowledge of Amy
and Justin? After all, the truth was out, and
still Tanner showed no signs of remorse, no
shame. "I met with your mother a week
after you left for Hungary. I wanted to talk
to her about . . ." *Careful, Jade. Careful.* She
heeded her own warning and her earlier
fears. "We . . . agreed to meet for tea one
afternoon."

Tanner looked puzzled. "And she told you
about Amy and Justin?"

"Yes!" Jade felt tears burning her eyes.
"How *could* you, Tanner? How could you
lie to me all summer long? And how could
you turn your back on those children?"

Tanner drew a deep breath and stood up.
He paced the floor from the sofa to the
kitchen and back. Finally he sat down and
turned once more to Jade. "First of all, I
never lied to you." He struggled to maintain
his composure.

"How can you say that?" He had lied a
dozen times, and now he was lying again.
Wasn't he? Everything Doris told her was
true, wasn't it? Jade had a strange feeling
about the entire conversation and tears of
anger and confusion streamed down her
face.

"The question I have for you is this: Why do you care about my brother's children? What in the world do they have to do with you and me?"

Tanner's words settled around her like a series of hand grenades. She sat motionless for a beat, unable to move or think. Unable even to breathe. "Your brother's children?" Flashes of light began exploding in Jade's mind. *It couldn't be true. . . . It wasn't possible. . . .* "Amy and Justin are . . . Your mother . . . she said they were . . ."

The emotions tore through Tanner's features until his face was a study of controlled fury. He came closer and took Jade's hands in his. "What did she say, Jade?"

"Amy . . . and Justin . . . she said . . ." *No, God, it can't be. . . .*

"My brother Harry is ten years older. He has two children, Amy and Justin. Now what did my mother say?"

One by one Tanner's words exploded in her heart until Jade's breathing came faster and her heart raced with uncertainty. *How could she have —* "What are you talking about? Your mother said . . ."

"My mother said what?" Tanner held her hands more tightly now, and Jade could see the anger building in his eyes.

"Your mother said you'd . . . you'd had

lots of women." Jade felt as though she were free-falling through space, as if their conversation were something from a disjointed dream. In that instant she hated herself. *You idiot! You believed that old woman and now* —

Tanner squeezed her hands. "What else, Jade? What did she say?"

Jade's breathing was quicker now, jerky, a desperate gasping. She was hyperventilating, and black spots danced before her eyes. *Calm down. You have to get through this. Help me, God. Please.* "She said they were your children, and . . . and you didn't care about them. You were . . . you'd been with many women and paid for their . . . abortions."

Tanner burst to his feet, and his voice boomed through the house. "What? She said that Amy and Justin were *my* children?"

There was nothing Jade could do. Everything about her entire existence was being sucked from her so quickly she was convinced she would die from the shock. Her teeth were chattering so that she could barely speak. "Y-y-yes."

Hot, burning rage filled Tanner's eyes, and he stared at Jade. "She told you that and . . . and you *believed* her?" He spun around and kept his back to her for what seemed like an eternity.

Jade struggled to breathe. *Calm . . . be calm. This can't be happening.* Her heart raced faster in response. How could she have believed . . . ? The woman was an evil, treacherous monster. Jade closed her eyes. No matter how hateful Mrs. Eastman had been, Jade knew she was worse.

She had believed the old woman instead of believing Tanner.

Jade heard him sigh, and she opened her eyes. He turned toward her and fell to one knee like a man who'd just been shot through the heart. His eyes looked like two open wounds. In a voice broken beyond description, he whispered the words again. "Jade? You believed her?"

Jade couldn't bear to see his pain any longer, and she closed her eyes again. *Dear God, what have I done? Why? Why did I believe Doris Eastman so quickly?* Then she remembered the faces of Amy and Justin, suddenly as fresh in her mind as the day Tanner's mother had shown them to her. Her eyes shot open and met his, imploring him to understand. "Pictures . . . She had snapshots. One of each of the children. She said they were yours . . . and . . . and they looked . . . just like you."

This time Tanner closed his eyes, and when he opened them his face was filled with regret. "Of course she had pictures. Harry moved to Montana the year you and your dad left for Kelso. He got married three years later and bought a ranch. He's lived there ever since." Tanner paused. "Harry sends pictures once a year."

Jade searched her mind but found no memories of Harry. Had she ever known about him? Even when they were kids? No wonder his mother knew the pictures would work. Jade's mind raced once more, desperate for an explanation. "Why didn't . . . why didn't you talk about him?"

"He's ten years older than I am. I guess he never came up."

This couldn't be happening. A lifetime of devastating choices couldn't possibly have been based on a pack of lies whispered on a quiet afternoon ten years ago.

"Did I ever meet him?"

Tanner wrung his hands and stared at the floor. "Probably not. He left home when he was eighteen. A year before you and I met."

Jade did the math in her head. Her teeth were still chattering, and she had the sense she might faint at any moment. "S-so that summer he would have been . . . in his early thirties."

Tanner nodded and glanced up at her. "Amy was about four then, Justin two."

"Why didn't you tell me about the kids? They're your niece and nephew." Jade was grasping at straws, still reeling from the shock.

Tanner shrugged and moved back up on the sofa next to Jade, his eyes glistening with unshed tears. "You never asked."

Jade was surprised she was sill conscious. *What have I done, Lord? How can this be happening?* She felt suspended in midair, as though there were nothing solid to stand on or cling to. She knew in that instant that Tanner was being completely honest with her — that he'd always been honest with her and that there had been no other women, no paid abortions. He had been truthful all along, and Jade thought surely the realization would kill her.

To think that every bad thing she'd believed about Tanner had been a lie . . . a lie concocted by a vindictive old woman whose heart pumped pure venom. And now he was marrying someone —

"I can't believe she'd tell you that . . . and you'd believe her." Tanner buried his face in his hands and when he looked up at Jade again, his voice was angry but quieter than before. "I thought . . . I thought you knew me better than that."

She had no response. She had been intentionally tricked, but she was without excuse.

Tanner met her gaze and held it. He softened his voice. "There was no one before you . . . no one since."

Jade's heart felt like a lead weight in her chest. All those years of misunderstanding. And now there was Ty to consider. No, she couldn't tell Tanner now. He would never forgive her. Besides, he was about to be married; his life was finally coming together. She would keep her promise to Doris Eastman and not tell Tanner about the child he'd fathered. Not now when it would only complicate matters and possibly put her relationship with Ty in further jeopardy.

"You . . . haven't slept with your fiancée?"

Tanner shook his head. "God's always given me control in that area. Leslie's been with two men before me — both boyfriends she dated for several years. But I told her how I felt. God couldn't honor our relationship unless we stayed pure."

Jade hung her head. She'd heard those words before. "You said the same thing to me, but . . ."

Her words drifted in the space between them until Tanner finished her sentence. "With you, Jade —" he placed his finger under her chin and lifted her head so she had no choice but to look at him — "with you I had no self-control. I'm sorry now just as I was then. Somehow it changed everything."

Jade nodded and thought of Ty. Tanner had no idea how right he was. A pang of fear coursed through her. He had explained his part; now it was her turn. There was only one place their conversation could go, and she wasn't sure she was up to the explanation. Especially a dishonest one.

Tanner drew a deep breath and stood up. He rubbed his neck and wandered through the room looking at Jade's family pictures. He focused on a snapshot of Jade and Jim and Ty, taken when Ty was three years old. They were smiling in the photo and looked like an all-American family. Tanner kept his eyes on the picture as he spoke. "My mother lied to you. And you believed her."

Jade wanted desperately to go to him, hold him, and tell him how sorry she was. But somehow it didn't seem right. Not now that he was engaged to someone else. "I'm sorry, Tanner. I don't know what to say." Jade remained on the sofa, her eyes trained on Tanner's back. He was crying. She could tell because his shoulders shook slightly, and for several minutes he said nothing.

Oh, God, what have I done? Why did I believe her without talking to Tanner first?

Finally Tanner drew a deep breath and turned to her. She saw his tear-streaked face then and wondered how much pain her heart could take in one night. "You believed her and . . . so you married someone else." Tanner's eyes narrowed and his voice grew hard. "I can understand that, Jade. After spending a summer with me, after sharing your conversion with me, after we bared our souls and . . . and everything else . . . I have no choice but to understand that somehow you believed my mother's lies and decided to marry someone else."

He searched her face, and when he spoke again his voice was choked with another wave of tears. "But three weeks after I left? Three weeks, Jade?"

A single sob escaped from Jade's throat, and she buried her head in her hands. How could she respond? How could she make him understand without telling him about Ty. *Help me, God. I'm falling apart. Please help me.* She expected Tanner to come to her side, reach out and put an arm around her. But he remained on the other side of the room, his feet firmly planted, his back to the series of photographs that had caught his attention earlier.

Tanner waited, and when her crying quieted, he asked again. "Help me under-

455

stand, Jade. Three weeks? What happened after I left?"

Jade wanted to be anywhere at that moment other than alone in her house facing Tanner and the truth about the past ten years. But she had no choice and she drew a deep breath. "Jim was . . . always around."

"You never mentioned him."

Jade could be honest with this much. "He wasn't worth mentioning. He was just . . . always around."

Tanner huffed. "Yeah, Jade, lots of guys hang around girls like you. You're gorgeous. That doesn't mean you marry the guy. Three weeks after . . ." He didn't finish the sentence.

Jade shook her head. "No, there were never lots of guys. Just Jim. Everyone at school wanted to date him. Big man on campus, that kind of thing."

"And he wanted the only girl he couldn't get." Tanner leaned back against the wall, avoiding the photographs.

"Right." Jade hated herself for having married Jim. But she wanted Tanner to understand. *I never stopped loving you, Tanner.* The words stayed stuck in her throat. "I, well, I was never interested, until . . ."

"My mother lied to you." Tanner's voice was calm again as he finished her sentence, his eyes clear. Jade studied them and saw a veil of indifference. As if she had hurt him too badly, and now he was choosing to be vulnerable no longer where she was concerned. Tanner sighed. "Still . . . three weeks?"

Jade was not proud of what she was about to say, but she needed to say it. "My father always told me I'd wind up with Jim Rudolph. Jim asked me to marry him when I turned eighteen and I refused. Daddy found out and said I was an idiot. After I learned about you, I guess I figured there were no other choices. Your mother told me you wouldn't want me. . . . She said she knew we'd slept together. . . ."

"What?" Tanner raised his voice again. "She told you that?"

Jade felt another pang of regret. *Not that, too, Lord.* She was beginning to understand. Anything Doris Eastman had told her was probably a lie. Including this. "She said she knew, said you told her before you left."

The topic was getting dangerously close to forbidden territory, but Tanner didn't seem the least bit curious. Apparently he believed Ty was Jim's son, and even this discussion about their last night together that summer didn't make him wonder. Tanner rubbed his neck again and stared at the ceiling. "I never told her about us, Jade. I never told anyone."

A new wave of hot tears made their way down Jade's face, but this time she didn't bother trying to hide them. She waited until she had Tanner's attention, and then she continued. "Jim wasn't a Christian. He . . . loved winning me over . . . but he never really loved me." She hung her head. "I wanted our marriage to work. For Ty's sake."

Tanner nodded, and when he spoke, Jade could still hear his intentional indifference. "And now?"

"He had an affair. A teacher he works with. Obviously we're not on good terms at this point." Jade was desperate to change the topic. "What about you? Your fiancée must be a wonderful girl."

Tanner exhaled slowly. "Jade, I don't want to talk about her. Not now."

"Okay . . . I'm sorry."

"No," Tanner sighed. "You're right. I want you to know. It's just . . . oh, never mind. I met her two years ago. Her name's Leslie and . . . we're getting married this summer."

Jade wished he would return to the sofa and sit beside her again. He felt so far away, standing across the room, his back stiff. "I'm happy for you, Tanner. Really."

She searched his face, and somehow she wasn't convinced that Tanner loved the woman he was set to marry. But that wasn't her business now. There was nothing she could do about the direction their lives had taken. And she was determined to keep the truth about Ty to herself. It was the safest thing for everyone involved.

Tanner hung his head, and again Jade wanted to go to him. He was a tall, strong, powerful man, an attorney feared by special interest groups across the country. But here in her living room he was broken by the truth of the past. His voice trembled when he spoke. "Why, Jade? Why would she lie to you?"

Jade understood what he was talking about. They'd been so busy unraveling the pieces of what had happened Tanner hadn't had time to analyze the truth about his mother. The woman had lied, and in the process, as she had tried to do so often back then, she had managed to change Tanner's life. "She didn't want me to marry you. It's that simple."

Anger flared in Tanner's eyes. "It wasn't her choice."

"But she lied all the same. And now here we are."

Tanner moved slowly back to the sofa and

settled into the spot beside Jade. He turned his body so that his face was near hers. "Was it so easy to marry someone else?"

Jade held his gaze. "No." Fresh tears stung her eyes. "I thought about you every day." Images of Ty came to mind, and she looked away, unable to meet Tanner's gaze. "I think about you still."

Tanner framed her face with his fingertips, desperately searching her eyes and positioning her so that she had no choice but to look into his again. "You did love me, didn't you, Jade?"

She nodded, her words barely audible. "Yes, I loved you, Tanner."

"In all my life . . ." He moved his face closer to hers, and Jade knew what was coming. She knew but was unable to stop it, didn't want to if she could. "I have never loved anyone . . . like I loved you, Jade."

He moved his mouth gently over hers and kissed her. It was a moment stolen from days gone by, a kiss that assured Jade had she not believed Doris Eastman's lies she and Tanner would be together still. Together forever. His hands wove their way through her hair as he pulled her close, kissing her like a man might kiss his bride before heading off to war. Desperately, hungrily, with an almost fatalistic certainty that this kiss would be their last.

Jade's hands found Tanner's face, his neck, and shoulders. No man would ever make her feel the way Tanner did, the way he still did. They kissed again and again, and sometime in the midst of the moment, Jade finally understood the Scripture from Jeremiah.

This man, Tanner Eastman, had been God's plan for her, the future and hope he had prepared for her life. But they had given in to desire, and after that she had chosen to handle the situation on her own — without trusting God's voice or heeding his warnings about not being unequally yoked. She had acted hastily in irrational fear and married a nonbeliever while Tanner was studying religious freedom halfway around the world. The life she had now was the punishment she deserved. Punishment for her many sins.

She had rushed ahead of God, and her sentence would last a lifetime.

Tanner pulled away first, and Jade saw guilt in his eyes. He was, after all, engaged. There was no way they could turn back the clock and pretend ten years hadn't gone by. "I'm sorry, Jade."

She kept her hands on either side of his face, her eyes connected with his. "Don't be. It doesn't change anything. I know that."

"You're right." His face was still inches from hers, and Jade found herself wishing he would embrace her once more. His breathing was raspy, and Jade could feel his body trembling beside hers. "I just wanted you to know the truth . . . I'll never love anyone the way I loved you, Jade."

The hours had slipped away, and Jade felt like Cinderella. Midnight was approaching, and it was time to return to reality. Time for stolen moments from the past to be put behind them forever.

"We shouldn't have . . ." Jade couldn't bring herself to voice the words, but she pulled back and caught her breath.

"I know." He stood up and reached for her hands, pulling her gently off the sofa. When they were both standing, he wrapped her in his arms and held her close. Her body screamed for him, and she was certain he felt the same way. There was something between them, a physical chemistry, an attraction that was stronger than either of them. It was the same feeling that had caused them to veer off God's course in the first place. Now life had moved on without them, and Tanner's plane was set to leave in ninety minutes. "I gotta go."

Jade pulled away from him and crossed

her arms in front of her. "Are you going to talk to your mother?"

Again anger flashed in Tanner's eyes. "How can I forgive her for what she did? She made up her mind I wouldn't marry you, and she did everything in her power to devise a plan that would keep us apart. A plan that worked. I'll struggle with that as long as I live."

"But you'll forgive her, Tanner." Jade's voice was gentle. Much as she wished Tanner could hate his mother for what she'd done, Jade knew that was impossible. Tanner loved God too much to hold a grudge of bitterness and hatred. "You'll forgive her. You couldn't live with yourself otherwise."

Tanner sighed. "Being with you tonight has made me doubt a lot of things." His eyes held hers, but she kept her distance. "My ability to forgive is one of them."

Tanner made his way to the front of the house, and Jade trailed close behind. He opened the door and turned to her once more. "We still have a lot to talk about regarding the hearing. It's in a week, and I'll probably be back up here at least once before then."

Jade nodded. "It'll be different."

"Yeah, I suppose it will be."

She looked in his eyes, and though she

kept her distance, she allowed her fingers to find his face once more. "I'm sorry, Tanner. I wish . . ."

His face grew serious, and fresh grief filled his eyes. "If only you'd believed me . . ."

She blinked and two tears slid down her cheeks. "I'm sorry."

Her apology settled over him, and she could see something change in his eyes. He forgave her. No matter that she'd doubted his intentions and believed horrible things about him. Regardless of the fact that she'd married someone else less than a month after his departure, he forgave her.

"At least we're not enemies anymore." Tanner leaned toward her and kissed her tenderly on the forehead. "Good-bye, Jade."

She pulled away. "Bye."

He left then, and she allowed her eyes to follow his car until it disappeared at the end of the street. Why had she ever doubted him? So what if the pictures had looked like Tanner? Hadn't she known him better than that? Hadn't she believed his love for her?

In that moment, with the damp breeze blowing through her hair and Tanner headed for the airport, she knew that had there been a way to go back, she would have found it. If it meant swimming the ocean for days on end or climbing a hundred mountains; if she had to walk the desert floor ten years straight, she would do it. Whatever it took. If only she could go back a decade in time and live life over again.

If she could, she would question everything Doris Eastman said instead of taking the awful things she'd spoken about Tanner as gospel. She would search out the letters Tanner had written from wherever her father had hidden them. Then she would wait for Tanner the way a drowning man waits for his next breath.

As though nothing in life mattered more.

THIRTY-ONE

Doris Eastman was alone in her condominium, chasing away invisible monsters in the night and praying for relief. Perched on her lap was an open copy of the Bible. Anxiety had plagued Doris before — terrifying, suffocating anxiety — but it had never driven her to read Scripture. It was the chest pains that had done that. Persistent, relentless stabbings somewhere in the vicinity of her heart. Doris was about to turn sixty-six, and in the past week the thought had dawned on her that perhaps this problem wouldn't be cured with diet and exercise.

Perhaps she was dying.

Doris had never actually considered death. It was an opponent she did not fear because as far back as she could remember she was certain she would live to be a hundred. She wore a seatbelt, had annual checkups, ate well and walked a mile each day. Death didn't happen to people like her. It happened to people like Hap who — cheeseburger after cheeseburger — built a gut around their midsection and refused to see the importance of exercise.

But now, though Doris had taken every precaution, though she was clearly the picture of health for her age, she had the distinct feeling she was no longer bulletproof. The chest pains were a constant reminder.

Doris had been to the doctor, and he'd given her a concerned look. Her blood pressure was high, and she seemed short of breath. He'd scheduled a treadmill test for the following week and sent her home with nitroglycerin tablets and medicine to control her blood pressure. She'd been taking both drugs for three days, but they brought little relief from the pain.

And no relief whatsoever from the fear.

Doris tidied her condominium while voices raged against her peace of mind. *Repent! Remember the height from which you have fallen! Woe to you blind guides. . . .*

Even with classical music blaring through her home and the washing machine running in the next room, Doris could not block out the incessant warnings. *I've done nothing wrong. I'm a Christian woman, for heaven's sake.*

But the silent echoes of Scripture she'd long since forgotten screamed in the foyer of her mind: *Broad is the road that leads to destruction and many find it. . . . And on that day he will separate the sheep from the goats. . . . Anyone whose name was not written in the Lamb's book of life was thrown into the lake of fire. . . .*

"Stop!" Doris shouted as she flipped off the bedside stereo. "Enough!"

She clutched at her chest and winced as she made her way across the room to her bathroom sink. She flicked on the light, poured herself a glass of water, and took two sips. Silence; that was what she needed. Time to reflect on the strange Scriptures that played constantly in her head. *What are you trying to tell me, God? I'm not the one you should be hounding. What about Jade? She's the one who tricked Tanner into sleeping with her. I did the only thing I could do under the circumstances.*

Woe to you . . . remember the height from which you have fallen. . . .

Doris squeezed her eyes shut and sank onto the nearest sofa cushion. From what height had she fallen? *Show me, God.*

A memory began to take shape. Doris was twelve, maybe thirteen years old sitting on

468

the bank of a creek in Williamsburg, Virginia. Her parents had been churchgoers, but they never actually discussed their faith. And that day Doris had found the family Bible and taken it with her to the quiet spot along the water. For three hours she sat there soaking in Scriptures, seeing her faith in a new light. Making it her own.

Though more than fifty years had passed, she could see herself clearly, hear her sweet, young voice as she prayed aloud asking Jesus to be with her always, to walk with her and talk to her and hold her close. It was that day that Doris realized faith wasn't the picture that had been modeled by her parents. It was a relationship with Christ. There on the creek bank she promised God that a day wouldn't go by without her meeting him the way she had that morning. They would meet together, talk together, and in time she would know the Bible by heart.

Doris blinked and the image disappeared. When had she stopped feeling that way about the Lord? Three years later? four? She was seventeen when she met Hap, and she remembered them discussing the Bible on their dates. But sometime before they married things had changed between her and God. The image of Angela Conner appeared, and she gritted her teeth. Yes, that's when everything had changed. When Hap gave in to Angela Conner.

God had allowed Hap to fall, and Doris must have decided she had no one to lean on but herself. The days of sweet fellowship with the Lord died a quiet death after that.

Doris never stopped claiming an allegiance to Christ. It wasn't that she disbelieved him. But she had never quite forgiven him for letting her down where Hap was concerned. Over the years, her hard feelings toward God grew into a distance that now — even with the chest pains — seemed too vast to cross.

Doris returned to her bedroom, sank into a swivel chair, and leaned against the back-seat. Her chest pains eased. Had she come so far from that day on the creek bank that she had actually stopped listening to God? Stopped loving him? She closed her eyes, and the Scriptures returned.

Anyone whose name was not written in the Lamb's book of life was cast into the lake of . . .

No! God loved her too much to threaten her with fire. Her name was there in the Lamb's book. Surely it was.

Repent! Repent or I will remove your lamp-stand. . . .

Another image filled Doris's mind, and

this time she stared at it in horror. A cross, anchored on a lonely hill bearing the shadowy figure of a dying Christ.

In that moment a tidal wave of remorse crashed down upon Doris, driving her to her knees. And though her bones ached at the odd position, she hung her head and felt the strangest sensation. Her eyes burned and grew moist, and Doris realized what it was. Tears. She hadn't cried in decades, and now a torrent of tears were fighting their way free from the depth of her heart, where they had been trapped so long they'd nearly dried up.

She had become a hard, ugly old woman. A person who preferred to play God rather than talk to him. A liar, a gossip, a slanderer. In that moment she knew she was without a hope should the chest pains grow worse and demand her life.

No wonder she feared death. She thought of the lake of fire, the eternal lake of fire, and suddenly she was desperate for God's saving grace and mercy. Desperate to know she was free from her calloused past.

"Forgive me!" She cried out the words, begging God to hear her. "I'm sorry. Please change me."

Doris sobbed, remembering the precious child she'd been, repulsed by the monster she'd become. As her tears slowed, she caught her breath and realized something had changed.

The fear was gone.

Confess your sins to one another so that you may be healed. . . .

Confess. Yes, that was it. It wasn't too late after all. She would call Tanner and confess. The realization should have brought her peace, but instead she was seized by a new kind of chest pain. This time it felt like an elephant was sitting on her chest.

Call Tanner, my daughter. Confess. . . .

I'll do it. It's what I need to do. Her breathing had become labored, and she struggled to find the energy to move. What was happening to her? The pains grew worse in response, and suddenly she knew.

She was having a heart attack.

She was going to die without having a chance to tell Tanner. He hadn't called her since his return from Portland, and somehow she was certain he'd found out about her lies. Fading in and out of consciousness, Doris gasped for breath and thought how sad it was that she would die at peace with God and at odds with her favorite son.

If only she could reach the phone and call him, let him know she was sorry. Tell him the truth about Jade's son . . . his son.

Again the pains grew more intense, and Doris fell back against the sofa. There was nothing to do now but wait. *This is it, the real thing.* Doris closed her eyes and accepted death without a fight.

If the Lord was going to take her home before she had a chance to make things right with Tanner, then she'd have to trust God that somehow, someday, Tanner would know the truth. And that he'd understand how sorry she was for lying in the first place.

"Forgive me . . . Tanner." Her voice was a frail whisper. "Forgive me. . . ."

A sense of peace washed over her, and she saw another vision: her name written in the Lamb's book. And she knew that despite her faithlessness through the years, despite the horrid thing she'd done to Tanner and Jade, God had been merciful. He had always been merciful. Her body slumped onto the floor, and then the sounds around her faded.

And in that instant, the world around her went dark.

THIRTY-TWO

Since returning to Los Angeles, Tanner had busied himself in preparations for the hearing. With the entire nation watching for the verdict, he had spent nearly as much time praying about the case as he'd spent researching it. By Thursday afternoon, Tanner had a peace about the hearing that whatever came of it, God would be glorified in the process. And that was enough for him.

The most difficult aspect of preparing Jade's case was the fact that his personal life was falling apart. He had been avoiding his mother and still had no idea when he would confront her or what he would say when he did so. She had lied to him, done everything in her power to manipulate him. And for that he would always struggle with his feelings of anger toward her and the possibilities of what might have been. In many ways she had ruined his life by sending Jade into the arms of another man while he was too far away to do anything to stop her.

But, Tanner knew he would have to deal with his mother later. First he had to deal with Leslie.

He had lain awake the past few nights imagining life with Leslie, being married to a woman who was not capable of giving her heart and all of who she was to him the way Jade had done. It wasn't fair to either of them that he would constantly compare their relationship with the one he'd shared with Jade. And years from now — even after sharing his life with her day in and day out — there was a certainty in his heart that Leslie would still come up short.

There would be no summer wedding. No wedding at all. As Tanner finished his work for the afternoon, he knew he had to tell her that night, before she made any more plans.

He'd considered whether seeing Jade again, whether learning the truth about their past and kissing her had driven him to this decision. He couldn't deny it: In some ways it had. But he would not attempt to rekindle a relationship with Jade now. She had changed since that summer ten years ago. She'd believed his mother's lies, and though Tanner had forgiven her, he could not imagine opening himself to her again.

No, breaking his engagement with Leslie was simply the right thing to do. He had known love once, a long time ago, and what he felt for Leslie was not love. Unless he loved that way again, Tanner would rather stay single.

The phone rang, and Tanner sighed. He was expecting a call from Jade, but usually she waited until he was back at his townhouse. They had talked about the case every evening that week.

"Hello?"

"Tanner? Good, you're still there." Leslie sounded upbeat, ready with another string of details. "What about meeting tonight for dinner? I wanted to talk about attendants, you know . . . how many ushers on your side, how many bridesmaids on mine. Besides, you've been so busy with that case you haven't given me the time of day. I'm a pretty fun date, Tanner; you ought to take me out sometime." She was trying to sound coy, and Tanner summoned his resolve. "Anyway, I sure hope things will settle down after we're married, but then I'm sure they will. You've got such a busy —"

"Leslie." Tanner hated to interrupt her, but he was so sure of his decision he could no longer pretend. "We need to talk."

She paused. "I agree. We haven't so much

as had a quiet night alone in I don't know how many —"

"No." His word stopped her cold. "I mean about us. We need to talk tonight."

She uttered a nervous laugh. "You sound so ominous, Tanner. Don't tell me you're getting cold feet?"

Tanner sighed. It wasn't his feet that were cold, it was his heart. And Leslie deserved more than that from a husband. "I'm sorry, Leslie. I've been doing a lot of thinking. Like I said, we need to talk."

"Listen, darling, I'm not one for surprises." The cheeriness had disappeared from her voice. "Why don't you just tell me what's on your mind."

She sounded angry, and Tanner knew she was covering the hurt. The things he needed to tell her would leave her world upside down. But eventually she'd find her way back to the surface, and one day another man would come along. One who would love her completely, the way she deserved to be loved. "I don't want to talk about it now."

"Fine." Leslie's voice was hard. "Where do you want to meet?"

"My place. Six o'clock."

She hesitated. "You're serious, aren't you?"

Tanner sighed. "Yes. I'm sorry, Leslie."

The conversation ended, and Tanner pushed himself away from his desk. A month ago he'd been ready to settle for a life with Leslie. She had been the kind of woman he thought would make him happy. But seeing Jade again, remembering what love felt like when it resided deep in his being . . .

Tanner knew he couldn't marry Leslie.

He thanked God for letting him see that truth now, before the wedding. And he asked him for strength to get through the evening. Then he packed his things and headed for home. Thirty minutes later Leslie was at his door.

"Come in." Tanner had changed out of his shirt and tie and was barefoot in a Princeton sweatshirt and faded denim jeans. He stepped aside as Leslie huffed past him and stormed into the living room.

"Okay, I'm here. What's so important that you made me drop what I was doing to come talk to you face to face?"

Tanner studied her, the way she shifted uneasily from one foot to the other, running her tongue nervously along her upper lip. She was frightened. Leslie was a pampered young woman, accustomed to getting her own way. When things didn't go as she planned, she fussed and fumed until they did. But that would not happen tonight, and by the look in her eyes, Leslie knew as much.

"Sit down, Leslie. Please."

Her gaze lingered suspiciously on him, and as she sat on the sofa he moved next to her, taking her hands in his. "I've been doing a lot of thinking lately, and, well . . . I have some things to tell you."

Leslie squeezed his hands, and a bit of her façade collapsed. "You still love me, right, Tanner?"

He hated what he was about to do, but there was no choice. "I love you, Leslie, but not like I should. Not the way a husband should love his wife."

Raw pain flashed across her face, and her eyes grew damp. She started to pull her hands from his. "You're teasing me, Tanner. Of course you love me that way. We're getting married in —"

"No." Tanner sighed. "We're not. I'm breaking it off, Leslie. I can't do it. It wouldn't be fair to either one of us."

Tears spilled onto Leslie's cheeks, and in seconds they had cut two trails through her perfectly applied foundation. Tanner realized that oddly it was the first time he'd seen her look flawed in any way. Leslie dabbed at her face, then excused herself while she got a tissue. When she returned she nestled against him, but he felt himself stiffen in response.

Her jaw fell and she studied him closely. "Wait a minute. You aren't giving me a chance here, Tanner."

Help me be gentle, Lord. "It's too late for chances. This has nothing to do with you, Leslie. You've done everything right. It's me." He stroked the side of her face in a gesture that was more fatherly than even remotely romantic. "I care about you a great deal, like I said. But I don't love you the way I should."

Leslie covered her face with her hands and cried softly, pressing her eyes with the tissue. She spoke in a muffled voice. "What did I do wrong? I thought everything was so good between us."

"You did nothing. It's all me."

"It's that woman in Portland, isn't it? You're still in love with her. . . ." She stared at the engagement ring on her hand and twisted it until it came loose. "I could tell you were still in love with her the first time you talked about her at dinner that night."

"This isn't about her, either. Like I said, it's about me. You deserve someone who loves you completely."

Leslie sniffed and slipped the ring from her finger. "Here. I don't want it. Not now."

Leslie straightened and stopped crying, and in that moment Tanner felt that perhaps she hadn't loved him the way she should have, either. Maybe all Leslie loved was the idea of being married to a man with Tanner's credentials. After all, she had been groomed to marry correctly since she was a very young girl.

She leaned over and hugged him. "You know, I almost expected this would happen. . . ."

"You did?"

"Well, you haven't been interested in the planning, and it's been months since you've called me just to chat." Leslie kept her hands on Tanner's shoulders. "Do you think there's a chance for us, Tanner . . . someday?"

He wished he could give her hope, but he had to be honest. "No." He shook his head. "You'll meet someone else, Leslie. Someone better for you than I ever was."

She smiled sadly. "It would have been a beautiful wedding. . . ."

"And you'd have been a beautiful bride." He pulled slowly away. "I'm sorry, Leslie. Can you forgive me?"

She thought a moment. "You know, I

think maybe I was feeling the same way you were. Like we were going through the motions, hurtling toward the big wedding day with little thought as to what we shared between us."

"Really?"

She nodded. "Really." Leaning close, she kissed his cheek. "Let's not be strangers, okay?"

Tanner nodded just as the phone rang. He rose from the sofa to answer it. "Hello?"

"Tanner Eastman?" Tanner didn't recognize the voice.

"Yes. Who's this?"

"This is Dr. Jeff Young of St. Vincent Medical Center. We have your mother here. . . . I'm afraid she's suffered a major heart attack." The doctor paused. "She's in the intensive care unit, Mr. Eastman. You need to hurry."

He hung up the phone slowly, bombarded by a dozen conflicting emotions. He still hadn't talked to his mother about the lies she'd told Jade, hadn't given her the opportunity to fill in the missing pieces. Now he might never get the chance.

His throat tightened at the thought of losing his mother now, when so much of his life was in turmoil. She had been his greatest fan as far back as he could remember.

Pushy, demanding, overbearing . . . but Tanner never doubted her love for him. Even now that he knew about the lies she'd told Jade. In some strange, twisted sense, that had been her way of loving him. *Help me forgive her, Lord. Don't let her die without giving us a chance to talk. Please.*

But there was something even more troubling now that she lay dying at the nearby hospital. Tanner wasn't sure if his mother was really a believer, whether she was ready to die and face God Almighty.

Leslie's face reflected the alarm she must have seen in Tanner. "What's wrong?" She was at his side, her hand on his arm, and Tanner was suddenly anxious to see her go.

"My mother's had a heart attack." He pulled gently away and reached for his car keys. "I'm sorry, Leslie . . . I have to go."

She nodded, taking his hand in hers once more. Tenderly she peeled back his fingers and slipped the ring inside. "Take this."

With a small sigh, he pulled her close. "We'll talk more later, okay?"

"Okay. . . ."

But he had the feeling they both knew there would be no reason to talk later. The relationship simply hadn't worked. It was time to move on.

He bid her good-bye, thankful she hadn't

wept loudly and carried on, hoping she believed what she'd said about it being for the best. Tanner wasn't sure if she did, but right now it didn't matter.

He had to get to his mother before she died.

THIRTY-THREE

To the extreme surprise of her doctors, Doris Eastman pulled through a rough night in which she suffered two additional heart attacks. During that time doctors determined that though her arteries were severely blocked, she was too weak to undergo major surgery. If she survived the hospital stay, certainly it would not be for long.

Tanner held a bedside vigil throughout the night, alerting doctors when his mother looked pained or when she began gasping strangely. By ten o'clock that morning she was heavily sedated, but her heart was stable. Doctors expected her to regain consciousness before noon.

"Of course, it's possible she'll never come out of it," one of the doctors told Tanner earlier that morning. "Her heart was severely damaged. At best she'll be a cardiac cripple."

"What's that mean?" Tanner still couldn't believe she'd had a heart attack at all. His mother was one of the strongest people he knew and seeing her small frame lost in a sea of hospital sheets and plastic tubing was difficult to accept.

"It means she'll never be the same."

The doctor didn't elaborate, and Tanner was left to wonder how the heart attacks had changed his mother. *Let me talk to her, Lord, please.* He prayed quietly at her side until finally at eleven-thirty, she opened her eyes and blinked slowly.

"Tanner . . ."

Her voice was scratchy, and Tanner could barely make it out. "Hey, Mom, how are you feeling?" He stood up and leaned over the bed, taking her now frail hand in his.

She motioned for some water, and he helped her take a sip from a straw, disturbed at what an effort it was for her. The ordeal left her breathless and unable to lift her head. Tanner tried again. "Rough night, huh?"

She made a slight nodding motion. "Have to talk . . . Tanner."

He weighed his options. He wanted to talk about the lies she'd told Jade, but it was more important that he talk about God. "I'm worried about you."

She frowned and shook her head, and Tanner felt his spirits lift. If his mother was showing her usual spunk hours after suffering three heart attacks, maybe she would survive after all. "Nothing . . . to worry about."

Her talking was improving now that she was more fully awake. Still she seemed unusually calm, and Tanner figured that was because of the medication. "How are things with you and God, Mom?"

A peaceful expression filled his mother's eyes, one that Tanner knew no medication could produce. "Good. Very good. We . . . had a talk."

"You and God?"

His mother nodded. "He wants me to . . . tell you something."

Tanner frowned. Was his mother thinking clearly? He leaned over her, searching her eyes. "Now?"

"Yes." She glanced at the bedside chair. "Sit down."

He did as she asked and waited.

"I want to tell you something . . . I'm not very proud of." She rested a moment. "Long time ago, when your father and I were engaged, Angela Conner was a waitress at the tavern. . . ."

Tanner was beginning to have his doubts.

This couldn't be good for her, rehashing age-old memories and mistakes hours after the heart attacks. "Mom, you can tell me later if —"

She held up a single, trembling hand. "Now. God wants me to tell you now."

Tanner sighed. "Okay. Take your time."

"One night, your father visited the tavern, and Angela Conner asked for a ride home. Our . . . wedding was still a year away, and when your father pulled up in front of Angela's house . . . she asked him in."

What? No one had ever told Tanner this story. Why was his mother telling him now, and what did it have to do with God? He took his mother's hand in his and stroked her pale skin. "I'm listening."

"Your father didn't plan for it to happen, but it did. He went inside and . . . one thing led to another." She coughed weakly, and Tanner helped her take another sip of water. After a moment she continued. "Your father didn't mean anything by it. He was weak . . . and later he was paralyzed with guilt. He came directly to my house the next day and . . . confessed."

"You still married him?" The Doris Eastman Tanner knew would have kicked the wayward Hap out of her house.

His mother inhaled slowly. "We broke it

off for six months, but eventually I forgave him. I figured it wasn't as much his fault as it was hers. . . ." She struggled to catch her breath. "From that day on . . . I vowed never to forgive Angela Conner."

Tanner was confused. "God wanted you to tell me that?"

His mother moved her head in a manner that was barely detectable. "I'm not finished." She sighed. "When Angela married Buddy and moved into our neighborhood, I did everything I could to avoid her. But then they had Jade and . . . you and Jade were inseparable. There was nothing I could do to stop the two of you from meeting together. Until that summer, when Angela ran off with my best friend's husband."

"The summer Jade and her father moved to Kelso?"

Doris nodded. Tanner could see she was getting tired, and he took her hand in his once more. "You don't have to tell me this now, mother. We can talk about it later."

"No. God . . . will give me the strength." She moistened her lips and appeared to be concentrating on the right words. "When Jade left I was glad. I could see where things were headed for you two and . . . I was determined that no daughter of Angela Conner would ever date you."

489

A heaviness settled over his shoulders. He had wondered why his mother hadn't been friendlier with Jade.

"When they moved to Kelso I thought I was rid of Jade Conner. Then . . . that summer, the two of you found each other again. I tried everything possible to make you change your mind about taking that internship in Kelso. I figured Jade would be a loose woman like her mother. . . . And I couldn't stand the thought of her bringing you down." She stared hard at Tanner. "Does that make sense?"

He shrugged. In many ways his mother had tried to play God where he was concerned. The truth hit him hard. "Go ahead, Mother, I'm listening."

She studied him for a moment. "You know about the lies, don't you?"

Tanner nodded. "Since Monday."

"I thought so. But God wanted me . . . to tell you what happened in my own words." She took a few moments to catch her breath. "Jade came to me that day, and I guessed that you'd been together. . . ."

Tanner felt like a little boy caught in some dreadful act, and he felt his face grow hot. "What made you think that?"

"If Jade was anything like her mother, then it didn't take much guesswork . . . to figure out the two of you had probably slept together."

"But she was nothing like her mother, never has been." Tanner rose quickly to Jade's defense, but his mother only nodded weakly.

"I know that now. God has . . . made everything clear to me, Tanner. Jade is a sweet, precious child who was . . . never treated well by anyone. Except you."

Tanner was silent.

"But I thought I was protecting you, so I lied. I told her you had been with many women, you had children you cared nothing for. . . . I told her you wouldn't care for her, either, now that she'd slept with you."

Tanner still couldn't believe the woman before him had said those things, purposefully destroying the one relationship that mattered to him more than any except the one he shared with God Almighty. "You showed her Amy's and Justin's pictures."

"Yes. I did that. It was the only way I could be sure I'd convince her."

Tanner stroked his mother's hand and allowed himself to grieve silently. If only Jade had stayed away, turned down the invitation to go to his mother's that day. . . . *God, help me forgive her. Help me forgive them both.*

"You'd better rest now, Mom. You said

what you needed to say."

His mother shook her head, more adamantly this time. "No." She coughed several times and was barely able to catch her breath. Tanner helped her with another sip of water and waited. "There's more."

He clenched his fists and noticed his palms were sweaty. "More?"

"What did Jade tell you about her son?"

Tanner's heart lurched. Alarm coursed through him, and he was suddenly unable to draw a deep breath. "What do you mean, Mother?"

Doris's eyes filled with tears, and Tanner was flooded with apprehension. His mother never cried. Not even when his father died. He watched her struggle to speak. "Did she . . . talk about him, mention him when she told you . . . about the lies?"

Tanner was terrified of the direction the conversation was headed. He shook his head. "No. She wants him back . . . that's the whole reason I'm representing her." *God, please, where is this going?*

Doris was silent, her lower lip quivering as she stared at her son. "I'm so . . . sorry, Tanner."

"Mother, tell me, what do you know about Jade's son?"

Doris swallowed hard, fighting for control.

"Promise you won't hate me?"

Tanner was losing patience. He knew his mother's condition was fragile, but nevertheless he could not wait another moment. "I love you, Mom. No matter what you've done to me, regardless of how you've manipulated my life I will always love you. Now tell me what you know."

She nodded, and in that moment Tanner thought she looked like a mournful child, confessing a sin too great for her to bear any longer. "I could be wrong, but I doubt it. . . ."

"Wrong about what? Please, Mom, whatever it is, say it."

"The boy . . . Ty . . ."

"Yes, what about him?"

Her lip was trembling badly again. When she spoke, Tanner could barely hear her. "I think he's y-y-your son."

Tanner felt himself spinning out of control, falling wildly into an abyss too dark and deep and narrow to ever climb out of. The child . . . Jade's son . . . was *his?* It was impossible, wasn't it? "But Jade's husband thinks . . ."

Doris shook her head. "He doesn't know. There's . . . there's more to the story." A teardrop slid down his mother's wrinkled cheek. "When Jade came to me that day . . .

it was because she was pregnant."

"What? She told you that?" Tanner's heart was beating erratically; his world had tilted, and he wasn't sure he could ever right it again.

"I guessed." His mother was breathless but determined to continue. "She wanted an emergency number where she could reach you. . . . I invited her over to discuss it."

"So she hadn't been with any other man?"

"No, Tanner. She loved you. She told me the two of you . . . were going to be married."

It was making sense to Tanner, more sense than ever before. "So she came to you for help and you . . . you lied to her. Is that right?"

His mother nodded, her eyes filled with remorse. "I told her you wouldn't want anything to do with the child . . . and I gave her a check."

"A check?"

"A cashier's check for ten thousand dollars."

"She took it?" Tanner couldn't imagine the hurt Jade must have felt, trusting his mother with her news, and then learning that the man she thought she loved was a —

His mother coughed loudly and struggled for a breath. "She . . . she didn't want to. But I convinced her she'd need it for the baby. I made her promise . . . to never tell anyone you were the father."

The shock was almost too much for Tanner to bear. But he understood now why Jade had married so quickly. He could hear himself asking her about children on that hot August day so long ago, hear her telling him she'd only want a child if she could give him the kind of life she never had. A mother and a father, safety, security. Then he left for Hungary, and she was alone, pregnant with no one to turn to.

And so she had wound up with Jim Rudolph, a man she didn't love, but who would give her the life she wanted for the child she loved more than anything.

Lord, I can't bear the pain. Help me, God. Please.

His mother was studying him, trying to convey her sorrow with her eyes. "Tanner, I saw the boy on TV. He . . . he looks just like you."

Tanner thought of the boy now, rugged and active, sandy blond hair and eyes the same shade as his. Why hadn't he seen it before? Jade must have thought him a horrible man for not at least wondering about the boy.

"Do you forgive me, Tanner?"

He stared at his mother and felt pity more than forgiveness. She had spent most of her days a hard, manipulative woman bent on controlling his life. Now, when her time was nearly up, she had finally seen the light and come clean. Tanner realized that if his mother had died during the night, he might never have known about Ty. But she had lived, and for that he would always be grateful. "I forgive you, Mother." He smoothed a lock of gray hair from her forehead. "You can rest now."

"Will you go to her?"

"Yes." Tanner had no idea what Jade would say, or whether she'd tell him the truth. After all, she'd had her chance the other night, and she'd said nothing about Ty then. He thought of the child he'd missed, the birthdays and milestones and miracles of his young life, and he wondered if the pain in his gut would kill him. "Pray for me, Mom."

"I will." She blinked and another teardrop fell. "I'll be okay. You go. . . . Jade needs you."

Tanner bid his mother good-bye, and in four hours he was on a plane back to Portland.

THIRTY-FOUR

Jade was finished with the dinner dishes and midway through a conversation with Ty. He called her every night at seven o'clock, and as the hearing drew closer, she could detect a growing sense of hope in his voice.

"I can't wait to get out of here, Mom." Ty spoke in a whisper so Jim wouldn't hear him. "It's going to work out all right, I know it is."

She closed her eyes. "Mr. Eastman is doing his best, Ty."

"I saw him, Mr. Eastman. He was on TV with you."

"You saw us?" A nervousness ran through Jade at the thought of Ty having seen Tanner. She chided herself for it. There was no way the boy would ever know. What harm was there in talking about him now. "He's a nice man. He's done a lot to help us."

"I heard what he said, how he stuck up for you." Ty maintained his whisper. "I like him, Mom. I wanna meet him."

Another wave of anxiety hit, and Jade's knees felt weak. She sank into a chair in the kitchen. "Okay . . . maybe. Sure."

Eventually their conversation wound down, and Ty grew quiet. Jade knew he was probably crying; he had cried every night lately. "Mom . . . I miss you."

Make it all be over, God, please. I can't take this. . . . Jade closed her eyes and struggled to find her voice. "Remember . . . even now I'm with you. Right there in your heart."

Ty gulped loudly. "Okay." He hesitated. "Bye. I love you."

"Love you more." *Enough to marry Jim Rudolph.* "Good night, honey."

Jade hung up and noticed tears on her cheeks. The house was so empty without Ty. She wandered about, idly straightening framed photographs of Ty and precious homemade trinkets he'd brought home from school over the years. She ran her finger over each one, removing the dust and savoring the memories they evoked. She and Ty would have been fine on their own; it was clear, now. *How could I have married Jim?*

In some ways, she was no better than Doris Eastman, who had lied and manipulated to protect Tanner. Hadn't Jade done the same thing? Promised a lifetime of love to a man she didn't care for, rushed ahead of God and made a miserable choice all to protect Ty.

Both she and Doris Eastman were wrong. And regardless of what hope the future no longer held, Jade knew from this point on, when a decision had to be made, she would seek the Lord's wisdom. She would never again rush ahead of him.

There was a knock at the door and Jade jumped. It was nearly eight o'clock, and her porch light was off. *Too late for advertisers or neighborhood Girl Scouts.* Jade moved cautiously toward the front door and peered through the lace panel covering.

Tanner.

Jade's heart skipped a beat. *What in the world . . . ?*

Jade opened the door, but before she could speak he ushered her inside, took her face in his hands, and studied her eyes. "Jade . . . Oh, Jade, I'm so sorry. . . ."

"What?" Adrenaline raced through her veins. He must have learned something about the hearing. . . . She was going to lose custody of Ty after all. She pulled back. "What's wrong? Why're you here?"

Tanner sighed, and Jade thought he looked haggard. Dark circles stood out underneath his eyes. "My mother had a heart attack."

Her insides knotted up. "Is she okay?"

"She's in bad shape, but that's not why I'm here." Jade watched his eyes fill with regret. "We talked this morning. She had something God wanted her to tell me."

Pulling away from him, Jade moved into the living room, tucking herself in the corner of her sofa, her legs pulled up to her chin. *Doris wouldn't have told him about Ty. Certainly not.* So why was her heart pounding so fiercely? "What . . . what did she say?"

Tanner followed and knelt before her, his face level with hers. "She told me you were pregnant when you came to her. . . ." His eyes filled with tears. "Is it true, Jade? Is Ty . . . ?"

Jade hung her head. She could not lie any longer. Whatever came from this they would have to deal with. Right now he deserved the truth. "Yes."

Tanner held her with his eyes. "He's my son?"

Jade lifted her head and met his gaze. He looked like he'd been shot through the heart. *Oh, Lord, how could I have hurt him like this? What kind of woman am I?* "Yes, Tanner. He's your son."

Very slowly, as if he'd been mortally wounded and was still fighting the final fall,

Tanner bent over his knees and settled in a heap on the floor. His first sob was more of an animal cry, the wail of a tortured beast. There were more that followed, and Jade felt her heart breaking as she watched the man she had always loved grieve for the son he'd never known.

The world was spinning, and Tanner could do nothing to stop it. He had spent the past ten years searching for Jade, thinking of her, wanting her. Wondering how she could marry someone just three weeks after he left town. And now he knew. She'd been pregnant with his child. And when she'd come for help, his mother . . .

Deep, consuming regret covered him like six feet of cemetery dirt, and he was unable to lift his head.

My God, how could I have been so blind? I'm a father . . . a father to a boy who doesn't even know me. He thought of Ty and his heart ached with the weight of this new reality. Had he really thought Jade could lie in the arms of another man so quickly after his departure? If only he'd found her back then. . . . The weight of the lost years was more than he could bear. *Help me, God. I'm dying here, I'm —*

"No! It can't be. . . ." His mother's lies

had cost him a relationship with his own son.

He was overcome, and he was suddenly aware of Jade moving. Her arms circled around him from behind, and she lay her head on his upper back. She began stroking his arms, and he could feel her shaking. *She's crying, too. We've both lost so much, God. . . . How can we go forward after this?*

Finally she spoke, and her voice was a choked whisper. "Tanner . . . I'm so sorry."

He sat up and pulled Jade to him in an embrace that spoke everything they were too devastated to say. They stayed that way a long time, and when he could finally speak, he pulled back and studied her expression. What he saw there was regret as deeply rooted as his own. He took her hands in his. "Why, Jade? Why didn't you tell me?"

His pain was so deep and raw she had to look away. "I promised your mother I wouldn't tell anyone. Not even you."

Tanner's face twisted and he set his jaw. Jade wondered if he was going to cry out again. "I'm his *father*." Every word pulsed with emotion, and Jade knew much of the blame was hers. *He'll hate me for the rest of his life for this.* "Didn't you think I had the right to know?"

"Your mother said you wouldn't care. She . . . she showed me the pictures and . . ."

"And gave you the check?" Jade could see he wasn't making an accusation, just desperate to understand what had happened that day ten years ago.

"I never touched the money. It's in a trust fund for Ty. . . . I was planning to use it to send him to college."

Tanner looked away, the muscles in his jaw tightening again. She watched as the emotions played across his anguished face: anger, regret, immeasurable sorrow. All the emotions she'd struggled with for so long. He turned toward her once more. "The other night . . . when we talked. Why didn't you tell me then?"

"Your mother told me if I ever told anyone, she'd take me to court. She told me with her money she'd win. . . ." Jade sighed. "I was afraid of her, Tanner." She glanced at her hands, still wrapped protectively in his. "Besides, it didn't seem like the right thing for anyone. You have your life; you'll be married this summer, and soon you'll have a family of your own."

Tanner leaned his shoulder into the sofa, and Jade watched him, worried. His jaw was clenched tightly, and he passed a hand over his eyes before looking at her again. "I broke it off with Leslie."

"What?" *Why had he* —

"I didn't love her, Jade. It would have been wrong to marry her."

Her head was swimming. . . . So much had happened in so short a time. "When was this?"

Tanner thought a moment. "What day is it?"

His question broke the tension, and Jade smiled. "Friday night."

"Then it was yesterday after dinner."

"When did you find out about your mother?" No wonder Tanner looked beat up. First Leslie, then his mother, and finally the truth about Ty. It was enough to push anyone over the edge.

"Leslie was still at my house. She left and I went to the hospital. I was up all night with my mother, and this morning she came to. That's when she told me about Ty."

Jade slipped her arms around Tanner's neck. She didn't blame him if he never forgave her, but she owed him an apology. After all they'd been through, all the poor choices and lies and missed opportunities, she needed to speak her mind before another moment passed. "I'm sorry, Tanner. I should have told you first, I . . . I was afraid of your mother."

His eyes were still racked with pain, but his expression softened.

"I didn't want you to think I was trying to ruin your wedding plans. . . . I was trying to do the right thing for everyone."

Tanner pulled away and stood up, pacing her living room floor and raking his fingers through his hair. When he stopped, he leaned against the wall and stared at her. As he did, the anger in his eyes was slowly replaced with a love for her that knew no limits. He reached out his arms. "Come here, Jade. Please. . . ."

She went to him, fitting her body against him, her face inches from his. His voice was a whisper that spoke directly to her soul. "So much has happened between us that I didn't know what I was feeling for you. . . ."

Jade felt tears sting at her eyes. "I'm sorry."

He shook his head and placed a single finger over her lips. "It's over." He tightened his grip on her waist. "It's behind us, Jade. Now . . ." He seemed to be reading her eyes, searching her soul. "I want to meet my son. I want to —"

Jade closed her eyes, and for a moment she couldn't hear what he was saying. *I can't believe this is happening.* Tanner was here, he was not marrying someone else, and he wanted to meet Ty. A rush of holy gratitude came over Jade, and she felt the arms of God's presence as if he were standing in the room beside them. How was it that God had taken everything that was so awful and turned it into this?

For I know the plans I have for you . . . plans to give you hope and a future. . . .

Jade opened her eyes and saw that Tanner was staring at her, his eyes filled with compassion and forgiveness. "So . . . you're not marrying Leslie?"

Tanner leaned forward and gently kissed Jade's forehead. "Did you really think I could be with you the other night . . . kissing you, wanting you . . . and then go back home and marry someone else?"

"I guess I —"

Again Tanner held his finger to her lips. "Shh. I'm here, Jade. I never stopped loving you, and now —" he paused and his expression grew deeply serious — "say the word and I'll never, ever leave you again."

The tears that had been building spilled down Jade's face, and she allowed herself to get lost in Tanner's eyes. "Please, Tanner. Don't ever go away again."

"Are you sure?"

He had suffered much because of her lack of trust, their weakness that summer. Jade felt the corners of her mouth lift slightly, and she buried her head in his chest. "I've been sure since I was a little girl."

Jade lifted her face to him, and their kiss was long and slow.

"I love you, Jade. . . ."

She pulled back slightly, and he kissed her chin, her throat. "I love you, Tanner. I never stopped loving you."

He found her mouth again, and his hands moved along her back, holding her closer still. "Let me go with you tomorrow . . . so I can meet him?"

Their words were breathless, spoken between kisses that were every bit as spellbinding as they'd been a decade earlier. "Okay." Jade sat up, looking at Tanner, studying his face . . . the face so like her son's. . . .

"Hey, wait a minute!" Jade's mind suddenly raced with the possibilities.

Tanner pulled back, his fingers tracing her cheekbones. "What?"

"Let's call off the whole thing. Get a DNA test and prove Jim isn't Ty's father! Then we can be done with it once and for all."

Tanner's eyes clouded with concern. "The whole way from Los Angeles to Portland I thought about that, but it's more complicated than it seems."

"How come?" The solution seemed simple to Jade.

"First of all, custody is a tricky thing. Jim's fighting for full custody based on the idea that living with you — a person of strong faith — would be damaging for Ty. If we walk in and present a DNA test, you can be sure everyone involved will be highly suspicious. Second, in many states fatherhood is less a matter of biological factors than it is familiarity. The courts have actually awarded custody to boyfriends on that basis. The question here will be who raised Ty? Who does Ty think of as his father? The answer, obviously, is Jim."

Jade listened intently. She still didn't understand why Tanner couldn't call off the trial now that he knew the truth.

Tanner leaned back into the sofa and stared at the ceiling for a moment before turning his gaze on Jade once more. "It's pretty clear here that Jim's not trying to win custody because of some deep love he has for Ty. My guess is that his reason is simple: He wants to make a point. That your faith is dangerous to your child. And if a judge is willing to give Jim complete custody because of your faith, then why wouldn't my faith be equally problematic? I mean, if you're a religious fanatic, what does that make me?"

"Worse?" Jade was beginning to understand.

"Much worse. And since I don't have a relationship with Ty, it would still be very possible for a judge to grant complete custody to Jim. And we can't have that."

The hope Jade had felt moments earlier was gone. "No, that would be awful."

"So I've decided to go on with the hearing. I think our best shot is to win custody back based on your religious freedom, your constitutional rights. If that happens, my guess is Jim will bow out fairly easily. Like I said, I don't think he's really interested in Ty."

"I get it. But it seems like we're playing games. And what if we lose? It could take months or years, and then —"

"Shh." Tanner cradled her close and stroked her hair, and after a minute he pulled back and kissed her again. "Let me take care of it."

"Even if we win, you can't tell anyone the truth, Tanner. Your career would be ruined."

"I don't care about my career. Jade, I've missed you so much. I can't believe I'm here. I feel like . . . like I'm dreaming."

His being near her made her body feel like it was on fire. She could feel the length of him and knew neither of them would be willing to let go if they didn't stop soon.

She pulled away first. They'd made this mistake once; she wasn't going to let it happen again. "You need to sleep, have you thought about that?"

"I need you. . . ." He reached for her and she took his hand. "Jade, marry me. When this mess is over and everything's straightened out. Please."

Her heart soared, and tears burned in her eyes. *Lord, is this what you planned? Is this the future you have for me?*

Yes, my daughter. For I know the plans I have for you. . . .

The Scripture sounded clearly in her mind, and she was overcome by God's mercy, his faithfulness. She and Tanner had gone against God's will, and in the wake of that she had chosen to go her own way. But still, through every nightmare in the past ten years, God had been drawing them together.

He was waiting for an answer, and with tears streaming down her face, Jade leaned her head back and laughed. "Yes, Tanner. Yes!"

He caught her by the back of the neck and drew her close once more, kissing her. "Jade, I can't believe you're here. Everything that's happened. . . ."

Flee, my daughter.

The warning was painfully familiar, and Jade knew better than not to heed it. She pulled away and made her arms stiff. "Stay back." Despite her purposefully light tone, clearly Tanner understood.

"You're right." He rattled his car keys. "What would you think about giving me directions to the nearest hotel?" He winked at her. "I've got an important date tomorrow with a very special little boy, and a little sleep wouldn't hurt."

"Motel Six, you mean?" Jade grinned and gave him directions. Suddenly everything in life looked so much brighter. They would get Ty back no matter what. After all, Jim wasn't his real father, and Tanner had promised. Whatever it took.

Tanner moved closer to the door and leaned back, his head resting against the frame. "What if he doesn't like me?" She joined him, and he slipped his arms around her waist.

"He'll like you." She brushed a lock of hair off his forehead and leaned her head against his chest. "He already told me so."

He pulled back a few inches so that their eyes met once more. "He told you that?"

"He said he saw you with me on TV, told me you seemed like a nice guy."

"Really?" Jade's heart melted at the concern in Tanner's eyes. How had she thought she could keep him from his son?

"Really. He told me he wants to meet you."

Tanner closed his eyes for a moment, and then opened them slowly. "You're still here."

"What do you mean?"

He nuzzled her neck. "I mean I can't believe you're here."

Jade leaned into him and savored the feel of his face against hers. "When Jim divorced me, I felt God allowed it to punish me for going against him. It only served me right for deceiving Jim. I knew how much God hates divorce, and I prayed he would heal the break between Jim and me. But Jim wasn't open at all. He'd had enough. Then, when I lost Ty —" Her voice broke and she swallowed hard. "Well, I thought God had forgotten about me. But he didn't." She met his eyes and smiled through the tears. "Despite my weaknesses, he had plans for me, remember our verse?"

"I remember. Jeremiah 29:11."

"Right. . . ." Jade ran her finger along the edge of Tanner's neck. It was hard to believe they were finally together, where their hearts belonged. "God had plans for us, but we went against his will and . . . I thought he was going to punish me forever."

"Ah, Jade." Tanner kissed her forehead tenderly. "God isn't like that. There's another verse you need to memorize. Romans 8:28: God works all things to the good for those who love him."

"Even this?" She snuggled close to him.

"Even this." Tanner found her face again, and they kissed once more. This time he pulled away. "I better get some sleep." He leaned close once more and kissed her again.

"It's hard to let go. . . ."

He drew in a deep breath and exhaled dramatically. "Tell me about it."

"Good night."

"Wait." The door was open, and the cool night air made her shiver. "There's something we need to do before I go."

"What?" Jade saw the serious look in his eyes, and she moved closer to him, appreciating the way he warmed her. He reached for her hands and folded his fingers over hers.

"Pray with me, Jade. Please. It's been so long."

They came together in prayer like they hadn't since that long ago summer. Only this time they whispered words of thanks and requests for strength in the weeks to come. After several minutes, Tanner ended the prayer.

"Lord, I want to pray for the first time ever . . . for my son." He squeezed Jade's hands. "Thank you that you have always been with him and thank you for letting me find him now. Please help me build a relationship with him. And with Jade."

He kissed her one last time before leaving. And as Jade fell asleep, she heard Tanner's prayer over and over again. *I want to pray for my son . . . for my son . . . for my son.* The nightmare was almost over, and when it was, they would finally be a family — the three of them.

The thought of it made Jade's heart swell to nearly bursting.

THIRTY-FIVE

Jade met Tanner outside the motel the next morning, and while she drove the five miles to Jim's apartment, Tanner fired one question after another. "What's his favorite sport?"

"Basketball." Jade's tone was light, teasing, but inside she was relieved that Tanner cared so deeply. Her son had craved fatherly love and attention, and Tanner wanted desperately to meet those needs.

"What about baseball?"

"Baseball's okay. Basketball's better."

"Did he play Little League?"

"Little League, flag football, and most of all —"

"Basketball." Tanner's grin lit up the car. "That's my boy."

"Anything else?" Jade glanced at him. He didn't look a day over twenty-seven. He'd matured into a very striking man, and again Jade ached at all the years they'd lost.

"Does he like to talk?"

"Yes." Jade laughed. "He comes by it honestly."

Tanner mouthed, "Me?" and pointed to himself in mock astonishment.

"Yes, you. You haven't stopped asking questions since I picked you up."

He smiled. "My way of reminding myself I'm not dreaming. Every time you answer I'm forced to believe it's true." He stared at her, the smile gone, his eyes glistening with emotion. "You're really here beside me."

Jade reached across the car and wove her fingers through his. "I can't believe it, either."

They pulled up in front of Jim's apartment and parked. The officers were already sitting in their patrol car, and Jade waved casually at them.

"Your monitoring crew?"

Jade uttered a brief laugh. "You guessed it. Just in case I do something really harmful — you know, like wield a Bible at Ty."

"I'm still amazed any judge in his right mind would —"

She put her finger up to his mouth. "Don't. It doesn't matter. Everything's going to work out."

When the engine was off, they faced each other, and Tanner's eyes were filled with love for her. "I still feel like I'm dreaming, Jade."

She felt the hairs on her arms stand up straight. "Don't look at me like that in public."

Tanner motioned to the apartment complex. "Come on. Ty will be waiting."

Jade drew a deep breath and squeezed Tanner's hand. "Okay. Let's go."

The sun was making a rare early spring appearance, and Ty raced out the door in shorts and a sweatshirt as Jade and Tanner made their way up the walk.

"Mom!" Ty raced to Jade but stopped when he saw Tanner trailing behind her. "Wow . . . I didn't think I'd get to meet him today."

Jade laughed and willed herself not to weep at the significance of the moment. "Ty, I'd like you to meet a friend of mine, Mr. Tanner Eastman."

Ty nodded shyly. "Nice to meet you, sir."

Tanner stooped down to the boy's level and placed his hands on the child's shoulders. "Nice to meet you, too."

Jade saw nothing uncomfortable in Ty's expression as he remained there, facing Tanner, his face cocked curiously to one side. "So you're the guy who's going to get me back home, right?"

"I'm going to do my best, buddy."

Jade saw the glint of tears in Tanner's eyes. In all her life she never imagined a scene like this one. God was good, and certainly he would see them through the hearing. Even if Tanner was worried about the outcome.

They settled onto the front porch steps, Jade on Ty's left and Tanner on his right. She had missed Ty terribly and normally would have been anxious to talk with him. Instead, she said little and allowed Tanner the chance to get to know his son.

"I hear you're a basketball fan." Tanner rested his arms on his knees and turned his head so he and Ty were facing each other.

"Yeah, hoops are the best." Jade savored the enthusiasm in her son's voice. How long had it been since Jim had asked Ty about his hobbies or interests? He probably never had. Yet when the hour was up, they would be forced to leave him completely in Jim's care.

It's not fair, God.

In response she felt a deep-seated peace that caused the clouds of bitterness to dissipate. Somehow, no matter how dismal the current situation, she believed that one day they'd be together as a family. It would not be easy, certainly. If she won Ty back, Jade

518

knew the bond between her son and his father would take time to develop. It would never be what it could have been if she and Tanner had followed God's plan instead of succumbing to their own desires. But if they did get their chance, she felt certain the life they would someday share would be true and real, and that it would last forever.

"Think I could come see you play?" Tanner's enthusiasm was genuine, and from where she sat watching them, Jade smiled.

"League play's over. . . ." Ty thought a moment. "But there's tournaments starting next month on the weekends. You could come then!"

"Deal."

"Hey, what's it like being on TV and stuff?"

Tanner laughed. "I'm only on TV when one of my clients winds up in big trouble." Jade caught the concern in his eyes. "Then it's something you forget about. I'm usually too busy helping my client to think about it."

"Mom's your client, right?"

Tanner's eyes met hers, and Jade felt a shiver pass over her. He had a way of seeing straight through her, down to the deepest part of her soul. "Yes." Tanner reached across Ty and squeezed Jade's hands. "Your mom's a client. And she needs a lot of help right now. Lots of prayers."

Ty frowned. "You mean because of the hearing."

"Right."

"You mean I might not get to come home?" Ty had been so happy, but now doubt clouded his face.

Watching him broke Jade's heart, and she pulled him close. "Mr. Eastman's going to do everything he can, honey." She exchanged a quick glance with Tanner. "One way or another we're going to get you back home. Okay?"

"Okay." Tears filled the corners of Ty's eyes.

"I'm not too worried about it. Best thing I can do is pray for help. When I get up there before the judge, God'll have to give me the words to say." Tanner ran the back of his hand gently over Ty's cheek. "You're praying, too, right?"

Ty ran his fists under his eyes and dried his cheeks. "I wanna go home with my mom."

This time Tanner slipped an arm around the boy and hugged him. "That's what we're going to tell the judge."

The door opened and Jim stood there, glaring at them. "Get your hands off my son!" He stepped out on the porch as if he might push Tanner, and in the distance the officers both turned their attention toward Jim. He noticed them and immediately relaxed his stance. This time he pasted a smile on his face and spoke in a quiet hiss. "I said . . . get your hands off my son!"

Jade didn't bother to get up. Let Jim look like a hothead in front of the officers. "He's my attorney, Jim. Besides, this is *my* time. Leave us alone."

The plastered smile remained, but Jim shot a vicious glance at Tanner and then turned back to her. "I don't care who he is, I want his hands off my son."

Tanner loosened the hold he had on Ty and leaned back. Jade wished he would say something, threaten a lawsuit, anything. But Tanner remained silent.

Ty glared at Jim and slid closer to Tanner. "I can talk to anyone I want."

Jade caught her son's eyes and gave him a look. *Not now, Ty. Don't be rude now.* Ty slid away from Tanner once more, and Jade was proud of him. The upcoming hearing was too packed with emotions and tensions already. At this point Jade, Tanner, and Ty needed to be agreeable.

"Go in the house, Jim. Everything's under control." Jade stared at him until finally he disappeared back through the front door. How she wished they could stop this nonsense, and that Tanner could look Jim in the eyes and tell him the truth.

But Tanner had already explained that to her. The possibility was too strong that Jim would still win complete custody because he was the man Ty identified as his father, and because he was more tolerant in his views than either Jade or Tanner. No, their best chance was to fight the case from the angle they'd already planned and hope that she'd win Ty back because of her First Amendment protection, her right to believe in God and teach his truths to her child.

The hour was up, and Jim's appearance had dampened the mood considerably. "Well, buddy, nice talking with you. I'm sure we'll talk again sometime soon." Tanner pulled Ty into a hug, and Jade was grateful. Tanner had his reasons for saying nothing to Jim earlier, but he was obviously not intimidated by him.

"And you'll come to my tournaments, right?" Ty's voice was no longer enthusiastic. It never was when the hour was up and it was time to say good-bye for another week.

"Right."

"Ty, we'll see you Monday at the courthouse. You'll be there in case the judge needs to talk to you. Okay?" Jade held her son's face in her hands and searched his eyes.

"Okay."

They said good-bye, and Jade waited until her back was to Ty before she started crying. Without saying a word, Tanner fell in step beside her and wrapped an arm around her shoulder.

"I don't want *my* boy —" his voice was strained with emotion — "living with that man one more day."

A tense and anxious silence filled the car as Jade drove Tanner back to his motel. It was painful to leave Ty behind, knowing the way Jim felt, his lack of love for her son, his anger for Jade.

Help me, God, I'm so afraid. The prayer passed through her mind, and she knew she wouldn't have survived the past weeks without her faith.

Trust in me with all your heart and lean not on your own understanding.

Jade forced herself to breathe slowly. *I'm trying, Lord. Help me trust you more.*

Whatever the coming days held, the waiting was almost finished. The hearing was less than forty-eight hours away.

THIRTY-SIX

There was no mistaking something of great importance was happening at the Clackamas County Courthouse that Monday morning. Media vans clogged the parking lot and well-dressed news anchors milled about outside, sipping coffee and bemoaning the dampness of spring in the Northwest.

Jade arrived at the scene alone, thankful Tanner had made prior arrangements. In an agreement with Jim's attorney she would park near the rear of the courthouse and enter through a private door. There she would go to Room 12, where she would meet with Ty in what was scheduled to be a private session.

She eyed the sea of reporters and prayed God would protect her from them. At least right now when she had just five minutes before meeting with her son.

Jade parked her car and thought about

Tanner. He had met up with his partner, Matt Bronzan, Saturday night, and the two had taken a hotel room near the courthouse. They ordered in meals and without other interruptions ran through every aspect of research and case history pertaining to the case. She hadn't heard from Tanner until late last night.

"Have you read the newspapers?" Tanner sounded concerned, and Jade felt her anxiety increase.

"No. I try to avoid them these days."

"They've done their homework, Jade. Big piece in *The Oregonian* quotes you as saying U.S. Department of Education should not be allowed to parent our children."

Dread filled her heart, "How'd they get that?"

"I'm guessing you said it during one of your school board meetings, right?"

Jade thought back. "You're right. Three years ago, I think."

"Well, they found it, and you can be sure they'll use it against you."

Jade didn't miss a beat. "It's true. They shouldn't be parenting our kids."

Tanner sighed. "I know that and you know that, but judges are part of the judicial system. And the judicial system is part of the U.S. government."

Jade felt sick to her stomach. "So it's me against them."

"Exactly."

"You're really worried, aren't you?"

Tanner paused. "Maybe because I know he's my son . . . because I've seen how Jim is around him . . . I don't know. But it's going to take everything we've got to win this time."

Remembering their conversation, she whispered a brief prayer. Then she checked herself in the rearview mirror and slipped on a wide-brimmed hat and a flouncy scarf, both of which helped hide her face. Her eyes trained on the ground, she climbed out of her car and headed toward the back of the courthouse.

The reporters kept their distance. Apparently they were assuming she would arrive with Tanner, so she made her way inside the building without pause and found Room 12. *Okay, Lord, give me the strength.* If she lost the hearing today, this would be the last time she and Ty would spend together alone for months. Maybe even years.

Tanner and Matt had arrived hours earlier and were going over their case one last time in a private office adjoining the courtroom. As Tanner had predicted early on, the hearing would be heard by Judge Susan Wilder, and that fact alone sent shivers of apprehension through Tanner.

In their research over the past few days the lawyers at CPRR reviewed the cases Judge Wilder had heard. She had ruled that a Portland woman, Anna Jenkins, who'd been injured in an auto accident was entitled to only minimal compensation even though she was not to blame in the collision. In her ruling she stated, "Ms. Jenkins was carrying out a work-related task and therefore should have taken into account the hazards of the job."

Matt had done further research and learned that the Jenkins woman was a volunteer with the local crisis pregnancy center and had been transporting handouts from the printer back to the center.

"In other words," Tanner concluded, "the judgment went against her, at least in part, because of her involvement in the Pro-Life movement."

There were other cases. A teacher at one of the public high schools allowed a Bible study to meet in his classroom before school each Wednesday. Time and again this same teacher was denied the stipend usually allotted to staff members who sponsor extra-curricular activities. When the case reached

Judge Wilder's courtroom, she ruled in favor of the school district.

"In accordance with separation of church and state, it is my opinion that the school district does not need to compensate this teacher for his involvement in an extracurricular Bible study. Other clubs are supported by the U.S. government as being neutral and in the best interest of the students. Bible study — while not something we can forbid — certainly crosses the line that separates church and state and therefore cannot be supported by the government or the school district."

After reading Judge Wilder's decision for half the day Sunday, Tanner had taken to pacing the hotel floor. "The timing is perfect for Jade to lose here, Matt. Are you seeing that?"

Matt sifted through the briefs on the table. "If it could happen anywhere, it could happen here."

"Jade's husband couldn't have picked a better judge if he'd paid for one."

They agreed there was just one way to argue before a jurist with such obvious prejudice. And to that end they had spent the remainder of the day and much of the night preparing.

Now he and Matt were already set up in

the courtroom. Tanner rubbed his eyes and knew that God alone had used that final preparation session to provide them the inspiration and ideas they would need to win the hearing. They were about to see if it would be enough to sway Judge Wilder.

An hour passed, and Jade entered the courtroom. She wore black slacks and a soft, blue blouse. Tanner smiled in approval. It would not help her cause to show up in a skirt with her hair in a bun. That was often how women with Jade's convictions were portrayed by the media, but Jade — like most women of faith — wasn't someone who fit stereotypes. It was important for the jury to see that a woman could appear very businesslike and intelligent and still have a deep faith.

The hearing was set to begin in twenty minutes, and when Jade looked at him, Tanner could see she'd been crying. He wanted desperately to go to her, hold her, and tell her everything would work out. But the reporters had begun to take their places, and every eye would be scrutinizing the two of them, looking for a chink in their very public armor of faith. They had dared to stand up for what they believed, and many members of the press would be anxiously looking for them to fall — in whatever way possible. A fall would mean conflict; and conflict made for breaking news.

Tanner understood the press well. He didn't believe they were in a conspiracy against people of faith so much as they held to a standard party line. An unfair portrayal in a handful of newspapers meant other editors would see the stories and run similar layouts. The media seldom seemed to report the truth on any topic. Rather, they gave a series of perceptions commonly held by the handful of people who assumed powerful editorial positions on newspapers and news stations across the country.

He looked at the reporters gathered there and thought about what they would do to him — and to Jade — if they knew he was Ty's father. It was something he would have to face eventually, but not until the time was right.

Jade made her way closer and took the chair next to him. Their backs were to the members of the press, and Jade leaned over and whispered, "I feel like a criminal or something."

Tanner gave a slight nod but kept his distance. "In the eyes of some people here, you are. We both are."

Jim and his attorney appeared and took their seats at the table earmarked for the plaintiff. By the time Judge Wilder entered the courtroom, spectators and reporters packed the seats.

Tanner had long since stopped relying on developing a rapport with the judges who heard his cases. He was openly conservative and an outspoken Christian. In other words, he was a marked man. The cases he won, he did so with the help of God and by leaning heavily on America's founding fathers and the ideas they had expressed when writing the constitution.

Today would be no exception.

For the first hour, they heard testimony in favor of the current custody ruling. Jim's attorney marched a handful of upstanding community members onto the stand, who one by one testified that Jade's views were extreme and bound to have a negative effect on her child.

"Why should a person's religious viewpoint make her an unsuitable mother?" Jim's attorney tossed out the question as if he were genuinely unsure of the answer.

The man on the stand, a long-time member of the local school board, raised his chin and glanced at Jade in disdain. "When a parent teaches a child to steal or kill, we have no trouble recognizing that as abusive parenting, and we do the right thing as a society. We take the child away." He paused and resumed eye contact with Jim's attorney. "Mrs. Rudolph is teaching her son to be insensitive to the diverse nature of our culture. She is teaching him to hate. And that — whether we're ready to recognize it or not — is abusive parenting."

Things couldn't have been going worse.

Matt took notes furiously while Tanner listened and provided cross-examination. As a rule, he stayed away from anything that might appear argumentative. They would not win this case by getting in a fighting match with the plaintiff's witnesses. Rather, they would have to present their facts in a manner both calm and approachable, assuring the judge they had nothing to hide.

Tanner knew too well that when a Christian flew off the handle or yelled out in court or showed up carrying banners with Bible verses, newspapers ran photos of the event across the top of the page. This fed the media perception that believers were extreme fanatics, which in turn fueled public perception. Tanner's job was to show these reporters how different Jade was from the right-wing image they'd bought into over the years.

The last bit of testimony presented in favor of Jim Rudolph was a journal entry written by Jim and dated just three weeks prior.

Jim was called to the stand to read it and verify that it was an accurate portrayal of the events as he understood them.

"Today I took Ty home from school after basketball practice. While we were driving, he asked me if I believed in God." Jim paused and glared at Jade. "I told him I did not believe and that this was my choice. I told him everyone was entitled to his or her different beliefs.

"At that point my son became alarmed and told me I was wrong. He said there was only one way to heaven and that was through Jesus Christ."

Jim practically hissed the last two words, and Tanner felt a stab of sorrow for this man who could so openly defame the one who had created him. At the same time Tanner was fiercely proud of Ty. And of Jade, for teaching him the truth.

Jim took a drink of water and continued reading his journal entry. "I told the child that not everyone needed to believe in Jesus Christ. Some people believe in other gods. Some people believe in themselves. I told him he should be tolerant of what other people believed because that was the best way for them."

Jim's attorney nodded in agreement, and Tanner thought he saw the judge do the same. Clearly this was the accepted doctrine in U.S. courts today. The fact that Jim had tried to correct his son with this modern-day "truth" would make him nothing less than a hero in the eyes of too many government officials.

Jim continued. "But Ty looked at me and told me again that I was wrong. He said he was worried that I would go to hell if I didn't accept Jesus and believe in him. He said he knew Jesus was the only way to heaven because that's —" he paused — "what his mother told him."

An almost imperceptible look of dismay crossed Judge Wilder's face. Tanner held his breath. *Dear God, let her be at least partially open to what I have to say. Please.*

He glanced at Jade, at her eyes filling with tears, and he mouthed a silent exhortation: "Pray."

She nodded and briefly closed her eyes.

The attorney directed Jim to other slips of paper that contained additional journal entries. In each there was a reference to faith and the fact that Ty had credited his mother with teaching him to believe.

When it was time for Tanner to cross-examine Jim, he decided to stick to the journal theme. "You brought lots of journal entries with you today, didn't you Mr. Rudolph?" Tanner forced himself to remain calm, casting a smile in the other man's direction.

"Yes. I've been very careful about taking notes for the past few months."

Tanner nodded. "Very well. Then could you locate the journal entries wherein you record your concern for the boy's safety?"

Jim drew a blank look and turned to the judge for help. "Answer, Mr. Rudolph." Judge Wilder adjusted her robe and crossed her arms firmly in front of her.

"I don't understand the question."

"Very well, let me rephrase it." Tanner wandered closer to Jim. "I assume that you are concerned with the child's safety. That you believe Mrs. Rudolph is a danger to the boy, is that right?"

"Yes. She's a danger to his mental health."

"All right then, did you bring any journal entries that describe episodes where you feared for the boy's safety?"

Jim shook his head.

"Answer out loud for the court, please." Judge Wilder's reminder was pleasant but firm.

"No, I didn't bring any." Jim all but snarled his response.

Tanner let his surprise show on his face. "You didn't bring any . . . or there aren't any? Which is it, Mr. Rudolph?"

Jim exhaled dramatically. "There aren't any."

"So are you telling this court that you have no record of any incidents wherein your wife mistreated the child in question?" Tanner stopped directly in front of Jim.

"She mistreated him all the time." Jim sneered in Jade's direction. "I just didn't take any notes."

The reporters scribbled furiously, and Tanner stared hard at the man. In that instant he would gladly have pushed Jim Rudolph over a cliff. After how he'd treated Jade and Ty, it was all Tanner could do to continue quizzing the man without losing control.

"Objection. The witness is answering beyond the scope of the question."

Judge Wilder glanced at Jim. "Sustained. Keep your answer specific to the question, Mr. Rudolph."

"No. I didn't keep track in the journal."

"Very well, Mr. Rudolph, since you've chosen to open the topic, please tell this court of any incidents where your wife mistreated or abused the child in question." Tanner couldn't bring himself to refer to the boy as Jim's son. Not now.

Jim squirmed on the witness stand. "Specific events?"

Tanner planted himself in front of Jim. "Yes. Whatever events of mistreatment or abuse you can recall."

Jim paused a moment. "I'm not sure I can recall them at this time."

Again Tanner nodded. "Very well. So is it correct to say that you do not have record of any instance wherein your wife mistreated the child, is that right?"

"Right." Jim mumbled the word.

"Speak up, please."

"Right!" Jim barked the word, his eyebrows angled toward the bridge of his nose. Tanner smiled. *Good. Get mad. Make the judge's decision that much easier.*

"And you also cannot recall any specific instance where your wife abused the child, is that right?"

"Yes."

"Thank you, no further questions, your honor."

Tanner expected Judge Wilder would take a brief break before he began calling witnesses in Jade's defense, but she plowed ahead.

"I am not unaware of the stakes in this case." She motioned toward the back of the courtroom. "Virtually the entire country is holding its collective breath outside those courtroom doors. Therefore there will be no breaks until I have heard all the testimony."

Tanner took his cue and called his first witness, Jackie Conley, Jade's friend from the Bible study group. Jackie had a master's degree in psychology and worked part-time as a counselor in a firm that dealt with high-level management clients. She was articulate and straightforward and delivered a glowing opinion of Jade as if she'd spent hours analyzing her.

Jackie was followed by Barry Burns, manager of a Portland convenience store, who had been thankful when Jade brought to his attention the content of magazines he'd been carrying on his shelves. He confirmed that she was merely looking out for the best interest of the community and especially the children.

"Do you think Jade Rudolph is a wacko, Mr. Burns?" Tanner managed to keep a straight face, but several members of the media snickered.

The old man on the witness stand grinned. "No, sir. She's a hard worker, though. I'll give you that."

Finally, Tanner put Jade on the stand. They had agreed earlier that Ty would remain in another room, spared the events of the hearing and from having to act as a witness. Jade felt it would be too much to put the boy through. Especially when he would soon find out the truth about Tanner.

Much like the press conference, Tanner walked Jade through a series of questions revealing the types of issues she had been involved in and her reasons behind them. Time and again, Jade's answer was the same. "I felt I had no choice but to protect the children involved."

"Has Ty ever said anything to you about where he wants to live, who he feels more comfortable with?" Tanner presented the question as casually as he could. He knew that Jim's attorney would pounce on this, accusing Jade of brainwashing her son, but still he thought the court should hear what Jade had to say on the matter.

She struggled for a moment, and Tanner willed her to be strong. *Help her, Lord. Put your peace in her heart.*

Jade reached into her shirt pocket and took out a folded piece of notebook paper. "I could tell you how Ty feels, the things he's said to me . . ." She held up the note. "Or I could read you this letter. He wrote it over the weekend and gave it to me this morning." She looked at the judge and the members of the press. "He wanted me to read it to you."

Tanner was speechless. Jade had said nothing about the note until now. A surge of hope welled up inside him, and he turned to Judge Wilder. "Your honor, we'd like to admit the letter from the boy as Exhibit A."

"Very well." Judge Wilder looked bored, as if she'd already made up her mind. Tanner prayed she hadn't.

He turned to Jade. "You may read the letter now."

Jade opened the paper near the microphone and the sound echoed throughout the courtroom. " 'Dear Miss Judge . . .' " Jade swallowed hard. " 'I wanted to write you a letter so you would know where I want to live. I want to live with my Mom.' " Again Jade struggled. " 'I know that you think she's forcing me to believe in God the way she does, but that isn't so. I will believe no matter where I live. I will believe because the Bible is true more than anything else.' "

Jade wiped a tear as it slid down her cheek, " 'I am in fourth grade now, and that's pretty old. I am old enough to know that my dad doesn't really care about me. He talks about the hearing all the time, and he told his girlfriend he wanted me to live with him to prove a point. Also so he wouldn't have to pay child support.' "

"Objection, your honor!" Jim's attorney was on his feet, his face beet red. "The child's letter is hearsay. There's nothing on the record to indicate the plaintiff wishes to discontinue paying child support."

Judge Wilder cast a look of reprimand at Tanner. "Objection sustained." Her eyes moved to Jade, "You may continue, Mrs. Rudolph, but please refrain from reading statements that are based on hearsay."

"Yes, your honor." Jade kept her eyes trained on the letter and exhaled slowly. " 'My Dad doesn't ask me about my day. He doesn't go to my games, and he doesn't even know my teacher's name, or that I want to be a missionary when I grow up. After I play college hoops, of course.' "

Tanner felt his heart melt at his son's words. *He wants to be a missionary, Lord.* Tanner watched several members of the media smile at the mention of college hoops. Ty wasn't a brainwashed puppet. He was like any other child in America, with dreams and hopes and a desire for his parents to be interested in him. Tanner couldn't wait to fill the role.

Jade drew a deep breath. " 'So, what I'm trying to say is, please let me go home to my mom. She loves me more than anyone. And if you want to know the truth, I think it's because that's the way God wants her to love me.' " Jade smiled sweetly at the words her son had written. " 'Sincerely, Ty Rudolph.' "

There was a lengthy pause while the child's innocent words hit their mark. Tanner turned to the judge. "The defense rests, your honor."

Jim's attorney tapped his pencil on the table and scanned his notes. Jade was certain at any moment he would take to his feet and cross-examine her, tear apart the legitimacy of the letter.

But instead he set his pencil down, rose, and announced that he had no further questions. Jade returned to her place beside Tanner as Jim's attorney presented the court with his closing remarks. He referred to the dangers of intolerance and the frightening place the nation would be if parents like Jade were allowed to continue brainwashing their children. He completely ignored any reference to Ty's letter until the end of his speech.

"Children say a lot of things that don't necessarily make sense to adults." The attorney smiled at Judge Wilder. "If children were able to make these decisions on their own, there would be no need for judges and courts." He hesitated and glanced at Jade. "But in this situation we have Jade Rudolph — a wolf in sheep's clothing. Her teachings and right-wing behavior will color the child's perceptions for decades, perhaps for a lifetime.

"It is at times like this that we need to step in and make the decision that is truly best for the child. Even if it is not a popular decision."

Jim's attorney sat down, and Tanner had to give him credit. His last line had said it all. Taking a child away from his mother because of her faith would not be a popular decision. But if it meant protecting future generations from the narrow-minded views of radical right-wing Christians, it might be the only choice possible.

Usually by this time in a hearing, Tanner knew which way the decision was going to go. But this case was different, more compli-cated. And the fact that he was so emotion-ally involved only complicated things that much more.

As Tanner stood to make his closing argu-ment, he had the sinking suspicion that if he didn't say the right things, Jade would lose this case. And her son. Their son. Matt handed him a brief. He had wanted to wait and see how the case went before deciding whether to use the information he and Matt had studied the day before.

Now he knew. The brief was their last hope.

Tanner addressed the judge and recalled character traits about Jade, elements that certainly seemed to prove she was neither fanatical nor extreme and definitely not given to brainwashing her son. As he spoke, he had the sense that judge Wilder was barely paying attention. He fell silent and walked back to his spot at the table.

There he picked up a one-dollar bill and held it high for the judge to see. He remained that way for a moment so that everyone in attendance had the opportunity to view it. "This is a one-dollar bill, printed by the U.S. government and recognized worldwide as the national currency of this country."

Tanner approached the judge and saw that she seemed slightly more interested than before. "In many ways, your honor, this dollar bill is what started these proceedings in the first place."

He gestured toward Jade. "My client takes a stand against violence, gets magazines removed from the store shelves, and someone —" he held up the bill again — "is out some money." He paused. "My client takes a stand against books that preach a doctrine of murder and suicide; books get removed, and again someone is out money.

"But when my client takes a stand against a commercialized program replete with questionable material, a program sponsored by the U.S. Department of Education, then suddenly she's crossed the line."

Tanner turned to face the courtroom. "Why?" He held up the bill again. "Because now the people who are out some money are the very ones who have the power to take away what she cherishes most of all." Tanner's gaze settled on Jade and he saw her trembling. "Her little boy."

Tanner stared at the bill for a moment. "It says here — on this bill printed by our government — 'In God we trust.' " He paused again and sought out Judge Wilder's face. "Is that so? Or is that only the way we *used* to feel, back two hundred years ago when it was popular to feel that way back when our country was first founded?"

He looked at the bill again. "George Washington's picture is on this bill, and I thought it would be interesting if we could put him on the stand, ask him what he thought about a country where a parent could lose custody of her child because of her beliefs."

Tanner scanned the courtroom and saw that the reporters were spellbound. "I'll tell you what . . . George Washington wouldn't recognize such a country."

He set down the dollar bill and held up Matt's brief. "We can't ask Mr. Washington to testify here today because we no longer have the benefit of his presence among us. However —" Tanner held up the brief — "we have the words he left behind."

Tanner glanced at Jade and saw the surprise in her eyes. She had not known what he and Matt had been working on in their hotel room, but from the gleam in her eyes he could easily see she approved. He positioned the document so he could read it. "In a public address in May, 1789, George Washington stated: 'If I could have entertained the slightest apprehension that the constitution . . . might possibly endanger the religious rights of any ecclesiastical society, certainly I would never have placed my signature to it.' "

Tanner let the comment settle over the courtroom. "Later that year in another public address he said this: 'The liberty enjoyed by the people of these states of worshipping Almighty God agreeable to their consciences is not only among the choicest of their blessings, but also among their rights.' "

The courtroom was utterly still, and Tanner felt as if the former president actually were on the witness stand. This time when Tanner spoke, he did so slowly and clearly, so that not a person in attendance could miss the message.

"Finally, in another public address in 1792, President Washington said this: 'We have abundant reason to rejoice that in this land, the light of truth and reason has triumphed over the power of bigotry —' " he glanced at Judge Wilder — " 'bigotry and superstition. And that every person may here worship God according to the dictates of his own heart. . . . It is our boast that a man's religious tenets will *not* forfeit for him the protection of the laws, nor deprive him of any right . . . whatsoever.' "

There was a lengthy pause, and Tanner saw a change in Judge Wilder's expression. There was something humbling about listening to the words of George Washington, something that seemed to bring a measure of perspective to a system gone mad.

"And so your honor, I ask you to take seriously the words of George Washington, a man whose signature is found at the bottom of the constitution. On December 15, 1791, the First Amendment was added to the constitution." Tanner read the Amendment in its entirety. As he let the last words sink in, he nodded slowly, facing the judge. "You will notice that it absolutely forbids the government to pass any law — or make any decision — that would prohibit the free exercise of religion."

He leveled his gaze at Judge Wilder. "It seems to me, your honor, that this court has already done that by taking Jade Rudolph's son from her because of her religious views. I ask you now, on behalf of Jade and the people of this country, to prove to this court and the members of the press that we are not willing to let go of the freedoms guaranteed us in the constitution. Rather, we will fight to the end to preserve them.

"Please, your honor, restore primary custody to my client so that the people of this nation can sleep easier tonight knowing their constitutional freedoms are safe. Thank you."

Judge Wilder called a ten-minute recess and slipped through a door to her chambers. Muffled conversations broke out across the courtroom as reporters compared notes and guessed about the outcome. Tanner noticed them, but only briefly. His attention was on Jade and the paralyzing look of fear in her eyes.

He sat down beside her, blocking her view of the reporters and of Jim and his attorney. He spoke so that his voice was just loud enough for her to hear. "Worried?"

Jade nodded. "I can barely breathe."

"She's in there making her decision. Let's pray."

They were silent a moment, and Tanner brought their collective fears before the Lord, blocking out the voices around him so that finally he heard the one he was listening for.

Well done, my son. All things work to the good for those who love God. . . .

Okay, Lord, but let Jade get Ty back. Please.

There was no response, and moments later Judge Wilder returned. She did not need to ask the court to come to order. Everyone in shouting distance was waiting breathlessly for her decision.

Tanner winked at Jade and mouthed a message to her: "Trust."

Judge Wilder glanced at a sheet of notes and cleared her throat. "You must first know that I felt honored to have this case in my courtroom. On a personal level, I have to tell you I agree with the plaintiff. I believe

549

we've reached a level of saturation as far as religion is concerned in this country. It had a place at one time but today is little more than a veil, a thin veneer intended to disguise the roots of hatred."

She paused, and Tanner felt his heart rate double. Was it possible? Had she really understood the importance of what he'd read in his closing arguments?

Judge Wilder exhaled slowly. "The day will come, mark my words, where a parent will lose custody of his or her child if his beliefs are not in keeping with the nation as a whole. Extreme beliefs are dangerous, pure and simple."

She stared at Jade, and Tanner feared for their system, a system that allowed a judge such obvious bias. "That said, the plaintiff in this case simply did not do a thorough job of showing potential for harm. Ms. Rudolph's views, while extreme in my opinion, have not been proven to be dangerous. She has not staged a sit-in at an abortion clinic, nor does she belong to a cult that requires her to ignore medical treatment. Those are a few of the many circumstances that would have caused me to uphold the lower court ruling.

"In addition, aside from recounting his estranged wife's extreme views, the plaintiff did nothing to prove any harmful behaviors on the part of Ms. Rudolph. For that reason, I have no cause to believe the child would be in danger if he was returned to his mother."

Judge Wilder looked at her notes again, then gazed across the courtroom. "I was intrigued and troubled by the remarks belonging to former President George Washington. Rather than mourn the loss of religion, I treasure such a shift in our understanding and believe we are a better country today because of it. The deciding factor in this case then, was not ancient rhetoric nor the childish plea from the boy. Rather it was the First Amendment itself. Unless a child is truly in danger, this court must uphold the constitution of the United States and allow no ruling or law that would prohibit someone their right to religious freedom."

Jade couldn't breathe.

She sat there, still, her hands clenched together, sure she would shatter into a million pieces if she moved.

A million pieces of pure, unadulterated joy.

When Judge Wilder had started talking about the "deciding factor," Jade had let herself believe for the first time that she'd won. Hope, wild and overwhelming, coursed through her. Tears spilled onto her cheeks, and when Tanner took her hand in his, she could barely contain herself. She focused her attention on the judge once more.

"Therefore, in a ruling that is against my better judgment, I am hereby overturning the decision in the lower court and ordering that custody be returned to Jade Rudolph. . . ."

Jade squeezed Tanner's hand to keep from jumping out of her chair and shouting her thanks to God. Ty would be hers in a few minutes. Tanner had told her that if she won, the bailiff would escort her to the room where Ty was waiting. The officer would then physically hand him over to Jade. No questions asked.

God . . . God, thank you! You are faithful beyond words.

The judge was still speaking. "Furthermore, since Ms. Rudolph was the primary parent prior to the divorce petition, she will remain the primary parent of record. I have deemed an eighty-twenty split where custody is concerned so that the plaintiff will have the child every other weekend. Are there any questions from the attorneys?"

Jim's lawyer was on his feet. "We'd like to

file a motion for joint custody, a fifty-fifty split."

"Duly noted." The judge wrote something down.

Tanner released Jade's hand, rose from the chair beside her, and nodded to the judge. "Your honor, I'd like to file a motion, but I must warn you it's going to seem very unconventional."

What was this? Jade's eyes followed Tanner as he moved closer to the judge. "Your honor, I'd like to file a motion severing the plaintiff's parental rights in their entirety."

Judge Wilder raised an eyebrow. "Do you intend to explain yourself?"

"Yes, your honor."

Jade's heart was pounding against her chest. What was he doing? Where was he going with this? Had he forgotten who was in the courtroom? Enough media to wipe out his law practice in the space of time it took to call in a headline.

"Go ahead, counselor." Judge Wilder looked frustrated, as though Tanner were ignorant of some unwritten protocol.

"Your honor, I have prepared a brief with various documents proving that the plaintiff should not be entitled to any parental rights because —" he paused long enough to glance at Jade — "the plaintiff is not the boy's biological father."

"What?" Jim bounded up from his chair and had to be held back by his attorney. "He's crazy! He doesn't know what he's talking about."

Tanner remained calm. He retrieved a brief from Matt Bronzan and handed it to the judge. "Everything's there. A DNA test has been performed, and the results will be available soon. At that time there will be no question as to the validity of this brief."

For the first time that morning, Judge Wilder seemed speechless. Jade didn't care. Her eyes were on Tanner, stunned by his admission and the fact that he'd prepared a brief on the issue. How could she have ever doubted him?

The judge sorted through the brief and then stopped, her eyes trained on an item near the back of the document. She looked up, fixing her gaze on Tanner. "You mean to tell me, *you're* the boy's father, Mr. Eastman?" There was mockery in her voice, and as if by cue, the members of the press moved a step closer.

"Yes, your honor. Ms. Rudolph and I were together that summer and . . . yes, your honor. There are a lot of circumstances involved, but Ms. Rudolph believed I had abandoned her. As a result, she agreed to a marriage proposal the plaintiff had made a year earlier."

Jim glared at Jade and sank slowly into his chair. Their eyes met, and Jade saw anger and humiliation there. But not surprise. And in that moment it became clear to Jade that her longtime suspicions were probably true — he'd known about Ty all the time.

If that were true — if Jim had known Ty wasn't his biological son — it was no wonder he had treated the boy with such indifference. Suddenly the custody battle made sense. Jim had taken her in, thought she'd come to care for him, only to discover that the woman he'd always longed for had betrayed him. With another man. It must have been abundantly clear to him that she'd come out of need, not out of desire. And that had been her greatest betrayal of all.

This — the hearing, the push to take Ty from her — it was Jim's way of paying her back for lying to him all those years. Jade felt a wave of remorse.

God, forgive me. Forgive me for bringing him such grief, such sorrow. Forgive me for whatever part I played in driving Jim into the arms of another woman with my dishonesty. He deserved a wife who truly loved him, Lord.

Tanner was still speaking. "Either way, the

information is all in the brief." He shrugged. "Also for the record, when Ms. Rudolph's divorce is final, I will be marrying her and claiming my rightful place as the boy's father."

Judge Wilder fell back against her chair and threw up her hands. "Why didn't you say so in the *first* place? We could have avoided this hearing altogether."

"Because Ms. Rudolph deserved to win this case as a way of protecting her constitutional freedoms. Now that this court has agreed with her rights, it must also know the truth before an accurate discussion of custody can be made."

The judge's face grew serious, and she sat up in her chair. "My decree regarding custody will stand until I have had time to review this brief and examine results from the DNA test. At that point all parties will be notified, and a permanent arrangement will be determined. Court dismissed."

The judge disappeared, and the courtroom erupted in conversation and a push by the media toward Tanner and Jade. Jim and his attorney stood up and headed for the side door.

"Jim, wait. . . ." Jade worked her way past Tanner until she was face to face with the man who had been her husband. "I'm sorry.

You deserved to hear that from me. Not here, like this."

Jim's eyes were cool, almost indifferent. "I was a fool to love you, Jade. To think you ever cared for me. As for the boy —" he shrugged — "I knew from the beginning he wasn't my son. I had an injury in high school, playoff football game my junior year. Doctor told me I'd never have children."

What? An injury . . . ? "Then why . . . ?"

The smile that tipped his lips was bitter. "You came to me, remember? I thought maybe if I didn't say anything . . ."

An ache developed in Jade's chest. *Dear God, what have I done to this man? Forgive me, please.* "I wondered if you knew, but I wasn't sure. Not until a few minutes ago. I'm sorry, Jim. I never meant to hurt you."

"You never meant to love me, either. You came to me pregnant, hoping I would give you security and a home for your child. I never knew who you'd been with, only that he was a fool to let you go."

Jade saw the anger cool slightly, and in its place was deep and profound pain. Their marriage had never had a chance. Jade's eyes remained locked on Jim's. "And when you realized why I showed up that day, you determined to keep your distance."

Jim nodded. "We should have split up a

long time ago, Jade. Your silence about Ty's father told me that whoever he was, you loved him the way you'd never love me. Problem was, I could never quite make myself stop loving you. But these last few years . . . well, I found someone who cared about me, and you didn't seem to mind. Most of the time you never asked where I was."

The media was moving closer, and Jade needed to get back to Tanner. He would join the bailiff in walking her to the private room where Ty was waiting for her. "You hate me, don't you, Jim?"

His gaze was unemotional. "I don't care enough about you anymore to hate you. This hearing was about what Kathy wanted. She thought Ty could be the son she never had." He looked away. "The boy mattered more to you than I did. Right from the day he was born. If I got full custody of him, then it served you right."

Jade felt a chill pass down her spine. If this man had won today, Ty would have been little more than a pawn. *Thank you, God.* . . .

"I'm sorry."

Jim's eyes narrowed. "You won. But then, you always do. Ty wasn't my boy; I didn't want him anyway."

Jade nodded. She knew Jim's words were in part to conceal the hurt she'd caused him, but there was truth there, too. "I know."

Jim ran his eyes over the length of her. "I'll never forgive myself for letting you get under my skin, Jade. But don't worry your Christian heart over me. I'll be fine." He smiled through cold eyes. "I got bigger fish to fry now. And don't worry about the judge's decision. I'm tired of fighting with you. You can have your kid back. I want no part of him. Or of you."

She wanted to apologize once more, tell him she never meant to hurt him. But there was no point now. After ten years of marriage they were nothing but strangers. "Good-bye, Jim."

Working her way back to Tanner, Jade saw the concern in his eyes. "What did you say to him?"

She held a finger up to his lips. "Later. Right now we have a little boy to pick up."

Tanner took her hand, and they managed to sneak out a side door without answering a single one of the dozens of questions being hurled at him by the swarming members of the media. A bailiff ushered them down a hallway void of any reporters and into the correct room.

"Mom! Mr. Eastman!" Ty ran to her and jumped in her arms. "Well? Did we win?"

Jade wrapped her arms around her son and snuggled her face against his. "Yes. Your — Mr. Eastman was wonderful."

Ty pulled back enough to grin at Tanner. "No offense, Mr. Eastman, but I knew we were going to win even if you bombed."

Tanner laughed. "How so?"

"Because I was stuck back here by myself, and I was doing a lot of praying. About an hour ago I heard the Lord whispering in my ear."

There was something unquestionably innocent about her son's faith, something that made Jade's heart swell with pride. She linked one arm through Tanner's and drew him into their circle. They were a family now, and even if Ty didn't know about Tanner yet, Jade was convinced everything was going to work out.

She kissed Ty on the top of his head. "And what did the Lord whisper to you?"

"It was really weird, a verse we read once in Sunday school. After that, I knew for sure we were going to win."

Jade exchanged a curious look with Tanner. "What verse?"

Ty stood up straight and recited it perfectly: "I know the plans I have for you . . .

plans to prosper you and not to harm you, plans to give you hope and a future."

Jade and Tanner were silent for a moment, and then their eyes met. Jade could read Tanner's expression, perfectly and she nodded in response. It was finally time. "Ty, honey . . ."

Ty hugged her close, at peace with his world once again. "Yeah, Mom?"

"Mr. Eastman and I have something to tell you."

THIRTY-SEVEN

The first Saturday of November presented itself with crisp, clear skies and an impending sense that soon — very soon — all would be right with the world. It was the kind of day when Doris Eastman didn't mind her body's weakness or the way her ailing heart slowed every move.

In some ways, she had waited all her life for this day.

She rose from bed and opened her Bible to 1 Corinthians, Chapter 13. Since giving her life back to the Lord, every word in Scripture was vibrantly alive and new. And there could be no better day to remember what God taught about love.

Patient and kind, not keeping a record of wrongs, not easily angered.

It was like a heavenly description of Jade and Tanner. Wherever they were that morning, whatever they were doing at this moment, they, too, had waited all their lives for this day.

Marti appeared with her morning water and pills. "Good morning, Mrs. Eastman." The girl was in her late twenties and had moved to Los Angeles from Italy the year before. After her release from the hospital, Tanner had moved her across country, into a condominium not far from his law office. Marti came recommended by a pastor at Tanner's church, and after a trial period, Doris and Marti became fast friends. The younger woman had moved into the bedroom down the hall from Doris's and worked for her full-time.

"It's the big day." Doris allowed Marti to help her to her feet.

"Yes, ma'am. Mr. Tanner's wedding day. He doesn't know you're coming?"

Doris felt a stab of fear. "No. He . . . thinks I'm too ill."

"Well, the doctor, he said you should stay in bed as much as possible, Mrs. Eastman." Marti's accent was thick, but Doris no longer had trouble understanding her.

"Not today, Marti. I wouldn't miss this for the world."

"I am glad to go with you today. You will tell me if you get too tired, no?"

"Yes, Marti." Doris appreciated the girl's concern; she would not have been able to attend the wedding without Marti. The water shook in her hand, and Marti helped steady the glass. It was always an effort getting the pills down each morning, but Marti's conversation helped pass the time.

"When did Miss Jade and her boy arrive in town?" Marti slipped Doris's robe off her shoulders and helped her to her feet.

"Her divorce was final two weeks ago. They arrived last weekend."

"They have somewhere to stay, yes?"

"With Tanner's friend, Matt Bronzan." Doris winced. Her bones had been aching more than usual, and she figured it was because she'd gotten so little exercise. It was, in some ways, a no-win situation. She needed to rest to conserve energy and protect her heart, but the more she rested, the weaker she grew. The doctor had told her it wouldn't be long now. She had cheated death once; it wouldn't happen a second time.

"They have a new house for after the wedding, yes?" Marti held Doris's elbow gently and eased her into the bathroom.

"Yes. Tanner told me about it. Four bedrooms, a big backyard. Only twenty minutes from his office." She would love to see it, but that was out of the question. It took all her energy just to visit with Tanner for an hour these days. The wedding would be her first outing since the heart attacks.

Meticulously Marti tucked Doris's hair into a shower cap. She knew the routine well and seemed forever one step ahead of Doris, anticipating her needs and struggles. "Hmm. Four bedrooms?" Marti's eyes twinkled. "They have just one boy, no?"

Doris smiled. "Yes. But not for long if Tanner has anything to say about it." She sucked in her breath as Marti led her to a nearby chair. The process of getting out of bed, of donning her bathrobe and a shower cap, left Doris exhausted. She generally needed a few minutes in the chair before she was ready to bathe. "Tanner and Jade are young. Tanner says they want lots of babies."

"Tanner seems very happy. You must be proud."

Doris thought about the pain she'd put her son and Jade through, the lost years her lies had cost them both. Marti knew none of those details, though, and Doris had no need to share them now. "Yes, Marti. Tanner and Jade are very happy." She hesitated and felt herself getting weepy. "I am very proud of them both."

And terrified at the same time. She remembered Tanner's visit not long after she was

565

settled in her condo. "Call Jade, Mother. She wants to talk to you."

But Doris had used her health as an excuse, both then and again weeks ago when Jade arrived in town. "I'd love to see Jade and Ty," she'd told Tanner. "But dear, I'm simply not up to visitors."

The truth was, she desperately wanted to meet Ty — her son's only child, her grandson. But guilt formed a barrier of shame she couldn't see past, and instead she had written a letter to Jade apologizing for her inexcusable lies, her wicked behavior. In turn, Jade had written back, assuring Doris of her forgiveness. Still, Tanner told her often that she should meet Jade face to face, talk things out and make amends in person.

"Don't run from this," Tanner had begged her. "Jade forgives you, Mother. But you two need to talk, face to face now that she's in Los Angeles. For both your sakes."

A small voice within Doris had told her that was true, but still she held back. What if it didn't go well? She shook her head. No, it wasn't right. She didn't want to do anything to mar this time for either Tanner or Jade. With that in mind, Doris declined her invitation to the wedding. "I'd ruin it for her, Tanner."

"That isn't true. Mother, she wants you there."

Tanner didn't understand. God may have forgiven her, but Jade . . . How could Doris look the girl in the face and apologize to her? How could Jade ever really forgive an old woman who had cost her ten years of happiness?

And yet, more and more over the last few days, Doris had felt the urging — almost as though someone were giving her a strong nudge in her spirit — to go. Finally, yesterday, she'd given in. She would go, trusting God to work things out.

Marti helped Doris up, carefully removed her nightgown and eased her into the shower. Doris could still bathe herself but the process left her drained and Marti had taken to staying within arm's reach. "You're so wonderful, Marti. What would I do without you?"

"God is good, Mrs. Eastman. Good to both of us."

When she was finished showering, Marti helped her dry off and for a moment Doris remembered how independent she'd been, how proud and hard hearted.

Now she was grateful for having help in and out of the shower. Although she missed her vitality, she knew better than anyone that the true condition of her heart was worlds better than it had been before the heart attacks. And for that she thanked God constantly.

Marti slipped the robe back over Doris's shoulders and eased her into the chair once more. "I'll be all right, Marti. You go ahead and get ready. I need some time with the Lord."

The girl smiled and then dashed out the door down the hall toward her room. When she was gone, Doris closed her eyes and thanked God for his faithfulness. He had brought Tanner and Jade back together, where they had always belonged. He had spared her life long enough to allow her to repent and tell Tanner the truth. And he had done something she still couldn't believe.

He had spared Tanner's career.

From the hospital bed set up in her Los Angeles condominium, Doris Eastman had scrutinized every article and news story she could find about her son. The newspapers had been so shocked by Tanner's revelation that at first their stories seemed almost ambivalent.

What had happened over the next weeks and months had been nothing short of a miracle. Rather than rail against Tanner for his immorality years earlier, the media learned the story behind Tanner and Jade and embraced him as a modern-day hero. A man of faith with whom the people could relate. Not perfect, but perfectly committed to God.

Since August, editorials in the Los Angeles *Times* had described a major groundswell of public support should Tanner Eastman decide to run for state senator. Tanner had talked about it with Doris during one of their visits, and for the first time he thought serving in a public office might actually be the path God was choosing for him.

"Matt's ready to take over the CPRR office." Tanner had been unable to hide his grin. "Who'd have thought there'd come a day when the idea of public office actually appealed to me."

Doris had enjoyed his easy banter. The two were much closer than they'd been before the heart attacks, giving her yet another reason to be grateful. "I always knew you'd be on the ballot one day. But of course you had to do it your way."

In reality she knew that though she would probably not live to see her son elected to office, or the children he and Jade might have in the future, she was no longer concerned with the choices he made. He had chosen to follow God's path, and from where Doris sat now, she would be eternally grateful.

She thought about the wedding and the fact that sometime later that day she would face Jade. It would be their first meeting since that afternoon in Portland. And then . . . she would meet her grandson for the first time. *What if Jade hates me? What if she asks me to leave?* Doris wanted nothing more than to make peace with Jade, but in that instant she was struck by a palpable sense of doom.

My precious daughter, remember nothing is impossible with God. . . .

The words filled her mind and brought with them an unearthly peace. Yes, that was it. With the Lord, nothing was impossible.

God had given Tanner the strength to follow him.

Now it was her turn.

The ceremony was to be held west of Los Angeles at Chapel in the Canyon, a stucco building with a Spanish tile roof situated amidst rocks and wild brush. The view from the courtyard was breathtaking, and Jade stood outside savoring a moment of solitude before the wedding began.

In a million years, she would never have

dreamed that this was what God had planned for her . . . that this was the future she —

"Jade."

The voice was weaker than before, but it was distinct all the same. Jade's heart skipped a beat. *No, it can't be . . . not now . . .* She spun around, her veil swishing gently behind her. "Mrs. Eastman."

A younger woman waited in the distance as Tanner's mother took slow, shuffling steps toward her. *What was this? She had come after all. Despite her failing health and adamant refusal to receive visitors, Tanner's mother had come.*

"Jade, I know you weren't expecting me today." She was out of breath, and Jade could see something different in her expression, something soft and genuine that had been missing the last time they spoke. Tanner had told her a dozen times how different his mother was, how her faith was new and alive and how everything about her had changed as a result. Now Jade could see that for herself.

Jade's heart pounded, and she struggled for the right words. "No . . . I mean, yes . . . we want you here, Mrs. Eastman. I'm so glad you could make it." The woman's eyes told Jade she had nothing to worry about.

This was not a trick or a trap like their last meeting. Mrs. Eastman was a changed woman.

Mrs. Eastman moved closer still and placed a hand tenderly on Jade's arm. "You're a beautiful bride, Jade. Tanner is a lucky man."

Jade was speechless, overwhelmed by the power of God's love and forgiveness.

"I'm sorry, Jade." There were tears in Mrs. Eastman's eyes, and Jade began to tremble. "I'm old and worn out, but God has been merciful. He allowed me to be here and tell you to your face. I'm so very, very sorry, Jade. What I did was . . . it was shameful. There's no other way to say it. I'll be sorry as long as I live."

The confession seemed to add years to Mrs. Eastman's countenance, and her shoulders drooped as she stepped back. "I won't bother you anymore. If you don't mind, I'll go inside and watch."

Too full of emotion to speak, Jade took Doris Eastman's hand in hers and squeezed it gently. "We all paid a price for what happened that summer." Tears sprang to Jade's eyes. "But God, in his mercy, has worked it out for good." Through watery eyes, Jade smiled her forgiveness at the woman. "I told you in my letter that I forgave you, Mrs.

Eastman. And I do. The past is over."

She led Tanner's mother to a side door near the back of the church and flagged down Matt Bronzan. "Get Tanner, please." Jade squeezed Mrs. Eastman's hand gently and smiled at her. "Tell him his mother is here."

Jade entered the building on Matt Bronzan's arm, and Tanner had to remind himself he was not dreaming. Jade was stunning in a simple, straight-cut ivory gown, and in her eyes he saw a love for which he'd gladly wait a lifetime. When he thought of Jade now, it wasn't with remorse for the years they'd lost. Rather it was with gratefulness to God for bringing them back together.

The minister was telling their few close friends the importance of keeping God in their marriage, and Tanner exchanged a brief smile with his mother, who was seated in the front row, in the place of honor that was rightfully hers.

"The Lord is more than a wedding guest," the minister was saying. He was a somber man, and his message hit the mark for Tanner. "He wants to be part of the marriage."

He told them that Scripture teaches how a cord of three strands is not easily broken. "With God at the center, you will build a marriage that will be a beautiful thing, a union that will draw people to the Lord." He looked at Jade and Tanner and smiled. "Why? Because the world so desperately wants what you already have."

Ty stood beside Tanner as his best man, and Tanner's heart swelled as he glanced at his son. He had taken Ty fishing and to breakfast and even hiking in the past week. After months of phone conversations and letters, the child willingly accepted Tanner as his father. The road ahead looked promising for all of them.

It was time for the vows, and Jade and Tanner turned to face each other.

They had agreed to say their own vows, rather than repeating something read by the minister. Tanner went first.

"Jade, you are the treasure of my heart, my friend, my lover, my past, my future." Tanner tightened the grip he had on Jade's hands. "I promise before God and our friends, to love you, honor you, cherish you now and forever, no matter what bends appear on the road ahead. God created man with a missing rib, a missing part."

Jade's eyes glistened and she tilted her head, her eyes locked on his.

"You, Jade, are that missing piece, the part I have searched for all of my life. From this day forth I will cling to you and you alone. From this day forth I am whole." He slipped a gold band on her finger and saw tears glistening in her eyes. "With this ring, I, Tanner Eastman, do thee, Jade Conner, wed."

Jade swallowed hard, and Tanner could tell she was struggling to speak. He squeezed her hands gently, encouraging her, and she gave the slightest of nods. Then she stared at him; her eyes lit up from all she was feeling inside.

"You, Tanner Eastman, are the one with whom my soul rejoices. You have given me hope when I had none, life when I was dying, and love when I thought I would never love again. On this day, with God as our witness, I promise to love you, cherish you, honor you, and respect you all the days of my life." Her hands trembled as she slipped the ring on his finger. "With this ring as a token of my promise, a reminder of my unending love, I, Jade Conner, do thee wed."

And in that moment, Tanner knew that whatever else lay ahead, they would never again be alone. Because God had brought them back together, and one day, in the sunset of their lives, God would lead them home.

The reception took place at the Bronzans' house in Malibu, with a view overlooking the Pacific Ocean. A seafood dinner had been catered in for the occasion, and Hannah Bronzan had decorated the house beautifully.

It was three hours into the party, and many of the guests had already left, but still there was no sign of Doris Eastman. Her nursemaid had taken her home moments after the ceremony with promises to bring her back for the reception if she was feeling up to it. Tanner had tried to call her twice, but there had been no answer.

"I'm worried about her." Jade found Tanner in the kitchen and leaned up to kiss him. "She should be here by now."

Tanner shrugged. "I'm not sure she's coming. She wasn't supposed to be at the wedding. Doctor said no outings until she's stronger."

"Well, I want her here. She wasn't in any of the pictures and . . ."

"And?" Tanner pulled her toward him and kissed her tenderly.

"She didn't get to meet Ty yet." Jade gazed out the window toward the ocean. "I want her to meet him before —"

Tanner held a finger to her lips. "God knows that, Jade. Don't worry about her. She'll probably be here any minute." He kissed her tenderly. "Have I told you lately how beautiful you are, Mrs. Eastman?"

Jade's heart soared and she returned his kiss. The nearness of him made her long for the morning, when they would leave for four days in Cabo San Lucas. Ty would stay with the Bronzans, and after that the three of them would spend a weekend in San Diego, deep-sea fishing off the coast.

"Have I told you how much I'm going to enjoy being Mrs. Eastman?" Jade snuggled closer to him.

"Okay, okay, break it up." Matt bounded into the kitchen with Hannah and Ty in tow. He wore a conspiratorial grin, and Jade couldn't help but smile. The Bronzans had become very dear friends, and she was sure they would only get closer in the years to come.

Matt and Ty squared up a few feet away while Hannah shrugged sweetly in the background. "Now —" Matt poked an elbow at Ty, and the child grinned — "Your son has a special request. Something about checking out the fishing equipment in the garage." Matt held up his hands in mock surrender. "I know it's not appropriate to talk about fishing on your wedding day and all, but . . ." He grinned at Jade. "If I could borrow Tanner for just a few minutes."

Jade laughed. "Go ahead. Hannah and I will stay here and talk about the joys of cleaning fish."

The last guests had gone home, and only Hannah's daughter, Jenny, remained in the other room studying for a high school English exam. The women watched as the men disappeared into the garage, talking all at once and sounding like three children on the verge of a great discovery.

When they were gone, Hannah leaned against the kitchen counter and smiled at Jade. "Congratulations."

"Thanks. You guys have done so much for us. . . ."

Hannah cocked her head. "You know, in some ways you and Tanner remind me of Matt and me. Love forged out of pain." Hannah hesitated. "Know what I mean?"

Jade knew pieces of Hannah's background, but not the whole story. She nodded. "Yours was much more painful, though. Tanner's told me about what happened. The collision."

There was a long-ago kind of sadness in Hannah's eyes as she gazed at Jade. "My husband and daughter were killed by a drunk driver." She paused, and Jade could see she was at peace with this. But it was painful all the same. "Matt prosecuted the case."

Jade reached out and squeezed Hannah's hand. She had the distinct feeling this woman was going to be a close friend someday. "Tell me about it, okay? When the time's right."

Hannah returned the squeeze and smiled. "It's an amazing story of God's faithfulness."

Jade nodded thoughtfully. "He's definitely that."

The men returned, and Matt carried with him a dusty guitar.

Hannah laughed. "I thought you were looking at fishing poles."

"We were. But we found my old guitar. Isn't that great?"

Hannah exchanged a look with Jade, and both women giggled. "You planning to use it as bait?" Hannah walked to Matt and ran her hand over the neck of the guitar.

Matt looked hurt. "No." He turned to Tanner. "Actually it was Tanner's idea."

"What?" Jade moved between Ty and Tanner and put her arm around them both.

Tanner kissed her cheek. "I thought we

could sit on the deck and sing while Matt plays."

Jade smiled. It was a warm evening; the sun was just beginning to set. "Perfect."

Hannah wrinkled her nose. "Matt, I haven't cleaned the chairs out there in weeks."

Jade cut in. "It's okay, Hannah. Really. It'll be the perfect ending to the most perfect day." She smiled at Tanner and then Ty.

"Do I have to sing?" Ty looked worried, and the adults laughed at his sincerity.

"No, son." Tanner tousled Ty's hair, and Jade felt as if her heart would burst. Any concerns she'd had about whether Tanner and Ty would bond had long since dissolved. Tanner led the way outside and the others followed.

When they were seated, Tanner grinned at Ty. "Of course, you haven't heard me sing before. We just might need your help."

The ocean stretched out toward the horizon, gentle swells glimmering under the setting sun. Matt tuned his guitar and then called for requests.

"I have one." Hannah gave Jade a knowing look. "My favorite song."

"Ah, yes . . ." Matt practiced a few cords. " 'Great Is Thy Faithfulness.' " He looked at the others. "You guys know it?"

Jade nodded and wove her fingers through Tanner's hand. It was the perfect song for her. And Jade had the feeling it was equally perfect for Hannah.

It had been a day to remember, but still it had been hectic at times. When Matt began playing the song, the strains carried on the breeze and soothed what remained of the wrinkles in Jade's soul.

"Great is thy faithfulness, Oh, God our Father, there is no shadow of turning with thee. All I have needed thy hands hath provided; Great is thy faithfulness, Lord unto me. . . ."

They had just begun the second chorus when Doris Eastman and her nurse appeared at the foot of the deck. A broad smile filled Tanner's face, and he rose to meet her. While the song played on, he helped his mother up the three wooden steps to a cushioned seat. Doris's nursemaid took the spot beside her, and Tanner returned to Jade's side.

"Great is thy faithfulness, great is thy faithfulness, morning by morning new mercies I see. . . ."

Ty tapped Jade's arm and motioned toward Mrs. Eastman. Jade nodded, and the boy crossed the deck and gently hugged the grandmother he'd never known. She held him close, her frail arms shaking, and then she moved so that he had room to sit down. Smiling innocently at the older woman beside him, Ty took her fragile hand in his and joined in the singing. Somehow the song magnified the beauty of the moment, and Jade's voice grew stronger.

At that moment, Tanner's mother caught Jade's gaze, and her eyes spoke volumes. Jade nodded to Doris and smiled. The old woman wanted to be her friend. Jade could see it clearly, and her heart melted. They were finally, completely at peace with each other, and, God willing, the future would hold many chances to talk.

Jade savored the words to the song, singing them in a prayer to God alone. As she did, Doris closed her eyes and raised an unsteady hand toward heaven, adding her voice to the others. "Great is thy faithfulness, great is thy faithfulness. . . ."

Jade understood. The song belonged to Doris, too. It belonged to all of them. God had kept his promise and given every one of them a hope and a future. All because his mercies truly were new every morning.

Jade clung to Tanner's hand and closed her eyes as the final strains of the song drifted out to sea.

"All I have needed, thy hand hath provided. . . . Great is thy faithfulness, great is thy faithfulness, great is thy faithfulness, Lord, unto me."

Dear Reader,

First, you must know what a privilege it is to have been handed several hours of your time as you followed the story of Jade and Tanner. I hope you have received much in return as you traveled with them through the abysmal pit of sin and regret to the peace-filled plains of God's mercy and forgiveness.

As with each of my novels, it is my prayer that *A Moment of Weakness* did more than entertain you. I pray it helped you — as it has me — to grasp one of God's many truths. In this case, God's truth about sin.

There are obvious lessons in *A Moment of Weakness* for those tempted by sexual sin. But perhaps you cannot relate to this temptation. Maybe you are one who has — with good intentions — stood in judgment. Someone in your church family or even your immediate family has succumbed to a moment of weakness in his or her own life, and you, like Doris Eastman, have led the contingent in seeing that he or she receives punishment in full.

I remember well the story of a preacher's young daughter who wound up pregnant. She was broken and repentant, still the congregation was split in their reaction. Some hugged her close and promised prayer and support. Others pointed fingers behind her back, whispering mean-spirited words and inciting outrage among that body of believers. The girl was a 4.0 student with a brilliant mind and, before her weakest moment, an equally brilliant future. Though she could have secretly had an abortion and maintained her pure image, she chose to take responsibility for her sin and move forward in God's grace. Today God has blessed her with a godly husband and several beautiful children.

I never feared the repercussions her sin would have on her own life. Not with her faith so firmly rooted in Christ and his saving grace. Rather I feared for those who considered themselves judge and jury, those who were ashamed of her and held a grudge against her. Scripture teaches us not to judge others or we, ourselves, will be judged. Forgive one another, encourage one another, build one another up. Love one another.

Please learn a lesson from Doris and remember God's grace the next time someone in your circle gives in to sin.

That said, I believe more of us relate to Jade and Tanner. Most people have been or will be tempted by the powerful pull of sexual sin. The Bible is as clear on this issue as it is on any that God feels strongly about. Scripture says flee immorality. Avoid sexual sin. Be pure. Be holy, set apart. Do not commit adultery. As with Tanner and Jade, God does not give these commands to punish us or dampen our pleasure. Rather he provides them so that our joy will be complete. Had Tanner and Jade waited until they were married, they would have been spared a decade of heartache and despair.

God's ways are always more satisfying than acting out what seems or feels right in our own moments of weakness.

Sadly, in America today, sexual sin — including pornography — has been cast into an almost comical light. This despite the fact that it has ruined people of authority and power on both sides of the political spectrum, people in Hollywood, and people in churches across the country. Our society seems to have bought the lie that somehow sexual sin cannot be avoided.

As a nation, we are wrong in this thinking, wrong for encouraging it, and wrong for celebrating sexual sin as a means of entertainment. It is time that you and I and all who would believe take a stand for holiness and purity. If that means turning off the television set or canceling your Internet service to maintain a healthy, holy environment for you and your children, then turn it off and cancel it. Remember, we are to hate what is evil; cling to what is good.

Finally, if you or someone you know is struggling with sexual sin, the time has come to seek godly counsel. There is glorious hope and a bright future for those who will get right with God, who will repent and turn away from this pervasive, addictive sin. Otherwise, there is only dark desperation and the consequences of sin as they are spelled out in Scripture.

In the meantime, I will pray along with you that each of us grows closer to God, his perfect Word, and his perfect plan for our lives.

Jesus Christ wants to be our personal friend and Savior. If you don't have a relationship with him and want to know more about becoming a Christian, making sure your name is written in the Lamb's

Book of Life, please connect with someone at a Bible-believing church in your area.

God is there, even now. Waiting, watching. Ready to forgive, ready to make us new creations, to welcome us with open arms into his everlasting presence.

As always, I'd love to hear from you. Write me at:

Multnomah Publishing
P.O. Box 1720
Sisters, OR 97759
Or e-mail me at: rtnbykk@aol.com

Karen Kingsbury

The employees of Thorndike Press hope you have enjoyed this Large Print book. All our Thorndike and Wheeler Large Print titles are designed for easy reading, and all our books are made to last. Other Thorndike Press Large Print books are available at your library, through selected bookstores, or directly from us.

For information about titles, please call:
(800) 223-1244

or visit our Web site at:
www.gale.com/thorndike
www.gale.com/wheeler

To share your comments, please write:
Publisher
Thorndike Press
295 Kennedy Memorial Drive
Waterville, ME 04901